The Ambulist

Max Adams

[signature: Max Adams]

beat&track
130/500

Original hardback edition limited to 2000 copies and published in 2016 by *beat&track*. Dunadd, West Law Road, Shotley Bridge DH8 0EH. All rights reserved ©Max Adams 2016. The right of Max Adams to be identified as the author of this work has been asserted in accordance with Section 77 of the Copyright, Designs and Patents Act 1988. No part of this publication may be copied, reproduced, stored in a retrieval system, or transmitted, in any form or by any means without the prior permission of the publisher, nor be otherwise circulated in any form of binding or cover other than that in which it is published and without a similar condition being imposed on the subsequent purchaser. Printed by Martins the Printers in Berwick upon Tweed. British Library Cataloguing in Publication data available.

ISBN (Hardback) 978-0-9935919-0-7
ISBN (ebook) 978-0-9935919-1-4

In memory of Thelma Adams

1929-2001

Chapter One

New moon

Two drunks came lurching out of the alleyway fighting uselessly, never a punch finding its mark, pawing at the air, cursing the living bloody daylights out of each other. It was a black December night; no moon, just an epileptic neon sign and a half-dozen feeble street lamps dashing shards of pale colour at the greasy cobbles in the market place. A wicked gale blustered in off the coast, a Norse raider looking for victims. It fell upon street litter: cartons, cans and wrappers, whipping them into vagrant squalls which scuttled for cover in doorways and dark corners. Rain had lashed the city earlier in the day and now the clear sky was like a strip-search. Christ but it was cold.

A freezing couple sharing chips out of a crumpled paper wrapper sat hunched on the iron bench beneath the emaciated plane tree which waved ragged branches in its state of winter undress. The girl, all legs and a skimpy little halter-neck, looked up as the shabby, hunched outline of Gaunt, working late and now heading for the pub on a mission to get drunk, flapped passed, fag in mouth, his coat undone and a hand on his hat to keep it there. Something on wheels swished past on its way up from the bridge and it must have just missed Gaunt for his old bones skipped a couple of steps and he nearly ran full into the drunks before disappearing into the depths of the alley.

The editor-in-chief of the *Courier* looked out from the cinemascope window of his overheated eyrie on the third floor with complacency: he had seen this show a thousand times. Sure the cast might change twice every night, but with an extra matinee performance on Saturdays you got your money's worth: not a line spoken out of turn, never an off-stage whisper from the prompt. That the actors did not know themselves to be on stage was what kept him in his job. And still Queedy, the young man hovering at his side, would not or could not appreciate the artlessness of it all. He might be better off, M. reflected, learning his trade as an apprentice playwright and not as a cub reporter: not here.

The drunks now faced each other, swaying, ranting from a safe distance. The younger one, in his fifties maybe, he could have been the son, stabbed the air with his hand in a bitter gesture that went deeper than the bottom of a glass. The older one, balding, fat, bandy-legged, opened his flies and pissed on the cobbles. The door of the pub on the corner opened and out spilled two pairs of lovers, arms wrapped around waists; either the shock of the cold or the spectacle of the two drunks stopped them in their tracks momentarily before they staggered off down the hill in the direction of the taxi rank.

Queedy stood watching, taking it all in, his face pressed against the window, hands at his back as if he owned the place, not listening to a goddamn word M. was saying. He was wearing a suit, Queedy was, an expensive Italian object which had cost money – not Queedy's money – and time pounding the miles on a treadmill. No one else at the *Courier* could have or would have worn such a thing, or a shirt with cuffs that bloody perfect or a collar that clean. He was a five-clean-shirts-a-week man, was Queedy, not like the rest of them. He would come round to their way of thinking in the end.

It was late, but M. pressed his point anyway.

        - See what I mean (he says)?

        - About what? (This is Queedy, pretending not to see what he means)

        - Learning the trade, Son, learning the trade.

        - There's no story out there.

        - Sure there is. If not that lot then of what, exactly, do you suppose a story to be composed? Do you think it's wrought from concentrated good and evil? From pure ill-faith or perfect rectitude? Do you think the big stories start big? Does Palestine start with the Bible? Does the French Revolution start with the guillotine? No, Son. All stories start with a courting couple, a time-expired hack and two blokes fighting over nothing. It's the history of the world. You either see or you don't see.

Queedy laughed in a thin sort of way that said he had heard but was not listening. He carried on staring out of the window with his sleek dark eyes and when M. got a bottle out of the drawer and poured them both a large one he took it and drank it. M. joined him at the window, nursing his glass while Queedy drained his in one, showing off. Queedy's thin body shivered. M. lifted the catch on the window and opened it just enough for a blast of wind and the sounds of the street to invade the office. Queedy shivered again. Now the younger man's eye was caught by another movement and he put a finger to the window, pointing.

        - Who might that be?

An immense figure, a giant, his long head of silver-grey hair flowing down over the shoulders of a greatcoat buttoned to the chin, had emerged from black shadows at the top of the street. He traversed the market place in irresistible slow motion, one hand thrust deep in the pocket of his coat, the other holding an ancient leather grip which looked dead heavy. You couldn't see the man's face at that distance and with the light the way it was, but his head was the shape of an outcrop of rock that had defied erosion, earthquake and ice. He was a boulder tumbling fatefully down a mountainside, brushing trees aside. He was a landslide; an avalanche. He was tectonic.

What age was he? Somewhere between fifty and seventy; it was impossible to tell in that blearing dimness. He might have been born before the flood. There was no sign of a stoop in his walk. His pace had the even swing of a pendulum and seemingly made no greater noise. He leant forward slightly as if braced against the wind which tore off the cobbles but it was a straight walk, a guiltless walk, unapologetic. A walk that could not conceal a lie. Was it military? No, it was not: it had purpose, sure, but no strategy; principles, but no objects. Nor did it describe the shortest distance between two points any more than a line on a chart measured by dividers describes the sea. It told the man into being; it spoke his existence, no more and no less. The simple fact of his presence was so overwhelming, so much more massive even than his physical bulk, that the couple on the bench stared at his wake as he passed. Even the two drunks stopped dead in mid-flow: silenced, in awe. He loomed over them, parting the liquid air like a bow-wave. He was mythic. And then he was gone.

> - A story there, do you reckon, Son? (M. tosses the words into the air like scraps cut from a Sunday supplement; after all, how can either of them know?)

Queedy looked at his empty glass and without asking went over to the desk and filled it again. He examined his watch for signs of time passing.

> - No story: a man just walked past, that's all. He caught my eye. I haven't seen him before. I thought you might recognise him. (Sometimes Queedy's voice is reedy like an oboe; now it is all maple syrup)

> - For Christ's sake, have you ever seen anything like that? (Why does this boy make M. so damned angry?)

- No, I haven't. But then I am young; what can I know of the world? (Now M. remembers why this boy makes him so damned angry)

- Do you not get a scent of the quarry in your nose? When I was your age I'd have chased him down the street, cornered him, milked a story from him, cajoled and moulded him into a story if I had to. All life is there, Son, and you have to take it with both hands and bleed it like a vein. Where has he come from, Christ Jesus, and where is he going?

M., letting go the iron grip he had on his own fist, went and filled his glass again and collapsed into the grand chair behind the desk. It would have swallowed a smaller man; now it swivelled heavily on its pivot. He so rarely sat there, it came to him almost as a revelation that the room could do with the loving hand of a decorator. One of the racks of shelves, which held periodicals and his library of reference works, was buckling under the strain – although he could throw most of that stuff out if he had a mind to. Where its frame leaned out from the wall a patch of fresh-looking paint showed how bad the rest of the walls were. The faded brown carpet, worn threadbare at the door and almost shiny next to the window, testified to the general shabbiness of the place. A picture of the Queen wearing a pastel twin-set and presenting M. with his gong these many years past, hung slightly askew, enough to annoy but not sufficiently for him to get out of the chair and set her to rights. He wondered vaguely where the medal was; in a drawer somewhere at home, probably. Maybe the wife had taken it, or thrown it off the bridge.

M. noted mechanically that his Lakeland Views calendar had stalled at October. The new one, proclaiming the start of a new decade, lay on the desk in its buff envelope, unopened. The clock on the wall said it was past midnight. He ought to pack the boy off and go home himself but he'd never been good at going home – even if Queedy drove him to thoughts of the hot bath and iced gin which waited there.

- What do you suppose his story is, then? I confess to being curious. (Queedy has a nice way of talking, at one and the same time trying to pick your mental wallet and show you how bored he is)

- You'll never know, Son. You'll never know. (M. has given up on Queedy for the night)

Queedy stared at his watch again, ignoring the clock. He was looking for excuses. He went back over to the window and tapped it, as if to mark the place where the epic presence of the man had etched itself on the glass.

- I have an early start in the morning. Gaunt wants me to interview a kiddies' party Santa Claus who used to be a welder in the shipyards, a farmer who's rearing reindeer for meat and a little boy who won't be getting any presents this year because his Mam and Da lost all their Christmas money in a stamp club which went bust. There's no time to chase a real story. Which would be a pity if this turned out to be the Second Coming. (Queedy is beginning to sound like an oboe)

- Don't get bitter, Son. It's a long life to get bitter before you've started. Gaunt isn't a bad sort. He's been around and has an old-fashioned idea that you've to serve an apprenticeship before he lets you off your leash. He doesn't know who your father was and if he did it wouldn't make any difference. You're the new boy. (M. is a provincial newspaper editor, Irish by birth and sensibility. He is nearer sixty than fifty, he has expensive children but no longer a wife, he is fighting a losing war against falling sales, and young men like Queedy piss him off. His hair has gone decisively grey, he has a bad back and his diet is worse than it was before the wife left. He is a good man.)

Sure, Queedy was bitter: young, vain and bitter and that's why he didn't follow so tantalising a scent that night. The world owed him. Chance, or was it fate, would give him another shot. Meantime he would toe the line, sire six quarter-columns a day from the mawkish festive scraps which old Gaunt threw his way and cursing the day he'd been born. He had no choice: he had committed a nearly unforgivable sin in his youth, and been disinherited.

The man whose brief passing they had witnessed in the market place was seen no more in the city. The *Courier* stumbled on towards its Christmas deadlines. A 'flu epidemic broke out in the city; hospitals ran short of beds. A trawler, the skipper a father with three sons on board, went down in a terrible blow: widows; orphans. Rumours of an energy crisis: fuel up five per cent, pensioners freezing to death in their own homes. None of these stories came Queedy's way. It was a week when M. was reduced to sleeping on an inflatable mattress on the floor of his office, wrecking his guts with take-aways and coffee and in terrible pain from his sacroiliac. One of those weeks when you age about ten bloody years.

M. discouraged Queedy from coming into his office so often. Sure the boy needed a father-figure but it could not be M., who knew too much and liked him too little. Besides, in a business whose stock-in-trade was prurience and tattle he would soon become his own story. It couldn't be allowed to happen. And still M. hoped that Gaunt would knock the boy into shape.

When the place emptied on Christmas Eve, Gaunt kept Queedy on at the night desk. Neither of them wanted to go home and anyway someone had to be there to answer the phones. Gaunt sent Queedy off to make coffee and buy his fags. He took him round to the nick to count drunks in the cells. He dragged him along to car crashes and bridge-jumpers, arson attacks and warehouse break-ins. In between, on long nights when the phone never rang at all, they drank whisky.

Gaunt talked and Queedy pretended to listen.

Gaunt had been around. His liver and his lungs were shot, his arteries ran sclerotic as the city roads in rush hour. He possessed two suits: one for interviews with people who mattered and one for all other purposes. Neither had ever seen a dry-cleaner's. The streets were his home. He knew the tramps and the grubby corners where the hookers and dealers hung out. He drank his lunch in dingy back-street pubs and went home to a shabby flat where a slovenly wife and attention-seeking cat waited, claws sharpened, to give him a hard time. He could count on tip-offs from every desk sergeant, traffic cop and taxi driver for twenty miles around. He had dirt on every councillor and on most of the city magistrates. He was the city's encyclopaedia of the hum-drum, of corruption and vice, the banal and the bizarre.

For twenty years Gaunt had tramped and trampled the *Courier's* corridors, always on the way somewhere or coming back from somewhere: unnoticed except when a really big story broke. Then he would stick his bottom lip out and run a rolled-up copy of the paper along the walls, flicking at windows and doors as he passed. He loved it when he got the whole front page to himself. In thirty years, the early ones spent working for cut-price press agencies in sleazy corners of the world, he had never won a single award for his writing; and the *Courier* would have folded without him. He was the *Courier*. If only Queedy would listen, well then what an education he might get at that man's hands.

Many a wet-behind-the-ears cub reporter had been schooled by Gaunt. He never socialised with them. He had never liked any of them. Nor had he ever disliked any of them. His small kindnesses were those of the NCOs who had tried and failed to turn him into a soldier in his National Service youth: letting him off spud-bashing the day his brother died, that sort of thing. It was necessary for him to deny such tenderness and for it to remain unacknowledged. On that basis he might put up with stupid young men and they might graduate from his tutelage.

Something of Queedy's fragility must have penetrated Gaunt's misanthropic armour. In January, when Queedy collapsed, M. was away from the office for a few days, nursing his bad back and being fed nourishing bacon, cabbage and mash among the green hills and pastures of his native Ireland. It was Miss Nixon who telephoned his sister Mary in Donegal. M. knew something was up. Miss Nixon, who had been his secretary for fifteen years and would always be plain Miss Nixon, had never called him there, so when Mary passed him the phone he knew it would mean packing his bags. He flew back to a city which lay under a suffocating blanket of murk, and stood waiting in a queue at the airport for twenty minutes before a taxi arrived. He didn't go home but made straight for the Infirmary. Miss Nixon's urgency, so out of character, had him properly scared.

The shock was not so much seeing Queedy in a high-dependency ward, for M. had seen him like that before; it was the visitor which threw him. Gaunt was at Queedy's bedside. For once Queedy was talking and for once it was the old man who did not listen. Gaunt had brought a magazine for the patient and was reading it himself, sitting on a plastic chair at the foot of the bed with his back to the window to cast what daylight there was on the page. He needed reading glasses but would not admit it. He was eating an apple which he had also brought for the patient. Queedy was propped up on pillows, his perfect hair no longer perfect and the bright dark eyes no longer shining but empty of all lustre; matt, almost. Somehow the head looked too big for the body in those hospital-issue striped pyjamas. A drip attached at the neck fed him drugs and a salt solution. He was wired up to a heart monitor which flashed orange numbers. His voice was the same colour as his face, a translucent grey, like dishwater. He was reciting the history of his heart condition, trying to reassure himself he wasn't going to die young and hoping Gaunt would agree. But Gaunt was nobody's uncle. It wasn't his way. This was one of his little kindnesses, being there but not saying anything.

M. said Hello Gaunt and the old sod looked up and nodded, threw the magazine on the bed and made to leave as if the relief watch had arrived. That shut the boy up because M. already knew about his heart condition and had nothing reassuring to say except had Queedy thought any more about a transplant. Like his old man, Queedy had a great fear of the surgeon's knife. Some said that explained why the old man had disappeared one day in his private plane somewhere over the Rockies; he had been given the thumbs down by his cardiologist. M. had his own ideas on that story.

Still, to give the boy credit he was bloody well determined to make his own way with no help from anyone, or at least anyone apart from M. No, he still didn't want a transplant. There was nothing wrong with him, a stupid fuss over nothing at all, he had just had a bad day and forgotten to take a couple of pills. What he needed was more action, not less. When was he going to be allowed to work on something worth writing about? How long did he have to put up with Gaunt?

As long as Gaunt has to put up with you, M. said, meaning it kindly. The temptation to call him an arrogant little shit was there all right but the boy was on the ropes and so he got away with it that time. Yes, in his way M. was a good man.

M. stuck around long enough to wring a cautious prognosis from the consultant and told Queedy he'd be back with grapes and something to read. Queedy was pathetically grateful, which made a change. When M. left, the boy's ears were plugged into music and his eyes were closed. He looked terrible. He bloody well worries me, that boy, thought M.

Queedy was in hospital for three weeks. They tried this new drug and that new drug on him, watched his heart, tested his blood, shook their heads. When he left he would have to avoid strenuous exercise and stress, nothing he didn't already know. M. thought about putting that to Gaunt and then thought better of it, because Queedy's life was his own to risk no matter what promises M. had made to himself and neither did he want Gaunt to wear himself out with little kindnesses. Gaunt's heart was in no great shape either.

Chapter Two

Giant

January's grip on the city and its river, on the fields and copses, peat hags, fells and mosses of the hill country, did not loosen. If spring inseminates humans with the urge to leave and autumn whispers the need to return, to retrace, then winter is the season of the hearth, a time for staying: for stories, for magic, for fear of the night and longing for dawn's unveiling. The dark of a new moon in winter is a paradox: at no other time of year is there less light at midnight – darkness seems to stretch without end in all directions and only the hearth offers comfort. And yet, without the moon's reflected glare, the heavens are at their most brilliant. It is now that dreamers feel they might walk forever under the limitless canopy in complicit harmony with the galaxies as they wander across the firmament. The constellations were first called into existence by wanderers, and although they may be peopled with angels they are still named after hunters and bears.

By the dark of a moonless night the megalithic form of a man with flowing hair, wearing a greatcoat and carrying a heavy grip, could be seen navigating treeless moors graced with a tourniquet frost, guided by Polaris overhead and with the seductive W of Cassiopeia drawing him westwards. No hearth called him. He cast no shadow. His spoor was the rhythmic imprint of hoary footfalls which lay in an unfollowed glittering phosphorescent trail behind him. His breath streamed out in milky starlit clouds. A vixen and her mate watched. The ghost of an owl momentarily broke the pattern of its reconnaissance and traversed his path out of routine curiosity.

In the deepest hour of the night the man came down off the freezing moor and found shelter in a birch wood close by a stream. The stillness of the trees, sheathed in white, was absolute. Here he made himself a small fire and, laying a blanket out on the stiff ground, he watched as the dry crack of blazing sticks shot sparks into the heavens to join those who had passed before. Steamy wraiths emanated from him and from the trunk against which he leant his grateful back. He rolled himself a cigarette with moist tobacco from a soft leather pouch, lit it with a burning wand and, settling to his pitch, pulled a bottle of whisky from the grip. The sweet rush of the burn at his feet was his company, the fire a prism for his living soul. Above him Cassiopeia, parting company, rode on into the indefinite night.

The sun did not break free from the earth until past eight o'clock in the morning. The man, waking stiff with cold, quickly rekindled his fire. With sweet clear water from the burn he brewed his tea and shared the crumbs of his breakfast with greedy robins. Blue-grey smoke rose rippling into a sky of dazzling purity. When he had eaten the man got up from the ground, packed his grip and, without a backward glance, left the failing fire behind. He followed the burn down its valley for a while and may have been enjoying the fraternity of its company, but as the gorge closed in before him he climbed once again onto the moor. The white land was perfect. He marked the spire of a village church pricking the sky to the west and let it draw him onwards with the feeble sun at his back. After that, who could say where he would go? The man himself may not have known, unless perhaps there was some unfathomable imperative urging him on.

What does it mean to walk forever? For the nomad the opposite of walking is not the act of standing still, for that is nothing more than a pause on the trail. The opposite of walking is dwelling, so that in autumn the urge is to close a door and in spring the need is to open it again. The human fear of darkness is suppressed and feigns domestication even though it has not been tamed at all, but is lying in wait. Dwelling offers security, the security of a chain. For the nomad, the hearth must be rejected because it fixes, enslaves, emasculates. The camp fire, which may be set in a moment and left behind to die like an old man past his time, is both more and less than a hearth. It is life itself, the fleeting life of the moment. Nomads and dwellers must make their choice. The transhumant, whose sheep and goats follow him to the high pastures every summer and back home again in the autumn, is one who has not been able to make that choice. Who can say which is the happiest of these?

If a man must walk forever it follows that he can never arrive, so that his destiny is not a destination, his aim can have no target, his purpose no objective. But supposing he has once dwelt, what liberation or repulsion has released or expelled him from the hearth: hope or tragedy, or something else?

The dweller must plan: the time of ploughing and sowing seed, labour for the harvest and the hoarding of food and grain for winter, for death, famine and plenty. To subsist in the future then, is the lot of humans who have chosen to settle, for they are condemned to live in their minds the next year before they have existed physically in this. The first settlers captured the motions of heaven and earth in stone to tame them and be tamed by them, forcing the rhythm of their shared lives into a cycle of mimicry. But if a man must walk forever, does he plan anything? Even death? And if not, is he truly human?

At the side of the old military road that cuts the land in two

from sea to sea a tiny church stands sentinel over a wide green fertile
valley of small farms, scrub woods and hamlets. The place is called
Heavenham. The church is squat and domestic, no more than three
hundred years old, the little belfry mounted at its west end seemingly a
decorative afterthought. There are no dwellings nearby whose families
might be summoned to prayer by its tolling bell. Beyond it to the north
are bleak carrs and scattered farmsteads which have stood time out of
mind, locked tight into the fabric of the land by drystone walls telling
tales of labour and self-enslavement.

The church and the plain wooden cross which stands nearby mark
the site of a battle once fought not far away between great warlords for
dominance over these lands. One of them came from the far north
with the blessing of Saint Columba's ghost and the moral right to his
father's kingdom. The other came from the south with hate in his heart
and an army gorged on despoliation. With the victor went the authority
to command the faith of the people and so the cross, raised by Oswald
Iding the night before his fateful battle, is the mark of Christian victory
in a great slaughter which many a mead-song gloried in. It was not the
last but the greatest conquest of man's relations with spirits who had
lived in the woods, rocks and rivers of these lands since the departing
of the ice. There is nothing remarkable about the church which stands
here now. But some relic of worship has stood on this piece for more
than a thousand years, and it must have been a fine place to pray and to
die among the glittering spears of an atheling's war host.

M. could not say why, on that particular early February day of
breathless perfection, he chose this place to break his journey home
from a meeting; but he had stopped here many times before and it
pleased him to feel himself unbound on such a morning. The church
with its low encircling wall, its desultory crouching headstones and
grove of wintering oaks protecting its chastity, sat like a coronet on
the modest rise. From the south, where seamless hills ran on forever
into the blue, the arc of the midday sun brazed its golden stone walls,

fusing them to the earth. Within, the echoing clank of the iron door-lever dropping in its catch surprised an old silver-haired woman intent on polishing brass candle sconces set into the walls. The noise seemed to tear the flimsy curtain of light that hung from the wooden vault of the chancel.

M. sat for a few minutes in a stall, indulging in the immediacy of the day. The quiet, once the woman had left, was effortless. M. ran his hand along the top of the pew in front of him and opened the hymn book which lay against it. Leafing through the songs, softly singing an odd phrase that welled up from the spring of his childhood, he tried to remember the last time he had prayed, and could not. A waking dream took him back to the lush emerald hills of his native land and although he had a simple love for the austerity of the English church, he could at that moment have wept for the timeless familiar intonation of the Mass, the hanging musk of incense, the gold thread of Roman paternity.

He became vaguely aware that the shaft of sunlight falling across the wall of the chancel had moved on and now struck a glancing blow against the yellow-grey stone of the pulpit. He raised himself from the stall and turned to leave.

Along the path from the road strode an ageless giant in a loosely-buttoned greatcoat with a heavy grip in his hand. His grey mane hung at his back and only his breath trailed behind in his wake. He wove a pattern between tree and gravestone, pausing to read an inscription here and there, describing a clockwise passage around the church until he stopped beneath the sundial mounted high on the stonework.

As M. left the porch he half-turned back and stretched out a vain hand to stop the door latch from striking again. At that instant he saw the man and recognised, if not his face, then his intensity of being. The grip he saw too, the tumbling cataract of hair and the massive coat. The giant figure stood unmoving beneath the sundial, watching with intent the thin shadow cast by its gnomon as if tracking the infinitesimal passage of time. His feet were planted in the earth, his back was rigid straight, his jagged features creased in the sun's glare. He turned his head slowly towards M. and his eyes were fathomless, wrought from the dark pools that lurk beneath cliffs.

- What is the date, please?

- February the fifth (says M., not knowing what else to say).

- And so, the sun will be fourteen minutes slow. Midday has passed already. Thank you. (The man is speaking to himself: the thank you is automatic, it does not apologise)

- How can you tell? (M. realises straight-away this is a stupid question; but, after all, he is a journalist)

- It is the equation of time.

The man's gaze returned to the markings on the sundial, etched in sandstone almost as old as time itself. Feeling perhaps a need to make a gesture of obeisance, instead M. half-ran down the path towards the gate. The voice had been hewn from the same block of granite as the face. It was adamantine; it towered like a vulture's fastness. *The equation of time.*

M. ran Gaunt to ground in the print room where the presses were hard at work spewing out the late city edition. Neither man had lost his love for the smell of printer's ink or the orchestra of the machinery, the changeless choreography of roller, cam, feeder and belt. Nobody there thought to acknowledge them. The presence of those two old hounds in the printers' lair was indulged the way a time-expired dog will sometimes allow its master the privilege of his own favourite chair. Gaunt had just pulled a copy off the belt, licking a black-stained finger before opening it to check his own by-line and cast his worn eye over the layout.

- What do you know about the equation of time? (M. shouts in Gaunt's ear; he knows Gaunt won't know, he just wants to get the conversation started)

- No idea. Better ask your boy in the Infirmary. (This is

Gaunt's way of saying he doesn't like M.'s indulgence towards Queedy; but then he doesn't know who Queedy is so M. lets this pass)

    - Much on?

    - In February? (Gaunt is incredulous; he does not look up from the Sports section)

    - Have you ever come across a fellah, he's enormous (M. gestures with a hand, carving the air horizontally a full three inches above his own head) wears a huge greatcoat, carries an old-fashioned grip, long grey hair, moves like an oil tanker? I've seen him around a couple of times. Might be something to him.

Gaunt thought about that for half a second before shaking his head. M., shouting again to make himself heard, asked Gaunt if he thought he could track him down. Sure, Gaunt could find him. Where had M. seen him last? Heavenham. Heavenham? Gaunt raised an eyebrow, stuck out his lower lip and nodded, or rather jerked his chin upwards a fraction of an inch. Whether Gaunt was aware that the man was to be tracked for the benefit of the editor's protégé, M. did not ask himself. Among hacks, asking why someone wanted to know something was an unspoken taboo. You would never get a straight answer.

It was the third week in February when M. next saw Queedy. This time he was sitting on the bed with his feet hanging over the side, wearing a fresh pair of pyjamas two sizes too big, chatting up a nurse who looked like she didn't mind a whole lot. He looked dead bored. M. had already been to see the consultants so he knew what they knew. Queedy had a bad heart. So what, how many hacks could say they had a good heart? M. was in no mood to indulge the boy. He'd had a lousy week.

    - I forgot the grapes, Son.

    - So it would appear. (Queedy is reading a magazine with

the pretence of interest)

    - They going to kick you out soon?

    - Another week. (M. already knows this)

    - Pity, you're needed.

    - I'm needed...? Does that mean Gaunt is sick of running his own errands? (This is Queedy's oboe voice: it resents, it complains)

    - What does the equation of time mean to you?

Queedy dropped the magazine into his lap and gave M. a look which was meant to say he could hardly be bothered to answer. But M. was not fooled because Queedy's back straightened and the light came back into his eye. Queedy was young and stupid but he'd had an expensive education.

    - The equation of time is the difference between the time told by a clock, which averages out over a year, and the true time as told by the sun's position in the sky. That is why Greenwich Mean Time is called mean, because it is an average. (Now the maple syrup voice: too sweet and sticky. It might be patronising if the victim would consent to be patronised but M. doesn't)

    - You bloody well lost me already (says M.).

    - Already? Don't you see, the sun would always be in the same place in the sky at the same time of day if the earth were not on a tilt and if its orbit were circular? Because these are not constant, the sun and a clock are only in agreement on four days in the year. Sometimes the sun has to catch up with the clock and sometimes it is the converse. (Queedy has lain back down on his bed and his arms are crossed behind his head)

    - I give up.

    - Why do you want to know? (Queedy cannot help betraying his interest)

    - I'm not sure I do (says M., who knows he has hooked

his fish and walks over to the window to show that he knows
Queedy knows too).

    - But you did ask. (Queedy will tug on the line for form's
sake)

    - You remember that huge fellah from the market...

    - The market? It seems rather a long time ago. We
confessed to a certain curiosity. (Note the 'We', drenched in
syrup)

    - I came across him in a churchyard looking at a sundial.
(A sudden image of the man staring right through him flashes
into M.'s conscious mind, then glides down his back like it was
a lightning rod, and he smooths his wiry hair down, trying to
compose himself)

    - Ah, a sundial. Hence the equation of time.

    - If you say so. Fourteen minutes slow, that's what he said
the sun was. How in Christ's name can he know that? (Queedy
closes his eyes and it seems as though he is doing a little mental
arithmetic)

    - So, this was about two weeks ago. (M. allows his jaw
to drop but says nothing and Queedy doesn't notice because his
eyes are still closed) Where is this going?

    - We know where he is. I'm offering you the story seeing
as he's given you a second chance. Don't want you to die
before you get a by-line.

    - Do we know there is a story?

M. turned from the window and walked over to Queedy's bedside
cupboard where he knew there would be a bottle of whisky. Pouring
himself a large one into a pink plastic beaker which lay on the table he
drank it off, putting a full stop at the end of their conversation.

    - Be in my office at ten tomorrow morning. (He throws
the line backwards over his shoulder as he leaves)

It had taken Gaunt a week, and fifty pounds in cash which he would have to find a way of getting back on expenses, to track the man down. He ran his quarry to ground in a pub nestling in a cul-de-sac behind a village square. There had once been a great monastic house here, its lands sold off after Henry Tudor's expensive divorce case. A later lord of the dissolved estate had picked the wrong side in the Jacobite uprising in 1715, and the land was forfeited to the Greenwich Hospital. The prim, unadorned stone houses, formed up on all sides like a battalion of line infantry, had been built by that charitable trust for retired sailors. Later, the village thrived on the promise of a lead-mining boom high up the valley. Now it was dying on its feet, bypassed except for a few tourists lost on their way to somewhere else. The pub had been in the same family forever and the inertia of its massive oak door laid down a marker for what was inside: chintz curtains, a low ceiling made lower by fake beams, the stench of tobacco; a patterned carpet dimmed by wear and spillage. When Gaunt walked into the bar stamping the cold out of his feet the landlord levered himself off the stool where he had been reading the racing form and moved slowly over to the counter. In a dark corner the quarry, with a full glass of beer in front of him, put down the book he was reading, glanced at Gaunt and rolled himself a cigarette.

Gaunt noted without being aware of it that the talk at the bar was of the month's guest bitter and its optimum cellar temperature. The landlord contributed a lethargic comment as he pulled Gaunt's pint and examined the low sun coming from the window through the clearing beer. Gaunt moved very deliberately over to the corner where the giant sat overwhelming his chair and installed himself at the next table. He took pains to record the name of the book the man was reading, a volume of Shelley, and turned his attention to the beer. It had lain too long in the barrel and he winced.

> - Cold (says Gaunt, who might be talking about the weather or the beer).

The man said nothing, which was perfectly reasonable because

Gaunt might have been a loony and in any case sitting in the dark corner of a pub suggests a wish for privacy or solitude. None of that mattered to Gaunt, who took a cigarette noisily from the pack in his coat pocket and lit it.

- I see you are reading Shelley. (Gaunt has heard of Shelley so he sees this as a safe bet, and may convince the man that he, Gaunt, is not a loony)

- I hate this place (says the giant, whose accent, Gaunt cannot fail to notice, is clipped; he wonders if he has spent time in the colonies and the thought is filed. Sometimes even time-served hacks find themselves lost for words. The obvious question forms on Gaunt's lips but won't come out and he withdraws to what he sees as safer ground).

- All the kids from round here want to live in town where the action is. They go to college and they don't come back. I remember when this place was a thriving village, blacksmith, bakery and all. Come far?

- Yes. (The man takes a last drag of his roll-up before flicking it expertly at the log fire that isn't a log fire but fake, like the beams)

- Been here before?

- Yes.

This time the man turned and looked Gaunt straight in the eye. Like M. before him Gaunt experienced intense discomfort, like the schoolboy guilt of being caught at something private and embarrassing.

- If you hate the place, why come back. (Asking the obvious question now)

- I have not come back. I am here again.

And so saying the man returned Shelley to his coat pocket, rose from his chair leaving a third of his pint un-drunk, picked up his grip and walked out. Gaunt was not a man easily put off or discouraged. The man intrigued him as he had intrigued M. and Queedy, though for different reasons. They had been affected by his physical and moral presence, his ageless immensity. Gaunt was not impressed by such things, if indeed he noticed them. He was interested not because he thought there might be a story in it but because the man had refused to allow Gaunt to get at him, to prise off the lid, regardless of what might be inside. This was now a professional challenge.

Gaunt's impulse was to have him trailed to find out where he went, what he did, how he lived, who he knew. There would be a pattern in his behaviour and Gaunt would soon be able to predict his movements, know where he lived, when he came and went. Pointless trusting a job like this to one of the juniors: they would fuck it up. There was no time like the present. Gaunt knocked off the rest of his unsatisfactory pint, promised himself never to return and ran down the street, coat flapping, fag in mouth.

It had not occurred to Gaunt, who was religiously a car man, that his quarry might elude him by the expedient of leaving the road. Gaunt, panting, could see him now, following the line of a hedgerow along the rim of a dark shiny brown ploughed field which sloped up from the road in an inimitably ancient curve. In a few minutes he breasted the rise and, briefly picked out like a monstrous scarecrow against the northern sky, was gone. It was some time before a combination of luck and his road atlas brought Gaunt up once again with the giant. The day was fading and a brilliant orange sun coquetted with distant clouds in a dazzling show-off pyrotechnical throw-away. Gaunt found himself in a small village divided into two parts by a broad shallow stream whose rippling blue-black waters shattered the sun's perfect rays into a million particles. He parked his car on a verge, waited and watched.

Above the stream's hurry the noise of a jingling bell came from a shop on the other side. From its door a woman emerged with a small child clutching a doll. The sweet, gripping scent of wood smoke drifted on the stillness of the air. A miniature arched stone bridge spanned the stream, barely the width of the carts for which it had been built. Once there must have been a ford here, for just below the bridge the water ran smooth and clear for a few yards over ashlar sets before picking up her skirts once more and dashing for the sea.

The man had been striding along the lane towards the bridge for some minutes, his outline fading with the light but still with the same rhythmic inevitability which M. and Queedy had seen from their window, weeks before. Gaunt turned on the light in his car and checked his map. If the man crossed the bridge, as it seemed he must, then Gaunt would have to drive three miles to reach the next bridge downstream that would take a car. By then it would be dark. Well, and so he would lose his man this time.

The giant was now almost upon him. Gaunt doused the light and hoped he would not be seen, for his car lay some yards beyond the bridge. But the man did not cross the bridge. Instead he came on as if to confront his pursuer. For one moment the giant silhouette, back-lit in Old Testament glory by the sun's last fiery rays, seemed to stop before him. Then, turning towards the river, he plunged off the bank into the water. Gaunt lost sight of him and, fearing the imminence of some terrible event, leapt from his car only to see the man emerge onto the other bank from the silky water of the ford. Reaching the road, he turned and looked back at the static, frozen Gaunt, whose shambolic frame was picked out in a delicate rose-pink glow. And then, enfolded by the creeping night, he merged into shadows and vanished from sight.

Gaunt's failure to bring his man to bay was manifested in a sense of affront whose immediate victims were his wife and cat. There were no little kindnesses at home; nor at work. At the *Courier* Gaunt took to sitting at his desk in the office which he had almost never been known to use. An atmosphere of uncertainty infused the corridors. His long liquid lunches at the pub dried up, as did the steady flow of insiders' tips that fed the news room's insatiable appetite and the paper's columns. In Queedy's absence there was no one to fetch Gaunt's fags so he took to buying them by the carton and smoking a packet at a time. Nor were the office juniors an adequate substitute for Queedy's irritating precociousness; they were barely worth shouting at and quite useless as far as news gathering was concerned.

M. was uneasy, more than uneasy: he was climbing the bloody walls. February was a lousy news month anyway. Christmas and New Year drinking were over and with them the fights, crashes, domestic episodes and other festive distractions that guaranteed three pages of news every day for a fortnight. There were no competitions to pull the punters in. Dark nights offered no promise of summer holidays. Money was short. Now this.

On the last day of the month M. went down to Gaunt's office, which lurked at the dingy rear of the building overlooking, if Gaunt had ever opened the blinds, the side street where the vans came every lunchtime to pick up fat bundles of papers for the city's newsagents. M. was determined to kick the old sod into action, so he didn't knock at the door. He wanted no defensive foreplay. Inside, only the sound of Gaunt's lugubrious voice penetrated a thick haze of smoke. He was on the phone, drawing another blank from one of his network of informants. M. went over to the window to open it but it had been painted shut years before. Looking at the battered filing cabinets and unsorted piles of folders and loose paperwork littering the room, he realised it must have been ten years since he had been in there. Gaunt waved him at a wooden chair choked by a full ash-tray and two half-empty bottles of beer, but instead M. positioned himself in the comparatively clean air of the doorway and waited until the old hack put the phone down.

- Christ, Gaunt, forget it.

- Shut that bloody door, it's cold in here (says Gaunt, paying no attention).

- I mean it. (M. also paying no attention)

- You wanted him.

- Not this much.

- Have it your own way (says Gaunt, lighting another fag and leaning back in his chair).

- We've got a Minister of State from the Home Office coming to meet the Chief Constable tomorrow. I want you to cover it.

- Junior ministers is it? I can write that one from behind this fucking desk. The minister will express concern over a number of policing issues and the Chief Constable will ask for better overtime payments for his hard-pressed officers and a commitment to increasing numbers on the streets.

- Nevertheless.

M.'s attempt at finality was left suspended in the haze as Gaunt's old-fashioned phone rang. Now M. went decisively to the chair, noisily removed the ashtray and beer bottles to the corner of Gaunt's desk and sat down. Gaunt, at first listening with routine patience, now pulled a pad towards him and began writing very rapidly in shorthand, saying nothing. His movements were entirely automatic. The cigarette in his phone hand wore its way down to the knuckle, un-smoked. The ritual ground-pawing of his brief conversation with M. over, Gaunt's face now betrayed the totally unselfconscious anticipation of a child waking up on Christmas morning. He existed only in the immediate present. His blood was up. His bottom lip stuck out. He ended the phone conversation with a rapid series of questions and then, putting the receiver down, lit himself a new cigarette which, for the first time in days, he enjoyed.

- You'll have to put someone else onto your Chief Constable. I'm busy tomorrow.

M. let the silence hang in the room, waiting. He thought of the empty tranquillity of his neglected house and pictured a large gin resting on the side of a hot bath. He thought of filling his retirement with contemplation and quiet, with Tuscan sunshine and food, with literature. He wondered for a moment if he would miss Gaunt and the smell of newsprint and decided that on balance he probably would not. He thought of Queedy in his hospital bed, of Miss Nixon, of his children's university education, but none of these was so real as the picture of the large cool gin resting on the side of the bath. Just the right amount of tonic, an amount never mastered by his wife. A thick slice of lime.

- What sort of busy?

- Story busy, column inches busy. I'll need a photographer.

- Go on (M. says, wishing he was only pretending not to care and still mentally in his hot bath).

- A young foal afflicted with something incurable is declared dead by a vet, is miraculously revived, a girl's tragic loss turns to happy-ever-after. Sort of thing you like around this time of year.

- There had better be more, Gaunt (says M., and he means it). Otherwise you wouldn't be interested. The girl had better be an orphan at the very bloody least. So far it's a one-day wonder.

- There is more, yes. (Gaunt is enjoying this: he pulls an old copy of the *Courier* off his desk and rolls it tightly in his rheumy hands, wringing it almost)

- Get on with it (says M., looking very obviously at his watch).

- Description of the miracle: (Gaunt doesn't bother looking at his notes, he already has it in his head) foal dies; accidentally poisoned, it seems. A man turns up at the family farm just as the vet is driving off – nothing more he can do. The man walks into the stable where the weeping girl is being comforted by her wealthy and doting parents, lays down beside the foal with no by your leave or any nicety and brings it back to life. Simple as that: brings it back to life. (Gaunt whacks the rolled-up newspaper against the side of his desk for effect). At first they think he's another vet because he's carrying this heavy leather bag, like vets do, only it's brown not black. Description of the man – this is the girl's description: very tall, rugged-looking but gentle, might be a tramp, deep-set eyes and says nothing all the time he's doing whatever he's doing to the foal. Afterwards, when the foal is up on its feet and right as rain, he's making to go and the parents stop him and offer him money. He refuses. They ask him how they can show him their gratitude. He says he would like to camp on their farm for a few days. This is Tuesday. He's still there. The locals think he's the fucking Messiah.

    - Maybe he is.

    - No chance. But he's mine and you can get someone else to interview your Chief Constable.

    - Where is this farm?

    - Twyford, place called the Tower House.

    - You can't have him. I want Queedy on this.

    - By Christ you will not! (Gaunt shouts, so angry he can't look M. in the eye. He slams the rolled-up paper on the desk with such violence that the full ashtray clatters onto the floor)

    - Here's the Minister's schedule (says M., calm as you like, tossing a call sheet onto the desk and shutting the door firmly behind him as he leaves).

That was the afternoon on which M. made his final visit to Queedy in the Infirmary. The following day, the twentieth of February, Queedy knocked on the door of M.'s office, once more restored to his sleek, shiny self and wearing his immaculate suit. M. asked him how he was feeling and Queedy said Okay. M. told him nothing of Gaunt's interest in his giant, only that the miracle-worker who'd materialised on the farm in time to save the foal sounded as if it was their man. He had written Queedy a few briefing notes; few, because Gaunt refused to give up his shorthand scrawl. Queedy would have to interview the vet, the parents, the girl, sundry locals and especially the man himself. M. gave him the telephone number of the farm, and an address. Wishing for the first time in a very long time that he was going out on an assignment himself, M. packed Queedy off to see Stokes, the duty photographer, who had the keys to the pool car and would drive him up there.

Queedy accepted his assignment gracelessly. He could not see past a mental image of a brat with pigtails and a silver spoon wedged in her buck-toothed over-privileged mouth. He did not doubt that she would wear jodhpurs. The parents would be insufferable Tories. He hated animals, the countryside and human interest stories and he doubted if the so-called miracle-worker would live up to promise. His only satisfaction would come from exposing the miracle as a fraud or a cheap trick, and from the freedom to work without Gaunt looking over his shoulder. He was careful to betray no gratitude towards M. It would have made him feel unworthy of the assignment. He was careful also not to show the fear which suddenly came on him, catching at his heart. The voice in his head calming him down had the reedy whine of an oboe.

M., in his office, took to wondering what sort of copy Gaunt would write from his coverage of the meeting between the Minister and the Chief Constable. His mind drifted. He stood at the window for a while, but the drama outside for once bored him. The state of his office depressed him. As the afternoon wore on and Gaunt's copy did not come through, M. found he had achieved nothing. He took to writing a list of things which needed doing to his office to give to the maintenance team, although the thought of a couple of weeks of intrusion, of paint pots and rags, drills and fittings was more awful to contemplate than the slovenly state of the place. A day which had never truly been light enough to deserve the name merged imperceptibly into a murky dusk. At last he raised himself from his chair, took his coat from the hook on the back of the door. At five o'clock, to the astonishment of the girls on reception, M. left the *Courier's* offices and went home, where he ran a hot bath and drank gin.

From a bloated, starless sky thick flakes of snow began to fall across the city, enveloping its offices, shops, public houses and dwellings in a silent, immaculate counterpane.

Chapter Three

Miracle

The two dogs emerged bounding from the covert ahead of their master, spraying fresh dry snow from their paws and flanks, ears at keen attention and pink tongues lolling. Impatient, they stopped and turned every few feet, imploring urgency with their dark eyes. Above them a magpie fluttered screeching in the naked crown of an ash tree. From the edge of the wood the ground dropped away towards the Tower-house, its gardens and outhouses, dark against white hills chequered with skeletal hedges stretching into a distance swallowed by the sky.

A stocky middle-aged man now broke cover. He wore a battered waxed jacket, fur-lined wellingtons and a home-knitted woollen hat. A shotgun rested in the crook of his arm. He came to a halt where his hounds had turned and scanned the land before him, breathing hard. The Tower-house: tall, unapologetically square, an architectural fist of bygone paranoia hammered into the smooth floor of the valley. It might almost be a megalith, not constructed but quarried from the living rock and hollowed out by an army of dwarfish miners. Its narrow windows framed in formal Tudor mouldings, its steep four-pitched roof, the front door set defensively at first-floor level at the top of age-worn stone steps: even from above it imposed, dominated. Its builder had conceived it to tame, or at least deter, and, standing stark against the snowfields, it brutalised the land. It was an unsentimental cenotaph to four hundred years of border warfare, blood-feud and sleepless nights.

Even so, its current owner saw it through indulgent eyes: the eyes of the dweller returning home. He knew the sunset glow of its yellow sandstone walls, the roar of its open fires, the warmth of his bed and the welcome that would come. He saw bright yellow lights burning in the kitchen window and imagined the smell of cooking. He felt the immense solidity of the structure, was embraced by it, and could no more have imagined leaving it to walk forever than he could have imagined flying to the moon.

His view embraced the outbuildings which huddled around the Tower-house: the stable and paddocks, orchard and walled garden in their deep-winter colours, cluttering and humanising it as small children mob an indulgent grandfather. Beyond, a scrub of alder, thorn and hazel snugly bordered a small lake that looked as though it were wrapped in a woollen scarf. Here, a thin column of copper-blue smoke rose from a small camp fire into the windless grey of the sky. A flight of nervous ducks came to a skidding rest on the deeply frozen surface of the water and the man fancied he could hear their indignant chatter. His world was as it should be.

This morning the view was almost more perfect than he had ever known; almost. A rusty vehicle which he did not recognise stood near the gate; fresh tracks snaked along the short lane from the road. One of the dogs barked at him now and he leant down to fondle its wet muzzle with a gloved hand, muttering quiet words of friendship. The brace of rabbits hanging from his shoulder fell into the snow at his feet and he bent to pick them up, leaving a tiny bright smear of blood flashing red against the white. Now both dogs barked and the man, smiling, gestured to them to lead him home. It was well past the hour for breakfast.

A scene of chaotic welcome in the kitchen: dogs wildly excited, rabbits thrown onto a sideboard, boots discarded, the scraping of a chair as Queedy stood to shake hands; a kiss between father and daughter, husband and wife.

    - We saw the badger cubs. They look fine healthy. (This is Jareld, the father: white beard, sun-brown face, blue eyes exploding into crows' feet, and untamed eyebrows; a fine healthy man himself)

    - What will you have for your breakfast, Jareld? There are fresh eggs and a fried fish if you like it. (Freya, the wife and mother: she has high cheekbones and deep eyes, irresistible red lips and dyed yellow hair tied in a loose bun; she wears an old apron over dungarees, her face is lined with many cares, with poetry and laughter and unmistakable traces of former beauty)

    - I like the sound of fish and eggs very much. (Jareld is an enthusiast: he throws his woollen hat carelessly into the air from where it is plucked expertly by one of the dogs, and sits down with a thump on his chair) Has our guest eaten?

    - Yes Jara, of course. (This is the daughter, owner of the miracle foal. Her name is Selena. Queedy has imagined her as a pony-club pig-tailed brat, but he has been proved quite wrong, except for the pigtails. She is a woman of twenty or twenty-two years, more or less his own age, taller than both her parents; and slender. She has a pale complexion, and does not often laugh. She has wide, grey eyes and her otherwise untroubled face bears the scars of a childhood illness, measles or chicken pox. She wears a floral print dress over faded jeans. She moves and speaks with careful slowness; she might be saving her strength, as if she only has so much to last her. How can such a limpid, graceful thing be the child of these earthy joyous parents?)

Queedy, by way of confirming that he had eaten, pushed his plate across the table and mumbled thanks. Jareld, fork in mouth, stabbed his knife amiably at Queedy as if to see if he would flinch, and then engaged him with a mouth still full of trout and egg yolk.

- And so, Mr Queedy, our newspaper friends have sent you to write a story about the miracle man. Have you met the gentleman yet?

- I am just about to, I believe. (Queedy sees his chance to make a getaway, but he is waved back into his chair and a fresh mug of tea is placed before him)

- You will find he is an interesting fellow, if you can get him to tell you anything that you would like to know. He talks quite a bit but doesn't say much, if you see what I mean. Does he, Mette? (This is Jareld's pet name for his daughter)

- No Papa, he says little.

- Has he told you his name?

- No, no, he has no name; I think he likes to have us guess – it is part of the mystery. I have decided to name him the Ambulist. I think it's a pretty good name. What do you say, Mr Queedy?

- Ambulist. An invention, I take it?

- Of course! You English, you love to make up new words. You must allow us foreigners to join in sometimes. Ambulist is good: I have decided it means a man who walks forever.

- Is that what he does?

- You have to ask him. (Jareld fills his mouth with another ambitious forkful of fish and eggs but cannot wait to finish it before firing off a parting shot) But he won't tell you! Ha! Am I right, Mette?

Sensing that he was too easy a prey for this garrulous man, and uncomfortable in the happy chaos of the steaming crowded kitchen,

Queedy stood up and began to look for his coat, which had been taken from him and immured within some distant passageway. One of the dogs licked his hand as he passed and he looked without luck for something clean to wipe it on. The girl rose too and, recovering his coat, led Queedy out of the kitchen and down the steps into the yard where Stokes, the photographer, was snapping away.

Stokes was hairy, overweight and crumpled. Like Queedy he hated human interest stories, the outdoors and creatures with fur. He was not much engaged by the beauty of landscape or the form of architecture. But he knew how an image worked on a page of newsprint and how it could be created through his lens. He understood light and composition. Above all, he made a virtue of speed and efficiency and he did not like to miss a meal. His editor relied on him in the same way that he relied on paper merchants and postmen. Stokes delivered.

Today was not promising. The light was terrible: flat, lacking contrast and right at the limit of his lenses' capabilities and of his fastest film. He had never worked with Queedy before and suspected him on principle of the sins of interference or philistinism or both. Worse, Queedy was so thin that he probably wouldn't care whether he ate lunch or not. Stokes reasoned that he should cultivate the acquaintance of the homely-looking woman in the dungarees, who had already noticed the size of his belly and smuggled him out a fat roll filled with thick bacon rashers, fried tomatoes and some previously un-encountered but perfectly acceptable sauce.

After the tropical warmth of the kitchen, the damp cold of winter air in the yard made Queedy shiver inside his expensive coat. The yard was flagged with uneven stone paving, lethally camouflaged under its white blanket. Queedy walked with great care, extending his arms in an attempt to improve his balance. On two sides stood low brick outbuildings with orange pantiled roofs just showing their ridges through the snow: a wood store, an ancient milking parlour, stables whence the shuffling of animals could be heard. A half-consumed bale

of hay lay under a canvas tarpaulin in one corner; here and there a
nondescript farm implement leant rusting against a wall. A heap of
straw and dung steamed gently. Hens, fat under their ruffled feathers,
pecked at loose grains through snow dirtied with footprints. A black
cat tottered past, now and then shaking its paws in disgust, on some
private, predatory mission. On the third side of the yard, between
the kitchen wall and the stables, were a wooden gate and a stone wall
enclosing a pen on the other side.

At the sound of snow-muffled human footsteps in the yard the
head of a handsome piebald goat appeared at the wall, sniffing the dank
air, its manic eyes sizing up the newcomers with intent which could
have been malice. It disappeared for a moment, gathering itself, before
vaulting the wall and skidding at alarming speed across the icy stone
flags towards the little knot of people. In a hopeless attempt at an
emergency braking manoeuvre it stuck its four feet rigidly out and slid
to a precarious rest with its head firmly pressed against Queedy's groin.
Queedy by pure instinct sprang back and the goat, sensing his recoil
as a provocation, lowered its head for a determined assault before the
girl, with deceptive speed, took hold of one of its horns and expertly
immobilised it.

- Billy, now, you mustn't butt people before you get to
know them (she says, reaching into her pocket for half a carrot
which the goat grabs boorishly).

- I take it (Queedy says, recovering his poise) that this is
the culprit.

- Yes, Billy is the culprit. You are a bad goat, Billy. (She
strokes Billy's idiotically lop-sided ears while he shamelessly
stares at Queedy's groin)

- As I understand it from what your mother was saying
(Queedy is careful to keep the girl between himself and his antagonist) the goat broke into a bag of feed which was lying here
in the yard, and the foal was able to get at it before you became

aware. (The rising tone implies a question)

- Yes... you see, normally we put the goat feed in the wood store and keep it locked. By the time we realised, the foal was already dying.

- And this is a donkey foal, not a horse? I had supposed...

- Oh, yes. Tigger is four months old, nearly ready to wean.

- Tigger (says Queedy, spotting some intended irony in the name but unsure if he should attempt some play on it. There is a short silence, as if the snow has sucked all noise from the air).

Queedy now took out his notebook and read from the shorthand he had already taken in the kitchen. The girl gestured the men towards one of the outhouses whose stable door was half-open at the top. She slid the bolt across and stood back for Queedy and Stokes to go in, but the goat was there first, eager to see his convalescing partner-in-crime, who lay engulfed by a landslide of fresh straw. Its doleful-looking mother stood stoically at its side. An oil lamp hanging from a rafter gave the scene a biblical poignancy which Queedy sensed and instantly dismissed. The foal raised its head feebly, recognised its friend and struggled to its feet. The goat butted its neck gently, and bleated.

- We'll just stay for a minute (says the girl). Can you manage your pictures without a flash? (This to Stokes, who makes a face but nods)

- This chemical Rumensin, the antibiotic present in goat feed but fatal to equines... did you know about it before? Are there warnings on the bags and so on? I will have to explain for the readers, you see. (Queedy, in the company of three live animals and a girl whose strange grace has put him out of countenance, wants to get this part of his business out of the way)

- Oh yes, everyone knows about Rumensin: it's often fatal in horses and donkeys, especially in a young foal. (She kneels down beside the foal and puts her arm around its neck, stroking its muzzle)

- And the vet?

- When we phoned and told him what had happened he
knew Tigger would be dead before he got here; but he came
anyway.

- I would like to talk to him. Perhaps you can give me his
number? I shall be interested to know what he thinks of your
miracle. (Queedy realises immediately that this sounds both
patronising and sceptical but he does not apologise and the girl
seems not to take offence)

The party was now outside in the yard again. From the kitchen
came faint sounds of laughter and barking. Queedy felt unwell and his
overwhelming desire to run away began to manifest itself in a nervous
cough. The girl might have been waiting for him to ask another
question for she stood quite still, her lips and cheeks now pink with
cold; but she did not look at Queedy. Her expressionless eyes were
cast down towards the ground. Was she caught, perhaps, in the void
between existence and memory whose emptiness was absolute. The
rough attentions of the goat brought her to life once more. Again she
found half a carrot in a pocket and let the goat steal it roughly from her
hand.

Now the girl looked directly at Queedy, her pale eyes searching
his face. He wondered whether suddenly she had become as it were
aware of his existence for the first time. Was she trying, perhaps, to
place him in a taxonomy of the creatures in her ark as if she sensed his
fragility, his need to be cared for? Perhaps he too needed to be petted
and quietly admonished, fed titbits from time to time from her graceful
hand. If so, the goat's resentment of him as a competitor for her
affections was comprehensible. The thought unnerved Queedy extr-
emely. For the second time his composure failed him and a sudden
thumping in his chest nearly brought him to his knees. Rescue came
with Stokes' impatient insistence that they now make the acquaintance

of the man who had worked his miracle on the foal: this Ambulist. The party made its way through the gate and down towards the copse of trees. The goat followed them, always keeping himself between Queedy and the girl.

At the edge of the lake the camp fire filled the air with now a biting tannin reek of oak wood and now the sweet caramel scent of frying fish. In this feeble winter light the fire's orange heart cast a livid glow onto the icy lake and onto the face of the man as he leaned over the flames, nursing a chipped enamel mug in his hands. A tin plate, empty and wiped clean with bread, lay at his feet. At his back, forming the flimsiest of lean-to shelters, stood an improvised bivouac of interwoven hazel sticks, baler twine and empty plastic feed bags, its only apparent luxury a floor of loose straw which must have been donated vicariously by one of the girl's creatures. Incongruous set against the bare veinous trees behind, it might have been proof against a light shower or the faintest of breezes, but no more. The most hardened nomad could not have levelled the accusation of dwelling against it, nor had any apparent craft or expertise been used in its construction.

Was this incompetence or did it testify to wilful negligence? Was it possible to believe that a man who walks endlessly denying the seductive chains of the hearth, the roof and the door cannot – actually cannot – fashion a weather-tight shelter? If so, was he then a mere vagabond? Did he fear that a concession to comfort would make it harder for him to leave? Or did this healer of humble animals practice a pure Franciscan asceticism; was he a Saint Godric, lacking only a pet viper? His apparently miraculous resuscitation of their donkey foal entitled the girl Selena and her parents to incurious acceptance of this contradiction. But Gaunt would want an answer, M. would demand an answer, and so would the prurient readers of the *Courier*. Queedy himself wanted to know only because not knowing discomfited him.

M. had warned Queedy of Gaunt's reception by his prospective interviewee. He feared that Queedy, in his city clothes, with his

patronising air and tactlessness, might dash himself against the
adamantine giant and be broken; feared and, perhaps, hoped a little. But
Gaunt had come at the man uninvited, and if Queedy could be tactless
his expensive education had conferred on him patrician manners which
he now self-consciously adopted, not for the sake of the Ambulist but
because he had felt Selena's measuring gaze on him ever since they
had arrived in the yard. As if surrendering to the role of orphan pet, he
sought her approbation.

The miracle-worker was expecting this delegation. Its arrival
was announced by the theatrical entry of the goat who, attempting to
snatch a mouthful of the titanic greatcoat in passing, went instantly into
the shelter and lay down with proprietorial complacency. The man had
raised no objections when Selena approached him with their request for
an interview. He may have acquiesced because, like Queedy, he found
the girl Selena enigmatic and strangely attractive. If he did not seek the
attention of the press, nor did he actively disdain it. A man who walks
forever may please himself and choose his company. Why should he
not talk about himself? Gaunt had encroached on his privacy, had
presumed. Selena, Queedy and Stokes came to his camp by invitation
and if his hospitality was necessarily Spartan it was nevertheless that
of the traveller: unambiguous and disinterested. His fire was their fire
– did they realise he was sharing his living soul with them? His tea, his
tobacco and his whisky were offered freely and with generosity. He
seemed almost to be childishly flattered by having his picture taken; he
positively posed for Stokes, whose malnourished lens now gorged on
the magnificent face.

There was one thing: the Ambulist – Queedy began to like
the sound of the word – would be grateful if the *Courier* could find
its way to replacing his map of the county, now in its last throes of
decrepitude. Queedy told him that the *Courier* on no account ever paid
for interviews; but he thought the paper might furnish a new map out
of incidental expenses.

Later, reading his elegant shorthand back to himself, Queedy was surprised to see how brief his notes were, because at the time it seemed as if he had barely stopped writing. At the top of a fresh page was an empty line for the title of his story; beneath it a list of facile thoughts scribbled down and struck through with his pencil. Then a note that the man would not give his name. He could have given Queedy or anyone an ordinary name which said nothing about him. But he would not. A name did not signify, he said. He had once possessed such a thing, but had left it behind with the rest of his belongings many years ago.

Below the space where he would have written a name came Queedy's rendering of a species of autobiography that teased and evaded, tempted, misled. Or was meant to mislead. When had he started walking? When he first kicked his mother's belly from the inside. About the mother... no memories of her, she died in childbirth. The father, then... an officer in the Indian army, always away, hardly known. He had spent some of his youth in the Punjab. Had he walked much there? Had India given him a love of walking? No, it had given him a love of rickshaws and elephants and a hatred of snakes. Schooling? He had never been to school, had learned with uncles, aunts, a tea-planting second cousin, and then... and then? He had joined the merchant navy, had travelled. He was vague on detail. He had married once but it had come to nothing, he had no children. In his middle years he had lived in Canada where he got a job on a train that ran right across the continent from Quebec to Vancouver.

He had not set foot in England until he was sixty. He had supposed it to be a small country made up of fragments of other countries stitched together like an old patchwork quilt and had been astonished to find it was not a country at all, but a tapestry of arcane stories woven together with thread that was an ancient, forgotten language. It had amazed him to find that there was no one left who spoke the tongue of the aboriginal inhabitants. He wondered how anyone could understand their past when they could not read the words the land spoke to them.

He had determined to learn this language for himself.

He began to believe he could read, to decode the wonders of this enigmatic tapestry and had travelled the length and breadth of the country by train. Then he came to see that if you moved too quickly in this land it spoke in tongues, you could not parse its grammar nor feel the rhythm of its poetry. One day he set out to study the land on foot. Every day he walked further and every day he found it harder to return home because when he did he would lose his place in the story. At length he came to the knowledge that he must walk the land until he became fluent in its ancient languages. Then England began to lay itself before him, to seduce him. He had learned to tell the time by the sun and to navigate using the stars. He studied houses, factories and roads, farmyard gates, allotment gardens. He came to know the shapes and textures of the landscape: the way trees lived together and with animals and flowers, the flow and form of fields and hedges. He followed rivers from the sea to their up-welling springs in the hills, he climbed mountains and began to feel that he might one day be able to locate himself anywhere in England merely by the smell or taste of the soil underfoot. He also sensed that he could never come to a perfect knowledge of this country and accepted that he must therefore walk forever.

As Queedy read the notes of this shifting, diaphanous tale, this fireside yarn spun to entertain and obfuscate, he felt that he was not the first to be enchanted by it. He resented the man's artistry, his self-assurance, but at the same time he had been absorbed by its magic. He could not be sure whether the man he was interviewing was simply a tramp, or what perhaps Queedy, certainly M., and for that matter the girl and her parents wanted him to be: a savant of some kind, a charismatic healer. In the first case, how dare he be so self-possessed when the modern world demanded property as a qualifying badge? How could a man who possessed nothing create the fiction that he in fact had everything? And in the second case? So far there was no second case.

The account of the so-called miracle, which began on the next page of Queedy's notebook, was striking largely on account of its banality. The Ambulist had passed through the village on the morning of the incident with the goat feed and seen the vet drive past at speed. He had noticed a sign at the top of the farm track advertising eggs – Queedy had seen the sign himself – and on arriving at the gate to the Tower-house had witnessed the vet getting back in his car and the distressed girl being comforted by her parents. Having some experience with animals – Queedy must interview him again: what experience? What animals? How? When? – he had gone into the stable to see if he might be of any assistance.

The next part of the story was told by the girl, Selena, because he – the Ambulist – claimed not to remember what he had done. According to her she went into the stable to ask him who he was and found him lying by the foal, one giant hand covering its muzzle and the other stroking its flank. Queedy had crossed out the word 'stroking'; the girl had corrected herself. Stroking was wrong: it seemed to her that he had been feeling for something under the skin, had probed with his hand. How long for? For some minutes, she supposed, it was difficult to say. What else had he done? Again, it was difficult to say. He seemed almost to have fallen asleep, when the foal opened its eyes, struggled to release itself from his embrace, and scrambled disoriented to its feet as Selena watched; whereupon its mother licked its head copiously and let out a most tremendous bray which brought the parents, Jareld and Freya, running into the stable. The Ambulist, she recalled, had lain for some moments before waking. He himself confessed to Queedy a feeling of confusion, as if he had emerged from a deeply convincing dream. Another question: what had he dreamed of?

Queedy felt the same frustration reading his notes back as he had when writing them. There was an affecting simplicity to the story which demanded to be accepted as truth. And yet the thing was absurd. Queedy would be interested, very interested, to know what the vet made of this. Surely the vet must have been mistaken when he declared the foal dead. What the Ambulist had effected was nothing more nor less than cardiac massage. The heart had stopped and he had started it again. What the girl, the man and the parents believed to have happened was incidental. Whether the man was an itinerant fraud who practised on the credulous remained to be seen. His refusal to take money, assuming this to be true and assuming he would not attempt to extort it later, mitigated, yes. But to accept the narrative at face value would not do.

M. stood at the window in his office staring out at a featureless white canvas which utterly obscured the market place. It disoriented him, gave him the feeling of being cast adrift on a great ocean waiting for something nasty like an iceberg, on which his office would founder, to loom out of the fog. Instead, his phone rang. It was Queedy, his oboe voice half-drowned by the background hum and clatter of the village pub, where a happy Stokes sat facing an over-generous plate of home-made pie and mashed potatoes.

> - See what I mean (says M., looking at the glass of his window, not through it)?
>
> - About what?
>
> - Learning the trade, Son. Or have I said that before?
>
> - Not sure I can help you: I've seen no brawling drunks or time-expired hacks, so maybe I don't have a story.
>
> - Did I never tell you about the other sort of story, the one that starts with a virgin, a manger and three wise men and ends with a resurrection?
>
> - I don't think the girl is a virgin. (Queedy can't tell if M. is being serious, but for that matter M. doesn't know either, so maybe it isn't important)
>
> - What about the resurrection?
>
> - Debatable (says Queedy).

- Aren't they always?

- Well, this one is cast-iron debatable. (M. likes this sort of irony, though from what he knows of Queedy it isn't intended, so he doesn't laugh but bats it straight back)

- It's a comfort, sure. Witnesses? Any passing Wise Men or shepherds?

- Do you want the copy I've written or do you want it straight from my notes?

- We'll start with your notes, Son. I like to hear my second-hand witnesses first-hand.

Queedy read the account of the so-called miracle the way the man and the girl told it to him, avoiding his own commentary not because he didn't have an opinion but because he wanted M. to ask him what he thought; wanted to hear M. asking him, like he was a real journalist. He was, for the moment, disappointed. M. wanted first of all to know what the vet had said. Queedy, who also wanted to know, was forced to admit he hadn't yet interviewed the vet, who was away on a call and couldn't be reached. M., suspecting a species of mission-creep, told him he wanted copy for that evening's deadline, so Queedy had better camp outside the vet's house and get his side of the story damn quick. He also wanted quotes from the locals. The old boys at the bar would do. That was why they were there; that and feeding Stokes. Queedy wanted to assure M. that he was being a responsible journalist. M. said he felt fully assured, and half-meant it. Queedy said he hoped it was all right if he paid a few quid for the replacement map the Ambulist had wanted.

- Stop calling him the Ambulist and find out his real bloody name.

- Will you let me off the name if I tell you I have his worn-out old map with me, a map covered in interesting marks, symbols, annotations and curious arrows? He wants it back, but I could have a copy made. (Maple syrup drowns the nerves

in Queedy's voice, almost)

    - You'd better bring the bloody thing here. And no. I want his name.

As a day of inexpressible gloom slid into a night like a thick curtain, the glare of an orange street lamp through the shuttered blinds in Gaunt's office illuminated the sulking hack's face. Otherwise the room was dark. Gaunt was brooding. He had known the boy would fuck this story up. He had the evidence in front of him, run through with his pencil like a blunt sword. It was full of shit. Half a column too long for a start, though he could cut it down easy enough. It prosed on like an undergraduate essay, missing the guts of the thing. It was too clever, too knowing, the style affected. It was a cub reporter's idea of a foreign correspondent painting a picture of a far-off land. And as for the title of the piece: the Ambulist. This was the *Courier*, for fuck's sake.

    Gaunt, for the first time realising that there was now insufficient light to read or write by, flicked on his desk lamp, inserted a sheet of paper in the long-superseded manual typewriter which even he hadn't used for years, and knocked out the copy that Queedy should have written. The copy that he, Gaunt, would have written. It took him ten minutes. It made a good little story. The man was a character; matter of fact Gaunt would still like to nail him over a beer in a bar. The disappearing act annoyed him. The girl, too, had mileage, from an editor's point of view. The family, the whole farm scenario had a rustic provincial flavour which city readers liked in their Saturday paper. It made them feel urbane and smug. It would have made a better story in the week before Christmas. A much better story. But he bet himself sightseers would start turning up at the gate asking for eggs and taking pictures, trying to get a shot of the man in the woods without getting too close for fear he might eat their children. Maybe he should go out there himself. If he did he would take his own camera: he couldn't do worse than Stokes, whose freshly-developed film contained a number of nice shots of the girl and her donkey but whose pictures of the man he had somehow managed to get out of focus. They were useless. Stokes was useless. Everyone was useless.

It was late. Gaunt didn't bother, or rather wilfully avoided, passing his new, better copy past M. The boss had probably gone home already, he said to himself. He ran the piece downstairs to one of the duty subs, grabbed a packet of fags and his hat and coat, and made his way through the dismal murk of the market place to the pub via the seductive bright lights and flashing screens of the bookie's. Did he feel bad about giving the piece his own by-line? Did he hell: it would teach the boy to listen. The little shit.

Upstairs M., still at his window, would have seen Gaunt pass into and out of his view of the market place had the fog not been so impenetrable. He would have wondered what had happened to Queedy's copy. He knew Gaunt would butcher it, both for form's sake and because it was not a good piece. That is to say, it was not a piece for the *Courier*. What could he have expected? Queedy was a rookie, it was a tricky story to tell right, and he – M., that is – would deflate the boy as gently as he could. He turned back to his desk, put his glass of whisky down and reached for Queedy's copy. No, in itself it was not right. If anything it was too polished and it sounded like it was supposed to be written for a Sunday national; it condescended in the way Queedy always condescended. Too long, of course. Altogether up its own end. But he was interested to read again what the vet had said when Queedy finally tracked him down. And he was forced to admit to himself that he rather liked the title.

The vet, on hearing what had happened and listening to the symptoms the girl described, expected the foal to be dead when he got there. It was a clear case of equine monensin toxicosis caused by ingestion of the antibiotic generically known as Rumensin. Typically this caused tachycardia, sweating, passing of dark urine, lassitude and cardiac arrhythmia. All these had been confirmed by the girl. When the vet got to the donkey foal it was barely breathing and immobile. Its heart stopped within two or three minutes and there was nothing to be done. When asked for his reaction to the animal's resuscitation, which he had already heard about in the village, the vet confessed to being astounded. This was Queedy's translation: what he had actually said was that he was very surprised, and delighted, because he knew the family well and was aware of how fond the girl was of the foal. Could he explain the revival? No, was his simple response. He could not. Was it possible that cardiac massage could have effected a revival? On its own, no: a lethal toxin could not simply be massaged out of a heart which had stopped. Had he ever met the man? No. Had he heard of him before? Again, no. What did he think were the chances of the foal surviving? The vet's reply was that he would be going over to the farm to give it a proper examination, but that if it had survived a case of monensin poisoning it could probably survive anything. And yes, he would be very pleased to meet the man who had succeeded where he had failed. Here M. spotted the forensic traces of Queedy's accusatory line of questioning; well, it was a reasonable question, he would have asked it himself.

M. put the copy down and thought to himself that Queedy might one day make a journalist if only he would bloody well listen to good advice. He and Gaunt had put each other's backs up, but Gaunt, for all he was an irritable, cussed, obstructive old sod, meant well. Sure, he meant well.

M. lumbered through streets which had somehow lost their familiarity in the oppressive gloom. The front door of his Victorian terraced house came suddenly at him through a swirling atmospheric soup. Peering at it, he read the story of its neglect in the peeling forest-green paint before even he recognised the number. He could hear his own thoughts as he turned the key and entered the hall. He felt for the light switch and as he flicked it the light bulb blew and he swore, fumbling along the corridor until he came to the open door which led down two stone steps to the kitchen. The neon strip light in the ceiling flickered uncertainly into life. He put the kettle on automatically and then, seeing there was no milk in the fridge, switched it off and instead ran himself a hot bath and poured a glass of gin which could not be described as mean. But, Christ Jesus, how had he run out of limes?

Chapter Four

The Ambulist

Darkness fell on the stillness of the lake. A three-quarter moon, the snow moon of February, perfect in its crystal whiteness, rose steeply above the eastern horizon. Through the thin veiling scrub of alder and hazel it clambered into a sky emptying of the day's last light as pioneer stars began to prick its deepening canopy. Scratching, shuffling, settling noises, betraying the chores of winter's hardy creatures, cut crisply through the intensely cold, windless air, deadened only by the mantle of snow which lay across the land. The sea fret which had muffled city and coast alike in its linen shroud for days had not penetrated so far inland, and even at this early hour of evening the arm-thick ice that held the lake under its battened hatch had begun answering the night's call with the sinister creak of a rope under strain.

The Ambulist, sitting motionless on the ground before his shabby bivouac, opened all his senses to the natural drama which he alone might witness because he would not or could not dwell. The penetrating musk of a fox's territorial scent, the faint sweet trace of

the goat's greedy muzzle on his coat, a hoary whiff of frost, came to
him on the rigid air. From the far side of the lake came a discontented
chatter of ducks and geese. The slow dance of blue shadows cast by
the moon tracking across the lake's imperturbable surface held him
entranced. Even so, the urge to set match to his fire, to rekindle his
living soul before he too froze, was strong. He waited until the moon
was clear of the trees, unconsciously naming the familiar features of
its seas and craters, before he indulged himself, announcing his own
entrance onto the stage.

The wanderer's camp fire is small: he does not try to tame the
night, nor beat it back with the consuming pyromaniac lust of the
back-garden bonfire-builder. He takes what he must of the earth's
abundance, and no more. The living tree's dying gifts warm him
and dry his clothes, raise his spirit and cook his meal; but the fire is a
solitary companion, not his tribe. And he knows, as his ancestors had
known since they first captured the wild fire of the bush from the great
darkness, that the secrets of the universe are held in its tiny roaring
heart.

Hours passed. The moon hung high in its southern arc, its milky
glaze veiling the navigator's guiding stars. The fire's embers glowed
a rich senescent red. The Ambulist's silent covenant with the land was
now broken by busying noises from the courtyard up at the Tower-
house: an accusatory bleat; the sound of straw being teased from a bale
and a wooden door being opened, then closed on its latch. Hints of
music, perhaps, from the open kitchen door and a bark as someone –
the girl? – went back inside. The door again... and the human noises
faded into the night's own unobtrusive sound-scape. And then...
movement on the path: light footfall in the snow, a swaying kinetic
melody which could only be the girl called Selena. Fur-lined boots,
loose trousers tucked in below the knee, a quilted jacket, plaits caught
unself-consciously in a hood at the back, woollen gloved hands which
held something heavy: Selena broke the circle of the fire's rippling

orange light bearing the gift of food.

    - I thought you might like to taste Jara's rabbit stew. There are potatoes, carrots and onions. And I have made some nice bread. It is still warm. (She waits until the Ambulist motions with his hand, and then sits, legs crossed, her soft eyes catching the glow of the fire, absorbing it but giving little back)

    - Ah. I have a great fondness for rabbit stew. Your father likes to hunt. I have seen him, out early with his dogs.

    - Yes. He likes to cook too. He likes many things. (She laughs, only it is more a hum than a laugh and is soon lost to the night)

The Ambulist leaned forward and took the lid from the iron pot so that a cloud of steam unfolded and rose billowing white against the sky. The overwhelming gamey smell of the rabbit simmering in its gravy seemed momentarily to transport him to another place and time so that he closed his eyes. And then, breaking a hunk of fresh bread in his giant hand, he dipped it into the pot and ate. The girl did not watch him but set herself to adding sticks to the failing embers until once more the fire began to crackle and spark.

    - You must keep the rest of the stew for your breakfast.

    - Thank you, Meisje.

    - Please, what is mayshya?

    - Ah, meisje is a little child. I do not mean it to offend you. In my homeland it is affectionate.

    - You told the reporter you were brought up in India, didn't you?

    - Ja, klopt, we will see if he believes everything people tell him. He is quite clever I think but he also is a child; a wounded child. Only not a meisje but a jonge, wet behind the ears. He needs someone to look after him. (The Ambulist, as if the girl has disarmed him, allows his voice to soften and the swallowed vowels of his native tongue now betray him)

- I think you have come out of Africa. (The shimmering heat of the fire's blaze transports Selena for a moment to a seductive fantastical landscape of baobab and acacia trees, of prowling beasts, chirping insects and a savannah camp fire)

- I think maybe you are a wanderer, like me. Like that old white fellah up there. (He nods his head upwards at the moon)

- I don't know what you mean.

- Maybe not. Who gave you your name, child?

- My parents, of course.

- When you were born.

- Yes. Why not?

- So. (He offers nothing more by way of explanation but lets the silence between them speak for him and the girl merely watches his face, which seems to respond like molten rock to the living flame of the fire)

The earth's ghostly companion continued its nomad arc across the winter sky, forever falling toward a western horizon which it would not meet until it was swallowed by the dawn.

Queedy, in his city apartment, woke perturbed. The ivory walls of his bedroom, high up in a red-brick building expensively converted from the skeleton of a defunct Victorian manufactory, were brilliantly illuminated by the sun, and he wondered stupidly if it was later than the hour shown by his clock. He rose and walked naked to the iron-framed window which offered such expensive views of the river and its bridges, the old merchant houses huddled along the quayside, the spires of churches and the ancient castle keep; but not this morning. Directly before him a Union flag hung solemnly still from the roof of the castle keep. Traffic flowed in double-glazed silence across the bridges and in the far distance, towards the sea, gigantic yellow, blue and red cranes peered like browsing giraffes above a celestial plain of pure white cotton: mist still lay thick over the city and the river below so that its houses, shops, offices and bars, the narrow roads, crossings and pavements appeared to have been erased from the city's map.

Queedy's sense of dislocation was not eased by a hot shower, from which he emerged wide awake but feeling slightly dizzy. He looked at his naked body in the mirror. Without the expensive clothes there was no hiding the brittleness of his insubstantial frame, which no regime of exercise or diet seemed able to forge into manhood. He dutifully swallowed his pills and brewed himself a potent coffee. An uncomfortable sensation grew on him as he dressed that perhaps, in his dealings with the Ambulist, with the vet, with the odd girl and her over-friendly parents, he had missed something. Or, rather, he had the feeling that he had somehow walked past an open door without pushing at it hard enough; without, he imagined, noticing it was there. A door that Gaunt, or indeed his unofficial guardian, M., would have had no hesitation kicking down. He had got the nub of the story all right, had treated it with a sophistication which even the philistine readers of the *Courier* would find refreshing. At the same time, he was not entirely sure he had got at the truth. The man coincidentally passing by the farm; his disinterested resurrection of the donkey foal: did he do this sort of thing often? Was it just another day in the life of a tramp? Was he a tramp? The rationalist in Queedy demanded that the Ambulist have a past, present and future and preferred the idea that he should be exposed as a sharp. Given the chance, it would be interesting to verify his story. Queedy consoled himself with the assurance that he had written an acknowledged column for the paper, that more would now surely follow. At the very least Gaunt would have to treat him with a new respect.

Queedy rushed his breakfast, for he was to present himself with the Ambulist's tattered map at M.'s office before nine, and ran down four flights of stairs rather than wait for the lift. He found himself, as M. had the previous night, ghosting along streets which had lost their familiar shape, length and direction. His walk became elasticated into a dreamy mile through a stifling chiffon world. The heavy glass doors of the *Courier's* entrance reflected only his mood back at him, and the morning's sombre atmosphere must have infected the girls on the front desk too, for they barely gave him a nod as he passed by towards the lift. To his surprise, he found that M. had not yet arrived at his office; it was Stokes, the photographer, who stood dishevelled and hairy at the window staring out at nothingness.

Stokes was cross; more than cross. He was humiliated. That he should return from an assignment without a printable picture of the main subject in the story was an affront. What was worse, he had seen the negatives of the film and could not explain why his shots of the Ambulist were out of focus. He found no consolation in the belated discovery of a dirty lens, a failed light meter: the equipment was in perfect order. No. Stokes had screwed up. He couldn't understand it and he couldn't take it: it diminished him. Queedy's 'Bad luck old chap' did not help. Nor had M.'s curt summons early that morning, which so unsettled Stokes that he had been unable to eat breakfast.

The incongruous pair stood silent, waiting for their editor-in-chief as the minutes passed until Queedy, his self-confidence returning and reinforced by this turn of events, felt emboldened to sit in M.'s voluptuous chair, oblivious to Stokes's look of horrified astonishment. By way of making himself feel better, Stokes asked Queedy if he had seen his story in the paper. No, he hadn't, but then, he had written it so he didn't really need to, did he? Perhaps not, Stokes replied, smiling to himself for the first time that day... perhaps not.

M., on reading Gaunt's version of Queedy's story for the first time that morning and inflamed by the old sod's arrogation of the boy's by-line, had run Gaunt to ground at the cavernous rear entrance of the building where the delivery van drivers were enjoying their bacon rolls and hot tea. Gaunt, cigarette in mouth, was yarning away with one of the men, knowing bloody well that M. would be after him and trying to put off the evil moment as long as possible. He was already working on a counter-offensive; even so, he knew he was for it.

- Christ bloody hell, Gaunt. (This is all the editor-in-chief can bring himself to say; Gaunt's mate, seeing the way the wind lies with the boss purple of face and clutching a rolled-up copy of yesterday's Late City edition in his raised fist, backs discreetly away and joins his peers at a distance)

- The little shit had it coming. (This is not brilliant from Gaunt; it is a defensive parry only; but it will do for now; and for good measure he sticks his bottom lip out in a gesture of pure truculence)

- This is a serious newspaper, Christ Jesus! I won't have you stealing by-lines and re-writing copy without my say-so. (M. pulling rank doesn't quite convince since it hasn't worked these last twenty years, and he doesn't suppose it will now; but he's got more than half a mind on Queedy's reaction when he sees the copy and doesn't want the boy back in hospital with a fit of the vapours. Besides, Gaunt has it coming)

- You're a bit bloody precious about that boy, aren't you? Don't remember you being so protective before about your snotties... Don't suppose he's your unacknowledged love child, is he, by any chance? (Gaunt spots his opening and sticks the knife in – and just for a moment it crosses his mind that he might have scored a bullseye, because M. flushes a full high-blood-pressure red)

- And supposing he was. (A brilliant recovery by M., his back up against the ropes; it brings Gaunt up with a round turn)

- I've got work to do. Somebody has to fill the fucking columns on this piss pot rag. (With that Gaunt stalks off in the direction of his office; a metaphorical bell rings for the end of the round and both fighters so to speak spit a tooth and a mouthful of blood into the second's bucket as they retire to their corners)

M., having in retrospect enjoyed his little bout with Gaunt, calmed himself sufficiently by the time he got to his office to compose his features with a facade of professional indifference.   Queedy, feeling slightly seasick, had left M.'s chair and was leafing through a biography of William Randolph Hearst by one of his mistresses.   On M.'s entrance Queedy glanced up at the clock as if to imply that he had been kept waiting.   In M.'s early years it would have cost a cub reporter a week's wages.   But the look on Queedy's face told M. that this cub had not seen Gaunt's copy, and so he stayed his hand.

Was it possible?   It was, M. realised with a sense almost of disbelief, entirely in character that this boy should fail to read the edited and printed version of his first published story.   It would not have occurred to him to reflect critically upon himself.   So be it.   Better not to disabuse him, for the moment.   The look on Stokes's face told the editor-in-chief that the photographer had arrived at the same conclusion, and the two old pros came close to sharing a silent joke. But this was no time for M. to be friendly with his staff, and Queedy's delusional failure to discover Gaunt's betrayal now presented him with a strategy.   His one hope was that Gaunt's downbeat treatment of the miracle would ensure that the story did not, had not yet reached, would not excite the interest of the nationals.   Not until the *Courier* had nailed it.

- Gentlemen, before the world's media descend on us and steal our exclusive nativity story, let's just get it right, shall we? Here we have the Second Coming of Christ, but we don't know what to call him. We have a bona fide miracle, but we don't have a picture of the miracle-worker. The report, if you can call it that, is written in the style of an Edwardian gentleman's memoir. I am trying to run a regional newspaper with a readership in terminal decline and here (M. is standing behind his chair, gripping its back with both hands as if he has all their futures in his hands) is my story of the decade. I want to know who this man is. I want name, rank, number, mother,

father, school, loves, life, vices, the whole bloody lot. Go back
to that farm and get me some facts and don't be satisfied with
the flannel he gave you yesterday. The man is in his sixties or
seventies, for Christ's sake. Where has he been? Where is he
going? How many other miracles have there been? Why have
we never heard of him before? What the hell is he doing here?

M. had once had pretensions to be a politician. He liked rhetoric,
it tasted good when rolled around the palette; and when he was in full
flow he was irresistible. He had a passion for storytelling, learned
at his Rathmullan granny's knee; he loved the Bible and the gospels
and the thought that these two standing in front of him did not seem
to care, did not understand, could not comprehend the nature of the
golden dust slipping through their fingers, enraged him. But now,
having worked himself up to full steam, M. waved them both away.
Queedy was too dumbstruck to offer up a defence and followed the
shuffling, emasculated Stokes out, meek as a lamb, leaving the copy of
the Ambulist's map on the desk.

Queedy's earlier discomposure now explained itself. The vague
sense that he had woken with, of something missing, once articulated,
was now blindingly obvious. He had been seduced by the deceptive
charm of the titanic vagabond; he supposed that the girl and her family
had too; maybe also the donkey had fallen for him and in its death
throes had simply yielded to his moral force. Very well, Queedy would
return to the farm and tackle the Ambulist again. He would turn the
story on its head. He would expose the man, and perhaps the rather too
genial inhabitants of the Tower-house, as fraudsters. M. would get his
story all right.

What still disconcerted Queedy, and it disconcerted him so much
that he had to make a diversion to the executive wash room to splash
cold water in his face, was that M.'s dressing-down had made him
feel physically sick. It had revived awful memories of his father's
explosive temper: the time in the Hong Kong hotel when he lost one

of his cuff links; the holiday arguments heard through bedroom walls; the humiliating punishments he had suffered for a bad school report. And then… that other school business. Queedy looked at himself in the wash room mirror and saw only his father's eyes stare back at him. He felt sick again. It raised the awkward question of what exactly M. was to him: a boss, or a surrogate father?

This, oddly, was the same question that M., at that very moment, was asking himself. Did his avuncular feelings for the boy amount to something like compassion or were they merely payment for a debt he was damn sure he didn't owe Queedy's old man? He was bloody well certain he had more important things to worry about.

Gaunt made his way to the *Courier's* personnel office well aware that he ought to be following up his interview of the previous day with the Chief Constable. He knew M. would not be satisfied until he had got a statement from a senior civil servant at the Home Office, received a response from the Association of Chief Police Officers and run a revised piece past the Chief Constable's own spokeswoman. Well, M. would have to wait.

Gaunt had at one time considered himself an admirer of Mrs Fenwick, who dispensed a sort of even-handed injustice from her throne in personnel. It was the admiration of a man of few social accomplishments who nevertheless knows quality when he sees it. From her carefully permed hair to the string of cultured pearls which adorned her starched blouse, the delicate lavender perfume and slightly seductive bi-focal spectacles, Mrs Fenwick was ladylike. She spoke well and applied her makeup judiciously without overdoing it. What was more, she was available, since her husband had died of emphysema. It was some time since Gaunt had attempted to seduce her. Now he thought it right to pay her a social visit. He might ask her out to dinner; that is to say, he would attempt to ascertain how she might react if asked out to dinner.

As luck would have it, Mrs Fenwick was absent from her desk.

Gaunt used her telephone to call one of the girls on reception and find out where she was. At the hairdresser's, was the answer; did Gaunt have any particular need of her? Had his pay-slip gone missing, perhaps? No, no, he would see her another time. When would she be back? Not until after eleven, the girl supposed. Gaunt, half-disappointed that he was not to have the guilty pleasure of flirting with Mrs Fenwick and half-relieved that he would not have to explain an expensive dinner bill to his wife, turned to the matter in hand. Extracting Queedy's personal file from the locked cabinet where all such confidential material was held (the key was and always had been taped to the underside of Mrs Fenwick's desk), he removed all the loose papers and, wrapping them in a copy of the *Courier*, took them back to his office, tapping the paper fraternally against each door as he passed it. Ignoring the ringing telephone which greeted him, he cleared a space on his desk, lit himself a fresh cigarette, and began to read.

M. should also have been attending to pressing matters of business. Instead he spread a blueprint copy of the Ambulist's threadbare map on his desk and made himself a cup of strong coffee. He switched on a table lamp and familiarised himself with the area covered by the map: more or less the whole of Northumberland from the river right up to the Border. He knew its geography: it was his adopted county. He had walked over most of it as a newly-divorced forty-something; from the sandy bays of the coast to the wild volcanic plateaux of the Border massif; through mossy forests and bleating pastures, church-hugging villages, peaty blue-black rivers, bridges and bastle houses; he could close his eyes and imagine flying over the land, following the lines of the Roman roads, surveying the indomitable houses and grand estates, the heather-purpled moors and ancient fastnesses of native tribes. Here was Twyford, where the Tower-house lay, just to the west of the Devil's Causeway – a Roman road subsumed beneath modern tarmac; straight as a die, careless of river and contour. South and west into hilly lead-mining country was Whitlands, where Gaunt had first run the Ambulist to ground. On the map, Twyford bore what must on the original map have been a pencilled mark: a cross – or rather an X. There were several crosses elsewhere in the county, mainly next to small villages: at Halstane, for example, there were two. The Ambulist had also, here and there, drawn small circles, some of them hollow and others filled in; whether they had all been of the same colour he could not tell. He cursed himself for not having inspected the original before having it copied. There were triangles, too; these were mostly on the sides of the sandstone fells so far as M. could tell: Lordencrags, Old Bewley, Roughtin Gill: beautiful, wild places that belonged to the wheeling buzzard, to seas of wind-ruffed machair grass, to the shepherd and his dogs.

Curious groups of arrows, some long and thin, others short and fat, some curved and some straight, seemed to trace journeys accomplished or anticipated through the landscape: along river valleys for the most part but never, M. noticed, over bridges. What rationale, what set of criteria lay behind them, M. could not say, except in one instance. He himself had encountered the man at Heavenham, on the north side of the Roman Wall east of Cholton. Here, the unmistakable mark of a D on its side with a vertical line through it indicated the presence of a sundial. Again, there were several such symbols on the map. The equation of time.

M., afloat on a sea of possibilities, told himself to apply first principles to the matter, to work from the known to the unknown. Queedy's so-called Ambulist showed no obvious signs of lunacy. He did not admit to any agenda; he was not apparently researching material for a book. He was simply walking. But if it were so simple, why annotate his map in such detail? Was it a personal record of movements and incidents made during his travels, or was it an itinerary of places yet to be visited? And for what purpose? How long had the man been in the county? Again, Goddammit, M. wished he knew who the man was, where he had come from; maybe then he would understand where he might be going. Not for the first time, M. wished he had the capacity to follow this story himself, but he immediately dismissed the idea. He must believe he had stung Queedy's pride sufficiently to stir the young man to action. Gaunt was now on the defensive. At least, for the moment, they knew where their latter-day Messiah was. M. straightened himself stiffly and, carrying his half-drunk and now cold mug of coffee, walked over to the window, where faint shafts of light playing on the glass indicated that the sea fret might finally be lifting.

Idly picking up the Hearst biography which Queedy had left on his desk, M. went to put it back on its shelf, which chose that precise moment to collapse onto the floor with a sound not unlike rolling thunder. M., cursing his bloody luck, stared at the disaster and wondered whether Gaunt had finished his piece on the Chief Constable's visit yet.

Gaunt had done no such thing. He had not given the Chief Constable a moment's thought. He was busy. He was trying to remember how M. had introduced Queedy to the staff at the *Courier*. It must have been nine months ago, give or take, but Gaunt couldn't remember when exactly. The file showed that he had been put on the payroll the previous August, but the boy had been around some time before then, Gaunt was sure. Open in front of him was Queedy's *curriculum vitae*, but there was no application form to go with it and for the life of him Gaunt couldn't remember the *Courier* advertising for new reporters; they had just made two redundancies. Gaunt might ask the fragrant Mrs Fenwick if she could offer any insight, but on the whole he thought he would not.

The *curriculum vitae* made interesting reading. Queedy had, it seemed, attended grade school in Washington DC until the age of thirteen, when he had been sent to Stowe School. That meant serious money; probably Pater was an old boy. He had dual American and British nationality. Well, Queedy was not a common name, it would be easy to trace the parents. Stowe had produced its fair share of lawyers, writers, politicians of all hues, so perhaps his father was in the public eye? If so, M. might know him and have taken Queedy on as a favour. Nepotism was a feature of English society that inverted snobs like Gaunt, a Secondary Modern boy who had never been given a leg up in his life, specifically detested.

For reasons unknown Queedy had not completed his education at Stowe, though he appeared to be a good pupil as far as exam results went. Nor had he gone on to any other school or university. He had simply left Stowe at the age of seventeen. The rest of the *CV* detailed a variety of short-term jobs in improbable places like a Florida marina, an Edinburgh hospital, a Soho film production company; they didn't much sound like Pater pulling strings. Gaunt smelled a rat. Had the boy been kicked out of school? Had Daddy been embarrassed by illicit goings-on in the dorms? Had the perfect prefect perhaps been caught peddling dope to the third-years? Now then... Stowe... Buckinghamshire... the *Bucks Gazette*. Harry Tanning. Gaunt flicked through his ancient card index until he found a yellowing entry for Harry Tanning, an old mucker of his from National Service days, last heard of at the *Bucks Gazette*. Gaunt dialled the number, more in hope than expectation. How long had it been since he had heard from Harry?

The return to the Tower-house of the reporter and his photographer, after a silent car ride along ghostly roads lit by low, piercing sunlight and almost empty of traffic, was greeted with equanimity by its inhabitants. In the steaming warmth of the kitchen the smiling Freya filled her large iron kettle and set it on the range. The two dogs yelped a welcome and licked Queedy's delicate hands enthusiastically, as those of a long-lost friend. Bacon, eggs, tomatoes were retrieved from the pantry and an early lunch was improvised in which the whole family joined. Jareld emerged from the mysterious lower floor of the Tower-house, spectacles resting low on his nose so that when he smiled over the top of them he looked just a little sceptical. The girl Selena, fresh from tending to her demanding menagerie in the courtyard, a faint flush of colour on her cheeks, set the table in front of their guests.

- They have come back to talk some more with our friend, Jara.

- Well, and why not? He is a fine interesting man to talk to. And I am most exceedingly hungry! (Today Jareld is not dressed for the cold; he wears an old shirt and corduroy trousers and he has sandals on his feet; a pencil sits neatly behind one ear. He is humming softly to himself a phrase which he turns over and around as if he had found a curious stone on the beach)

- Mr Stokes, you look as if you have not eaten since yesterday; I fear for your welfare. (This is Freya. Placing a large plate in front of the photographer and putting her hand on his shoulder, she points at a fresh loaf of white bread and urges him with her beatific smile to help himself. Stokes needs very little encouragement, and tucks in as though it might be his last meal)

- And you, Mr Queedy. Are you quite well? (Selena sits opposite Queedy at the table and examines him intently. She reaches out a pale hand and touches him. He is cold. To his own surprise he does not take his hand away but leaves it there, taking in her warmth. The girl absently strokes it, the way she rubs her donkey foal behind the ear)

- I think Mr Queedy finds our happy chaos perhaps a little too happy and perhaps a little too chaotic. I imagine your house is very orderly and tidy, and I think it will be a little quiet. Will you pour the tea? (As if she too senses Queedy's vulnerability, Freya feels the urge to draw him into the familial orbit)

The residents of the Tower-house, for all their indifference to formality, their apparent disregard for routine, seemed to play along to some sort of orchestral arrangement whose workings, or at least notation, might be apparent if only one looked from the right direction or listened carefully enough. To Queedy and Stokes the complex rhythms and harmonies of their lives were as mysterious as the movements of the stars and planets were to the ancients. After their lunch, without

any apparent plan, Selena escorted Stokes down to the lakeside to
recapture the Ambulist's lost features on film, Freya disappeared to the
upper floors of the house, and Queedy found himself being ushered by
Jareld Arnesen down a set of tight, curving stone steps into the recesses
of the ground floor – a sealed basement whose massively steadfast
foundations bore the vast weight of the tower above.

   - I want you to listen to something; I am not sure if it is
   quite right; I need a clean pair of ears. (Jareld speaks over his
   shoulder as he reaches the bottom step and switches the lights
   on. Even before they come on a faint red glow creeps up into
   the stairwell with a low hum of valves and transistors)

Queedy wished later that he could remember what he expected
to find on the lower floor of the Tower-house. Whatever he had
imagined, he was wrong. He ought, perhaps, to have allowed for the
existence of a grand piano, whose marked and battered walnut casing
was eccentrically in keeping with the ambience of the house. He had
certainly not conceived of the variety of other instruments set up and
ready to play: drums, vibraphone, a semi-acoustic guitar – or resting in
cases along the far wall: a double bass, a trumpet and a trombone, by
the look of them. Nor had he expected the glass-fronted booth housing
a twenty-four-channel mixing desk, whose pin-sharp lights burned
feebly among the massed rank and file of faders, pots and switches.
Microphones hung suspended from a superb vaulted stone ceiling or
were clipped onto angled stands. Baffles, screens, carpets, monitors
and amplifiers disported themselves around the studio, lending the
whole an air of laconic anticipation. Wondering who the musicians
might be to populate this cavern, Queedy's eye also took in the rear
wall of the booth, on which were mounted framed discs in silver, gold
and platinum. Without making it obvious Queedy could not read the
citations and he now felt foolish that he had not researched the Tower-
house's owner any better than he had its guest. He looked at his host
now with fresh eyes.

Queedy's immediate supposition was that he had been brought down here to admire, to wonder; he might also have speculated whether Jareld wished to have a quiet word with him about, say, the Ambulist or possibly even about his daughter. If so, he would have been wrong again. Jareld sat down at his piano and, looking earnestly towards his guest for a reaction, began to play a phrase, whose variations he had been humming when he emerged for his impromptu lunch.

- Listen… (Jareld plays an arpeggio with his left hand, then the chord and a right-hand melody alongside it)

- And then, maybe this. (He plays another chord, then an inversion, searching, feeling for the harmony; his head is inclined to one side, as if to hear the right true notes beyond mere noise)

- Would you play the whole song? (Queedy supposes that he really is here to help, to listen, so he intends to do the situation justice. It will give him time to think. The idea is less traumatic than mere chat, which is beyond Queedy's competence. The music, underpinned by a logic which Queedy comprehends as effortlessly as he does the equation of time, is infinitely preferable to a discussion about the Ambulist or Selena and, as a journalist, he also supposes that he should conscientiously research any local background)

- Very well, it is a sad song, but in D mixolydian – not so-so sad. The opening is like this (he plays three strong rising chords) and then we run down from G to F sharp minor to E minor, then back to F sharp minor. So far so good; but do you see, the bridge is not quite right. (He plays the next few bars, stops, tries another inversion. Queedy can see him straining, his fingertips reaching out for the right phrase)

- What is the song called? Does it have words?

- It is called *Chasing rainbows* – not a very happy title and not very happy words, but sometimes we have to make people cry, it is pathos. I very much like pathos! (Jareld plays the whole song through, accompanying it softly with words which are indeed sad; they speak of a betrayal which Queedy finds hard to attribute to Jareld or his wife)

- You could remove the third chord in the bridge and run straight up from B minor to C for the start of your chorus – there is a certain mathematical elegance that way. I confess to feeling more comfortable with numbers than with pathos. (Queedy has in a moment been transported back in time to excruciating lessons in musical theory at school; he has no ear and cannot hum a tune, but finds harmonic theory mathematically interesting. And, despite himself, he would like to please this enthusiast)

- Oh! Yes, I see what you are saying. (Jareld works through Queedy's variation, nods his head with a grin, and plays the bridge through to the chorus; annotates the score resting on the piano with the pencil retrieved from behind his ear, and claps his hands) So! Simpler and as you say, fine more elegant. We might indulge in a C seven, though, what do you say? Mr Queedy, I am justified in my opinion of your talents. You are a musician! A credit in my sleeve notes and all the bacon and eggs you can eat!

By the time Queedy emerged from the basement several songs later, without, disconcertingly, having noticed the passage of time, Stokes had taken his precious pictures and left, nervous and impatient to get them developed in the *Courier's* darkroom. This time he would do it himself, to make damn sure nothing else went wrong. Queedy, for his part, might have wondered if the girl, if the whole family, had colluded in keeping him and Stokes apart, sensing perhaps the tension which lay between them. In truth he felt only relief that he could now interview the Ambulist without the distraction of the camera's eye. Once more the girl accompanied him down to the lakeside bivouac; and once more Billy, the green-eyed goat, acted as their half-hostile chaperone. The sun's brilliance had done little to warm the day and now, as it began to set, a stiletto chill seemed to emanate from the very earth, as if it could take no more of winter's rough diet; would rather starve. And wait.

The moon, obeying its own clockwork, would not rise tonight for close on another hour; where the sun had set Venus now shone in chaste silver perfection, while in the east Leo's faint spots breasted the scrubby trees on the far side of the lake. Higher, unmoving, the North Star shimmered like the mariner's beacon, his true friend in a universe of fatal possibility and uncertain hope. Already the Ambulist's fire was alight. The goat ran ahead, reserving its station of comfort and surveillance in the straw berth of the shelter. The outline of the Ambulist, old as the earth and more than proof against its elements in his greatcoat, could be seen illuminated from fifty yards away in backlit magnificence as he leant forward and lit his cigarette from a burning stick.

- I thought you would be back. (The Ambulist, by way of welcome, has filled his pan with water and sets to make tea. Queedy hands him a fresh copy of his map, along with the dilapidated original)

- My editor thinks I haven't yet quite done you justice. (Queedy sits awkwardly on the hard earth, knees drawn up to his chest, his city coat hitched up)

- Ha. (The Ambulist's eyes sparkle and his mouth smiles a smile of satisfaction) Justice. It is a nice word. What did your animal doctor say?

- He thinks you must be a very clever man. He would like to meet you. But I have not come about that. (The Ambulist passes Queedy a hot mug of tea. It is a formal gesture of traveller's hospitality which Queedy might mistake for friendship) Thank you. (Queedy does not want the tea but he knows he must accept it and drink it. The Ambulist has

sweetened it with two spoonfuls of sugar, which Queedy feels
obliged to appreciate. The girl watches him and the goat stares
malevolently at his back)

    - I want to know more about your background. My editor
thinks the last time I interviewed you, you made it all up; that
is to say, about your parents, and India. And he wants to know
where you are going and why?

    - And you, Mister Queedy? What do you want to know?
(The Ambulist turns and for the first time looks Queedy directly
in the face. It is a look that could crush a man, the look of all
men who have ever lived under the stars; the look that asks a
man who he really thinks he is and whether he knows himself)

Selena rose without a word and disappeared into the darkness;
only the goat, interrogating her briefly with its eyes, seemed to notice.
Did she fear the conflict, the bolt that must fall? Was it that she could
not bear to see pain inflicted on this vulnerable young man? If, on her
soundless walk back to the Tower-house she expected, or feared, to
hear raised voices from the men behind her, she was spared. No noise
followed her but for the gun-shot crack of a spark being spat from the
fire.

    Gaunt had waited so long to hear back from his old mate Harry
Tanning that he felt obliged, almost, to complete his column on the
Chief Constable. It was not a brilliant piece of journalism and Gaunt
did not care. The Chief Constable's spokeswoman would not tell the
truth; nor would the Minister's civil servant; and neither would Gaunt.
That was the way these things went: a series of expedient fictions
designed to prevent the public from knowing what was happening.
But it would keep M. happy: he would get no flak from any of the
interested parties. What M. really needed, his story of the decade, lay
almost within reach. But perhaps not quite. The nativity scene at the
Tower-house, if pitched right, was about as good as it was going to get,
short of a major fire, a bridge collapsing into the river, or the city's

team winning the league – something that had not happened these few decades and was not likely to happen in the foreseeable future. Unless there should be a miracle.

Staring at his phone, Gaunt had failed to notice that he was chain-smoking, that it had gone dark outside, that he had not drunk his usual liquid lunch nor indeed eaten anything that day. Coffee and fags would have to get him through the evening too. It was past eight when the call came.

– Gaunt, Harry Tanning. Got your message. How's tricks?

– Soldiering on, Harry, soldiering on. Yourself?

– Mustn't complain. I don't suppose trade is much better up where you are?

– It's dying, Harry. We are the last lot, I reckon.

– You are not wrong, Gaunt. Nobody wants quality regionals any more.

– That's right.

– So, you want to know about an alumnus of the posh school, do you? What's he been up to?

– Nothing of that; he's one of us. I mean to say, he is definitely not one of us, but he's on the strength. Wants his come-uppance.

– Say no more. You think he did a runner from Stowe?

– Could be.

– Well, the name Queedy doesn't set any flags waving around here, I've asked. Checked the archives too.

– Not what I wanted to hear. (Gaunt shifts the receiver from one ear to the other so that his right hand is free to massage the deeply rutted lines of his forehead)

– No. But there was a to-do at the school about the right time for the departure of your young friend.

– Oh? Do tell. (Now Gaunt reaches for his shorthand pad, lights another cigarette, and sticks out his bottom lip)

- It was something and nothing, really.

- Always is, Harry. That's how the best stories start, with something and nothing.

- There was a house-master, nice man, I knew him myself. Ex-Rifles, Singapore and so on, well-liked by the kids and the other masters. Name of Stevenson. Maths teacher. Found floating in the school swimming pool one day.

- Oh yes....?

- No silly stuff came up at the inquest, you know; he drowned. Turned out he couldn't swim; must have fallen in, maybe after a lunchtime tipple and phhht!

- I'd like a little bit more than that, Harry.

- Sure you would. Here it is. Some weeks after the inquest two photographs are found in a senior prefect's locker during the long vac: what they call summer holidays. Only a handful of boys around at that time. One of the caretakers has taken the locker off the wall to do some painting, these pictures fall out of the back.

- Are we interested in the caretaker?

- No, we are interested in the pictures. Point is, the photos show the dead teacher: first one shows him in the water alive, fully clothed this is, looks like he's waving but maybe he's drowning. Second one shows him floating face down. It doesn't look good, does it?

- It looks good from where I'm sitting, Harry.

- Luckily for the school almost everyone is away on their hols in the Riviera with their posh parents, so it's all nice and quiet. Well, so the police fetch the boy from wherever it is he's spending the vac, America if I recall, and have a good long chat with him. And he tells them a story.

- I'll bet it's a good one.

- You wouldn't put your name to it, Gaunt.

- Go on then.

- All right, the boy whose locker it is admits, after a bit of the third degree, that he took the photos. The first one, he thought the teacher was having a lark, just playing; he had been passing the pool and heard shouts and went in, had his camera on him. Waves back at the teacher, all good larks. The boy and the teacher are both in the school camera club; sort of school that has a camera club, you know?

- No I don't, Harry.

- Anyhow, the boy tells the police he went off thinking nothing of it, and then when he passed by the pool again he looked in to see if the teacher was still larking about. And there he is, dead. The boy takes another picture, he says, to show that he had nothing to do with it.

- Only that's not what it looks like.

- Exactly. So when the police ask him why he doesn't report the fact that one of the teachers is dead, he says, well, he realises it doesn't look so good, and he can't do anything and feels terrible, so he just shuts up. But he keeps the pictures, which he's developed himself in the school's dark room.

- That, Harry, is a crock of shit.

- That's what the police thought. But there's no jury will convict, is there? Got to be a reasonable doubt.

- Not on my end of the phone, there doesn't.

- No, but the case never gets anywhere. Not a shred of proof that the boy killed him. Well, course he is removed from school and not seen again in these parts. The school hushes it all up as far as possible; and these institutions, you know, Gaunt, are pretty good at that sort of thing.

- And did the *Bucks Gazette* cover it?

- Sure we did, but between you and me, Gaunt, the boss here doesn't like to ruffle too many feathers down there, given that the Chairman of the School Governors is a shareholder.

- He would be. Anything more?

- Want to know the name?

- Oh yes. (The hairs on the back of Gaunt's old neck stand to attention in anticipation; in his mind he reaches out for a touch of the glinting treasure… and then….)

- Smith. John Smith. (There is a pause. Harry Tanning sucks his teeth)

- Oh, bloody helpful, that is. You going to tell me what else?

- No, Gaunt, I'm going to leave you with the name for a bit. You let me know where it leads you, and in a week I'll tell you what's what. You'll kick yourself. Cheerio, mate. (With that, Harry Tanning hangs up, leaving Gaunt feeling like he's chewing on a piece of prime steak but can't swallow it)

Once more a repertoire of off-stage noises, doors opening and closing, and a gently swaying footfall betrayed the arrival of the girl at the camp fire. Again, she brought food. This time she entered into the circle of the fire's pumpkin glow and sat without being asked, for the Ambulist and his interviewer were in full flow. Without a word she ladled soup into two bowls and cut thick chunks of bread which she laid on the Ambulist's own wooden board. Again she revived the dying fire. And now she sat with her steady gaze on the un-noticing Queedy, whose eyes were bright with the spark of conversation and imagination. His city coat could no longer be seen, for he was almost entirely wrapped in a woollen blanket which his host had produced from his grip. An empty bottle of whisky stood at his side. Selena had not seen Queedy animated before. His small, fine hands were describing elegant motions in the firelight: the motions of a conjurer or a plate-spinner at a fair. The Ambulist interjected, agreed, disagreed, waved his massive fist in synergistic orchestration. He briefly caught the girl's eye in his, and they exchanged a half-smile of knowing and surprise.

Freya and Jareld lay in each other's arms on an enormous couch before a home fire whose intense heat was soporific. Its lazy yellow flames caressed the logs as they consumed them. Freya stroked her husband's hair in unconscious imitation. The sweet smell of burning apple wood was intoxicating. Before the hearth the two dogs slept shamelessly, sprawled in attitudes of abandonment.

On the first floor of the Tower-house, looking out onto the wooded hills, was a sitting room of gorgeous warmth and colour swathed in Arab carpets, its windows lost behind damask drapes, its sandstone walls the colour of a desert. A high ceiling was hidden between joists of oak hewn by adze and stained the deepest black by time and smoke. Above the lintel of the cavernous stone fireplace a panoramic gilt mirror threw the room back on itself. Paintings grouped exuberantly together checked the austerity of the stone. A sculpted head, it might have been that of Jareld in his youth, looked out from the top of a bookcase. Two oil lamps, their globes casting lunar shadows across the floor, provided the only competition for the firelight.

Freya and Jareld heard quiet steps on the stairs and looked up enquiringly as Selena came into the room, flushing red from the sudden heat.

      - Well, and have they come to blows?

      - Oh no, they are the best of friends. (Selena laughs; it is almost the giggle of a girl in skirts. She makes a space between the dogs and sits with her legs folded beneath her and her back against the couch, stroking the golden-coated ears which have subliminally registered her presence)

      - Oh? (This is Freya, half sitting up) I am glad. I thought they might fight.

- What are they talking about? (Jareld takes his wife's hand in his and closes his eyes)

- Something they call the equation of time.

Chapter Five

Trails

I met the enigmatic miracle-worker, whom locals have churlishly christened Saint Francis of Twyford, on a farm deep in the country-side, wrote Queedy. There was snow on the ground and it was well below freezing. He kept a small camp fire going and sat there in his shabby coat as if it were the most natural thing in the world. He would not tell me his name, and he wants to keep his past secret. He was not born in this country but somewhere in Southern Africa, judging by the accent which his deep voice occasionally betrays. His apparent resurrection of a donkey foal at the farm owned by Mr and Mrs Arnesen is something he would rather not talk about either. It is not that he is embarrassed, or that he wants to keep his healing 'method' secret; rather, it is something which for him is not worth talking about. He shrugs it off with a gesture which says, Ask me something more interesting. I press him to tell me about his early life. All he will say is that his parents were Protestant farmers, that he was brought up in the 'back country' and sent to the city to be trained as a lawyer; but he will

not say where, or when. It is impossible to tell his age; he could easily
be sixty – or eighty, even.

The 'Ambulist' – a name coined by Mr Arnesen, owner of the
Tower-house and well-known musician, to mean 'one who walks forever' – seems almost uncomfortable talking about himself and would
rather speak of the natural world. His knowledge of the moon and stars
is extraordinarily comprehensive; when he speaks of the constellations
it is as if they were his cousins. He understands the movements of the
stars and planets – something of which your average school geography
teacher is painfully ignorant – and to him this 'music of the spheres' is
a nightly promenade concert, one of which he never tires. He knows
the names of the moon's seas, valleys, mountains and craters; they are
very much members of his social circle. Long into the night we discuss
such wonders as libration, the precession of the stars, the lives of the
comets.

It was no good and he knew it. Queedy looked up from his notebook as the lumbering grey-green bus swerved to avoid an oncoming
lorry and its momentum pressed him against the bulkhead. A thin,
diluted sun struggled to penetrate the filthy windows. Warm dry air
blowing up from the grubby vent beneath his feet smelled of burning
dust and mould. The other passengers: a workman with black stained
hands and a bag of tools on the seat beside him, a grandmother with her
fidgeting granddaughter, a scruffy young man hugging an old guitar
case, wore looks of resignation. Queedy was almost hypnotised by
the tired racket of the growling engine, periodically drowned out by a
swishing surf of melting snow thrust aside by its rolling, ever rolling
wheels or the straining pitch of the gearbox as it took on a another hill.

A thaw had begun to set in with first light, and Queedy imagined
the Ambulist busying himself about his camp, watching and listening to
nature's unfolding drama: dripping trees, fluffing feathers, the calls of
rooks and crows, the first almost noiseless hint of the ice letting go of
its grip on the lake; the Tower-house, immune to the passing seasons,

monumental and unyielding, thin veils of vapour rising from its roof in long-suffering exhalation. Queedy also imagined the girl, whose steady, unjudging gaze made him feel both intensely uncomfortable and frighteningly exposed. She would be brushing, feeding, refreshing the bedding of her adoring charges; she might touch the goat's ear just as she had touched his hand, and once in a while the light would catch a wisp of hair falling against the white nape of her neck. He saw in his mind's eye Freya's warm shining eyes, her lips, her studied grace in movement, the worn beauty of her hands; the cosy, seductive fug of her kitchen. He thought of the painfully energetic and optimistic musician Jareld, at the same time promising himself he would research that man's career. He wondered, also, what it would be like to belong to such a family and felt it would be a terrible responsibility to have to love them in return. How could one afford to be loved if it meant having to love them back? It was a cross to break a man's back. With that thought his heart thudded the way it sometimes did when he thought he was going to die imminently; he screwed his hand into a tight fist to make the abysmal sensation go away and gradually, with the sympathetic trundling of the bus, his heartbeat returned to something like its normal rhythm.

On and on towards the city the bus droned, down through a sodden, exhausted country chilblained and blotchy, aching for spring, anaemic, dispirited and hopeless. Only humans, Queedy thought, who knew that the sun was even now well advanced on its northward migration towards the equator, could afford the luxury of hope, could believe in a future. All else anticipated the coming season by long-learned rote or else responded to its oft-repeated notes. Even now Arctic geese would be flexing stiff wings, itching to take to the air and head for their distant breeding grounds. Far away to the south, in the Ambulist's homeland, cattle farmers would be watching the parched land and the sky waiting, waiting for the rains to come. Did anyone there wait for him to return?

In small, silent, leafless villages veiled in wood smoke the bus pulled up reluctantly, opening its doors with a hiss to refugees fleeing winter's wretched bleakness for the neon equinox of the city's shops and libraries, banks and markets, doctors, dentists, coffee shops and galleries. Queedy leant his heavy head against the window, his breath misting it. Scarecrow ranks of telegraph poles, swaggering dark against a distant sky which was now bleached and hazy, danced across his view. Parallel lines of white snow dazzled in plough furrows as his eyes flickered to and fro across lifeless fields.

Now the bus, with a consumptive roar, swung out onto the main road and the verge receded from him. The highway stretched ahead straight and true, a river drawing them on. And so... Queedy would return to the *Courier* and admit to M. that he had failed in his assignment. The golden dust falling grain by grain through his hands was not precious metal but sand. He would return to his perfect, empty, heartless apartment. He would be surrendered once more into Gaunt's callused hands to serve his time on the streets. And he would remember to buy a new pair of boot laces.

Queedy looked down at his notes. As I prepare to say goodbye to this man, he wrote, who has shared with me his fire and his thoughts, he pathetically makes me promise to bring him a new pair of laces for the boots which carry him so many miles; his old ones have perished in the winter mud and ice. I promise. I wonder how he has survived the cold and damp in this faraway land and suppose that this nomadic life must take its toll on body and spirit. We do not shake hands, and he does not watch me as I leave but sets himself to adding a few more damp sticks to his small fire. For the Ambulist the idea of leaving or, indeed, the notion of coming back, does not really exist the way it does for us dwellers. Every day is its own journey lived entirely in the present. Goodbyes are pointless. There is no See you again. Who knows where he will go next; or for that matter, where he has come from? It seems as if he will walk forever. His solitude, his lonely path, his uncertain future, remind us how lucky we are to know that we have homes, and loved ones, to come back to.

    - I suppose you know Stokes's bloody pictures didn't come out again. (Queedy, having returned to his flat to discard his now quite earthy clothes, has run M. to ground not in the office but in a small restaurant called A la Casa on a dingy side street, where he often lunches because the waiters know him and the chef doesn't have to be told how to grill a steak. Queedy, steeling himself for another dressing-down and wanting to get it over with, is not sure what to make of it when M. waves him into the spare chair at his table and orders the waiter to fetch another menu)

    - I am beginning to think that nothing about our Ambulist will surprise me. (Queedy's spirits are rising with the warmth, the faceless buzz of table chat and M.'s reassuring news about Stokes. He begins to study the menu with purpose and does his best to bathe his words in maple syrup)

    - What have you got for me, or should I not ask?

    - Sand. (Queedy pushes his notepad across the table, realising that his shorthand has suffered from the bus's lousy suspension and is probably unreadable. But for the moment he is rescued by the arrival of M.'s steak. M. eats and reads and takes the odd swig from his wine glass; his workmanlike chewing masks any emotion, so Queedy takes the opportunity to order himself langoustine ravioli in a truffle sauce, on the long-standing principle regarding the privileges of the condemned man. He realises he is starving)

    - You know, Son ... (M. wipes his mouth and, whether deliberately or not Queedy cannot say, throws down his napkin on top of the notebook) this is not a story. It isn't even the bare bones of a story. It's sure as bloody hell not what I wanted – or asked for. And you are not a journalist. I mean... (M. pauses, mostly for effect, to pick a thread of steak from between his teeth. Queedy, anticipating the blow, unfolds his napkin and spreads it subconsciously over his vulnerable parts. M. fails to finish his sentence)

- You mean....?

- I am going to print it. It'll be the first in a series of feature sketches, one every Friday – a little something for the weekend. A story for the Nineties, anticipating the Millennium. Hint of the Second Coming and all that. You can do one on that improbable family at the Tower-house, if you like. You will follow your Ambulist when he chooses to move on, pass the time of day with him, walk with him; watch the stars with him and debate the equation of fucking time with him for all I care. See what he gets up to. Make the readers want to follow him with you; take them on the journey; he can be our pet eccentric. Get his trust. And then get the truth. Better get a pair of decent boots and a set of waterproofs – the *Courier* won't pay for them, by the way.

- Are you saying you like the piece?

- No.

- Then, why?

- It'll piss Gaunt off, so it will. (M. has other reasons for wanting Queedy to follow the Ambulist, but pissing Gaunt off will do for now. And he is absolutely certain that Gaunt will blow a gasket when he sees the piece with Queedy's by-line next to it under a new feature banner, personally subbed by the Editor-in-Chief)

- By the way, I want you to mention somewhere in your sketch that the camera will not take a picture of him; part of the enigma, see? You had better think what name you are going to use.

- For the Ambulist?

- For you.

- What's wrong with Queedy?

- This is the *Courier*, Son. Your mother's name makes you sound like a fucking lawyer fresh out of Great Expectations.

- So, plain John Smith, then.

- Sure. It's a novel thought using your own name. Man of the people. One of us. John Smith's Friday Sketch: I quite like it. You have nothing to hide. Do you?

Neither man saw Gaunt shuffle past the window, head down to keep the bullet rain, which had begun not so much to fall as to volley-fire from the barrel of an angry lead-shot sky, out of his bloodshot eyes. On any other day he would have turned his head automatically to scan the punters at the Casa on his way to the pub for a lunchtime beer or two. You never knew who might be talking to whom, whose dirty little business might be on show for those who could read the runes. If he had, Gaunt would have seen Queedy's insufferably prig expression as he leaned back in his chair having eaten well at the boss's expense. He might have paused long enough to misread M.'s pointing finger as a gesture of admonition. He might well have stuck out his bottom lip and grunted with satisfaction. But today he was too busy chewing on a story about a school prefect, a drowned house master and a photograph.

Gaunt's lunchtime haunt was the Crown, a famously long and narrow bar at the bottom of the hill, just a few yards up from the quayside. It was all polished mahogany and brass, over-elaborate plaster mouldings and snug corners. After-hours the place filled with professional types putting off the journey home but at lunch there was generally a spare stool at the bar. Today the place was dead. The landlord was reading a cheap red top laid open on the counter. Looking up at Gaunt's entry he reached without a word for a glass and filled it with the local poison with which Gaunt abused his liver. He took Gaunt's money and went back to reading his paper. Gaunt, with thirty years of practice behind him, began involuntarily to read the headlines upside down. Same old scandals, nothing new.

Gaunt's lunch proved unsatisfactory. He sat and drank his pint; would have had two if there had been any other punters in. He needed someone to talk at, a dummy to pin his rough-cut thoughts on. Someone unconnected with the *Courier*, with the business. His mate Jimmy, more often than not in here at this hour, would have listened to Gaunt turning the story over in his head, shaping it, manipulating his facts, tailoring the best fit between fabric and form. Jimmy was good like that. He let you buy him a drink and in return would listen without interrupting; sometimes nod, make a face, shake his balding head in sage agreement. He never interfered in Gaunt's line of reasoning. Never. It had been a while since Gaunt had seen the old bugger. Seen Jimmy, he asked the landlord. No, hadn't seen him. Gaunt buttoned his coat against the day and left the landlord to his paper.

The City Philosophical Society boasted the oldest library in the region, built and funded in the days when mining engineers, railway barons, shipping magnates and men of letters discussed the fortunes of empires while they smoked cigars and cast grand schemes in this crucible from the steel in their souls. Those men mused over the world's news when the correspondents of the *Courant*, the *Courier's* predecessor, carried almost daily dispatches from Stettin and Batavia, from Boston, Valparaiso and the Cape. Not like the consumers of today's thin media gruel. And they reckoned the world had shrunk. Gaunt laughed almost out loud as he turned the brass door knob of the Society's polished oak doors, pausing on the threshold to compose his hair and his equally disorganised breathing. A rack full of umbrellas with half-furled spines, dripping water copiously onto the marble floor of the atrium, might have brought to a more poetic mind the sight of swans or geese drying their wings after a storm. Gaunt, oblivious, head down, climbed the generous, sweeping staircase to the first floor with the aid of a banister rail whose flourished curves had been fully intended by its architect to inspire a sense of intellectual and economic awe. Gaunt stuck out his bottom lip and with eyes resolutely on the ground entered the Reading Room.

Southern visitors to the library, used to patronising provincials, might be taken aback by its dusky grandeur; might delight at the shafts of thin light which, on sunnier days, played down through drifting motes of dust upon apparently endless stacks of books from the magnificent glass and cast-iron dome forty feet above; might be surprised too that the somnolent hush habitually associated with books, with learning and with age, did not rule in that place. Far from it. The Society's members, though many of them could be said to be past their prime, did not slumber in their afternoon armchairs. They sat round elegant tables donated, or liberated, from redundant Regency dining rooms. They drank coffee which was and had since the dawn of time been served by an ancient trout from a small hatch above the staircase leading down to the music room and reference library. They were forced by the clinking of cup and saucer, the crunch of biscuit upon denture and the inadequacy of their hearing to talk to each other in raised voices. They debated. They discussed; sometimes they shouted. Fists were thumped on the table top; chairs were scraped against the floor in response. The philosophical traditions of the Society respected and demanded that the library be its servant, not the other way around. The members were proud of their traditions and defended them against all modernity. Gaunt hated the whole bloody lot of them, the daft pompous old sods.

One more pint over lunch and Gaunt would have been defeated, labouring up the tight spiral of the iron staircase which afforded access from the floor of the reading room to the gallery high, high above. The balcony was narrow, its low railing unnerving, the thought of the drop onto the shiny heads of the philosophers below unattractive. As it was, Gaunt felt light-headed with the effort of the climb and he wheezed. But he knew the stack he was after and his eagle eye found its mark on the binding of *Paton's List of Schools*. This annual, an indispensable work of reference for well-heeled parents regardless of whether their money was old or new, was no longer quite so commonly consulted by the men of this city as it once had been. Their black diamonds exhausted and the river emptying of shipping, the flow of money, like the peaty silt of the moors, these days flowed unstoppably towards the sea and now paid for little more than the case-bound octavo memory of material glory.

Gaunt knew he would not find Queedy in these pages. What he sought was a clue to the name; some line or pattern which would draw his eye towards unknown parents. Why Stowe? Why not another school? Why not Rugby or Winchester, Harrow or Charterhouse? And where, he wondered, had the money come from? Not from around here; he would bet on that. Gaunt might have taken the book back down to the reading room or to some cosy alcove out of earshot of the philosophers. He might have presented the book at the desk and had it stamped, had he been a paid-up member. But he was not. Instead he put the volume into the inside pocket of his coat, descended the spiral stairs and shuffled unnoticed from the building. Useful thing to have on the shelves, anyway. Save coming again.

Queedy, after his sumptuous lunch and unexpectedly satisfactory interview with M., was in the business of a more benign mission. His first port of call was the covered market in the heart of the city where, between the cheese shop, the greengrocers, the butchers, haberdashers and formica cafés, he was sure there was also an old-fashioned cobbler who would be able to supply him with the exact make of boot lace required by the Ambulist. The nomad's stock now stood high in Queedy's estimation. Interesting and mysterious he had been in any case; he was now tangibly valuable: he was the means of Queedy's liberation from Gaunt and the drudgery of missing children, reindeer farming, shop thefts and drunken weekend idiocies. The Ambulist must be kept sweet. Queedy was careful to produce the threadbare originals and have the cobbler identify and replicate them as exactly as possible. And so elevated was Queedy's mood that afternoon that he bought not one but two pairs of boot laces, so that his Ambulist might indeed walk forever.

Queedy himself had only, for the present, to make his way down to the library of the City Philosophical Society, where he missed the emerging Gaunt by a mere few moments. Queedy was a member of the Society. He recalled vaguely that the girl on the loans desk had been very persuasive when she suggested he join on a previous visit. She had filled most of the form in for him. The same girl, a lovely dark creature with wild curly hair tumbling down over her shoulders, whose only concession to bibliophilia was a pair of sensible, quiet shoes, flushed helplessly when Queedy approached and took it upon herself to lead him directly to the current volume of *Who's Who*. Queedy condescended to favour her with a practiced smile in thanks and as further reward for her solicitousness he sat at a table close by, where she could watch him, date stamp in hand. Queedy, at his most beautifully sleek and self-conscious best, leafed through the pages slowly, licking his finger every now and then in a manner characteristic of a certain fifth-form literary clique at Stowe School. But he did not have to leaf far to find the entry for Arnesen, Jareld.

Who could say if it was the moon's waxing face or some other urge which drove the Ambulist to take his bag up once more and walk? Did he, like Queedy, fear the responsibility of being loved, of being possessed, of belonging? Had the inhabitants of the Tower-house affected him with their generosity, pained him with reminders of home and hearth? Or was the constant invisible tug, the draw of road, field and fell a force whose incessant teasing could not, would not be resisted? The Ambulist did not say. No sentiment, no farewell escaped him. Even the goat, furious at the inconstancy of its new friend, was left behind without so much as a valedictory pat. It took its anger out on its mistress, whose own distress manifested itself in an inability to eat. Instead she over-fed her menagerie, over-cosseted them and spoke only to them, to the dismay of her parents. The donkey and its miraculous foal brayed almost constantly in a gesture of solidarity, as if they felt her pain. Her delicate, pale features began to lose their lustre and became, so to speak, translucent. With the Ambulist all gaiety seemed also to desert the Tower-house.

The stone from which the fortress had been forged so many centuries before was quarried from a line of hills that locals knew as the Fell Sands. They rose to the surface of the earth, secretive, among the corn fields of the coastal plain and swelled steadily westwards in seductive undulations across oceans of moor and crag before crashing wave-like against the foot of the Cheviot massif. From the crest of this wave, the volcanic hills of the Border must have appeared to the earliest explorers of these blessed lands, the sunrise at their backs, as the plateaux on which heaven had been created by an Olympian of terrible love and creative power. His light poured in floodlit cataracts down canyons riven through onrushing head-height flocks of clouds onto a maiden land of perfect virgin green, voluptuous in form, bearing the promise of fertility and doom.

In that selfsame light, breasting the ridge – the breaking, plunging surf of the wave – the Ambulist saw this, his grey mane streaming to the wind, his eyes beads of amber, his arms spread in supplication, or was it greeting – greeting the generations upon generations with whom he shared in this moment the eternal solidarity of the nomad. Tears welled in his eyes for all he had lost and for all he knew; for all the land had lost and for all it knew. He bowed his head with the weight of sorrow and shame.

At this transcendent place – at his very feet – the Ambulist's predecessors had made their arcane mark on the land. Into the surface of the smooth bare rock some ancient sculptor had incised a pattern of rings and channels in low relief, so that the first and last light of the day should etch them in shadows which must fade at the sun's full height and at dusk. To the Ambulist, present at this diurnal display as if by careless invitation, the pattern shimmered in and out of focus. He laid his bag down on the ground and knelt, feeling for the sense and magic in the carvings. His fingers traced the time-worn lines of this unearthly map, probing for some sense of its author's esoteric purpose. Pale green, white and yellow freckles of lichen, nature's own adornment, graced the figures. The wind caressed them as if it, too, sought to read their message; and as it did so it sang the faint refrain of a song as old as the hills themselves.

The rain of the day before had passed overnight and although the air was brittle with chill, the sun's gathering energy penetrated the clouds and the Ambulist sensed its ephemeral warmth in the rocks under his touch. Were these circles gifted by ancient hands to the sun as a gesture of thanks and assurance? Did they tell of wonder or of woe? He could not say. No key, no hieroglyph existed to tell the meaning of these marks. For three thousand years or more, the wisdom or whimsy behind their creation had been lost, cast away by those for whom they had no use.

The Ambulist took up his bag and his trail once more and strode northward along the ridge. His heart was full. He closed his eyes and let his feet take him where they might. Before him he saw only a vision of his childhood. Summer's heat lay dense and enervating on the veldt. All sound was deadened; tall grasses, desperately parched, stood brittle, desiccated, paralysed. The overwhelming light seemed almost to pierce the very earth; shadows cowered beneath the few trees that clung to the plain. A San hunter, an old and trusted friend of his father's, had one day taken him blindfolded to a cliff above a most sacred cave where, kneeling down, his fingers were first shown how to read and listen to the songs of the circles. The vision was palpable. The raking prick of acacia thorns on the skin, the rancid assault of lion spoor on his nose and hot, hot dust between his toes, all were real to him again; and in his ears still the low, clicking whisper of the bushman, awed by his own imagery of poetry and fear. On the roof of that cave had been painted, in years not so far past, the liquid form of an eland springing alive from the bush, its flight traced by a hunter's arrow. The artist had brought forth life out of charcoal and ochre and, unleashed, the eland flew across the face of the rock. This beast, prized above all others by the San, remained trapped and at the same time liberated in that airborne instant and imprinted forever on the Ambulist's imagination.

The forests, glades, streams and hills, mosses and fells of the ancestral landscape through which the Ambulist travelled now were hunting grounds no more. The wolf and the bear, the beaver, elk and wild ox were gone. The footprint of the settler: his metalled roads, which ossified the lilting sine of the hunters' trail, bridges which denied rivers their rights as earth's own boundaries, fields and hedges whose greedy shears cut the land's cloth regardless of its flesh; his dwellings. These imprints of his studded boot seemed certain to erase all memory of the wanderers who had gone before. Even so, the Ambulist could sense the echoes of their footfall across the millennia. Onward he walked. And descending the scarp through a forlorn flat of pine trees whose wind-ripped branches seemed to applaud his exit from the stage, the Ambulist found the shelter of a little glen where a melt-water burn, in spate, dashed through a tumble of boulders. He followed the sound of the burn's voice and presently came on a tiny churchyard where he sat and rested his back against a gravestone. Here was shelter from the wind. The gravestone bore its own hieroglyphic tale to tell of life's long trick, of memory, of loss and hope for the hereafter. The hourglass and the snake swallowing its own tail, the death's head and the reaper's sickle: these were just another sort of equation of time.

The church was simple and ancient: it boasted no tower but a tall austere nave pierced by three high narrow round-arched windows on either side; a modestly elegant dog-toothed chancel arch; an apse, lit from within by three miraculous candles, flames perfectly unmoving, which stood in a silver gilt candelabra on a dark purple altar cloth trimmed with silver thread. The half-domed roof of the apse was painted the colour of a summer's night sky bearing a canopy of gold-leafed stars flickering in the candlelight. The Ambulist stood before the altar looking up at this firmament, his breath veiling the stars like the Milky Way, and once more tears came to his eyes. This time they were tears which flowed not for loss and shame but for beauty and faith. Again his vision blurred and it seemed to him that the stars might be a million miles and more away; that the ceiling of the apse was unutterably vast, the compass of the heavens unimaginably immense in time and space. The entirety of what had gone before now opened like an abyss before him and all became dark. For a few moments he was lost to himself and the present and was forced to feel for the surety of the altar rail, to steady himself and recover. As he left, heavy-limbed and burdened with thought, his eye was caught by the pages of a visitors' book lying open on a table close to the font. He took up a pen which nestled in its fold and inscribed the day's date in the left hand column. Next to it he wrote, I passed this way today and was moved to think of the ages of man and what came before. He stumbled out half-blind into the light and as he did so a gust of wind bearing down off the hills caught the clapper of the church's single bell and it tolled faintly.

Queedy took the news of the Ambulist's defection with new found equanimity. As a companion piece to his first John Smith's Friday sketch, the revelation that the quarry had flown and the obvious corollary of Queedy pursuing and running him to ground would have a satisfactory feel to it. He would tease his readers, draw them into the Ambulist's world. When he caught up with him, Queedy would be able to draw another, even more intimate portrait of this living enigma; he would subtly trace the details of the man's early life, his days on the road. In the meantime Queedy would entertain the *Courier's* readers with features on Jareld Arnesen, the once-famous popular music sensation, and his wife Freya who, Queedy's researches showed, had been a celebrated fashion model and was now – he read – a highly-regarded sculptor.

If the family at the Tower-house dreaded or resented Queedy's return they did not show it. Did they hope he would somehow bring the Ambulist back to them? They might, rather, have sought distraction. Father and mother may also have hoped that Queedy would be able to coax, or annoy, their daughter out of her disturbing malaise; he was, to be sure, a good-looking young man of charm and talent, and if he was a little over-formal and diffident he at least had age in common with Selena. Did they perhaps also feel, wish even, that Queedy's indefinable aura of vulnerability might touch Selena's heart?

Reaching the farm – another dreary bus journey: fields flooded with ditch water and rain, a flat grey sky and not a trace of colour anywhere in the land; the walk down the lane from the village past the lake – Queedy went first to the abandoned bivouac hoping that the Ambulist had left behind him some clue which might tell his next destination. There was nothing but the ragged shelter, the remains of the camp fire and a thin carpet of straw which the goat, in its vengeful capering, had spread among the trees along the lake's wooded banks. Moorhens and coots were now busy gathering the stalks for their new nests with the rabid enthusiasm of wreckers happening on the unwonted bounty of some maritime disaster. Around its edges the lake's icy lid had begun to melt.

Queedy's search of the yard, of its stables and pens, his brief and awkward reunion with the donkeys, his hurried avoidance of the goat's malicious, possessive glare, yielded no sign of Selena, so he climbed the steps to the kitchen door and knocked. Jareld opened the door with the dogs baying behind him in welcome; took Queedy's bag and greeted him with an enthusiastic smile and a slap on the back. Somehow the memory of the kitchen's informal cosiness had been a comfort to Queedy, at home alone in his flat and on the bus. Now even he sensed that it had lost its familial atmosphere of laughter and nonchalant shabbiness.

- Have you eaten, Queedy? I have no rabbit stew for you today, but there are fine good fish, eggs... (His voice trails off as Queedy shakes his head and sits at the table. Jareld sees that Queedy no longer wears his expensive coat and suit, but is dressed in a crisply new green waxed jacket over a cream polar neck jersey and brown corduroy trousers, with shiny polished brogues on his feet. He wants to smile but instead nods and places the kettle on the range. He joins Queedy at the table)

- Where are Selena and ... umm... your wife?

- Selena I do not know. Freya is in her studio, you must go to say hello to her. She will be fine happy to see you. (There is silence between the two men for a few moments and the space is filled by the slow spitting hiss of the kettle on the range, the ticking of the old railway clock on the wall and the slavering of one of the dogs as it works on a ham bone). So now, Queedy, will you look for our Ambulist again? Will you find him?

- Do you ask because you are interested, or because you wish me to bring him back?

- You ask me a good question, Queedy. Perhaps I do not know the answer to it. Suppose I am just interested.

- My editor wants me to write more articles about him.

- That is some sort of an answer. (Queedy bows his head in assent) We hope you won't let any harm come to our wandering friend. We think he is an excellent man and we will not like to see him misunderstood because he chooses an unfashionable way of life. It is sad to see him go, but to tame a wild thing is not a happy wish.

- My editor also wants me to write a story about you.

- A story of me? (Jareld looks appropriately astounded, opens his eyes wide) Do you think your readers will want a story about a fallen star, with his grey beard and his rabbit stews?

- My editor thinks they will. (Jareld says nothing while he considers this, but purses his lips beneath his whiskers. His eyes, peering over the rims of his glasses, stay fixed on Queedy's face, looking for a trace of humour. Queedy pretends to hear a noise outside and looks towards the door)

- Queedy, you know we worry about you. (This is disconcerting for Queedy. What precisely worries them he does not, perhaps, want to know)

- How is your song coming along? (Jareld does not respond immediately to this defensive prod, but reaches out for his wellington boots and heaves them on over thick wool socks. Immediately the dogs' ears come to attention; they scramble to their feet barking in unison, tails wagging; the ham bone is abandoned)

- Let us go for a walk in the woods, Queedy. You must make those clothes of yours look a little less new, and I will tell you about my song. You may write some notes for your readers. Come, dogs, we will show Mr Queedy where all those rabbits live. You don't mind if I take my gun? Do you like to shoot?

Gaunt sat rigid in his chair looking down at hands that did not seem to belong to him. The fingers were fat and swollen. They trembled like he had the DTs or something. The knuckles on his right hand bled, the skin gone. A ragged cut across the other palm oozed dark blood and he couldn't remember how he had done that. There was no pain to speak of. He felt a warm drip tracing a line down his forehead and couldn't tell if it was sweat or if he was bleeding there too. He wanted to reach up and touch it, wipe it away before it ran in his eyes, but neither hand would move. There ought to be a box of tissues on the desk, but the desk lay in fragments, some on the floor in front of him, some against the wall, some in the corridor. By a stroke of luck a half-smoked packet of fags lay more or less intact at his feet and he leant slowly forward and down, managed to coax it from the floor using both hands as a sort of grab. He pulled a cigarette out with his lips, realised he wouldn't be able to use a lighter or matches and spat it out. He began to wonder why all the noise hadn't brought anyone from down the corridor. He was sure they would have heard, his room having no door now.

Gaunt was a dangerous man when he got angry. The staff at the *Courier* had learned the hard way over the years to steer clear or keep their heads down. Behind the glass doors along the corridor they swapped nervous looks and spoke in whispers. The smart ones, the ones who'd read John Smith's Friday sketch fresh from the print room and had seen this coming, had found jobs to do in town or suddenly remembered urgent dental appointments. The rest, those whose work tied them to their desks, kept very bloody quiet, and waited. Someone thought to dial M.'s extension and let him know there had been a disturbance downstairs.

Whisky had a calming effect on Gaunt. He managed to get to his feet and open the filing cabinet where he kept an emergency bottle and unscrewed the cap with his teeth. He now sat on the floor leaning against it, drinking. One of the angular metal handles dug into his back. He shifted as well as he could and then settled to an acceptance of discomfort. As sensation returned to his hands the moments of rage began to come back too; he winced as he tried to flex his knuckles and with the arrival of throbbing waves of pain he began to think more clearly. With his right foot he was able to scrape towards him the copy of *Paton's List of Schools* which he had taken from the library. It hadn't told him anything new or useful. Not first time, anyway. Not until he read John Smith's Friday Sketch.

Gaunt now knew what he hadn't known before – apart from M.'s skulduggery and the fact of that cock of a boy's arrogance, which had been there all along. Two things. One: Queedy and John Smith the teacher-drowning public school psycho were one and the same person. Did M. know? The thought had occurred to Gaunt to go and tell the delightful Mrs Fenwick in Personnel. Maybe, but not yet. He would keep that ace up his sleeve where it was worth more. Two: the boy had left another footprint; or rather someone as yet unidentified had, someone Gaunt would track down before the day was out.

With the bottle in one clumsy fist and *Paton's List* resting in his lap, Gaunt thumbed roughly through its pages until he relocated the entry for Stowe. Boys, six hundred and twenty-seven, masters seventy-five etc etc... the Annual Review, now twelve months out of date, blah blah... prizes, scholarships to Oxford and Cambridge; sporting achievements... the shooting club, Southern Champions for the third year in a row... a shooting club for Christ's sake... Buildings and Grounds... Endowments... special events for the year, which Gaunt reckoned was two years after the Long Vac when Queedy must have been kicked out. Now, here, this was the interesting entry: the Astronomer Royal, a special guest at a ceremony for the commissioning of the school's new astronomical observatory which had cost... well, a small fortune. If Gaunt's bottom lip hadn't hurt so much – how had he hit himself in the mouth, he wondered – he would have stuck it out now. Over the page... the generous benefactor behind the building of this state-of-the-art observatory with its sixteen-inch Newtonian reflector blah blah... the Roanoke Foundation. The name meant nothing to Gaunt. But it would. A call to Companies House would yield the names of the Trustees. Queedy – or Smith – had shown his hand. His feature article betrayed his too-expert knowledge of space and the stars and moon. Typical of a stuck up little shit like that to parade it in front of the readers to impress them. Well, that observatory had something to do with him. To do with his crime. It was expiation for sin. Gaunt slapped the book shut with a noise like a gunshot which had the edgy staff down the corridor jumping out of their skins, and took another heave on the bottle of whisky whose hot hand reached down his throat into his heart, punching it back to life.

By the time M. appeared in the doorway, not looking at Gaunt but surveying the damage, Gaunt knew who Queedy was. That is, he knew who his father was. The American press baron, Carew Smith. Jesus Christ Almighty, that changed everything. No bloody wonder his mate Harry Tanning had thought it sport to keep him in the dark; the only wonder was that Gaunt had not seen it before. Now it was bloody obvious. Everything was bloody obvious. Gaunt, already half-cut and once more feeling no pain, looked stiffly up at M.'s silhouette in the doorway; would have laughed at him if he could. Who would have thought it?

- There you are, Gaunt. Sure I'm sorry to bother you, with you so busy and all. I was going to ask would you go out to the farm at Twyford and pick up the trail of our Ambulist. (Now Gaunt does manage a laugh, a wheezy, choking guttural chortle which goes on for about twenty seconds. M. is about to pick his way past the debris and back down the corridor, when Gaunt calls him back)

- Story too much for your boy? (Gaunt is slurring his words but they still sneer with contempt. The temptation to tell M. what he knows is strong, but he is going to play this once-in-a-lifetime hand very smart)

- In a way. He's had a heart attack. You look like you are in line for a coronary too and you bloody well deserve it. I think I'll maybe cover this one myself. Have somebody fix that door. (This time M. does begin to walk up the corridor, the sound of glass crunching under his feet like frozen gravel on a garden path as he makes no attempt to avoid it).

- Will you now? (Gaunt shouts after him) We'll bloody well see about that. (This in a croaking whisper, so that M. does not hear it)

Chapter Six

Second miracle

M. had not been so fit, nor had he felt so healthy, these many years past. On his days at the office he took advantage of evenings slowly lengthening into March and left work early. He would drive north from the city with the Ambulist's map, a notebook and a pair of binoculars. He would leave his car in one of the places which the wanderer had marked with an enigmatic cross, circle or triangle, and walk.

Map in hand, M. took in the lay of the land, tried to see it through the eyes of a nomad. He stood still and rotated the map. He held the map steady and rotated himself. He climbed hills and church towers for a better view. He formed theories on the significance of each place and tested them by pacing, by lining up viewpoints with one eye shut. He contemplated standing stones and Roman roads. He drew his own lines on the map to see if there might be a geometrical symmetry to the Ambulist's calculus. He read and re-read the county's histories; was the nomadic miracle-worker following in the trail of one of the ancient saints: Cuthbert? Oswald? He began slowly to decode the meaning of some of the Ambulist's marks; or thought he did. He slid down river banks, crossed bridges, wove many a path through churchyard and field in pursuit of clues to the whereabouts of the vanished giant. The light would fail, sometimes suddenly under a bank of grey-blue still-wintry cloud, sometimes almost unnoticed just after dusk with impossibly high tendrils of delicate icy cloud clinging to the sun's last rays. Then his dweller's chains would tug him back to the city and his empty house.

On Saturday or Sunday, when he had the whole day to himself, he would be early on the road, a flask of coffee and a breakfast roll wrapped in brown paper on the passenger seat, his walking shoes ly-ing on a sheet of newspaper in the boot. Sometimes he would pass a figure on the road, packaged against the North Sea's salty blast, and consider for a moment if it might be the monumental bulk of his prey. Driving on, he might throw logic aside and let his imagination, or it might be intuition, take him. Not once did this amateur divination lead to a sight of the quarry. At village shops he would buy himself a newspaper or chocolate bar and pass the time of day with the owner, mention the distinctive-looking friend he was supposed to meet close by, and draw blank after blank. He rarely returned to the city before dark. When he did so he was exhausted, but his joy at waking with only stiff limbs to complain of instead of a bad gut and a worse sacroiliac had taken ten years off him. He was often hungry and took to cooking himself a wholesome meal of an evening instead of eating, as had been his practice, out of packets and tins. His staff, most of his staff, appreciated their new, improved editor. M. smiled at them, asked them how they were. They bent to the journalistic wheel with renewed effort and some began to believe, as he sometimes did himself, that the *Courier's* declining fortunes were not, after all, irreversible. In more ways than one the Ambulist might be the saving of them. Only Gaunt, billeted on Mrs Fenwick in Personnel while his office was reconstructed by workmen, resented the air of levity which breezed along the *Courier's* corridors on a Friday afternoon and Monday morning. He was forced to endure a sort of torture, working alongside the fragrant and genteel Mrs F. now she had a new beau in her life.

M.'s affair with his adopted county blossomed. The careless days of his liberation from a long, mistaken marriage came often into his mind as he turned a corner and saw an inn, or it may be a telephone box or roadside bench, where he had turned to poetry and to thoughts of finding someone else. Woods in whose leafy bowers he had camped wild, rivers in whose lyric waters he had swum, came upon him as vividly as ever they had done in his Donegal childhood, fresh and exciting as if discovered for the first time. The air of the hills, the great rolling sweep and fold of the land intoxicated him as never before. The fall of light, early or late, in long shadows or through scudding pink-white clouds, raised his spirits to the sky. The thought of retiring and spending his days roaming with no greater purpose than a lust for the day whetted his desire to break free of the *Courier* and its shackling drudgery. He began, even, to envy the Ambulist his state of absolute, reckless, perilous freedom, that lust for liberty which must come close to something like a compulsion.

And yet M. was also spurred by a bone-deep desire to capture and tame the object of his search, if only in the features columns of his paper, so driven was he to own the story on whose trail he believed himself to be closing. Here he was, grasping for what might be The Story, and every time he believed himself to be within touching distance of his man it evaporated into thin air. Every day was a day of renewed hope and reaffirmed failure. Frustration led to thoughts of his own flight, of escape. Might he, dare he, throw the straws of this story to the wind, toss his keys into a burn and, like the Ambulist, embark upon the walk that never ends except in death? Was it possible that he could endure a life without the warmth of a hot bath or the cool seductive note of clinking ice in a tumbler of gin? He might have reflected that at the present time he did rather well to have it both ways; that he still had a business to resurrect, staff to manage, a house to wrest from the control of dust and mice and dirty dishes. There was, in any case, something to be said for collapsing into an armchair of an evening, switching on the heating and a reading light and musing on the collective wisdom of the county's poets, historians and geographers.

If the sin of pride had not stood between them M. might have enlisted Gaunt's help in his search. Gaunt had found the Ambulist before; his web of sources and informants cast a fine-meshed net over the county, which M.'s enthusiasm and affection for his adopted land could not match. M. must rely on persistence and the map, and hope that chance would cast the dice in his favour. For three weeks there had been no sign of the nomad. Where had he been sleeping? Where had he been buying his food? M. was almost tempted to enlist the readers of the *Courier* in his search. He stayed his hand because, in the first place, he would not want to answer to the Ambulist for such a strategy – he could imagine the man looking through him as he had once done at Heavenham, and the thought unnerved him – but also because he had now cast himself in the role of sleuth, or bloodhound. The quarry was his. Gaunt was unworthy of the pursuit, Queedy presently incapable.

Once, on a day when the map had led him to visit three churches, all lying on the south side of ancient river-crossings and all dedicated to the miracle-working Saint Cuthbert, he believed himself to be on the point of decoding the pattern in the map. If nothing else he was convinced that the Ambulist was, like himself, a student of the county's serpentine past. But even as each clue seemed to lead from the last, he was no nearer to predicting where the Ambulist might next turn up.

Even on a late evening, driving home along the back lanes hugging the western edge of the Fell Sands, when he stopped to reacquaint himself with the exquisite little Norman church at Old Bewley and found what was surely an entry in the Ambulist's hand in the visitors' book, just a week old; even then, he knew that the trail ran no more than lukewarm in his hands. And the catastrophic thought came to him that the Ambulist, knowing himself to be pursued, might by now have disappeared forever; might have vanished whence he came.

The same thoughts had probably occurred to the inhabitants of the Tower-house. Normal life had not returned for them. Without any fuss or fanfare a room was made up for the recuperating Queedy, whose coronary condition was stabilised for the time being by an adjustment in his drug regime. He was accepted, as the Ambulist had been, entirely on his own terms; even so, he changed the pattern and rhythm of their existence. During long evenings when he was asked to join the family before their fire in the sitting room there was a constraint to the atmosphere, not so much because of Queedy's awkwardness in their company but rather because he made them feel abashed in their hearty love for one another. After a while he took to spending evenings in his room, unless Selena could persuade him to join her in a gentle stroll around the lake in the company of the dogs and her ever-attentive goat.

M. was grateful that Queedy hadn't died, grateful too that he was being cared for; that he, M., did not have to play the uncle. Queedy cut a diminished figure, for his sleekness was gone and fatigue had wasted his curiosity. He had, however, been able to write a successful feature on the Arnesen family to supplement his first Friday sketch on the Ambulist, his now-curious readers mollified by the promise that the Ambulist's story would soon be taken up again. Now and then Jareld would consult him on musical matters and they would descend into the cavernous basement. Jareld used him as a sort of companionable sounding-board for his ideas. Queedy, content not to have to think much, acquiesced and said the right things. He was not allowed to walk in the woods with the dogs: Jareld and Freya feared another disastrous collapse, blaming themselves for Queedy's first crisis which he had suffered while helping Jareld split logs in the yard.

Selena, with the natural unaffected sympathy that the swineherd has for the runt of the litter, now more or less fully adopted Queedy as a pet. He was allowed to help her with light duties in the yard and the stable, and in his still-pathetic state he was grateful for the attention and for her distracting way of looking at him. He could not reconcile himself with the ruder functions of the animals; his original antagonist, the goat, marked his extended presence with sulky reproaches towards its mistress. Queedy's only ally in Selena's ark appeared to be the miraculous donkey foal Tigger, whose ears Queedy had become accustomed to stroking and who seemed to require having his back scratched by his fellow-outpatient. Queedy was too weak in mind and spirit to reflect upon his adoption and too feeble to contemplate the burden of the family's disinterested love, let alone attempt to carry it with him, or resist it.

The temporary sanatorium occupied by Queedy overlooked the yard from the second floor of the Tower-house, where Freya had her studio. It offered a satisfying sense of elevation like his own apartment in the city, except that he now shared the treetop world of rooks and wood pigeons. Evening light flooded the room with yellow warmth; in the morning the air inside was still and noiseless. The view Queedy had exchanged for his panoramic cityscape included, below him, the pleasingly uneven roofs of the outbuildings and, far to the left, the lake with its fringe of trees, just hinting at faint signs of bum-fluff greenery which told of sap's rise and the earth's faintly pulsing warmth. Beyond, over a rise that had once been the motte of a Norman keep, more roofs: the huddled cottages of the village and its squat Saxon church. From this height Queedy's eye reached even further, into the purple-misted hills beyond with their darkly rippled fields and curving hedges, wayside trees and flocking lapwings.

Here, in the afternoons, Queedy could sit and scribble shorthand in his notebook or work on a sketch for the *Courier*. Through the yard-thick wall behind the fireplace he fancied he could hear the sculptor at work, cajoling, kneading, punishing her clay, bending it to her purpose, writing and rewriting the sight-lines of her subjects, feeling for the truth beneath their skin. Her studio reflected the cheerful anarchy of the kitchen downstairs. Unfinished pieces – studies of hands or heads, half-completed nudes – lay on benches or propped against the bare walls. Stripped pine shelves sagged under the weight of books: modern art, renaissance sculpture, the Vienna movement; and film – Bergman, Joris Ivens, John Marshall. Oddments which she must have picked up over many years stood cluttered and dusty on cupboard tops and sills: tiny bronzes from Africa, a graffito on a plank of wood smuggled out of East Berlin, an Aboriginal pointillist churinga. Drawer after drawer half-open held inks and paper, bespoke and improvised tools, glazed firing samples, brushes, colour swatches. Dust cloths, filthy and crusted with plaster daubs and fingerprints of paint, hung from stepladders or curtain rails. A radio played, for the most part unlistened to. A fire roared and spat in the hearth. Natural light from the north-facing window illuminated her work.

Freya Arnesen had been much admired for her beauty, the perfection of her body, the ingenuous grace of her walk, the frankness of a face that men wanted to believe could not lie to them from the cover of a magazine. Couturiers had fought for the privilege of dressing her. Her face and body had been captured on film a thousand times. Freya knew the secrets of beauty, of the human form. She had not been passive in the creative process which had made her a wealthy and celebrated woman. The naked body, which she had seen and felt at its most sensuous, most defenceless and exposed, was her own passion.

In her late twenties, after her marriage to Jareld, Freya revolted against the industry which had made her fortune. Jareld tired of being forever on the road, of being in constant demand, almost as public property; he grew out of the rock and roll lifestyle: drugs and beer, highs that were too high and lows that were too low. They hid, the two of them, in an old weather-beaten pine cabin on a remote island in the far north of Norway. There they spent three years among forests and in their ketch sailing the fjords, rarely seeing or being seen by others. Jareld, exhausted by the strains and duplicities of the music industry, composed songs but did not record them. His new audiences were migrating flocks of wild geese overnighting on the water. His stage was the lapping shore or the porch, lit by a thin sun skimming the southern horizon or the boreal shimmering of the aurora on winter nights that seemed like they would never end.

Freya came to the secrets of light through the lens of the camera which, for the whole of her life until then, had been pointed at her. Light was precious, liquid gold here. The foreknowledge of its autumn departure, the poignancy of its return, were almost unbearable tethers to the relentless cycle of the seasons. The sun's transhumant wandering stole Freya's light from her in October and returned it grudgingly in March. During long winter months lit by oil lamp and firelight, when Jareld and Freya were forced on each other's unremitting company, she came finally to explore the world through her hands, feeling her way into the soul of the mountains, forests and water where she could not see. But the couple's arts kept them somehow apart, disunited. They sought contentment, or tolerance, in themselves, not in each other.

On the birth of their daughter Selena, so ephemeral a creature, so limpid, so passive and unearthly that they believed she might not survive, they were forced to move south to the city. There Freya found her true subject in the studio attic of an apartment where she could work without ever being far from the child. Giving her energy to the sculptor's clay in her hands, Freya massaged the life back into her daughter. Jareld nursed and nourished the little thing in song and in his joy for her life, cradled in his lullaby arms. This tiny delicate child, absorbing her parents' emotions and creativity day after day, month after month, nourished by their collective devotion, completed them.

In clay, in plaster and in bronze, Freya explored the body. She came to visualise the human soul as pure form. From time to time, on days when her strength of purpose, invigorated by the love she bore for her family, became almost overwhelming, she believed she might mould the souls of the living into new, more beautiful forms. The young, fragile and tainted Queedy, whose jarring awkwardness she could feel even through the walls of her studio might, she felt, become a subject for her art. But not now. Not yet. In the early weeks of March, her creative energies were concentrated on the bust of a magnificent, titanic human head, a form whose essential being transmitted energy as if it had been forged in an ageless crucible wrought by giants. The Ambulist was an irresistible subject: so strong and with such life in him. And yet, there was something: she sensed in him a rift, a flaw, which time and defences could not fully conceal. As she worked her clay, Freya probed beneath the man's skin, divining the nature of the scars she sensed were there.

Gaunt was taking advantage of Mrs Fenwick's absence – the hairdresser's again – to use the telephone which lay on her desk. He found through practice that he could balance the phone on the arm of her chair and lean back with his feet resting nicely on the low side table where she always kept a vase of cut flowers. Today it was pinks. Very nice too. He liked a flower, did Gaunt. Privacy was on short ration since M. had deployed the workmen to his room. Not content with ordering the installation of a new door and desk, the editor had decreed a decorative refurbishment which induced a cull of the room's shelves and filing cabinets, carpet, lights and blinds. It was a personal assault. Gaunt knew it. He dialled Harry Tanning's number.

      – That you, Gaunt?

      – Yes, Harry.

      – You still in quod?

      – I am. He's going to have them string it out for bloody weeks. I can't even smoke in here.

- And the charming Mrs F.?

- Out having her hair done. More likely out holding hands with the new boyfriend. Least it gives me a bit of peace and quiet.

- What's new?

- Our young friend is still getting his brow mopped out in the sticks. I shouldn't wonder if they're setting him up with the girl. They want to watch out, see he doesn't bump her off, with a nice framed photograph of the deed for them to remember her by.

- You'd like that, Gaunt.

- Maybe I would, too.

- What can I do you for this fine spring morning?

- Spring? Not up here it ain't. Freeze the balls off a brass bloody monkey, it would. What I'm after, Harry, is the gen on old man Smith. I mean, I know about the plane crash and I know he owned half the Yankee press. I know what the networks were saying at the time, that he killed himself because of the court case; I know all that stuff. What about the rest of it? You did all the leg work when the boy was kicked out of school.

- I did, Gaunt. Well, the widow, that is to say your young friend's mother, she now lives with a very swanky lawyer in San Diego; that's where they all go when they have too much money and don't know how to spend it. The other child, the daughter, she must be five years older than the boy, she's now in charge of the business. The whole lot was left to her, lock and stock. She's a right hard nut too. Fired half the board within a week of the plane wreckage being found. I reckon she couldn't hardly believe her luck, him topping himself. And then, who's to say he crashed the plane all on his own account? Who's to say he wasn't helped on his way to the dark regions? There was talk of him doing a bit of spying for the Feds, you know.

- Point taken, Harry. Point taken. Anyhow, I can't see Queedy, or should I say Smith junior, being too pally with Mum and his sister these days, can you? Otherwise what's he doing here in this tip? Why haven't they dished him up a nice plate of plum pudding? He could own a dozen rags like the *Courier*.

- True. Question is, Gaunt, was the boy disinherited because of the little difficulty at the school or was he out of the picture anyway? That's something. And we might also ask, how does your boss come to know the boy? If it's through the father, how did they know each other?

- Well, Harry, that's for me to find out. And I will. What I really want to know is, what did the old man do before he took over the world? Where did he come from, and how did he get to be such a big bastard in the first place?

- That, Gaunt, is another matter. He was a Yank citizen when he died and he was born in Ireland, that much I do know. He'd already been over the other side of the pond a good while when he made the bid for Global. The wife is a bona fide Yank, by the way: Ivy League. Before that he owned the Banner Group in Dublin. But there's a lot missing in between and beforehand.

- Telling me. Dublin must be the connection, cos that's where the boss was before here. Any chance Smith went to the same school as his boy?

- No, I don't think he was born with a silver spoon in his fat gob. He made it all himself. Be nice to know whose bodies he trod on to get there. And where he learned the trade. You don't get to own half the world's press being mister nice guy.

- Well, someone must know.

- You are right, Gaunt. You might ask your boss. Or are you still not talking?

- Sore point, Harry.

- Tell you what, I've got a great fat bundle of cuttings concerning Mister Smith senior, sitting in my loft at home. Be doing me a favour if you took them off my hands. That's if the mice haven't done me the favour already.

- All right, I will do you that favour, Harry. Send them up here and I'll see how Mrs F. likes having her office floor covered in cuttings. It might speed the buggers up a bit and I can get back into my nice new place and have a fag in peace.

- Tell you what. You come down and fetch them, Gaunt, and we will partake of a few beers for old times' sake. The wife'll cook. She's been on at me about those papers for ages.

- I don't mind if I do. There'll be a way of chalking that up on expenses.

- I don't doubt it, Gaunt. I don't doubt it.

Gaunt, conscious of the time and knowing that Mrs F. was due back, ended his satisfactory conversation with Harry Tanning, swept a dusting of his dandruff off the cover of the chair and went back to his own temporary desk in the far corner of the office behind the filing cabinets. He had a feeling Harry's bundle of cuttings would make interesting reading. In the meantime he was going to have a bit of a look at M.'s own career, see if there was a link with Carew Smith; a crossing point where the two might have met or worked together. The offices of the *Clarion* in Dublin might not be a bad place to start. Who did he know there? Where was that card index of his?

A long straggling line of children wound its way up through the trees and along the path which led from the school house. Their brightly-coloured coats gave the procession an air of carnival. Some held hands and all of them carried bunches of flowers: pansies, crocuses, snowdrops and primroses. Their teacher, Miss Davidson, handsome and silver-haired but looking faintly absurd in a combination of tweed overcoat and red and pink polka dot wellington boots, brought up the rear. Her attention was firmly taken up with two small boys, neither of whom wished to be seen carrying flowers under any circumstances. The snaking column lengthened as the steepness of the hill before them began to take its toll. A coterie of fat, pregnant ewes scattered ungainly and nervous ahead of them. The air was dry and cold; high cloud teased the sun whose heat, even in its elevated spring arc, had yet to penetrate the remoter valleys of the county. Here, cut flowers aside, small signs of spring had begun to show in understated native blooms among otherwise wan fields, hoary trees and hedges.

The pair who reached the gate first knew very well that they were to stop and wait there for Miss Davidson. But such was the eventual press behind them, and so far behind was their teacher, that more than one precocious soul began to egg them on and, in a chaotic mêlée, twenty-five or so children swept through into the enclosure, during which several ragged flower heads fell to the ground and were crushed underfoot.

The enclosure, bounded by a mossy drystone wall to keep stock out, was dark within and had the children not been perfectly familiar with the perpetual gloom of Saint Paulinus's Well, it might have scared the fainter-hearted among them. Rhododendron bushes of impenetrable thickness hemmed them in on all sides casting a deep, sinister shade. A ring of colossal beech trees, much scarred by graffiti, canopied the grove: ragged parasols filtering the light. Last autumn's leaves still lay in a rustling bronze carpet on the ground. A chaste statue of the Virgin Mary, which had stood next to the pool these hundreds of years, looked forlorn: moss-dressed, crumbling, her features cast down. One of the children delicately balanced a flower in her frozen hand as she passed by. The surface of the pool, some twenty feet across, was milk-flat, sky and trees perfectly mirrored. The water was clear glass two feet thick. In the centre, on a stone plinth, stood a cross of Celtic design.

The sweetness and purity of the spring were famous and proudly cherished by the villagers of Halstane. Every year at Easter, time out of

mind, they had gathered here to celebrate Bishop Paulinus's conversion
of the pagan English Northumbrians to Christianity in the days of King
Edwin; and, in an unconsciously pagan gesture, they came to thank the
spirits of the hills for the life which the spring brought them. At the
far side of the pool, against a dark green rhododendron, stood a wicker
framework which must have been placed there recently. Formed into
an arch with a pitched roof above and a bower below, it had been firmly
pegged to the ground; beside it on the leaf-covered earth lay a basket
full of string ties, wooden clothes pegs and ribbons. It was to this
bower that the fresh spring flowers were to be attached, in a design
conceived by the children with help from their teacher. Against the
back, the figure of Bishop Paulinus would be picked out in pansies:
purple for his robes, yellow for his mitre, pink for the face and hands.
The background would be white snowdrops. The bower's roof and
walls were to be multi-coloured crocuses intermingled with green
leaves, which the ladies of the village church flower committee were to
provide later in the day.

    - Who are you? (The child largely responsible for the
premature invasion of the enclosure walks unabashed up to a
man who sits on the dank slope at the back of the pool, drinking
from a battered silver metal flask. The man is old, a perfect
model for Saint Nicholas except that his greatcoat is dark, not
bright red, and his flowing mane grey rather than white. On the
ground next to him a large leather bag looks as though it might
hold treasure, or gifts. The man is used to being asked his name
and expert at deflecting the curiosity of strangers, but the simple
direct question of a ten-year-old boy with a very obviously
missing front tooth and dimpled, freckly cheeks disarms him)

    - My name is Pieter.

    - My name is Peter too. How old are you I'm ten and a bit.

    - It is nice to meet you, Peter. I am too old to remember
how old I am, but I remember being ten and a bit. It is a very

good age. The best. Now, tell me what you young people are up to. (The Ambulist immediately finds himself surrounded by a score of parti-coloured children, all thrusting handfuls of flowers towards him. He smiles and holds his arms out and his eyes almost disappear in the creases of his face) You have brought me flowers? (The children all laugh and begin to shout, telling Pieter that the flowers are not for him, but for the well. Doesn't he know about the Easter well-dressing?)

A more diffident or inexperienced school teacher than Miss Davidson might have been put out of countenance by the sight of this ragged giant holding court to her children as she came through the gate accompanied by the last of her wards. But she was too old and too wise to judge on first impressions. Her father had been a colonel in an Indian regiment. They were old county stock. She had been brought up self-reliant and thoroughly Anglican in outlook. Her first thought was to hope that her children had been polite to the stranger.

- Children! You were told to wait at the gate. Now, line up here and stop that racket this minute. Rachel Armstrong put that stick down. Good afternoon, Sir, I do hope the children haven't disturbed you? (Miss Davidson walks towards the Ambulist, who stands up and offers her his massive callused hand in greeting; the children, seeing him for the first time at his full height, are awed into unaccustomed silence and take a united, involuntary step back towards the edge of the pool)

- Your children are very fine. I thought they had brought me flowers. (The Ambulist smiles at the children, some of whom cover their mouths with their hands and giggle stupidly. The small boy called Peter scowls at them)

- Miss! Miss! Peter made us come in and he asked the man his name and the man's name is Peter too.

- Be quiet, Pamela, and don't be a tittle-tattle. You must excuse their agitation, Sir, they are very excited about the Easter

well-dressing. (Miss Davidson turns to the children and begins
to organise them with martial efficiency)

The Ambulist had traced an obscure path from the little church at
Old Bewley to the well at Halstane. These were the remote uplands of
the county, in former times the haunts of robbers and cattle-raiders, of
marcher lords and moss-troopers in the days when a hungry housewife
might serve up a dish of a spur for her husband's dinner to remind him
that her larder was bare. In earlier centuries praise of great and terrible
deeds had been sung in stone halls and bastle houses in the hills which
crowded in on all sides of these dales. Many a thief had been pursued
and taken in the narrow defiles that led here from the high peat lands.
Long before, the Roman legions had driven a road past this place and
must have paused to drink the well's sweet water; but they had not
cared to dwell or to pray. The first wanderers to come across this
spring may have believed that its water had magical properties. Flint
arrowheads, the traces of their hunting parties, might still be found in
local plough lands.

The Ambulist, keeping to the high ground, had walked for many
days among relict fields and sheep stells, passing his nights sheltering
in the empty shielings of long-dead shepherds and drovers. The 'plain-
ing curlew and the crow, the buzzard, fox and stoat yet scraped their
livings among the grasses and dwarf oaks, along dancing burns and
sucking bogs, but no humans lived up there now. Sensing winter's
end, the Ambulist had longed, like the herds of gravid heifers cooped
in their valley sheds, to be on higher ground, to see better and sooner
the new season looming from the south. He felt the urgency of the
northbound geese flying above and ahead of him, and saluted them.
His own urge drove him on: to compass this land, its rocks and soils,
woods and streams, its primeval geomorphic script and the history
of its people. In coming here the Ambulist hoped, vainly perhaps, to
catch the faint notes of an ancient song, for the well had been sacred
long before the arrival of any Christian missionary priest. He filled his

flask and drank long, exulting in the water's extraordinary purity. He might have guessed that he would find no silence here, for such bounty had attracted settlers and pilgrims from the earliest times. He might share its purity and accept the din of excited youth, but then he must move on. Kneeling down at the pool's edge he ran his hand through the water, spoke a few quiet words to himself and picked up his grip once more. Neither the children nor their teacher noticed him depart.

That night he slept under a sky clear of rain and lit by a moon within two days of the full. He found a quiet corner among the walls of a ruined priory long abandoned by its own silent brethren and, when he woke, set himself to a new direction, one that would take him far from people. He felt, though, a reluctance to travel long that day. He kept to the valley and traced the course of a stream through woods awakening to the colours and sounds of spring. A dazzling emerald green haze of ramsons, of wood sorrel and anemone jewelled by golden yellow star-burst flower-heads of celandine, clouded his eyes and drew him into a reverie so profound that he lay down in a small glade away from the path and could walk no more. He slept through midday and into the evening, as it were stupefied by nature's overwhelming resurgence.

As darkness fell the creatures of the wood began to busy themselves. The Ambulist, waking, stiff and for a moment confused, raised himself and, gathering such dry sticks as he could find, lit a small fire. As he did so he contemplated the trail ahead, but for once it did not draw him on. He opened himself to his unconscious thoughts as the fire-shine waxed and waned. A sense of unease which was neither fear for the future nor the dulled-chisel anguish of passing years, crept up on him and yet here, in this wood where spring crouched poised in its blocks, was life renewing its immemorial cycle. In the midst of creation his soul was filled with uncertainty, with unrest.

The nomad has a refined sensitivity to the passing of each season, to its flow and ebb, its melodic phrasing, its delicate, telling scents. The dweller walks out one day to find that the world has changed in his absence and he accepts it; it surprises him only as a knock at the door might. It causes no pain to his dulled senses, it cannot change him. His rhythm is set from birth by switches and clocks, by calendars and anniversaries which he is force-fed. To the nomad it may seem that the dweller can barely feel at all. But it now came to the Ambulist that he had missed something; had failed to catch a note or perceive a movement, had ignored some signal that might have mattered. Where and when this had happened he could not say. But as his old confidant and companion the moon rose white and almost perfectly round above the trees, wreathed in its icy halo of purity, he knew he must return to the well, to drink again, to be silent, and to listen. What was it he had failed to see, to feel, to hear?

When the Ambulist woke again in the hour before dawn with the wood's native life already stirring itself, his mood of the previous night had passed. He felt strong, and the urge to revisit the spring fed his desire to be on the trail early. He did not light a fire but ate stale bread and cheese and drank from the flask whose sweet water beckoned him to return to its source. He gathered his bag and found the path; but as he hit his full stride he tripped and stumbled and, realising that his sight was clouded this morning, paused for a moment and leant against a tree. He dropped the grip to the ground and rubbed his eyes. They would not clear and so he walked on, blinking and uncertain in the bright sunlight that now lit the winding path in front of him. Only slowly did his sight come back to him. The dappled forest floor, the penetrating polar blue of the sky and rippling sun slowly fed his spirit. His pace quickened with the exuberant sounds of birds calling for their mates or seeing off a rival suitor, the titanic momentum returned to his stride in grand rising chords, his breath funnelled in clouds behind him.

The Ambulist came again to Halstane late in the morning. Emerging from the shadows of the valley he heard from half a mile ahead the bell of the little village chapel ring out, proclaiming Good Friday, the day of resurrection. A small group of sober elderly people could be seen leaving the churchyard. Some wore narcissi in their button holes; they were clothed against the cold even though the sun was high now and its heat was tangible on the skin. As the giant passed, a knot of them looked up at him and he could hear a ripple of whispers behind him as he strode on. At the centre of the village, where drab strings of bunting had been hung in a seeming hurry between the eaves of the houses, a panting bus disgorged a crowd of chattering folk who made great haste along the path that led to the well. Villagers in tight family groups joined them, parents shepherding children impatiently with their hands as if they feared they might miss the festivities. Cars were parked askew on verges, their owners nowhere to be seen. The Ambulist saw, with a sinking heart, that he would find no solace, no quiet at the well today. He hesitated in his stride, unwilling to turn back but reluctant to go on, and at that moment he saw, and was recognised by, the familiar shabby bulk of the *Courier's* photographer, Stokes, who now ran shuffling towards him, followed more sedately but with no less enthusiasm by the paper's editor-in-chief, notebook in hand.

The Ambulist's instinct now was to avoid both the crowd and the attention of the *Courier*. He turned, but as he did so a clatter of small voices cried out to him and his ten-year-old gap-toothed namesake, Peter, who had so unselfconsciously made his acquaintance two days before, ran up and clutched his hand. He was immediately surrounded by a flock of cheering schoolchildren who had shed their coats in the sun and were now dressed in uniform claret and grey. They led him willy-nilly up the path towards the well with Stokes in determined but wheezing pursuit and a newly-fit M. gaining on them with every stride.

An extraordinary number of people was crowded into the enclosure, far more than could be accounted for by the village and its surrounding scattered farms. The well, its habitual and ancient sanctity shattered, now gave off an atmosphere of carnival excitement inexplicable to the Ambulist. The Easter bower, beautifully and festively decorated with such loving care by Miss Davidson and her charges, was almost swamped in the throng and in danger of being overturned by the press of humanity cramming against it. As the children led, half-pushed the Ambulist onwards, the crowd spontaneously parted with a hushing sound like a prairie wind. The by-now widely circulated description of the miracle-worker leaving no doubt that He had returned to savour his triumph, the mass of onlookers, celebrants, mystics and villagers drawn to the well fell almost silent, leaving a chorus of children to cheer him on.

Half in horror and half in wonderment the Ambulist, his little apostles clinging on to him for dear life, looked down aghast at a pool now teeming, brimming, with hundreds of glittering silver-brown fish. The moment was caught perfectly by the red-faced Stokes, armed with no less than three cameras.

It was not the Ambulist, nor the children, but Miss Davidson who explained to M. in perfectly lucid and admirably precise English the sequence of events that had led to the revelation of the Good Friday fish – certainly enough of them, some wag had noted, to feed five thousand and more if only the old village bakery had still been open to provide the bread to go with them. M.'s own interest in Christian mythology and the region's heritage meant that he was perfectly familiar with the story of the well and Bishop Paulinus's seventh-century conversions. He readily assimilated Miss Davidson's description of the Ambulist's appearance there, his effect on the children and what she saw as his obvious hand in the miracle, with a strong and immediate sense of his own, as well as the Ambulist's, destiny. He did not have to be reminded of the fishermen and fishers of men among Jesus' disciples or of the story of the loaves and fishes. The aptness of the shoal appearing on Good Friday, as Miss Davidson was sure he would know, was that fish could be eaten on the fasting days of Lent.

If M. had prayed for a miracle to save his flagging newspaper from oblivion, the Ambulist seemed definitively to have provided it. This was too good to be true. Headlines filled his head; pages of features and follow-up stories from children and villagers, bishops and assorted freaks. And yet... and yet. Was it possible that the whole thing had been staged, was a stunt pulled off by the man in collusion with these apparently guileless villagers? Could these children have been so convincingly tutored in their parts? M.'s head was so full of possibilities, of risks, of the impact which this story would have on readers, not just of the *Courier* but across the country, that he failed in his journalistic duty and missed the moment when the Ambulist, appalled at being the centre of so much unwanted attention, made his escape.

Down the path to the village he stumbled, his eyes again straining to focus on the ground in front of him. Ignoring cries from those who had seen him leave the enclosure, and barely knowing which path he should now take, he half-ran past the bus whose complacent driver sat on its step smoking a cigarette, past the chapel with its still-tolling bell, and towards the wooded valley that would give him cover, at least temporarily. He half-noticed as he passed that a police car had pulled up, the officer trying and failing to listen simultaneously to three enthusiastic informants and a resident angry at not being able to park in his own drive. Head down, he pushed on, his blurring vision bringing tears to his eyes, until his way was suddenly blocked by a Land Rover pulling across in front of him. The passenger door swung open and voices urged him to get in. Panicking almost and scared, like a hunted animal trapped with no way to turn, the Ambulist squeezed his giant frame into the vehicle and it drew away.

 - Where shall we take you? (The voice belongs to the girl, Selena, sitting at the wheel)

 - I do not know. Anywhere. (The Ambulist's head has sunk onto his chest; he is weeping and his immense hands cover his eyes)

 - I have brought you your bootlaces. (Queedy, sitting in the back of the Land Rover, frail and nervous, can think of nothing better to say)

M. had telephoned the Tower-house early that morning when the first word of the so-called second miracle reached the *Courier's* news desk. He roused Stokes from his breakfast in the café across the street and drove him at reckless speed along the old Roman road which drew its inexorably straight line from the city up through the Borders, desperate to be first on the scene. Jareld Arnesen, receiving his call, thought for some minutes whether or not to pass M.'s message on to Queedy. First he consulted his wife and then the two spoke to Selena in the yard. The girl was adamant that Queedy must be told, that she must take him to the scene of the miracle and that they must find the Ambulist. Queedy, after all, was the one person in whom the Ambulist seemed to have confided. Selena immediately saw that if the wanderer was identified with a second miracle he would be vulnerable to unwelcome attention; that he might need to be rescued. Her parents begged her to offer him sanctuary at the farm. Queedy, woken at what was for him a rude hour, was bundled into the Land Rover wrapped in a quite unnecessary blanket; even so he had the wit to remember the Ambulist's new bootlaces, and his notebook. Freya made up a hasty hamper of food and a flask of coffee and this strange couple set off, arriving at Halstane, as it turned out, in the nick of time.

We took him, wrote Queedy in the sketch which was printed in the following day's weekend edition of the *Courier* alongside Stokes's brilliantly evocative photograph, to a remote spot which he knew of, high in the hills. A hundred years ago it had been the site of an old whisky smuggler's still. No one will find him there. He seems genuinely shocked that people should believe he had anything to do with the appearance of hundreds of fish at Paulinus's Well, of which readers will no doubt have heard during yesterday's furore in the media. He cannot explain their arrival on the morning of Good Friday any better than the oldest residents of the village, who say that nothing like this has happened in living memory. The village schoolteacher,

Miss Martha Davidson, who was interviewed by this newspaper's correspondent at the scene, was at the well with her class when our Ambulist, whose name we now know is Pieter, first appeared two days previously. It has been traditional for many decades that local school children should come to the well at Easter to dress a wicker bower with spring flowers. On Good Friday morning, the vicar leads a procession from the chapel to the well and performs a blessing much like that which the priest Paulinus must have done when he converted the pagans here fourteen hundred years ago.

Miss Davidson clearly recalls the first time she saw Pieter. He was speaking with the children – one of whom, incidentally, was the bright spark, and namesake, to whom the Ambulist confided his Christian name – about what they were doing. She also saw him fill his flask with water from the well, say some words which she did not hear, and trail his hand through the water. It was a gesture, she thought, of reverence. She says that the mysterious stranger had an aura about him, that the children responded to him as if his appearance were completely natural.

The fish, which the Trust that owns the well have forbidden visitors from catching, are thought to be rainbow trout. They appear to be entirely healthy and thriving in this legendarily pure fresh water. According to local anglers the nearest place to Halstane in which they are usually seen is at least a mile downstream. No one can suggest a rational means by which the fish have ended up in the well and there is a feeling among some, perhaps understandably, that this is a sign from God; a sign of what, they are not prepared or able to say. For the time being locals are taking it in turns to watch over the well to prevent any of the fish from being poached, but I understand there is now a police presence in Halstane, intended to deter petty theft or vandalism and souvenir-seeking by the large number of tourists who have descended on the village. An anonymous American millionaire is said to have offered several thousand dollars for the catch. The local health authority warns against anyone drinking the well's water until a decision is made about what to do with all the fish and until tests have been carried out on the spring.

Fish are an enduring symbol of Christianity, the piece continued. Aside from the parable of the loaves and the fishes, and the Galilee disciples who became fishers of men, the fish was used as a secret symbol among Christians during their persecution in the early centuries AD. The Greek word for fish, Icthys, was employed as an acronym for *Iesous Christos Theou Yios Soter*, meaning *Jesus Christ, Son of God, Saviour.*

And so the feature went on, filling, with Stokes's picture, the entire front page of Saturday's *Courier* beneath the headline – not of Queedy's contrivance – Fishy story: is this the Second Coming? Queedy's own sceptical slant had been toned down – or up – by M. in the editing; readers were encouraged to make up their own minds. The paper assured them that the Ambulist, whilst his privacy was to be respected, would feature again soon in John Smith's sketches – EXCLUSIVELY in the *Courier.*

On Sunday a national broadsheet weekly carried the story at the bottom of its front page in an abbreviated account with no picture. The same day John Smith's piece was syndicated more or less unadulterated in the *Boston Globe* and was translated for *Le Figaro, El Pais* and *Corriere della Sera* for a very large sum of money by the *Courier's* own parent company, exclusivity having been surrendered to the irresistible demands of public interest.

When he was not answering his telephone, M. spent the long weekend in his office drinking coffee, grabbing sleep when he could on the put-up mattress – sacroiliac notwithstanding – and basking in the knowledge that, Second Coming or not, the *Courier's* and his immediate futures had been secured by the re-appearance of the Ambulist. He sent one of the office juniors out for a bottle of gin, another of tonic, and a net of limes. More than once he treated himself to a glass, but only one at a time. It was like old times; only different.

On Sunday it seemed as though the telephone's nagging ring did not stop until the middle of the evening. M. was almost alone in the building. Exhausted, standing at his window glass in hand, half-listening to the faintly pealing bells of the cathedral down the hill, M. flexed his tortured back muscles, winced and looked down from the window upon the bare, still market place. Had he known, that black night in December? Had he felt something, the whiff of sensation, even then? Had his old instincts been working, smelling the faint, seductive perfume of a story trailing behind the man they now knew as the Ambulist? Now, more than ever, M. needed to know where he had come from, his career, other miracles if any, his history: his essence. He had by now dismissed the possibility that events at Halstane had been staged: it was impossible. He brushed aside the briefly attractive thought that the Ambulist had waved a wand and effected a bona fide New Testament Easter miracle just to show what he could do. It was equally plain that the Ambulist had not anticipated this dramatic manifestation of his powers. The whole thing could be a natural freak – the sort of Act of God that insurers shelter behind, rather than a genuine deus ex machina – but, both professionally speaking and as an Irishman, M. was disinclined to follow the thought.

An idea came to him that perhaps Pieter was a refugee monk, sent forth or expelled like Goldmund or the blessed Saint Columba from the sanctified bounds of a monastery. Was he an accidental saint whose golden touch brushed those whom he passed without intent or self-knowledge? A Midas? Could he help it? Here, M. cast his mind over the pantheon of saints for some sort of precedent. Or was he seeking redemption for sins committed against his order? As a monk he would know the lives of the ancient saints of this land. Did he now, M. wondered, follow in their footsteps in search of guidance, or wisdom? How far could M. allow Queedy a free hand with this precious asset whose gifts – let alone his value in circulation figures –

might disappear over the next hill at any time, to be lost forever?

The clutching fear that M. might lose his Ambulist was distracting. He had spent three weeks on the trail himself. He knew how utterly hopeless the pursuit had seemed. He, the *Courier*, could not afford Queedy the responsibility. God only knew Queedy was not up to the job. The boy hadn't a clue how to handle a subject, to lead him on, to tease out the threads of his testimony, to hold on tight when the thing was in his grasp. And then again, who knew when Queedy might collapse? M. could not indulge himself in the time to find out, now that the spotlight shone bright and searching on his paper. Who else, then, might he trust with his story? Christ, he could not bring himself to give it back to Gaunt, now reinstalled in his own painfully white and shining office. The old fucker. That would be especially galling since M.'s moral authority over Gaunt had been so hard-won.

M. crunched a last, half-melted ice cube in his mouth, put his empty glass down on the desk, and looked at the time. He could do with some fresh air; a walk, maybe. A few minutes later he found himself standing shivering inside the porch of the cathedral, submerged in the monstrous racket of its bells ringing a full peal. He counted the changes as they worked their arcane, magical rotations again and again, never the same twice until the final resolution of their age-old calculus. Wishing for once that he could share the burden of his job like the ringers, M. let his thoughts go free. Peace came with the stupefying rhythm of the bells; but no solution.

At twenty minutes past eleven the next morning – Easter Monday, when all Christian citizens should have been at home or visiting sick relatives – M.'s phone rang for the hundredth time. Since Miss Nixon was religiously resting for the day, the call came directly through to his office. He had just made himself a coffee, cast a weary glance over some trivial copy from the business editor, and was standing again at the window looking down on the familiar scene. His mind's eye registered, as he lifted the receiver, that the plane tree overhanging the iron bench had come into leaf without him really noticing; surely it had been bare the week before. And there, trotting lightly across the road, was Mrs Fenwick in a new-looking coat, off to some appointment or other. She looked pretty good for her age, M. thought. He was glad she hadn't let herself go after her husband's death. Maybe old Gaunt had been flirting with her, down in Personnel.

- Am I speaking to the editor of the *Courier* (says the voice on the end of the line)?

- Sure you are. To whom am I speaking?

- I understand you know the whereabouts of a man I want to interview.

- If you mean my miracle-working nomad, I have no intention of revealing his location. We operate a strict policy of respect regarding his wish for privacy. Who did you say you were?

- I am a reporter from the *Star* in Johannesburg. I am looking for a man whose description bears a strong similarity to the man referred to in your newspaper as 'The Ambulist'.

- I see.

- The man I would like to interview is aged about sixty-five or sixty-eight. He is a white male of Southern African origin, six feet four inches tall; long grey hair. His name is Pieter Jäger. He is known to have arrived in your country some time within the last five years. He has no fixed abode. Sounds like your nomad, wouldn't you say?

- Plenty of men like him wandering the countryside. I could find you another just like him. What sorts of miracle does your man indulge in?

- Do you call murder a miracle?

- I might. If the accused was nowhere near the victim I might.

- This is not a subject we in South Africa take lightly.

- Sure. What is your Mr Jäger supposed to have done?

- I am investigating events surrounding the murder of eleven people in Ongandjera, Namibia. There was a massacre in a crowded market place in a small town near the northern border with Angola. It was a car bomb. Have you ever been near a car bomb when it went off?

- Once or twice. (Yes, once or twice, M. mutters to himself. Belfast, for example; Derry) Have you?

- Intelligence gathered by South African police linked the bomb with the South West Africa People's Organisation: SWAPO. Jäger had links with senior SWAPO figures and fled the region immediately after the atrocity. He was imprisoned, but he escaped. We have been on his trail for some time. Your Mr Jäger is a known terrorist and in our country we take the view that it is our responsibility as journalists to track these people down and see them brought to justice. It is important for our new truth and reconciliation policy. I have the full backing of the authorities. Now will you tell me where he is, please?

Chapter Seven

Prevailing wind

M. had not moved from his desk since the telephone call; had not, in fact, been aware of where he was for some little while. His coffee had gone cold in the cup. Now, as if waking, he made an involuntary move towards the half-full bottle of gin in front of him and unscrewed the top, then screwed it back on again, opened the desk drawer and put it away. It was no time for that. He leant back in his chair with his hands clenched behind his head and stared at the ceiling, where a stray hanging cobweb wafted idly back and forth on some un-sensed current of air. Could he in his mind's eye picture the Ambulist as a bomb-wielding revolutionary? Maybe and maybe not. That he was capable of murder M. did not for one moment doubt: he had seen the look in the man's eye in the churchyard at Heavenham; but murder in a cause? Supposing he had committed, contemplated or been complicit in such a deed, would M. be inclined to hand him over to a journalist from a foreign newspaper, supposing the caller to be who he said he was? No, he bloody well would not. The Ambulist was his. But then, he, M., the *Courier*, had just sold the Ambulist on the open market. Unwelcome interest was, he knew, part of the price. The question was, who was going to pay and how high would the price be?

M. pulled a notepad towards him and wrote in rapid shorthand. He drew lines, arrows. The notebook began to look like the Ambulist's map, which M. now took from his desk drawer and pored over again, but with no greater insight than before. He re-read his notes, then tore the top few pages from the pad and fed them into the shredder at the side of his desk. He could not remember the last time he had used it. He stood up and walked over to the window. It was a bright airy day, brisk spring sunshine flooding the market place and etching a deep crenellated shadow along the middle of the cobbled alley opposite. To and fro across the market place floated in Brownian motion the stratified society of the city, from barristers and cathedral clergy to street cleaners and tramps; capitalists, professionals, transients, workers, hangers on, the cast of an impossibly complex plot in which each character knew only their own part and no other, performing under the direction of a force or forces unknown with a penchant for scrambling tragedy, farce and the banal into a compelling but impenetrable and endless narrative.

Queedy. Queedy was the rub, both as M.'s direct line to the Ambulist and because of his own baggage. Queedy must be kept away from the *Courier*, probably away from the Tower-house too. He must go to ground, and the best place for him was with the Ambulist up in the hills – killing two birds with one stone, that was. The Ambulist would be under Queedy's nose – no more buggering off into the wide blue yonder – and Queedy wouldn't have to answer any awkward questions. But did the boy understand, did he really understand, how to cover his tracks, to trail his coat? And supposing he could, did he also have the nous, the experience, to draw from the Ambulist the truth of his career, supposing he had one, as a terrorist? M. shook his head. Yes, Queedy was a bloody problem, not for the first time. Did M., in his musings that morning, consider that the boy – that any of them – might be in physical danger from the Ambulist? No, he did not.

The sight of Mrs Fenwick skipping like an adolescent girl across the cobbles on her way back to the office brought to M.'s mind the possibility that Queedy's file might in due course be of interest to curious eyes. He picked his keys up from the desk and, for the first time in many years, locked the door behind him as he left. He caught Mrs Fenwick just as she was hanging up her coat. He mistook her flushed complexion for the effects of fresh air. Her nervous apology for popping out to the post-office might, on another day, have awakened his interest in her comings and goings, but he soothed the air with a patting motion like a confessional priest's. It was Easter Monday: she should be away from the office, enjoying herself. No, no, she had some few hours to make up and, the office being quiet, it was easier to work. M. would know what she meant. Yes, he would at that.

Mrs Fenwick did not know, could not conceive, that any of her files might be missing from their proper place in the cabinet whose key, as ever, was securely taped to the underside of her desk. M.'s enquiry was entirely routine, he assured her; he just wanted to check something in Mr Queedy's contract: matter of bonus payments for by-lines and featured articles. Did Mrs F. know, off-hand, what would be the procedure for revising an employment contract to turn it into a freelance agreement? Mrs F. felt sure that such a thing could be arranged, so long as the documentation was properly signed off. Would Sir – apart from Miss Nixon, Mrs F. was the only member of the *Courier's* staff to call the editor Sir; the printers and van drivers called him gaffer and everyone else was too much in awe of his station to address him at all – like her to contact Mr Queedy? No, she needn't, he and Mr Queedy were due to meet that week. If he could just have a look at the file…

Mrs Fenwick's face did not at first betray her perplexity at the sight of the empty file-hanger.

- I'll just check I haven't re-filed it under S for Smith.

(She gives M. her best Miss Jean Brodie look, closes the M to R drawer and in her ladylike way adjusts her rather too tight-fitting skirt before bending down to reach S to W at the bottom. She already knows she isn't going to find the file and is flicking through the tabs front to back as slowly as she dares while she tries to work out just where it might have got to)

- No hurry, Mrs Fenwick (says M., admiring with a certain detachment her shapely calves).

- Are you certain you haven't had cause to remove it yourself, Sir?   (Mrs F. is now racking her brains to think how the file could have been removed without her knowledge and may be feeling a cold prickling sensation running down her spine as she shuts the drawer and stands up to look M. unapologetically in the eye)

- I am absolutely certain, Mrs Fenwick... (And as M. is about to form a question on his lips, they both do the mental arithmetic in their heads and reach the same conclusion. There is an awkward pause)

- Perhaps... (she begins, but M. raises his hand again, this time to stop Mrs Fenwick before she says anything).

- Not to worry, Mrs F. I'm sure it'll turn up. (And with that the editor smiles winningly, closes the door behind him and marches down the corridor towards the far end, where there is a still-strong smell of emulsion)

The crisp, clinical whiteness of Gaunt's refurbished office had something of the mortuary about it, the black slab-like desk squared exactly in the centre of the room failing to relieve its sinister icy brilliance. There was no sign of Gaunt, nor any evidence that he had ever been there. The new powder-coated metal shelves were empty of paperwork, files or books. No pencil-sharpenings or bent paper clip, no scrap of waste paper sullied the pristine white plastic bin. No cup of coffee or glass of something stronger had been spilled upon the cheap but serviceable beige carpet. Taking this in with a glance, M. slammed the door shut and marched back up the corridor swearing loudly in Gaelic. The very few incumbent staff working on either side, so recently accustomed to M.'s more amiable moods, might have speculated among themselves that Gaunt and the editor had fallen out over Mrs Fenwick; something, at any rate, was up. No one was brave enough to call out after the boss that Gaunt was away for the long weekend. He had gone down to Buckinghamshire to collect some documents. The boss must have forgotten.

Old Bostock leaned heavily on his blackthorn crook, face tanned like saddle leather, eyes creased tight against the early sun. His threadbare grey worsted jacket, cuffs worn right through and collar turned up, was buttoned tight against a chill wind that came prowling up the still-shaded valley side below. A bony hand held a match up to the bowl of his pipe and he drew on it until the crisp redness of the burning tobacco glowed against his cupped palm. The briar let out a gasp of sweet grey smoke and, satisfied, the man looked down to the peat-black earth beneath his feet. He scuffed at it with the toe of his boot, kicking up a small cloud of dust. At his heel stood a panting collie, eyes alive to its master's every move, wet nose twitching as it sampled the air with forensic obsessiveness. Its morning's work was done: mother ewes and their gangling newborns now fanned out from the gate at the mouth of the drove way, baahing and bleating at one another to stay close. The dog, like old Bostock, was hungry and ready to eat. Why did his master delay so?

The giant human resting with his elbows on the top bar of the gate and talking to, keeping his master, was unknown to the dog. A friend, surely, from his greeting and the small titbit he had found in his pocket for the dog; but nevertheless a person who did not seem to realise that they must leave, that they were in a hurry to be home – who did not appreciate the urgency of the matter. The Ambulist, in apparent denial of this canine crisis, now rolled himself a cigarette and lit it as if he had all the time in the world. The two men, in unspoken harmony with the day, cast their gaze not at the sheep, nor at the fidgeting dog, but at the recumbent feline pose of the hills to the west, stretching lazily away across the Border into the creamy blue-green haze of spring. Far into that distant landscape a casual ribbon of tarmac, seeming to flow uphill through a cleft routed deep between parallel hedges, glinted silver grey, drawing the eye ever onward. No dwelling could be seen; the few farmhouses in these parts hid nestling in the depths of the valley. Few houses, and fewer trees; just the odd dwarf hawthorn, stripped of its last berries, buds urgently swollen but yet to trust the promise of spring. A solitary berry-eyed robin came darting out of the sky to rest on the gatepost, chirruping its pleasure in rare human company. From somewhere behind this unlikely band the tragic ululating wail of a curlew rode the living swell of moor and cleugh. It was a time and place beyond words.

Ignorant of M.'s plans for him, Queedy's innocent entry onto this stage was signalled by the barking dog, sensing an opportunity to stir its master from his reverie. Slowly up the lane Queedy came, not so much unsteady on his feet as diffident, each footstep a carefully calculated mark on a map with which he might navigate a foreign land. His still shiny brogues and too-new country clothes excited no comment either from the farmer, tapping his pipe out on the heel of his shoe, or from his companion. Only the dog's quivering nose and uncertainly wagging tail suggested the reserved welcome of the native to the newcomer. Queedy, now at least partly trained by his keeper at the Tower-house, bent down to greet the dog with an open hand and tousled its ears; to the farmer he nodded an inaudible Good Morning, and towards the Ambulist he aimed a sort of bow.

With no more than a jerk of his head the farmer and his dog departed for their waiting breakfast. Queedy opened the gate, struggling with the heavy catch. As it closed behind him with a metallic clatter the Ambulist, saying nothing, bent to his stride with Queedy trailing in his wake, up along the edge of the sheepfold. The fold was bounded on the east by a drystone wall of dubious antiquity, ill-constructed and failing in places, whose function was to keep livestock off the bracken and heather of the high moor. Now and then the Ambulist would stop and effect some minor repair to the stonework. It was a small service he had promised Bostock in return for staying on the land, but he would have done it anyway. It gave Queedy the chance to keep up, to catch his breath.

The Ambulist had taken temporary possession of an old summer shepherd's cottage, once also the site of an illicit still but long since abandoned to sheep and rampant nettles. It had neither roof nor door nor windows but its high gables kept out the worst of the wind's persistent blast. The lime render had crumbled from its rough and ready masonry to be replaced by moss and lichen, and the nests of small birds. A sheet of rusting corrugated iron nailed to the fireplace lintel had at one time made a perfunctory shelter for a previous wanderer. Now it flapped, clanking in the breeze. The Ambulist's only mark was the charred remains of his small fire in the centre of the single room, which had served as kitchen, living and sleeping quarters for a shepherd during the months his flock grazed the high pasture. Bostock himself remembered when the last shepherd had left after the war. The cottage had once possessed a walled garden where a twisted plum tree still grew, stunted, its bark polished to a shine by sheep rubbing their rumps against it.

The cottage was partially sheltered from the east wind by the Rigg, a blunt, square outcrop of volcanic basalt which had defied the ages. A knot of hardy pine trees clung to crevices in the rocks, their trunks leaning, yearning for the distant sea. Beyond, a grove of birch trees surrounded a shallow peaty tarn. In centuries past the monks of a great monastery had brought their bees to this place in the summer, to feast on the heather and provide them with honey for their mead. No monk, no tourist now came this way.

The Ambulist set to brewing tea for himself and his guest. Queedy, grateful to sit down, if only on the sill of a window, took from his pocket a small volume wrapped in brown paper and, not knowing quite how to present this new donation, left it on the ground beside the two enamel mugs.

- A gift, Mister Queedy?

- Yes.

- I did not ask for anything.

- Nevertheless. It might be of interest to you. A collection of poems and sermons by John Donne.

- Ah. You are maybe having some fun at my expense, Jonge.

- How so?

- No man is an island; that is John Donne, is it not? You think I am an island floating in the sea, is that it? Lost and lonely?

- Not a bit. (Queedy flushes)

- So. (The Ambulist pours tea and as he squats down to drink he pulls the package towards him and opens it. Queedy, a man with a sweet tooth, takes from his other pocket a jar of honey, fragrant, dark local honey from the heather with a generous slab of honeycomb floating within. He stirs an overflowing spoonful into his own tea and offers the jar to the Ambulist, whose eyes sparkle at the sight of such luxury). Now! Here is a royal gift (says the Ambulist, looking carefully through the honey against the sun and smelling it). I will read your poetry Mister Queedy, but I will thank you for the honey. Above all things I value good honey.

- I am glad (says Queedy, smiling to himself). Keep the jar, do.

- And when you have drunk your tea I will show you something in return. For now, you will tell me please how is that meisje, the girl who is so thin she might one day drift away on the breeze, like the seed of the dandelion? You be good to that girl, Mister Queedy (he says, pointed a great bony finger in Queedy's direction and at the same time taking the lid off the honey jar and drawing in a lungful of its aroma. Honey drips stickily from his whiskers).

- I believe she is sad that the wanderer who camped by the lake has gone; she seems out of countenance. (To this the Ambulist has no reply; he secrets the jar of honey in a fathomless corner of his grip, shakes his mug out, and rises like a leviathan emerging from the ocean's depths)

- There is a bird in my home country, Mister Queedy. We call her the honey guide. She finds a bees' nest in the bush, somewhere on the edge of the great desert. She does not care for the honey. She is after the wax and the larvae which the queen has laid. But she cannot get at them. She needs a helper. The honey badger will do, but if she can find a human she will lead him to the nest. The human must break open the nest and smoke the bees out and he will be stung, sometimes very badly, all for the sake of the honey. And the bird, she waits and waits until it is safe for her to eat the larvae.

- The point being (says Queedy)?

- Ja, seker. The point being.

The Ambulist led Queedy over to the rocks, whose God-given form was a series of slabs like steps leading up to a sloping table-top. Climbing silently, at speed, the Ambulist mounted the Rigg until he stood like Moses at the summit, leaving Queedy, nauseous and breathless with the effort, toiling below.

- Hey (the Ambulist calls out to Queedy). What is the matter with you? You are weak, Mister Queedy. You never done a hard day's work? Don't they make you play rugby at school in this country?

- Bad heart (Queedy manages, sitting down and breathing hard to get air back into his lungs).

- Bad heart? What sort of a bad heart? (The Ambulist is not watching Queedy but shades his eyes with his hand and screws them up, seeing as far as he can into the deep fading distance where hill and cloud become one)

- Weak aorta, thin ventricle walls, faulty valves. Bad heart. I need a transplant.

- Man, that is heel slecht, Jonge. You want me to fix it?

- I thought you didn't do miracles.

- Natuurlijk, I do not. Who makes fish appear in a well, verdomme? No, I cannot make miracles. I can fix your bad heart. Up to you. I'll fix it if you want me to. Not because I like you, because I can. But now, stand up on your weak heart Mister Queedy, and look at what you have been sitting on.

The Ambulist pulled Queedy to his feet and the two men – so incongruous a pair, silhouetted against the sky like statues erected to some fickle god – looked down together at the great slab of basalt on which they stood. Here, as on the crest of the ridge at Old Bewley, ancient hands had made their mark in the living rock: a hypnotic rippling maze of spirals, rings, flowing curves, incised dots, a hallucination in stone. It flowed across the slab, ebbed as a solitary migrant cloud passed across the sun, and flowed again.

- Ancient graffiti. A nice place to while away the Stone Age.

- You talk with a city voice, Mister Queedy. Think again. Look. Your artist Mister Turner, the one who painted the railway locomotive chasing the hare, ja, that one: he says, all you have to do is look, but look properly.

- Very well. It took a long time to make these and perhaps more than one artist, if you want to call them artists. It is a primitive map of the heavens, I suppose.

- Primitive? No, Mister Queedy. The man who wrote down all the numbers to say how the stars and planets move, your Mister Newton, he in his way was primitive. To desire control over nature is primitive. To reduce her to numbers is primitive. The men who made these signs understood their place in the nature's orchestra.

- Don't tell me it is a calendar or an observatory.

- The people who made these had no need of such things. These are not farmers who need to know when to plant their crops, Mister Queedy. These marks are made by hunters following herds of deer or maybe bison. They have come here to ask for guidance, guidance from the ancestor.

- You make it sound as if they might come by again any day.

- Ja. (Does the Ambulist know he is being satirised; does he care?)

- How do they know the ancestor is here? (Queedy will play along for the time being; he is beginning to hope that his subject will open up to him at last)

- Have you ever seen a face in a cloud?

- It is natural: humans look for faces everywhere.

- Very well. When you see this rock and these trees from the valley, what do you see?

- Not a face; it looks a little like a tree stump, with shoots growing from it.

- So... we will say it is a tree stump, and our hunter will say that the ancient tree offers wisdom to those who seek it. He comes here when the hunting is not so good maybe, and asks for guidance.

- And the ancestor tells him.

- He might; the hunter has to wake the ancestor from his slumber; he must bang his drum and caper around and go into a trance and then ask very nicely and then there will be a long conversation; you might say they are negotiating.

- What does the ancestor get in return for his wisdom?

- His sacred places in the landscape are protected, looked after.

- And the carvings?

- This is what the hunter sees when he is in his trance; when he wakes he does not remember the shapes or how he made them.

- But he knows where to look for his deer...?

- Ja, klopt. The ancestor teaches him the dance that the deer makes when it moves and now he knows where to find him; the words of the song which he has heard in his trance tell him.

- It is a good story. A pity they are all dead. No bison, no deer, no ancestor and no hunter.

- Maybe they are and maybe they are not. But I can hear the song still. Can you not, Mister Queedy? (Queedy does not reply but looks to the horizon for inspiration; to change the conversation, perhaps) I think maybe you have to be taught young, to learn to listen to the song in the stones.

Queedy's return to the Tower-house from his oddly unenlightening visit to the hills coincided with M.'s arrival there. Not for the first time he believed himself, in looking back, to have missed something, an essential truth in the Ambulist's words which he could not divine. What had the Ambulist been trying to tell him? What was the purpose of his stories about songs and hunters? And what had he meant with his apparently disingenuous proposition to fix Queedy's heart? Queedy was not adept at metaphor, was more comfortable with the spherical trigonometry of the stars' movements in the heavens; how was he to convey to his readers the mystery of the man when he himself did not understand it?

M. had not met the Arnesens before. Queedy, strangely, had come to accept the Tower-house as a sort of self-consistent fantasy within whose walls a special set of rules applied. Not his rules, but rules one could learn to play by. Queedy had adapted to Jareld's almost unbearably earnest smile and to his adoption as a pet by Selena, if not entirely to the probing, compassionate eyes of Mrs Arnesen, who gave him the feeling now and then that his psychological wallet had been picked by a dipper of rare talent. How could he know that she was even now contemplating his soul in the clay between her fingers?

For M., seeing Queedy almost comfortable in the damp, doggy clamour of the over-warm kitchen, it was a moment of revelation. He, with his Donegal aunties, sisters, grandparents and innumerable collateral kin, some of them too closely related for comfort, felt as if he had come to a home from home and it made him realise with a dull but forceful ache how little love there was in his life. Jareld, the father, was just like many an old fiddler or piper in a Dublin bar, all smiles and tunes and hidden emotions to which you would only be privy when he was dead drunk. The mother, yes, he had also known women whose loveliness gushed from a well of strength a mile deep, just like his Auntie Eithne whose husband had beaten her because he loved her so and feared to lose her. He had known girls like Selena, too, wild-haired gypsy colleens with green eyes from the islands who belonged not in this world but in a better or more magical place. He had known for sure since he was a little boy that these girls were mermaids, and not to go near them for fear of being taken under the sea in their arms and turned into kelp. Queedy, though, he now saw in a new light; for the young man, though still unbearably arrogant, seemed to be losing, or shedding – or was it being stolen from him by a siren – his infuriating aura of certainty. There was nothing certain in the lives of this family except their love and acceptance of one another. They had accepted the Ambulist exactly as he appeared to them; had not questioned or mistrusted him. They had offered the same open unjudging welcome to the annoying Queedy in what seemed a wholly disinterested act of generosity – as if the cup of their happiness overflowed and could be shared by all.

Nothing in M.'s professional life had ever surprised him more than Queedy's offer to introduce him to the miraculous donkey foal. Queedy's need to pet the foal, to rub its silky ears, scratch its mane and feel its warm muzzle against his hand was countered by an urgent desire to speak to his editor in private. What, he wanted to know, did M. think of the Ambulist's offer to fix his bad heart? Was he trying to exert moral authority over him, to put him off the scent as he had done so successfully before?

- Whyn't you let him fix it if he says he can?

- You think I should let him practice witchcraft on my malfunctioning ventricle? (Queedy reverts to his oboe voice: it betrays his fear not of death but of things he does not understand and cannot control; that is to say, of people)

- Sure it would make a great story. A third miracle, a holy trinity, wouldn't you say? If he can cure a donkey it's not much of a step up, is it? (Queedy cannot tell if M. is serious. In his intense discomfort he leads M. from the stable out into the yard and is instantly confronted by his old antagonist the goat, eager to make M.'s acquaintance and alert to any opportunity to renew its enmity with Queedy)

- Christ Jesus but he's a handsome, evil-looking fellah (says M., giving the leering goat a friendly punch in the side of the head and instantly disarming it). My Uncle Diarmid had a goat with squinty eyes just the same, a right little bastard it was, would eat the trousers right off your arse given half a chance.

What has this fellah got against you?

    - I believe it sees me as a rival in love.

    - A rival in love is it? And the girl; does she see you as a potential replacement, or is she just stringing you along to keep the goat faithful and true? (With that the editor-in-chief of the *Courier* gives the goat another fraternal whack across the muzzle and almost chokes laughing at his own joke) Christ Jesus, rival in love with a fucking goat, so he is!

The editor's temporary spasm of levity, triggered by nostalgia and erupting in the ludicrous presence of Queedy in this idiosyncratic Ark, only briefly displaced the urgent need to instruct the boy in his new role. Down to the lake they now walked. For once the goat, confused by the introduction of a second as it were co-respondent and nonplussed by M.'s cheerful bellicosity, did not follow. Ragged shreds of plastic, bailer twine and straw clinging to a loose pyramid of sticks were all that remained of the Ambulist's bivouac. The crisp surface of the lake, now that immigrant flocks and natives alike sensed the arrival of warmer weather, was constantly shattered by taxiing birds, courtship dances and squabbles. Along its edge among the alder and birch, sorrel and anemone, honeysuckle and celandine had freshened the winter-dirtied earth and the trees' first leaves were beginning to break free of their buds.

    - D'ye see now, Son, with all these other hacks on our trail you need to go to ground with your miracle man, keep him out of the way for a while. (M. hugs himself and kicks his heels together, trying to keep the cold out; he is under dressed for the outdoors, with just his everyday jacket and no overcoat)

    - He doesn't do miracles.

    - Sure he does.

    - You want me to stay with him. (It is not a question, but an awful acceptance of fact which makes Queedy shudder)

    - I do. What will you need?

- I don't know. I will have to think. I confess that until now I have spent every single night of my life in a warm bed behind brick walls with doors that can be locked (says Queedy, thinking out loud) with modern sanitary facilities and a refrigerator with fresh food in it. I will need a tent of some sort, I suppose; some supplies. Does food keep outside or does it go off – I don't know. All the jars of local honey you can lay your hands on. I imagine the Arnesens might know what camping involves. (Queedy sounds as if he is in shock; maybe he is. Writing about the Ambulist is one thing; leaving the safety of the Tower-house has him feeling like he's staring into that deep dark hole all over again and it makes him dizzy. He sits down on the ground)

- If we get the girl to bring the stuff out to you and pick up your copy... can we trust her?

- Yes, completely. (Queedy waves the question away, concentrates on not being physically sick; he puts his head between his knees and waits until a constellation of stars stops swimming before his eyes)

- And the parents?

- Yes. (It is all he can manage; his voice is now hollow).

- Shall I speak to them?

- No, I will do that.

- Anything else?

- Yes.

- What is it, Son, you've gone the nasty grey colour, so you have.

- Tell me... should I let him fix my heart?

- Only you can answer that, Son. Get yourself up to the house and into the warm. I've work to do at the office. And by the way, you're going to have to get at his background. I mean really, properly. I need to know what he was up to before he came here. I want to know about his politics.

The Arnesens needed little encouragement to conspire in M.'s espionage as Queedy explained it to them. From unsuspected stores an old army tent, complete with tin stove, was produced and erected in the goat's paddock, tested for leaks, tears and mould and pronounced fit for the hills. Jareld's National Service army sleeping bag and billy cans, primus and pocket knife were likewise dug out and loaded into the Land Rover. Extraordinary quantities of food – tins, dried hams, fruit, cereals, whisky – were packed into a chest, an old flight case covered with fading stickers, labels and stamps recalling Jareld's career as a global music star.

Freya, sensing perhaps not the change of season but that the prevailing wind in all their lives was about to change, to blow from a new direction, insisted that Queedy stay with them one more night, that he share a family meal with them before beginning his adventure. With characteristic charm she induced him to help her prepare supper. He was sent into the garden to pull almost the last onions and leeks from their rows of rich black earth, and to the outhouse for old roasting potatoes. He was despatched to the pantry to choose a ham, a wonderful pungently ripe beast of a ham, dry-cured and salty, and a case, a whole case, long ago laid down, of a powerful Bordeaux. In the kitchen he was set to sharpening, peeling, scraping, slicing, washing, carving, pouring. At all times he was escorted by the two dogs, solicitous, attentive and patient. He found himself aproned and scrubbed, biddable and obedient, caught up in the elaborate perspiring theatre of Freya's embracing, smothering intent. He was apprenticed, bonded, initiated as kinsman into the heart of the clan so that he might not forget, so that he might return and belong. He had need of them, this rootless, brittle young man. And, perhaps, they had need of him, a sponge for their liquid golden love.

With door of the range having closed on ranks of roasting trays within, Queedy was now to shed his apron and take a glass of wine to

Jareld down in his plutonic fastness. Not for the first time, Queedy was uncomfortably aware of being conveyed by intangible hands, blindfolded almost, into a labyrinth of nurture and dependence, of being carried along on a vessel of dubious construction but unerring purpose. He descended the steps with a brimming glass of the ruby Bordeaux in either hand. Expecting to be met with an over-enthusiastic slap on the back or some such, he braced himself, evicting the dogs from each step below him with a careful foot so that he should not trip. Jareld, though, was not to be seen either in the studio, where Queedy envisioned him sitting peering at a score with fingers on keys, glasses perched on his head and pencil behind his ear; or, apparently, in the booth. Queedy put the glasses down on top of a warmly humming valve amplifier and allowed the dogs to run their master to ground. Jareld emerged backwards from below his mixing desk, his head wreathed in multicoloured cables and leads like a Medusa, only grinning.

- Queedy (he shouts, as if partially deaf) you have been emancipated from culinary bondage and sent to keep me company! (Queedy nods and smiles and it is a genuine smile; how can one help it?)

- I have been sent to bring you wine. I doubt that I have been emancipated.

- The more I know you Queedy, the more I like your sense of humour.

- I'm not sure I have one.

- You see? I like it very well! You have not poured us tap water and turned it into Bordeaux yourself, have you Queedy? (Jareld lifts the glass to his nose and draws deeply on its intoxicating, harvest bouquet)

- Not my job. I have a friend who does that sort of thing.

- Ha. You are joking. So am I. This is the 'eighty-two, what do you think?

- It is superb. Were you having a problem with your

wiring?

- What? Oh, no, not problems so much as an experiment, one of those teenage moments one still likes to indulge in. I was trying to see if I could take a feed from the piano microphone and put it through the Marshall to give it that lovely warm valvey sound, then loop it back through the piano mic without getting feedback. It was a ridiculous idea and now I have restored everything to the way it was before. I have wasted an entire afternoon, though I confess I have had a fine wonderful time. One must have fun, Queedy! (And he claps his hand on Queedy's shoulder – but gently, so as not to spill any of the Bordeaux)

Supper's indulgent frivolities and good humour, in which Queedy, despite himself, participated with real pleasure, might have given an outsider the impression that the whole family was about to set off on some daring adventure; was to join a caravan traversing the desert towards some semi-fantastical Timbuktu. This ironic celebration of dwelling, distilled to its essence by the parting feast, echoed a thousand and a million such acknowledgements of the march of seasons spread across millennia. Those left behind must hide their sadness and loss in song and wine, in time-honed stories of the trail and the homecoming. Those who leave to seek and taste the brief, sweet transhumant freedom of summer take energy from the food and courage from their friends but they yearn for the hearth even before they have bidden it goodbye. At the Tower-house songs were sung into the night with good cheer. Even so, the Arnesens' vicarious anticipation of Queedy's experiment in nomadism filled their hearts with nervous apprehension, and Queedy's with a cold fear.

The acoustics of a city change with spring; not just because windows are thrown open or because the people in the streets are shedding their winter coats. It is more a quality of the light. The sun's steepening arc, its new-found intensity, reflects a higher volume of light off its glassy steel skyscrapers, off the stone of its churches and monuments, civic mansions and public edifices, and on to the streets below. The very air begins to stir. Even the neglected corners – the doorways, passages, vennels, basement areas and yards – even these start to echo the sounds of spring. Scaffolders, painters, groundsmen, street cleaners busying at their chores all add to this aural freshness which city dwellers often do not notice and which country folk take for something else.

M., returning to the city, did notice; and a very real and potent image of spring in Dublin on the banks of the Liffey, noise spilling from the bars, streets and cafés and spreading out across the river, made him pause for a moment at the entrance to the *Courier's* premises and listen. On his way along the third-floor corridor he poked his head into Miss Nixon's cubby-hole to see if there was any new mail or urgent messages, rather hoping there were none. No, no messages… but Miss Nixon had let Mr Gaunt into his office; she hoped Sir didn't mind. He had a rather large bundle of old newspapers which he wanted M. to have and did not care to leave them lying around. She gathered they weren't all that important.

Chapter Eight

Bush meat

PRESS TYCOON DISGRACED, read the triumphant broadsheet headline in seventy-two point bold. Underneath: a grainy photograph of Carew Smith, Queedy's father, vainly shielding his face from the flash of cameras as he walked down the steps of the United States Supreme Court building in Washington DC. It didn't do him any favours, the picture. Smith was the same age as M., the same age within two weeks, and they'd both been around a bit, but Smith looked like he was broken; like the fight had gone out of him. There was nothing like the prospect of attacking one of their own to get the press hyenas working as a pack, hunting in self-righteous blood-lust. The copy that went with the headline was purple: a ready-written obituary of Smith cast as Icarus, a suitably Greek parable for a man whose stellar rise, now he had fallen from the sky, was in retrospect a manifestation of hubris.

This story, this particular edition of a national daily, had been purposely put on top of the string-bound bundle of newspapers, magazine features and assorted cuttings so that M. should be in no doubt. No doubt of what, though? Of Gaunt's new-found knowledge, of imagined power over his editor? Of his determination to expose, to undermine, to wound? Of his declaration of war? And, if so, against whom: M., Queedy or the *Courier*? Was this supposed to fire a shot across the bows or strike with a torpedo below the waterline? And what, exactly, did Gaunt think he would achieve by it? Was this the prelude to some sort of blackmail demand, and if it was, what did he want? Whatever it was he bloody well wasn't going to get it.

M. cut the string on the bundle with a pair of scissors and opened out the top sheet. Sure, he remembered that day: three years ago but it seemed like mere months. The call from Smith's lawyer – yes, the call on this telephone, in this room – confirmation that Smith had been convicted on appeal in the Supreme Court of raiding his company's pension fund, of violating the interests of free market rules on competition. What they meant was, he had stiffed the competition. All of it. He had used his muscle to price other papers out of existence. He had attempted to influence legislation in his own favour. When he over-reached himself his workers' pensions had gone into the pot to pay for one last look at the cards. The sentence was five years in a correctional facility, suspended for five years because he had already served nine months between conviction and appeal and because he already had cancer. A huge fine went with it, to distance the politicians he'd had in his pocket from their erstwhile friend and ally. Two months after the trial, the same papers were reporting Carew Smith's disappearance in his private jet and, a month after that, the body found in the wreckage. The bastard had had his last laugh.

By the time the old man killed himself for fear of the surgeon's knife, if that was what really happened, the boy had already been disinherited. He had turned up on M.'s doorstep out of the blue, just like that. Just like his father had twenty-five years before. In America he was the subject of constant speculation in the papers and gossip columns; in England no one knew who he was and, if they had known, they wouldn't much have cared. Here, the body in the swimming pool at a toffs' school was old news and few would have thought to make the connection. Taking his mother's name had been M.'s idea.

Why had M. taken him in? He didn't owe the boy any favours and he was damn sure he didn't owe the father any. Nor was it for the sake of the past. There was history there, to be sure. Yes, there was history. Maybe it was just because the boy was so like his father at the same age. Did M. unconsciously believe that the son might redeem the father, give him another chance in death? Did he hell.

History began at Trinity College, Dublin. They were both reading English, both determined to be journalists, poets, critics, maybe even politicians in some distantly perceived future. They met in the first week of their first term in the great library where they read some of the same literature – Yeats, Joyce of course, George Moore – and where M., but not Smith, came to love the Christian works of ancient Ireland, of Iona, Kildare and Durrow; the Táin Bó Cúailnge and the Brehon Laws. They were the best students in their year. They competed, they raced to be better at everything than each other and everyone else. They edited Trinity's most celebrated literary magazine together; and a clear memory presented itself to M.'s mind of the two of them arguing over a review of the premier of *Godot* which they tried to write together but which would only work as two separate pieces; so they had published both and sent copies to Beckett. He had condescended to a nicely-worded reply, encouraging but not too encouraging.

They smoked and got drunk in all the right pubs. They brawled in back streets with the local thugs, wore their skinned knuckles and matching black eyes like badges and laughed all the bloody time. They took turns walking the same girls along the banks of the Liffey, kissing them and making them promises.

Where had it gone wrong? They had not known when to stop. They believed themselves invincible and indivisible in everything they did. Their mutual self-love was fed by senior common room gossip, which flattered them with comparisons to Sheridan and Leigh Hunt. They did not see it themselves, but to everyone who knew them or knew of them they were the Trinity Twins: same clothes, same haircuts, same mannerisms. In the third year they took turns getting the same girl pregnant – and her from a good family, and who was going to pay, and the law wouldn't let her have an abortion – and who was going to take it on the chin and be the father; and in a state of drunken exhilarating panic they flipped a coin. Yes, they had flipped a coin to decide which of them should wed her and take her child as his own. M. remembered, not that it mattered now, that he had called tails and it had been heads. The pact had been... yes, the pact had been: whoever brought the baby up and married the girl would be paid by the other to help support them for sixteen years. When sober, Smith had found the pact not to his liking even though he had won the toss. He did not sit his final exams. He left Dublin and Ireland and disappeared.

M. did not see Smith for a decade. M. went to work for the nationalist *Irish Clarion*; married the girl called Siobhan and had two more children with her. After long years of graft, too much coffee and too many fags he became the *Clarion's* deputy editor. He bought a nice doubled-fronted Georgian town house on Baggot Street and was forgiven his sins by her parents. He knew and Smith knew that Siobhan would rather have been with Smith. M. would rather she had been with Smith. Out of the blue, when the oldest girl, Geraldine, was ten, Smith appeared in Dublin one day, in M.'s office. M. had said nothing in that moment of flashing emotional turmoil but had taken up his coat and walked with Smith along that same old river bank, and they had spent the afternoon in a bar – not one of their old ones but a rather exclusive place, out of the way. They drank and Smith talked, not about where he had been all these years and not about Siobhan or her daughter but about Dublin and Trinity and great writing and how wonderful those days had been, as if he were with an old chum on an alumni reunion.

For a short while M. allowed himself to believe that Smith had come to see the girl who may have been his daughter. But he hadn't. Smith was in trouble, on the run from something or someone. If it was another girl he did not say. He would only say that he had been working abroad as an investigative journalist, that things had got a bit dicey and he needed somewhere to start again. He needed work. M. gave him a job in the marketing department, selling space in the paper, looking after circulation. M. knew he would do the job well; he was that sort. He invited him home for dinner because Siobhan wanted to see how he had turned out, but they didn't tell Geraldine he might be her father and Siobhan didn't say afterwards whether she would still rather have been with Smith. The silence on all sides said it better even than Beckett could have said it.

M. was not blessed with the gift of foresight. He did not see that Smith would use the chance given him by his old comrade to buy first the newspaper, then the whole of the Banner Group, within three short years. Smith had been furious at the insult to begin with. Marketing was beneath his talents – how like the father the son was. But he was good at it. He saw that the Irish news media were far behind the rest of the world in adopting new technologies, new distribution methods; that their advertising sections were tired and orthodox, inefficient. He persuaded the editor to let him start a glossy coloured supplement, to cast aside the *Clarion's* insular nationalist viewpoint and become a newspaper for all Ireland. He engineered a showdown with the print unions and after a bloody six months' battle of picketing, rising nationalist tensions and disastrous sales he had won, cutting the paper's circulation by twenty per cent and its overheads by a half. By Christ, they had nearly all gone to the wall that year.

Smith got himself appointed to the board and then somehow, M. never figured out how, he raised the funds to force a management buy-out. He floated the paper on the stock exchange, using his own holding to launch a bid for the parent group; all this with breathtaking speed and without anyone really grasping what he was up to until the deal was done. It was prestidigitation on a grand scale, Christ Jesus so it was.

After that, Ireland was too small. Smith headed west with his talents and profits and became America's greatest press baron since... well, yes, since William Randolph Hearst. M. stayed on in Dublin for a few more years until the children were old enough for Siobhan to leave him without ruining their education or their prospects. Smith had gone to America twenty and more years ago, and in that time he had constructed an empire from the empty shells of companies, of lives he had cast aside, men and women he had robbed, destroyed or trodden upon. He had been good at it. And, unlike Saint Columba of blessed memory, he had never looked back over his shoulder towards Ireland.

And now... now Smith was gone and all that Dublin past with him, and M. had ended up at the *Courier* for his sins. Smith had walked away from trouble twice, probably more than twice if the truth were told, and had got away with it every time; almost every time. Flicking through the assorted cuttings M. asked himself again why he had taken the son under his wing. Not for old times' sake, he knew that much. And not because Smith's lawyer had sent him a cheque for the money which Smith said he owed him. A cheque for sixteen hundred pounds, a hundred pounds a year for Geraldine's childhood, which M., for all he could use the money, still kept in a drawer at home.

An unpleasantly perverse thought now came to him for the first time: that he might have adopted the boy to punish Smith, even in death, for rejecting his son, just like he'd rejected Geraldine even before she was born. An odder thought still was that the two of them, Queedy and Geraldine, might be half-brother and sister, over ten years apart, but still. Maybe he ought to introduce them. His sister Mary would know where Geraldine was. Mary would know where they all were.

A brilliant spring day announced itself. A skylark sang an exultant celebration of the sun's first yellow rays from high, high up in the deep glassy blue of a transient seeping dawn. Invisible from the impatient earth, he nevertheless called on all those creatures bound to it to rise, to rise. Queedy, lying half-asleep in his absurd boy scout tent, heard but did not understand, or did not wish to understand, the message. The farmer, abroad with his dog, heard but did not listen, too intent on locating the sound of a lame ewe bleating, distressed and unable to keep up with her gambolling offspring. The Ambulist looked up from the fire where he was boiling stream water for his tea and tried to pick out the lark's flight, but could not. Now the day was upon him he cast the blanket from his shoulders and hung it over a cord which he had tied between the walls of his modest palace. Two rabbits which he had taken from his snares already that morning hung from the cord too and they now bounced gently up and down in a macabre dance as the cord responded to the weight of the blanket. The Ambulist poured tea into two mugs and to each he added milk and a spoonful of honey, Queedy's precious honey, which he prized above almost all else.

From the dying fire, where all the old stories are kept, came into his mind the fate of the eland, brought into being from the red dust of a dried-up waterhole by the *kaggen*, the wilful mantis spirit of the bushman. The *kaggen*, entranced and made covetous by the majesty of the animal, fed the growing eland on milk and honey so that it should be the most beautiful beast in all Africa, so that it should be strong and have a fat heart. But the Bushmen hunted the eland and killed him, not just because he was beautiful and had a fat heart full of blood, but because they were jealous when he ate all the honey which the *kaggen* should, by rights, have brought to them. Many Bushman songs and stories tell of the eland's regal nature, of his imperious attitude towards other animals, referring to him as the master. They admire his speed and grace in flight; they value also his meekness, his fatal lack of stamina, his mulish refusal to run after he has once become winded. His spirit has greater potency than that of any other animal; many rituals must be observed when hunting him and in the treatment of his carcass.

A rabbit was no eland, not even as good eating as the partridge which English country gentlemen liked to slaughter by the thousand in autumn. Still, it was good meat for the pot. The boy had brought with him from the Tower-house the Arnesens' generous provisions, but the Ambulist had forbidden him to eat their dried hams, smoked bacon or sausages. The pig and the cow, domesticated animals, were no food for the nomad. Queedy must learn to catch animals if he were to learn respect for them. An animal penned and herded from birth had no dignity; the meat tasted ill from its confinement, just like any prisoner carrying the smell of death on him. Queedy was not yet competent to set a snare, but he would be taught to skin a rabbit or he would not eat.

The Ambulist took up one of the mugs and carried it away to Queedy's camp on the far side of the Rigg. He breathed deeply and in that moment, when he imagined himself following the spoor of a wounded eland on the edge of the great desert at dawn, he gloried in the bounty of the pristine light. Queedy's tent could not be seen from the Ambulist's roofless shieling and that may have been because, so unused to the paradoxical privacy of his exposure to nature, he did not wish to feel himself observed. Or Queedy's exile might have been imposed by the Ambulist out of naked embarrassment at the boy's home-from-home, which reminded the African of a rich man's safari. Too much equipment that could not be carried; too much food that could not be eaten; too many things the young man thought he needed but did not. But no, Queedy's exile was for moral instruction – it had been at the Ambulist's absolute insistence, if he were to allow Queedy to infringe upon his solitude. Queedy had obeyed, but had not slept at all for three nights for fear of demons and those nameless wild animals who prey on the minds of dwellers when they close their eyes under the stars.

The Ambulist did not patronise or condescend to his guest; he did not indulge Queedy's fears and neither was he blind to them. But he would not countenance Queedy's surrender to them. The gift of tea was not servile; it was a notice to Queedy that the Ambulist was to walk that day, and soon. If Queedy wished to join him, he must rise now. It was thus that the young man passed into the hands of a new educator. Like Gaunt, and M. before him – and for that matter like Carew Smith – the Ambulist resisted the idea that he should become a father to this boy.

A young man used to showering and taking freshly-pressed clothes from a wardrobe every morning of the week is in danger, when confronted with life's wholesome simplicities, of acquiring feelings of revulsion for himself until the moment comes when the smell of earth and body, distilled to a sweet blend by sweat and toil, comes to feel like armour, a shield against the world. Queedy was resistant to the pleasure of the moment; resistant also to the idea of leaping naked into a river or pool as an alternative to domestic plumbing. He was miserable in his new un-shedding skin. The ground on which he lay at night was hard and lumpy. He was either too cold when he sat still or too hot when he walked. He felt bitterly the insecurity which night brings to those who fear life. The Ambulist did not pity him, or feel compassion for him. He accepted Queedy's discomfort as a ewe accepts the gangling incompetence of her newborn. It did not touch him.

Like the day-old eland faun, Queedy must in any case learn to walk, and walk fast; not, in his case, because he might be taken by a predator, but because the Ambulist walked at a pace honed to the kinetic harmonies of the land, not the traipsing shuffle of the window-shopper or commuter whose life is ruled by clock and appointment, by the artificial cycles of diary and wage, by the rainbow commands of the traffic light. Queedy must keep up or be left behind. The Ambulist's, and now Queedy's, cycle was that of the celestial elliptic, of the equation of time which the wanderer felt and responded to deep in his soul and which the journalist knew only by mathematics and Mister Newton's calculus. Queedy, because he was tuned to the complex and technical patterns of city life and because he was recovering still from his latest collapse, struggled to measure himself to the Ambulist's oceanic stride, his relentless progress. But he accepted that in his new incarnation he must play the part of obedient pupil once more. Gaunt had had to be endured; M. had to be pleased. The Ambulist's moral presence demanded that he be followed.

- … but you were not born in a bushman camp, I do not believe. (Queedy, breathless, aims his question at the Ambulist's back; they are following an old drove way, sunken below its bounding walls, which snakes its way up the side of a hill erupting in an acrylic yellow storm of gorse flowers. A symphony of bees, hover-flies and fluttering birds accompanies them. The sun now has real heat in it and even Queedy, sweating, feels the gift of its energy soaking through his clothes into his fragile bones)

- No, I am not your Mowgli raised by wolves or wild men. We were good Christian farmers, what you English used to call Boers. My father was a friend to the bushman, and the bushman to him. We had a farm. For my father the bushman was a blessing on the land. He believed it a special privilege and honour when the kleine mensen, the little folk, chose to spend part of their year with us. He knew the land was theirs, that the fence and the ranch house were insults to their ancient freedoms. (The Ambulist is talking to the sky and to himself, perhaps; Queedy might not be there, invisible, trailing in his wake)

- In his day he must have been an exceptional man.

- Ja, seker he was. Not many white men were on his side, the bushman. When I was young the Boers used to hunt bushman children and take them back to their farms. The mothers and fathers would come after them and then they would be taken into slavery too. Terrible crimes have been committed against those people. My father thought they were wonderful, the guardians of the earth; before I could walk he set me to learning their ways. There was an old woman whose child had died, she carried me on her back when she went into the bush; ja, I learned a long time how to use the digging stick. When I was older the men taught me to hunt the eland, the gemsbok and the hartebeest; they showed me the stars and told me the stories that are kept in their fires. Here now, Mister Queedy, we go through this kloof, what the farmer calls cleugh. There is a stream at the bottom, the water is sweet and we can drink. (The Ambulist leads Queedy down from the crest of the hill into the cool shade of a steep-sided narrow valley, dense with hawthorn and birch and soft with moss underfoot. In a small clearing by the burn they stop and Queedy sits down gratefully on the coat which he rolls up; they drink from the stream and the Ambulist splashes his face with the cool water)

For mile upon mile the two improbable companions bestrode the pulsing land as the morning matured and ripened to early afternoon. Queedy, inhabiting a dream-scape somewhere between exhaustion and trance, was drawn along, captivated, as forest and farm, hedgerow and wall, moor and vale marched past him on either side, the future parting like a curtain in front and closing behind him. The world was alive. It was as if the earth, so recently crushed by the burden of an unending winter, blanched and soaked, starched, beaten and leached of all goodness, now breathed in great gulps of reviving air, basked in the new warmth, and purred. Its breath rose in veils of mist that caressed the copses, hedgerows and walls before dissolving into the deep azure sky of an unsurpassed day.

The Ambulist knew the shapes and tastes, smells and sounds of this land in confounding intimacy. He knew where there would be a patch of parasol mushrooms growing beneath a holly tree; where the sett of a badger could be found and if any residents were at home. It was his back garden, his living room. He left no sign that Queedy could detect of his own passing, as if he merely shadowed the surface of the land like a wisp of wind; and yet, his massive bulk and immense presence were themselves a geographical entity. He was both Atlas and the earth itself.

- You did not wish to follow your father and become a farmer; you chose to follow the bushman into the desert. Can you tell me how you came to this decision? (Queedy, almost fainting with the effort of keeping pace with his quarry, cannot take notes while he is walking; he has to trust himself to remember, to grasp the essence of what he hears, and weave it into the fabric of a sketch when he can)

- Does a man choose his destiny? I am not sure, Mister Queedy. Have you chosen yours?

- Not yet.

- Not yet? Man, I think maybe your destiny chooses you. I had two older brothers. In Afrikaner families the oldest boy is sent away for an education and the second learns to herd the cattle and keep the pigs. Ja, he follows them up the koppies and onto the veld and runs after them when they make a hole in the fence. If he does his job well the father allows him to keep some of the newborn for himself, to raise and sell when he needs to marry.

- The third son?

- He runs around with nothing on and makes friends with the bushman and the coloured servants; he does not matter so much and this means he is free. On the great trek I think not many third sons survived; not enough food for three. The third son got left behind, maybe, somewhere on the veld, an offering to the leopards. Nobody cares about the third son.

  - But your father did care, I think.

  - Ja, my father did care and my mother too. I was strong and they loved me.

  - And so?

  - And so, my brothers died, first the second brother, then the oldest. I was fifteen years old then. My father fetched me back out of the bush and put a suit of clothes on me and sent me to Windhoek to get some learning. (He says nothing for a few moments, either allowing Queedy to accept the meaning of his words, or allowing himself to remember. The measured tread of his pace acts as a beat to think by) Man, I hated that suit.

The sun spun its daily thread through time's equation and, now it had migrated north of the equator at midday, it rose and set a few degrees to the north of east and west. The trees and flowers knew it somehow, for they accelerated their growth with the longer days. The Ambulist knew it, too; he sensed the shortening nights in his waking every day just after dawn, when the sun mocked him for oversleeping; in the autumn he would wake before the sun and watch it rise, taunting it in return sometimes for its slackness. Queedy had yet to teach his body to keep pace with the natural day, just as he struggled to play in time with the Ambulist's bass rhythm.

With the piety of the acolyte, Queedy harboured a hope that the Ambulist, deploying some magic of his senses, would bring them by a circular route back to their camp before nightfall. But now, as the sun slipped towards the distant line of hills to the northwest, even he knew that home, what passed for home, lay far behind them.

At a place which the Ambulist called the Roarin' Linn, in the last pinkish-orange minutes of sunlight, they came upon a giant slab of rock standing proud of the earth at the edge of a wood. It was tilted towards the east so that the carvings upon it should appear at their most prominent at this time of day. Ancient sculptors, feeling the importance of this place in the stories of their ancestors, had drawn into this stone the concentric essence of their universe, telling perhaps the story of their creation so that none should ever forget. The Ambulist said nothing but knelt and ran his hands over the rings and swirls, channels and pits, as if in reverence for the ghosts of their makers. Queedy, grateful for the break in this route march, leaned his back against the rock. Did he feel anything too? No, nothing beyond pain.

Rising after some minutes, the Ambulist led Queedy along a narrow path which in high summer became invisible, overgrown with brambles and honeysuckle, guelder rose and elder. The path dropped suddenly down to a stream which they followed for some hundreds of yards, the noise of water dashing itself against rock growing all the time. The Linn, when they came suddenly upon it, indeed roared with a thunderous deep note that echoed around crowding black rock walls dripping with moss and ivy. A great dark boulder rose from the shattered surface of the pool, some erratic pebble thrown down long ago by an angry – or was it playful – deity. High above them, amplifying the gloom of the fading day, immensely ancient oak trees from all sides joined the fingers of their canopies together as if to contain the force, the fall's superhuman natural power, and prevent it from escaping. With every fistful of water, jostling, flying out and down to its fate in the black linn below, order descended into chaos, day into night.

No sun penetrated here and Queedy shivered with the clamping cold around him. The Ambulist stood dead still for some minutes at the edge of the pool, drawing on the falls' profound energy and liberating leap into the cataract, feeding on it. His arms hung loose at his side but his great bony fingers flexed and spread. His head was tilted back and his eyes were closed, everything was sound and the touch of spray on his skin. As if Queedy were not there at all, did not encroach on his relations with the magic of the place, the Ambulist took his clothes off, cast them aside on the ground and, clambering on to the boulder, threw himself ungainly but magnificent into the depths of the linn.

From the comparative comfort of his tent, late in the morning of the following day, Queedy began the fourth of his Friday sketches. The Ambulist's shamelessness in his naked plunge into the pool was itself shaming for the unliberated, city-dwelling man, he wrote. Unburdened by door or debt, encumbrance of material wealth or personal ties, the nomad was not only free to do as he pleased, he was truly free, free from the self-consciousness which the writer and his reader must acknowledge as invisible chains. The author himself felt something of this liberation – he lied – sleeping under canvas in sympathetic harmony with nature. How often, he asked his readers, did one wake up in time to see the dawn? How alive did the city-dweller ever really feel?

Queedy's zealous prosings on the subject of freedom were excised by his editor without, so to speak, a backward glance. The *Courier* was not going to alienate its delicately-held readership with an insight so uncomfortable. This was not the age of enlightenment. But, trimmed to a thousand words, the rest of the piece would do very well. M. liked the material on the Ambulist's childhood – it had a simple ring of truth and its conversational aspects gave it an intimacy which increasing numbers of followers of his story would find touching. So, he hoped, would the syndicated outlets. The Letters page and the accounts would tell if he was right.

Queedy's description of his camp, shorn of all possible references to its location, was unconsciously comic. His account of the exhausting night-time hike from Roaring Linn back to the camp at the Rigg was evocative and touching with moments of self-effacing farce. The Ambulist had been recounting to his apprentice the Bushman's knowledge of the constellation of Orion. The belt was an arrow, the stars of his sword three zebras descending a trail in single file. A spirit had shot at them with his arrow but it fell short and lay there still. The unharmed zebras set foot upon the earth as their stars touched the western horizon each night in May. Queedy, staring upwards at the stars while he walked and suddenly losing his balance, had stumbled, fallen face first into a ditch in the pitch black and, fearing he had broken his arm, such was the immediate stabbing pain, had been hauled out, set on his feet and patted on the head by the Ambulist as if he were a four-year-old child. Yes, this disingenuously informal attempt to connect with the reader might yet emerge as a bankable trait in Queedy's otherwise awkwardly prolix style. Sooner rather than later, however, Stokes would have to be sent to get a shot of the two of them together in their little safari. How they were going to get Stokes there was another matter: he'd never make it up that bloody hill.

Queedy's modus operandi had been agreed with M. He was supplied with envelopes and stamps and would take his sketch to a post box which stood lonely like a sentinel at a remote crossroads five miles or so from the camp, two days before the copy deadline for Friday's paper. There would be no other communication unless Selena brought out fresh supplies or a message from M.'s own hand. In his current light-headed and bewildered state even the sight of a red post box, an icon of the civilising influence of Victorian imperialism, struck Queedy with a force equal to the moment when any indigenous tribesman saw his first white man – more so, perhaps, because the post box seemed at once both utterly alien and absurdly familiar. Still less was Queedy prepared for the sight of a car parked on the verge next to the box, a car in which M. sat eating a sandwich and drinking from a flask of coffee with a map spread before him against the steering wheel. M., sensing rather than seeing movement along the road, looked up to see Queedy, thinner than ever but ruddy in complexion, unshaven and lank-haired, wearing no more than a thin shirt, unwashed muddy-kneed corduroy trousers and scuffed brogues, carrying an envelope in his hand.

> - Do you have any chocolate (says Queedy, getting into the car without so much as a Good morning or a What the hell are you doing out here)?

> - Chocolate is it, son? Sure I can't tempt you with a juicy rasher of bacon in a buttered roll? I worry you're starving

yourself. You look thin, so you do, but you've a fine healthy colour.

    - Domesticated meat is tainted. I would rather not. (Queedy opens the glove compartment in front of him, knowing that M. will have an emergency store of chocolate there. He finds a Mars bar, unwraps it and consumes it in two bites while his editor stares at him, half a smile on his face)

    - Domesticated is it now? What, you catch your own, you and the Messiah – skinning rabbits and tickling trout...? Christ, I never thought I'd see the day.

    - What brings you up here? (Queedy stares ahead through the car's windscreen, licking his lips and sucking the last sweet traces of chocolate and caramel from between his teeth)

    - This. (M. reaches into his knapsack on the back seat and fishes out the newspaper with the headline and Queedy's father's face staring out of the picture, which he drops into the boy's lap) Gaunt. I can take you back to the Tower-house for a few days if you like. If you're going to have another heart attack I'd rather you had it there.

Queedy did not return with M. to the Tower-house; nor did his porcelain soul shatter under the twin blows of Gaunt's assault and the memory of seeing that headline the first time round. M. had measured carefully the responsibility for exposing the boy to Gaunt's treachery; more carefully, in fact, than he had the potential risk of sending him on an assignment with a wanted man who was probably capable of extreme violence. He had lost sleep over it. Worrying about the boy had, not for the first time, ruined the pleasure of an early evening bath and the taste of his gin. He concluded that he could not protect the boy from either his own shady past or his father's reputation. Not now and not in the future. There would be other Gaunts. The boy would take it or drop dead or he would run away, start again somewhere else. If he took it, stood up to it and stayed, then what more could Gaunt

do? Gaunt must have hoped to humiliate the boy. His knowledge of
Smith showed he knew, also, of Queedy's distasteful school history; he
must also suspect M.'s connection with the old man. It was in Gaunt's
character, M. reflected, to want to punish, to pick at a scab; there was
something of that in the business of journalism. The newsroom had
a culture which attracted the type. Knowledge pursued to its limits;
strength to be tested until it failed; secrets to be sniffed out and quarry
to be run down because the nature of the beast was predatory. This was
not the sort of knowledge that M., in his romantic youth, had thought
he was searching for. He had looked for the truth in Yeats and found it.
He had found a certain sort of knowledge in *Godot*, even in Joyce. Was
not Master Shakespeare full of unchallengeable truths of frailty and
honour, of dark souls and heroism? These were truths of acceptance,
knowledge of uncertainty, hard evidence of an imprecise world of
shifting realities which rarely deserved the surety of fact. And then,
here he was, M., an old greying hack with a bad back whose pursuit of
knowledge had turned into a hunt for sales and the quiet consolation
of a hot bath.

Did Gaunt hope that M. would pay him in some way to keep his
knowledge quiet, or would he be content to have inflicted pain, to have
shown what he could do in spite of them all? Was M. finally going to
have to sort the old sod out? If either M. or Gaunt believed that Queedy
would be haunted by the ghost of his disgraced father or embarrassed
by the exposure of his association with the death of a schoolmaster, they
were wrong. He had not felt guilty about the drowning of his teacher
because he believed himself innocent, at the time, of the knowledge
that there was anything wrong. He similarly reasoned that he could not
be held responsible for the sins of his father, whatever the Bible might
say about the matter.

The cold steel blade which now began to twist itself deep inside
Queedy's bowels, as he sat on the side of the road watching M.'s car
disappear from view, was the pain of remembering what his father had

been to *him*. Or had not been to him. The young man had come to accept that his life was empty of love, but the photograph of his father on the front of the newspaper was a reminder in grainy black and white of the father's legacy to the son: that he was absolutely incapable of loving, of accepting love, of acknowledging that he was loved. Did the Ambulist sense this? Was that what he had meant when he offered to fix Queedy's heart? Was that his secret? Was he trying to say that in the wandering of the nomad could be found solace for those who could not love? And, if that was so, did Queedy share with the Ambulist the dull insistent ache of amputation, the scar where love had been removed?

The light from the fire in the old shieling bathed its skeletal walls in a livid abysmal glow. The Ambulist, on his satanic throne, leant with his back against the gable wall and smoked, watching with dispassionate interest Queedy's maladroit apprenticeship in the art of rolling a cigarette. Queedy had done well that day. He had skinned a rabbit and constructed something resembling a stew. He had foraged for wood and made a neat pile of good dry sticks, enough for two days. He had boiled water from the stream and re-pitched his tent on softer, higher ground which would not flood so easily when it rained. He had busied himself, hardly pausing. If the Ambulist had been the boy's NCO he would have allowed himself to believe that Queedy had at last been broken to his duty. His obedience was exemplary – not a word of discontent, no questioning of his senior.

> – Mister Queedy, when you have made that thing so it will light and smoked it and gotten off the fairground ride going on in your head, you had better tell me what your editor has said to you.

- Nothing (says Queedy, but the oboe's reedy note betrays him).

- Oh ja? (The Ambulist is too old to play games but he remembers what it is like to be a boy and, besides, it is a long night to be under the stars. He can wait)

- When you said you could fix my heart...

- I am not going to fix it tonight, Mister Queedy. I need to make a preparation. It is not the same thing as making a stew. Has it broken again?

- What I meant to say was (and now Queedy holds up his shambles of a cigarette to his mouth and lights it, coughs convulsively and spits out a lumpy strand of tobacco) were you speaking metaphorically when you said you could fix a broken heart?

- Mister Queedy, are you suddenly a poet? Have you been reading Mister John Donne? There is a girl, I take it? Seker, it must be a girl. (The Ambulist gets up from his seat and sets to boiling a kettle for tea. The last light has faded into the west and Venus now shows her jewelled face above the hills. The Great Bear's silver skillet is high above, pointing at the north star around which all else circles. Cygnus, summer's herald, looms low in the northeast)

- No, not a girl. (The Ambulist does not respond; Queedy throws his unsatisfactory cigarette into the flames and stares after it) Is your father still alive?

- He would be a very ancient man if he was still alive. I buried him thirty years ago. It is a hard life, Mister Queedy, farming on the edge of a desert.

- My father killed himself.

- Go to your tent and fetch a jar of honey. (Queedy rises instantly, now so inured to the practicalities of the night that he does not even bother to switch his torch on)

Queedy returned with his honey and set the jar before the Ambulist, who doled a spoonful into each mug. In the boy's absence he had rolled two cigarettes and now he gave Queedy one with his tea. The two men smoked in company, one leaning back on his throne, the other squatting on his heels before the fire, holding his hands out for warmth and maybe also for reassurance. Their breath rose in wreaths above them. The air was now cold, the cloudless sky sucking all warmth from the land, and so clear that the sounds of the night could be heard from far across the moor.

- So, Mister Queedy, you are still young not to have a father. It is a hard blow to take. Your heart was broken by this act of cowardice, maybe.

- No. It was a relief, actually.

- You did not love him.

- He beat that out of me. I don't mean physically. Actually, I think he did not notice me until I was old enough to be sent to England to a boarding school. He didn't think I was up to much; not enough backbone. Maybe he was right.

- You should maybe not judge your father too hard. Perhaps he did not know how to love a son and perhaps already you did not want to be loved.

- Hard to say.

- Ja, it is a hard thing to say. I cannot say what your father felt for you. I have not met him. It is easy maybe to read neglect in an absence. In that respect I have been lucky.

- But your father sent you away from the farm. How did that make you feel?

- Feel? I knew my father loved me and I had many friends among the Bushmen. I missed them, like I missed my dead brothers. My father did his duty and I had respect for him. He was a fine man.

- My father was not a fine man. He was a predator.

 - A hunter is a predator. There is nobility in hunting if one respects the prey.

 - Nobility in a lion, perhaps. Nothing very attractive about a hyena.

 - The lion is a lazy fellow. Leave him alone, he leaves you alone. The hyena has to make his living, Mister Queedy. You journalists, you are like the hyena, always following, always waiting for a mistake, never giving up. The bush needs its hyena, he keeps the other animals strong. He is an intelligent fellow and he loves his children, maybe more than the lion does.

 - My father did not love me.

 - Did you know him well enough to say these things, Mister Queedy? If you want to forgive him I think maybe you need to know him better. Think that you did not know him before you were born. You think yourself better than other men?

 - I suppose I do.

 - So. You have brothers?

 - A sister. Older than me. He kept her very close. She was groomed to succeed to the empire. I was supposed to become a lawyer.

 - Ha. You and I both, Mister Queedy. And look where we have come to. We are sitting under the stars holding our own court, and we are not the lawyers but the judges. Here, do you have whisky in your tent?

M. had given Queedy a bottle of bourbon, more out of guilt than compassion and in the hope that it might loosen both men's tongues: Queedy's so that he might appear to be human and the Ambulist so that he might talk of his life. Queedy now brought this unopened bottle back to the fire where the Ambulist still sat ingesting its paltry warmth, his magnificent eyes intent on his own hand which he held at arm's length before him as if in scrutiny.

 - I must tell you now, Mister Queedy, that fixing a broken

heart is a dangerous thing to do. (The Ambulist takes the bottle offered by the boy and drinks deep from it; screwing his eyes shut and relishing the burning in his throat)

- I'm not sure I would have much to lose. Life is dangerous. (He leans across the fire and takes the bottle of bourbon from the Ambulist).

- Ha, you are a fool, still, sometimes. I do not mean for you. It is dangerous for me and for the spirit. What the Bushman calls the !kia is a tremendous energy. When you call on this energy to cure, it is like the power that the eland draws on in the moment of flight, it is an explosion in the stomach, the kleine mensen call it n'um, it boils inside you. Man, when that stuff is released it can cook your brain. You don't want to use it too often.

- Perhaps there is something to be said, after all, for the surgeon's knife.

- Ja, there is something to be said for it. More danger for you, less for him, eh Mister Queedy. (He passes the bottle. Queedy takes a slug and this time it catches in his throat so that he coughs explosively)

The night's black heart swallowed all sound. Numberless infinities of stars pirouetted in their unconcerned cosmic ballet overhead. From the eastern horizon an evil-looking gibbous moon rose leering, fat and bloated, above the Rigg. It might have been the corpse of the earth's stillborn child, pockmarked, pecked clean, scavenged to the white bone and tied down to remind men of their fate.

Chapter Nine

The wind's eye

The train swung across the points, its steel wheels clanking, squealing. Arching its stiff spine, spanning the tight apex of the curve, it straightened: squared itself for the bridge ahead. Low cloud and a grey industrial murk hung over the birthplace of the railways. The grunting diesel locomotive reached the centre of the bridge, a hundred feet above the matt-brown river below, and came to a stiff juddering halt before a last signal which glowed boiled-sweet-red. Its train of carriages snaked behind in Indian file, stoical, waiting. A southbound service clattered past it at military medium, for a few moments blocking the monochrome view of the city. Those passengers returning to their home town, unconcerned with the familiar roof-scape, the broad dun band of the incoming tide, the snail trails of traffic stuttering across the bridges, the seductive sweep of the valley to the west, merely gathered their belongings and stood.

The man with the bright red freckled face and incongruous ginger crew cut, conspicuous among the white faces and dark hair of the natives, checked his watch. He had not yet moved from his window seat. He carried no luggage except for a polished wooden case which could hardly have contained a suite of clothes but must have held something more precious: a musical instrument, perhaps. It lay on the seat beside him. The man did not need to retrieve his coat, for he had not once taken it off in the three hours of the journey. An empty right sleeve remained pinned across his chest. For a hundred miles and more the small girl with the pink-ribboned ringlets sitting opposite him next to her sleeping grandfather had been unable to take her eyes off it. She had stared shamelessly at him and he, unconcerned, had watched the flat plains and low hills rolling past, hour after hour. He seemed almost motionless, unblinking, his eyes narrowed from long exposure to the African sun flicking from side to side, tracking each passing feature of the burgeoning spring, his mouth set in what might have been half a smile. His fingers tapped out a faint, noiseless rhythm on the table and only otherwise moved when he raised his hand to look at his watch.

As if from fatigue the train came sighing to its halt along the platform beneath the immense wrought-iron cave of the station roof. The building echoed with bustling noises of engines and trolleys, of whistles, shouts from reunited relatives and friends, the blaring of the tannoy. The man with the red face edged along the aisle towards the end of the carriage, case in hand, forced to pause for a moment before climbing down as the heavy door swung back towards him. His foot reached out instinctively and with no more than the toe of his shoe he steadied it. Looking out, his eyes and ears took in every detail of this foreign city, every nuance of the physical language of a new culture: the clothes of the young and the old, the oblivious gaze of slap-happy lovers, the watchfulness of the lonely and the criminal. At first sight the man's pause at the carriage door might have been mistaken for diffidence. A young soldier in a maroon beret and a crisp khaki uniform leaning waiting against a pillar looked up at him and seemed about to come forward, to offer the man help; but he changed his mind.

An announcement blared out, drowning and drowned by the growling of the locomotive at bay. The soldier involuntarily turned his head away to look at the departures board and when he looked back the red-faced man had disappeared, swallowed by the crowd.

The streets of the city were new to him but, having negotiated the swishing traffic before the station, he seemed unfazed by the labyrinth of medieval streets which encircled it at one remove, keeping a respectful distance from the station's grandiose arcades, its need to be admired. Looming beyond the narrow vennels with their steep-pitched pantiled roofs, the city's stolid mercantile offices and warehouses were cloaked by the day's greyness in a mantle of gravity which would have suited the men whose money had built them. Dark orange brick, narrow windows set back like deep eyes, gabled roofs and turrets, minarets of the high church of capital: an egregious imposition on the visitor, crowding in upon the eye, browbeating the visitor. The man with the red hair and empty sleeve pinned against his chest walked unhesitating and direct through the passages that opened out onto the market place. He took in with a single sharp glance the stage, the actors, the scenery of M's perennial theatre: early lunchers sitting on the bench beneath the plane tree with their newspapers; delivery vans disgorging supplies for the cafés and bars; a refuse collector emptying bins with as much racket as twenty years of practice could effect. A gusty wind rolled tin cans along the pavements, shook the nascent greenery of the trees and toyed with the coats and hairstyles of shoppers and lunchtime office workers.

On the steps leading up to the entrance of the *Courier's* offices the man almost ran full square into Gaunt, head down and coat flapping as always, on his way out. Neither man looked the other in the eye, neither felt the brush of fate's hand; the newcomer continued up the steps and pushed open the heavy glass door. Inside, the sound of receptionists answering calls with automatic politeness produced a sort of melodic drone. The front desk was staffed by a young, fresh-looking man, a student of journalism marking time and earning a crust during the Easter vacation. Receiving the red-haired man's request to see the editor, he inquired if an appointment had been made and, on the slow, unapologetic shake of the man's head, he placed a call to Miss Nixon. Miss Nixon knew perfectly well that the editor-in-chief had no appointments today, for he was not in the building. Nevertheless, she checked his diary and told the young man at the desk to tell the stranger he was not available. She suggested he ask what the man wanted and see if any other member of staff might be able to help. Alternatively, he might make an appointment for another day.

Nearly twenty minutes passed during which the man, whose insistence on seeing the editor had begun to attract the attention of senior members of the *Courier's* staff, demonstrated an implacable determination not to be fobbed off on any junior reporter. It was Miss Nixon herself, therefore, eventually summoned to preside on M.'s behalf, who suggested that the stranger, unwilling to reveal his purpose, might like to talk to Mr Gaunt, a very senior reporter who enjoyed the full confidence of the editor and who, although he was not in the office just now, might reliably be found at this time of day at the Crown, down the hill by the Quayside. It was not, she might have reflected later, a very professional way to deal with an off-the-street inquiry; but then, Sir would go rushing off to London just like that in pursuit of a whim and then, what could a secretary do but draw on her long years of experience and handle the situation as she saw fit?

Gaunt and the stranger recognised in each other a type. Gaunt had not pounded the streets and the keys of his typewriter for thirty years without knowing a copper, or at least an ex-copper, when he saw one. With some it was the shoes that gave them away – even undercover coppers couldn't bear not to look after their shoes. With others it was the collar, always too tight, or maybe the way the hair was cut. This one had definitely been a copper. In his case the eyes said everything. Gaunt's theory was that it was having the power of arrest:

the knowledge that you could take a man from off the street, bind his hands and lock him up; chuck him down the stairs on the way too, if you felt like it. Yes, it gave you a look all right, that power. This one would be hard as nails too, missing arm or no missing arm. The polished wooden case which he had laid so unselfconsciously on the bar had a look of, well, menace. Gaunt felt even in those first moments a sense of danger, of risk, of opportunity.

In Gaunt, the red-haired, red-faced man with the strangled colonial accent also saw opportunity. He saw in the jutting bottom lip and jowly cheeks, the double chin and the fingers stained with nicotine a self-important cynic, an unhealthy man who probably liked a bet, whose principles, if he had any, could be bought. He saw an informer, a lover of conspiracy, a man for whom knowledge was power: knowledge of secrets, of dirty washing, of peccadilloes, of weakness and vulnerability. He would want to belong, to be taken into confidence, to be party to private knowledge. A thousand of this sort had been through his hands over the years. The man would help. He would want to help. What would he want in return? Whatever it was, he would probably be disappointed.

    - Gaunt. (This is not a question, it is a statement. Gaunt looks up from his pint and the racing form and sizes the stranger up in an intuitive instant, hears the accent and straight away it comes to mind when he has heard something like it before, not so long ago only in another pub in another place)

    - You are...?

    - I am looking for someone.

    - I'll have another of these. (Gaunt drains the last drop from his pint glass and pushes it across the bar towards the landlord)

If the stranger had been so inclined, he might have imparted to Gaunt a history similar in most respects to the one that, even now, M. was absorbing in the comfort of a first-class carriage, heading north at a hundred miles an hour through the sunlit fens of eastern England. If his train had left the capital two hours earlier he might have arrived back at the office in time to intercept the stranger, to prevent Gaunt from meeting him. How could he have known that the man to whom he had spoken on the telephone would turn up on that day, unannounced, that he would be guided by the ingenuous Miss Nixon into the arms of the most dangerous man possible? M., not having the gift of clairvoyance, was thus absorbed in reading a species of biography of the Ambulist, unaware of the fatal liaison now being forged in the bar of the Crown. The documents he had been sent, which included newspaper cuttings, an envelope full of press agency photographs and notes culled from more discreet sources, had been prepared by researchers contracted to the *Courier's* parent company at their Johannesburg office. They had been intercepted by the British Government and vetted. M. had been forced to collect them in person and to sign a copy of the Act there and then. These were delicate times in the history of a nation undergoing rebirth.

M. began with the notes: dates of birth and death of various members of the Jäger family, a copy of Pieter Jäger's passport issued in Windhoek, Namibia. The father, as M. already knew from Queedy, had been a farmer in what was now eastern Namibia on the edge of the Kalahari desert. Three sons, two of them dead in their late teens, one in a truck accident out in the desert, the other from typhus in his first year at college in Windhoek, the capital. The third son, Pieter: the Ambulist-to-be. Sent to school in Windhoek in 1938. From 1942 until the end of the war he read law at the University of the Cape of Good Hope. He returned to Windhoek, joined a legal partnership and practised as a barrister until his father's death in 1955. In that year he gave up his practice and went back to live on the family farm. The future nomad and wanderer, miracle-worker and mythic giant bestriding the northern hills of England yoked himself to the plough and the saddle, corralled his cattle and sheep and looked after his mother in her declining years.

In 1961 he was a signatory to the founding charter of the Western Kalahari Game Reserve. In 1964 he was arrested and charged with illegal marriage and sent to prison for six months. In 1965 he was named as a member of a proscribed organisation, the South West Africa People's Organisation, SWAPO, based on intelligence received from a press source. In 1968 he was arrested for a second time in the aftermath of the Ongandjera massacre two years earlier, taken to Pretoria and imprisoned without trial. So, the Ambulist had spent time in a South African jail. It was not a pleasant thought but it might begin to explain his love of freedom, his hatred of the idea of confinement behind walls. But these thirteen years between his father's death and his arrest for conspiracy to murder: here was a gap in the Ambulist's career which needed explaining, and a void in M.'s knowledge of history that had to be filled.

M. set aside the briefing notes and opened his shabby but once-stylish leather briefcase, a legacy of his days at the *Clarion* when he still harboured vague pretensions to cut a dash in the streets of Dublin. Another brown envelope, its foolscap shape and string ties telling its provenance in Her Majesty's Stationery Office. M. had obtained a copy of the Foreign and Commonwealth Office's restricted diplomatic briefings on Namibia – the sort of document that might have been thrust into the hands of novice attachés before they set off on a new posting to the far corners of some other nation's colony. As black fen gave way to the greening tree-dotted wolds of Lincolnshire, M. applied himself to the history of the former German protectorate of South-West Africa, a part of the globe to which he had previously given little thought.

Gaunt, enjoying his pint at the expense of the red-faced stranger, already knew something of the sorry history of that part of the world, having done a stint as a correspondent in Angola during its seemingly perpetual civil war. He knew something of the conflicts between German settlers, Boers and native tribes and of successive campaigns of repression and genocide in both countries. He knew that apartheid

South Africa's League of Nations mandate to run the former German colony had expired in 1940; that South Africa had declined to give up its mandate. He could not remember when, but some time in the late 1950s the policy of urban apartheid had been extended to South-West Africa. A programme of resettlement and segregation followed, bitterly resented by the black population who now became radicalised by the example of the anti-apartheid movement in South Africa and by those of the white colonists who thought the policy disastrously regressive.

An indigenous black independence movement was formed in South-West Africa and, in the early 1960s, SWAPO emerged as a motivated, organised and effective terrorist organisation which ultimately forced South Africa to grant independence. It had taken thirty years. The scars had barely begun to heal. This new country called Namibia was a fragile child of the African experiment with freedom and reconciliation. Gaunt remembered the Ongandjera massacre in '66. He remembered it well: an ugly car-bombing in which eleven innocents had died, along with any hope of a political compromise. He had tried to cross the border to wire a report from the scene and the border had been closed. The revelation that the Ambulist was one of its instigators came as a shock even to him.

- Your editor was not very forthcoming about Jäger's whereabouts. (The stranger has bought Gaunt a second pint; he has joined him with a glass of orange juice. He is careful not to question Gaunt but to offer him opportunities for a frank exchange of information)

- Not surprised... been his pet project since the winter. Sort of an obsession, thinks he's the Second Coming of Christ. I knew there was something up with the bloke. A right queer bugger to talk to. (Gaunt nods in self-affirmation, takes a cigarette from the pack on the counter and offers one to the stranger with a glance. The stranger ignores the offer; he does not smoke)

- I dare say you would know where to look for him.

- I dare say I would. (Gaunt knows he is dealing with a clever man; does not intend to sell himself cheap and, besides, he has a trick or two up his sleeve. He can hardly believe his luck in gaining the whip hand over his editor with such a decisive coup; he will savour the moment.)

- You understand, Gaunt, I have no intention to harm Jäger. For the sake of national reconciliation I need to talk to him about some of the people he used to know. He is respected by those terrorists and if he will help us to bring them in, persuade them they will not be prosecuted, he will be doing his country a great favour.

- His country or your country?

- We are all Africans.

- Listen, you do with him what you like. You can string him up as far as I'm concerned. No skin off my nose. He is nothing to me. Of course, if you want him found quick, if you need to get back and report to your CO pronto, I can speed the process up a bit. Just a bit more expensive that way.

- But he can be found.

- He can be found. You came to the right man for that, Mister...

- You can call me Albie.

- All right, Albie.

- This reporter, this John Smith, supposing that is his name...

- Real name? That's bloody funny, that is. Real name. It's his real name all right, I guarantee you. Another one of the boss's little projects, but that's another story.

- Another story? An interesting other story or just an expensive one?

- Don't get me wrong. Only interesting to me.

- And he is a freelance, this reporter.

- I couldn't say he is, as a matter of fact. But if you've a funny idea of turning him with a few bob you can forget it. Quite the boss's pet he is. Oh yes, quite the boss's pet.

- And he would live here in town.

- He has a flat here. Couldn't say where.

- Couldn't or wouldn't.

- You and I understand each other, Albie. But he won't be there. Hasn't been around for a while. Living rough out in the sticks with your wild man of the woods, I reckon.

- They are together, then.

- That is my information. Somewhere out there in the wilds of the Borders. A big place to search. They could be anywhere, really.

- But if you found one you would find the other.

- I would think so. Kill two birds with one stone.

No star had been seen in the night sky of the Border hills for days. The waning moon's lowering pearl-white horns were invisible behind a thick gruel of cloud that seemed inexhaustibly to replenish itself from the southwest, fed by a wind that dipped, swirled, swerved, poured itself unmeasured into every cleugh and farmyard, buffeting crag and copse, sweeping hill and moor as if a vast blanket was being shaken out by some matron household deity in a grand gesture of spring housekeeping. It was a rhythmical, pulsing wind which sang now a deep bass-drum thud that seemed to shake the earth, and now a whistling call to arms that in former times would have had the Border men reaching for their spurs. It was a riding wind, a wind to make war with.

Sheep huddled together in the shelter of tumbled walls. The farmer and his dog sat close to their hearth. Trees braced themselves and leaned back in defensive limbo. All birds and wild animals had long since retreated to nest or burrow. Queedy too was oppressed by the roaring force of nature, was bullied by it, shaken to his bones. His ungainly tent, hopelessly ill-designed to withstand such an onslaught, flapped and ripped, alternately seeming to shrug and crouch, tearing at itself, pulling its pegs from the ground like a hobbled steed wanting to be away, to flee. Queedy wished he could run too. He saw a vision of himself, his outstretched hand turning the key in the lock of his front door, the stillness of the air within the four walls of his apartment, the immovable sturdiness of the brick building, the push-button security of light switches and gas rings, the silent motes of dust hanging in the limpid overheated air. The vision replayed itself again and again so that he could think of little else. He was the first cave dweller, looking for nature's emergency bolt-hole. He was every dweller since, hooked on controlling his environment. He was an animal, driven to the edge of madness by the relentless pummelling blows of a Mistral or a Harmattan, hunted to exhaustion and submission, surrendering to his fate. He cowered in his tent, unable to function. He was numbed by failure and fear and detested the endless instant of his misery.

The Ambulist was not unmoved by the elemental blast which bore down upon them. Like a tree he drew strength from it, bent to its wrath, but did not submit to it. Like a sailor he rode it, accepted it, breathed it in and gave himself to its ursine embrace. He did not shelter behind his stone ramparts; nor were his senses overwhelmed by the brutality of the noise all around him. He had no fear of conflict, nor of madness. Since the first upright human had left the safety of the rainforest and walked out upon the open grasslands of the African savannah, wanderers had learned to coexist with the forces of wind and rain, storm and flood. The great adventure which, like a siren, called humans to explore, to risk, to create, also called on them to forge relations with the lion and the leopard, with drought and deluge, with baking sun and freezing night.

The Ambulist, who had lived in and on the edge of a great desert, did not contemplate fighting nature any more than he would fight with his own kin. There were tribes, warrior peoples to the north, who had shaken their spears at the wind, had tried to drive it off with a show of bravado. No such conflict existed for the bushman, who was of the world, not against it. Nature, like the big cats, was a neighbour to be greeted with respect, to whom gifts and honours must be offered in exchange for bounty and harmonious relations. The gift might be a name, a gesture, a song: a recognition of the equal right to be, to go about one's business. Even man's greatest art, the discovery of fire and its secret powers and evils, did not entitle him to arrogate possession of the earth. The Ambulist did not know these things the way Queedy knew his fear. He felt them, they were him. Now, as Queedy tried and failed to hide from nature, the Ambulist stood, arms spread wide to the horizons, fingers stretched out, on the squat black slab of the Rigg, head back, his grey hair torn back by the wind and his eyes brimming with tears. He sensed, through the whole of his giant frame the opening of the door which separated men from their gods, that he might fly through it on wings like an eagle's. Now was the moment and all moments were in this now.

The Ambulist would not play father or protector. Queedy's fears were those of a man who does not know himself and the Ambulist could not lead the boy to self-knowledge. His own experience was of a childhood in which freedom, neglect, exile and love were a plaited twine binding strength and knowledge together. The cords that fastened him to his land and his kin were also the threads that guided him through dark passages, the ropes by which he could haul himself up, always coiled across his shoulders, never failing in either strength or suppleness.

    - Come, Mister Queedy, we will walk. (The Ambulist sweeps the whipping flap of Queedy's tent aside and stoops, lowering his head and wild mane and addressing not Queedy but his dwelling, turning the young man's fear with absolute moral authority)

    - Yes, anywhere. (Queedy, grey of face and unable to look directly at his rescuer, laces his muddy brogues and follows the Ambulist, stumbling stupidly out into the maelstrom)

Had the Ambulist attached himself to Queedy with a thin line he might have flown him like a kite, so ephemeral was the figure of the young man in that landscape of turmoil, so little did his presence seem to matter. The Ambulist himself, breasting the wind's crests and troughs, brought his charge down off the moor into the lee of the Border ridge, down again to the valley bottom and a scrubby birch wood which likewise enjoyed its shelter. Madness subsided to racket, gale to breeze, ocean to lough. Finding their way steeply down to the edge of the burn, its waters dancing unperturbed and in sympathy with the breeze which bent the feathered catkin-laden branches of the trees, the two men followed its winding course. The first green heads of a congregation of bluebells offered the distant promise of a glorious May. Nesting tits and goldcrests, nuthatches, even the normally solicitous robin, all too busy to notice intruders, graced the chords of wind and water with their amorous melodies. Queedy, calming, began to measure his pace, walking with the ground underfoot rather than upon it. His tread was now light but sure. His aching heart found company in the rhythm of the trail. The Ambulist felt the change in his step but did not look behind him. Nor did either man speak.

    They were silent, the sound of their thoughts drowned by the overwhelming orchestration of the air above them, following the twisting course of the stream ever downward, sometimes south and sometimes west, sometimes out in the open and catching a careless slap as they strayed into the whirlpool of the wind's eye; but for the most part they kept to the trees. Only when the parent burn joined the shallow frenzied blue-black waters of its daughter did the Ambulist come to a halt. He squatted on the bank where there was shelter from a copse of venerable alder trees and drew a handful of the peaty water to his mouth. He rolled himself a cigarette and lit it, passing his tobacco to Queedy who reached out and took it. Queedy rolled his own inexpertly, lit it and drew deep on it, passed the pouch back. Two exhaled clouds of smoke, synchronised, were plucked by the gale and propelled downstream, vanishing into the mass of air.

From his pocket the Ambulist now took a slab of bread and a piece of cheese and, dividing them, passed a share to Queedy. Queedy, in return, reached into his jacket and from it pulled a chunk of honeycomb wrapped in waxed paper. The Ambulist's face exfoliated into a great toothy grin and his companion returned a more modest smile of acknowledgement. They sat there for some minutes watching the hypnotic unchanging chaos of the river until the Ambulist, rising, made off downstream with the water rushing at his heels and Queedy shadowing them both.

They came to a bridge in the middle of the afternoon. It must have been built more than two centuries before, a humpbacked stone packhorse arch which any modern vehicle would have struggled to negotiate. The Ambulist ignored it, plunging, as he had done once before in the presence of Gaunt, into the foam of the river and wading across with the water splashing at his knees. Once he stumbled, as if unsure of his footing, and his arms stretched out as if to feel for some non-existent support, but he recovered and made the opposite bank. For a brief moment he looked agitated and rubbed his eyes as if his vision had blurred for an instant, as if he had been subjected to a personal insult.

Queedy had not before witnessed the Ambulist's hostility to bridges, and he stopped halfway across it to lean on its parapet and con-template this eccentric manifestation. The wind funnelling down the dale hit him full in the face but it seemed no longer to bother him and, not for the first time, the Ambulist, like M. and Gaunt before him, was astonished at Queedy's capacity to recover his self-assurance. Perhaps it was the bridge that reassured him, the unshakeable solidity of human endeavour which had survived and would survive, like the Ambulist, seemingly proof against time.

The water dashed beneath the bridge towards its tidal fate like the first spouting froth off the top of a beer keg. The granite footings thrust into and against each bank were like fists spoiling the river's flow, a gesture of useless defiance against its elemental power. In their slipstream the river's turbulent disdain was written in ink the colour of harvest ale. Queedy stared at the Ambulist like he was waiting for an explanation. The Ambulist looked back expressionless at Queedy on the bridge. The un-posed question formed on Queedy's lips but the Ambulist did not wait for him to get it out. He strode off and Queedy was forced to run to catch up. Speaking over his shoulder he told the young man how rivers hated bridges, their geomorphic right to divide the land, to segregate mountains and plains, animals and plants arc'd, short-circuited. Thus emasculated, rivers were no more than drains.

Could Queedy take this seriously? Could he really judge the weight of the Ambulist's words, their expense, their value, their cost? Were they, indeed, capable of evaluation or was Queedy in fact merely playing the static part of a boulder, marooned in mid-stream with the meaningless words flowing over him?

- Ja, Mister Queedy, you think this old man is an old fool.

- I am intrigued. You are not offended, I hope, by my taking the bridge?

- Jonge, it is not me who is offended by your use of the bridge, or by the bridge itself. It is out of respect for the river that I do not use it.

- In what way does the river demand respect, and in what way is it offended by the bridge?

- If you had been brought up in the wilderness you would not ask that question. Rather, you might ask why, when nature offers her bounty so freely, anyone would want to build a wall or a fence and claim ownership of any part of it.

- I can see how the bushman, the Lapp or the aborigine might fail to appreciate barbed wire or a stone wall. I imagine something like our Roman wall would not go down too well with a hunter or a herder.

- Ja, klopt, that is for sure. I think you should take the stones of that thing and wrap them up one by one and send them as a present to Rome. It was nothing more than a fiscal sphincter on the arse-end of a military empire. (Still Queedy cannot tell if he is being made fun of)

- But if you are saying you do not like these boundaries, well then, the bridge is surely in sympathy with you, it subverts the whole concept of the river as boundary.

- True, Mister Queedy. But you see the river must go where it will and it has a right to divide the land as it sees fit.

- That is perverse. A pathetic fallacy.

- Are you telling me that barbed wire is not perverse? That dividing one country from another is not a fallacy?

Queedy, even Queedy, had nothing to say for some minutes while they walked on, leaving the river behind and following the pack horse trail as it traversed the steep side of the hill. But he was not satisfied and he now dared to ask the Ambulist if he was not living in some sort of prehistoric delusion, if he actually thought the world of his childhood, of uncorrupted Bushmen living in blissful conspiracy with the birds and bees, was more real than the dweller's world of electricity, of roads and railways and bridges, of brick buildings and showers and refrigeration.

- Do you know, Mister Queedy, that every war has been fought over grass, that every five generations all the land has to change hands, that it has rained every spring since ten thousand BC? The Bushman, he was not living in a delusional garden of Eden. His practical knowledge of the world, of the real relationships that exist between us when we do not shelter behind possessions and structures, was profoundly real. The delusion is that of settlers and those who make war on nature, because they are only waging war on themselves. Are you so sure you are not living in a contemporary delusion? Read a newspaper from front to back. I have not seen one in ten years but I bet you every single story is about the fight for resources, for ownership of something which someone stole from their neighbour ten thousand years ago. And you think I am living in the past? Verdomme, we all live in the past, my friend.

For the second time that day the young man at the front desk in the foyer of the *Courier* found himself at the centre of the action. The awkward business with the slightly sinister and overly-persistent stranger had been uncomfortable but no doubt character-building. Miss Nixon running past his desk and out of the building in floods of tears that same afternoon must, in its way, have been more disconcerting. Several members of the public queuing to hand in competition coupons looked uncomfortably at their feet and the young man felt obliged to apologise to them and to the world in general on the paper's behalf. The receptionists, who had seen and heard most things in their time, carried on stoically taking calls but several of them flushed with embarrassment and concern. The departure shortly afterwards of the editor-in-chief, red-faced and with a furious look on his face, raised more questions in the staff canteen than it answered. Speculation swung between a contretemps involving Mrs Fenwick and Miss

Nixon over the affections of the editor, and fallout from the morning's business with the stranger and Mr Gaunt. No one, except the editor himself and Miss Nixon, knew the truth. Mr Gaunt, who might have shed interesting light on the matter, had not yet returned from lunch at the Crown. He did not, in fact, return that day.

M. regretted his outburst at Miss Nixon. How he would make it up to her he did not know, but he would, somehow. Not now, though. He drove fast, maybe too fast, heading north from the city. His thoughts ran ahead of him. He was oblivious to the wind buffeting the car from side to side, unheeding of the sky's violent reflection of his purple-grey mood, but as he approached the narrow lane leading to the Tower-house he was forced to brake sharply and steer the car around a large branch which had become detached from an overhead tree and now lay treacherously in the middle of the road. Jareld Arnesen, out with his dogs and, having seen the fallen branch, on his way to remove it, saw the car coming and recognised it, flagged it down. M. brought the car to a halt and wound down his window.

> - A fine lively day! We did not expect to see you. I will
> join you up at the house. (Jareld waves him on and drags the
> branch onto the verge)
>
> - Get in. (M. stretches across and opens the passenger door
> and Jareld leans in. A look at M.'s face tells him something is
> not right so he does not say anything but opens the back door
> for the dogs to jump in and M. drives them the two hundred
> yards or so up the track to the farmyard)

M. found some relief from his mental turmoil in the prospect of a council of war at the Tower-house. Arnesen was a practical man and no fool, whatever evidence of harmless buffoonery he proffered to the world. Freya spread calm about her; she would not rush to an opinion and whatever she said would be drawn from deep reserves of insight and humanity. And the girl... the girl was interesting, she would say and think unorthodox things that would not perhaps occur to her parents, or to M. himself. M. had come to the right place for help.

    - Let us eat something. Sit, sit and I will fetch a fine fresh loaf of bread and some cheese. I have a soup maturing on the stove. You look hungry. (Jareld busies himself about the kitchen. Selena, trotting up the kitchen steps from the yard, takes a towel and rubs the dogs down. Freya has seen M. and her husband arriving from a window and, intrigued, has come down from her high place where, like the Ambulist in his own way, perhaps, she has been working on Queedy's head)

    - Thanks. I'm hungry, sure, haven't thought to eat today but soup and bread will be good. We've got a bloody great problem on our hands.

    - Tell us. Is it John's health?

    - No, the boy is fine. That is, he was fine last time I saw him. (M. pulls from his briefcase the envelopes containing photographs, notes and briefings, and spreads them on the table for Freya and Selena to look at. Jareld returns from the pantry and ladles the wonderful-smelling soup into large earthenware bowls. The bread he cuts into inelegant chunks on a wooden board. The fug of the kitchen, like the warmth of the welcome, seeps reassuringly into M.'s consciousness and he sets himself to eating)

    - Pieter is not a terrorist. (Selena's passive, listless voice possesses a sureness which does not invite contradiction, and her parents are too used to her modest assertions to doubt the truth when they hear it. Besides, neither of them can believe that the Ambulist has hate in his heart and the guilt of murder on his hands)

    - He may be or he may not be, and I'm inclined to agree (says M.). I've known about this massacre, or at least the accusation, for a couple of weeks. (From the sink Jareld turns his head to look at M. and raises an eyebrow, catches his wife's eye too but does not say anything) I had a phone call from a man who said he was a reporter from the *Johannesburg Star*. He wanted to interview our Ambulist regarding his murky past. The reason I sent the boy to go and mind him was that I wanted to keep any nosey journalists off his back. I did it to protect my story, don't get me wrong. I thought this was just another good angle. Sure I have a black heart and I feel the weight of it so I do. Read this. (M. leafs through the pages of his Foreign Office briefing notes to a paragraph which he has marked with a big red ballpoint pen. He passes the notes to Freya, who reads them and passes them to Selena. Jareld comes over from the sink and reads them in his turn, peering over the top of his glasses. The paragraph contains the description of a man, formerly of the South African Defence Force and latterly regarded as a rogue element belonging to an ultra-nationalist white supremacist party disinclined to accept majority black rule. Despite losing an arm in a bomb explosion he is regarded as a capable marksman. He has a known interest in the man called Pieter Jäger)

- This man described here, you think he is the man who posed as the journalist and called you? You think he is in this country?

- He was at the offices of the *Courier* earlier this afternoon.

The Ambulist and his companion, careless of the extreme danger to which the stranger's conference with Gaunt now exposed them, had broken their trail at the foot of a stone cross fully the height of three men, which seemed as if it must have grown organically from the dark earth. Its slender black form tapered with chaste perfection up, up into the sky; even the jagged fracture at its top might have been sculpted by divine hands. No wind, no earthquake had brought it low in thirteen centuries, although the delicate lace work of its carvings and the arcane runes incised along its edges had softened with age. Its circular head had long ago been broken into pieces, not by the forces of nature but by those of the iconoclast Cromwell. The nobility of its solitary exposure, its fidelity to the men and women who had prayed here in this remote churchyard, was unshakeable.

Queedy sat at its foot, exhausted, breathing great gulps of the air which had so assaulted him. The Ambulist leaned his head against it, probed it with his fingers as he had done the prehistoric carvings of the Rigg, of Roarin' Linn and Old Bewley. The runes he could not decipher, though he felt in their execution not just the zeal of the evangelists who had set this stone here but also the expert pride of the craftsman. He knew too that the vine scrolls and leaves, the fantastical birds, beasts and scenes of apostolic pastoral care told of a greater truth, an older truth, than the vengeful God of the settlers of Israel.

    - Here, Mister Queedy. You see here our mason has carved us a fine sundial on this cross to keep us to our duties. (The Ambulist points to a half moon carved into the south side of the cross, divided like a protractor into segments. At its geometric centre a hole drilled into the stone allowed for a small gnomon, it might be as simple as a stick, to be inserted)

    - An equation of eternal time? Or time to go fishing for men?

    - Maybe. Maybe for rabbits and deer too. I do not think they were confused like the city people of today who think a tree dies when you cut it and the hunting of an animal is a sin. Your ancestors, like the Bushman, knew the difference between a good story and filling the larder with food so your family can eat.

    - Speaking as a lawyer, you should know.

- Ha. Mister Queedy, I have hopes for you. Humour is a good tool to have in your survival kit.

- Haven't you noticed, I can hardly speak for laughing.

- Ja, I had noticed.

- Tell me, what did you do with your law? I like to think you were the champion of the lost cause.

- I went back to my home and became a farmer.

- There is an irony there somewhere.

- Ja, there is an irony. My father died, my two brothers were dead, my mother needed help with the farm. There were many people to feed from the land. So I became a farmer. The farming was not good there any more. The wells were drying up. It was hard.

- And the Bushman? (Queedy has recovered his breath enough to stand and now he too examines the carvings on the four faces of the cross. There is a simple intensity in them which matches the bleak location. It is too high here to grow anything except the rough grass that only hardy long-haired highland cattle can eat. Winters are long and hard and spring comes late, sometimes not until the end of May. Two or three farmsteads cluster together on a plateau that offers no shelter but the church in whose shadow the cross stands, and the shell of a castle whose builders were godless rustlers)

- The kleine mensen were still there, like they had been for a hundred and fifty thousand years, but the farmers and the politicians wanted to move them. They wanted to put their barbed wire across the desert and herd their cattle. They wanted to mine the metals beneath the earth. The politicians in Pretoria wanted to put these wild people into corrals and tame them like goats and sheep. The Bushmen were driven out of the desert. Many of them came to my farm.

- What did you do?

- My mother and I helped them to stay and we tried to tell the politicians that they should be allowed to go back and live in the old way. For five years we worked with the Bushmen and the agencies to make a big reserve in the west of the Kalahari so the animals they hunted and the plants they gathered, the waterholes where they camped, would be protected from the farmers and the miners.

- And?

- Ja, we got them their reserve.

- What happened?

- Tourists came to look at the animals and kill some of them and take pictures of them, and they brought lots of western dollars too so the poor areas could be developed with roads and electricity. Then the tourists complained that the Bushmen were hunting and eating all the animals they had come to see and were begging for gifts and tobacco from them, and the tourists did not like the way the Bushmen smelled, so the politicians took them from the desert and herded them into concentration camps for their own good. Now the bushmen are all drunks and they kill each other with knives and guns. You know, Mister Queedy, before I was born no Bushman had ever carried a knife? Now the tourists can enjoy their game reserve without the bad smell. Come, we will go again to our camp.

The long spring day passed into twilight with no sign of the setting sun. The unrelenting wind at their backs, the two men crossed fell and burn, river or bridge, through forest and scrub wood and up again, up onto the dark moor, until the silhouette of the Rigg, sitting waiting squat and stiff against the blue-grey horizon, signalled that their camp was near. Queedy, desperate to stop walking and to rest for a few minutes before trying to set a fire, walked on to his own camp. He could hear no tearing sound now, no wrestling of canvas with wind. Where his tent had been only a few tins of food, his torch and a box full of jars of honey remained. The canvas shell of his dwelling had been torn from the earth, had been swallowed by the sky. Now, only now, in this moment of shattering loss and helplessness and in the realisation of his naked exposure to nature, did Queedy fall to his knees and cry like a child.

Chapter Ten

Blindness

No wind ever rocked the brute square fastness of the Tower-house. No raider, not even in the calamitous sixteenth century when no king's writ ran here for four generations, had ever taken it by fair means or foul. No flood or earthquake might shift its foundations and no siege would exhaust its supplies. From the hill on the edge of the woods, where every tree but the oak and the ash had flung out its exuberant crop of yellow-green leaves, even the furze of spring foliage surrounding the tower on all sides could not have softened its stiff, uncompromising lines. From the south the sun, gliding towards its gentle evening touchdown, bathed it in a sympathetic pool of liquid gold, but from the north this back-lighting only hardened its charcoal imprint on the skyline.

Above the kitchen, in the imperturbable security of the sitting room before a roaring fire, with the glancing rays of the sun coming in at the window, a council of war was in progress. M., sitting forward, perched almost, on the edge of an enveloping armchair, stroked the head of one of the dogs, whose muzzle rested, deeply contented, in his lap. Selena knelt close to the fire with the other dog stretched out asleep beside her, her pallid face glowing in the saffron light cast by the flames, eyes bright berries of attention. Freya and Jareld reclined on their sofa, not in each others' arms but facing out to their guest. A bottle of wine stood breathing on the hearth. Another lay empty. The heat was soporific, would have sent them all into slumber had not the conversation been of such moment. Shadows playing on the walls behind them gave M. the feeling they were being watched, even that they were being judged. By whom? The ghosts of all his other mistakes?

- What will you do with your renegade reporter?

- He will be sacked tomorrow and I'll have the lawyers slap a confidentiality order on him so he can't spill this to any of the other papers. The old sod should have been retired ages ago, by Christ so he should. The God only knows he is a dinosaur.

- Is John safe, do you think? (This is Freya. Her concern for Queedy, until now conferred exclusively on his soul, now extends to his physical self. The clay that lies on its pedestal a few feet above them is beginning, she believes, to yield to her penetrating touch, to expose the vulnerabilities which M. is only too familiar with and which she feels with visceral certainty)

- From Jäger? Yes, I believe so.

- I meant from this man Rooi. Pieter is harmless, or at least to John he is harmless. (Freya dismisses the thought with an graceful wave of a hand).

- You know, he has offered to fix the boy's heart? I mean, actually physically fix it, heal it, make it new.

- So! What an extraordinary man he is, I wish he would have stayed longer with us. What a fine clever fellow. He is a shaman, I think. (Jareld's enthusiasm for such wizardry is that of the musician, praising another man's art with open admiration)

- Papa, I do not think he can just fix John's heart. It must take a terrible toll on a healer to do something like that. For him to take such a risk, I think he must have become fond of John, don't you think?

- It is hard not to be fond of that young man. He is like a ten-week-old cub, he tries to chew off your hand and you laugh and pet him on the head. He knows nothing of himself and cannot be harmed, his world is full of curiosity. You just wish he might not do something reckless to see what will happen, like a dog jumping off a cliff.

- John has been terribly harmed in his life, Jara. (This is Freya; she holds her husband steady in her gaze and touches his hand lightly) I do not know how or by whom, but he is quite broken and I do not know if he can be mended. Perhaps Pieter can make his heart work better so he does not die, but there is a mortal wound in his soul. I fear no-one can fix it except the one who broke it in the first place.

- Too late for that (says M.). It was his father. I knew the father long before he was born. I promise you he did a great deal of harm to many people. The boy is a fragment of shrapnel with sharp edges, flying through the air, and who knows what damage he might do?

- The father is alive?

- Dead. (M. shakes his head) Killed himself three years ago. Probably killed himself, that is. But definitely dead. Plane crash, Rockies. (M. makes a motion with the flat of his hand, spiralling down towards the floor; the dog muzzled in his lap brings an ear and an eyebrow to vague attention and then, realising that M. is not going to move, sighs contentedly and subsides once more into his lap) John Queedy's father was Carew Smith.

- So! To be the son of a father like that, it is not easy I
think. (Jareld looks at Freya, who holds a hand over her mouth
as if to stifle a cry; her thoughts flash to the clay head upstairs
in her studio and an almost painful sensation of enlightenment
flashes into her mind) But this is for another time. Now, we
must speak of our Ambulist. (Jareld raises himself from the
sofa and refills glasses, throws another log onto the fire and sits
back down; this time, like M., on the edge of his seat)

- Rooi is going to hunt Pieter down and try to kill him, isn't
he? (Selena seems incapable of dissimulation. Her parents are
used to this. M. has come across such a girl before, but even
so he is taken aback by her direct statement of what they are all
thinking and it comes to him that Selena would make a terrible
newspaper editor, although a refreshing one)

- Sure I think he will try. There is history there and it
might be personal.

- And your man Gaunt is going to help him. (Jareld is
already thinking ahead, feeling for the practical which must
emerge from the immediate shock and fear)

- Gaunt will be dealt with before he can do any more harm.

- And we, we must do something. Here we are sitting in
a fine great house like a castle, which no one can come into if
we don't like it. He can come here. Shall we bring him here?
(Jareld is thinking too fast, and almost immediately he sees why
this cannot work) But no, it is not possible, of course. (And he
looks over his glasses first at his daughter, then at his wife, and
now at M., who shakes his head)

- Jara, it is a beautiful thought. But you know he would
never be able to leave if he came here and knew that man was
waiting for him somewhere as soon as he stepped from the
door. It would be like keeping a pet tiger, it would kill him just
as surely.

- Darling you are right, of course. But we must warn him and we must take the young man away from him because he will worry more for Queedy than for himself.

- Jara, it is right that we warn him. I think he will know best what do to if he is pursued. I think it has happened to him before.

- Good (says M. slapping the arms of his chair and this time disturbing the dog, who raises its head, turns with an extravagant yawn and slouches off to join its twin on the carpet by the fire) We get John away. Jäger must look after himself. Rooi might not find him so easy to track down on his own patch. I'll go out and see if I can't make contact with the boy.

- No. I will go (says the girl, and the others look at her and then at each other and none of them says anything because there is no point).

M. should have gone back to the office that night. He should have apologised to Miss Nixon, taken her flowers, bought her dinner, implored forgiveness for his outburst, or at least explained it. He should have seen Gaunt off the premises, should have ensured that his own files and paperwork were secured, that Gaunt did not try to gain access to M.'s room where the Ambulist's map lay vulnerable in the desk drawer. He should have placed a call to the *Courier's* lawyers and arranged for them to take out an injunction against Gaunt publishing or selling any material relating to the Ambulist or the *Courier*. He should have warned the paper's board members and trustees of the storm about to break.

He should have done all these things, but he did not. He found comfort in the reassuring bosom of the family who dwelt at the Tower-house, as Queedy had before him. He drank wine with them, ate their homely, nourishing food and talked of many things long into the night. Queedy's history, and some of his father's and M.'s, were laid before the Arnesens over dinner. A family held together by love found many things painful and difficult to hear. That such guilt and bitterness should exist between father and son, that such friendship should end in betrayal, were affirmations of their own love for each other and of the compassion that they felt for the broken-hearted Queedy. But still... but still.

M. returned to the city and to his desk the following day to find two national newspapers carrying a front-page story about the wandering miracle-worker now exclusively exposed as a wanted terrorist; to find that the Ambulist's map was missing from his desk; that Gaunt had already left; and that his, M.'s, immediate presence was requested at an emergency board meeting of the *Courier's* directors. The chief executive of the *Courier's* parent company wanted to know why he had not already offered his resignation. The absurd thought that crossed M.'s mind in those hours of craziness was that if Carew Smith had been alive he might have lent him a good lawyer and somehow got him out of this mess. As it was, it looked as though he would be hung out to dry on a very long, very high line.

The *Courier's* corridors bristled with silent anticipation; the air crackled with tension. Every footfall along every passage, every banging door was pregnant with menace. The delivery van drivers smoking out at the back entrance, the old-timers in the print room, the typesetters and reporters, all of them keeping the conversation on other things like the racing form or the week's football; only nods and raised eyebrows conveyed the general sense of unease. Even gossips like Mrs Fenwick kept their mouths shut, waiting to see what would happen next, waiting for their lunch hour so they could talk in private. Only the receptionists, overloaded with calls, gave the impression of enjoying a normal busy day. The young student on the front desk must have wondered if all days in the newspaper business were going to be as exciting or as terrifying as this. Miss Nixon, who would have taken the day off to show how hurt she was had she not been summoned in panic by Archie Stubbs the newsroom chief, held the fort as she so often had, wondering at the same time where on earth M. was and whether any of them would have a job come Monday morning. The time for apologies was now past. M. must fight for his paper and his professional life.

Queedy's last sketch, describing his time with the Ambulist, was never published. In it, he wrote of Jäger's life as a farmer on the edge of the desert east of Grootfontein, a whole day's truck ride from the edge of civilisation, the Omatako river. He painted a picture of a whitewashed weatherboard house bleached by the sun, of the kraals where cattle were herded before being driven off to market; of Jäger's mother worn to a thread by care and the loss of so many of her men in that hard land. He wrote of his personal shock at finding that the Ambulist had been married at the age of thirteen to a ju/'wasi girl; that they had been in love. The courtship had been informal, just a boy and a girl holding hands and exchanging small gifts – a bracelet of beads from her, a woven gathering bag and an ostrich egg from him. His parents and hers had spoken and agreed to the match. The ceremony, like all bushman marriages, had been short, a small gathering after sunset and the preparation of the girl's new marital shelter, her tshu. Both parties were free to dissolve the marriage but neither had ever sought another partner.

The girl waited for her husband when he was sent to Windhoek to be schooled. She waited for him during the long years when he was at University in South Africa, seeing him only for a few weeks during vacations; he, for his part, had never chosen to be with a white girl. The Ambulist, Queedy noted, lapsed into the clicking sounds of the bushman tongue when he described people or places in the bush, and pronounced his wife's name N!ai with an extraordinary softness and evident affection.

When he moved back to the family farm in 1955 after his father's death, he spent part of his time at home and part in the bush with his wife and her mother's family. The group had what amounted to ownership, or n!ore, of the rights to a small waterhole. When he was with them the Ambulist hunted with the men and danced with them at the full moon or when there was a special healing dance. At that time Jäger was intimately involved with the establishment of the Western Kalahari Game Reserve. He was pilloried by the black independence movement for helping the bushman to adapt to a mix of sedentary and bush life, acknowledging that the old way was gone forever. The independence movement believed he should have armed them and fought the white apartheid government in South Africa. His controversial approach to the indigenous people and his marriage, so offensive to many whites, attracted to him the label of a notorious liberal and worse: a kaffir-lover.

Disaster had befallen the Ambulist and his wife: he was arrested for illegally marrying a non-white under the new urban apartheid rules imposed on the Protectorate of South-West Africa. He spent six months in prison. When he was released he found his wife had been resettled in one of the government's corrugated iron villages, where bushmen were fed on food aid which they found inedible, wasted by western disease and corrupted by alcohol. The Ambulist found her and took her back to her homeland and there they had lived for two more years before he was arrested again.

This much Queedy had discovered. He still did not know what had happened to the wife because the Ambulist would not speak of it. He hoped his readers would understand his discretion on the matter. Queedy compensated with a dramatic account of the night of the gale when his tent had blown completely away, never to be found. He admitted that at first he had found life under the stars strange and uncomfortable; that he was now more or less used to it and that it had helped him to bond further with the fascinating man whose company it was his privilege to enjoy. Besides, with the warmer weather and a few days of glorious sunshine, it was hard to feel at odds with the world. It was a beautiful spring.

Queedy made his camp not with the Ambulist in the relative shelter of the old cottage but close to the former site of his tent, in the lee of the Rigg. He built a shelter, under the Ambulist's guidance, from two or three small birch trees cut, formed and bound with twine, then roofed with fresh spring heather, and he would have admitted to no one a childish pride in his achievement: the shelter stood up and was vaguely waterproof. With the longer days it might gradually be improved. In a note attached to his latest sketch he asked M. for some more practical equipment: a good bush knife, a small saw, some twine and a light tarpaulin or basha such as soldiers used, for emergencies. He wanted more honey too, and more tobacco. The Ambulist had freely shared with his companion an extraordinary wealth of knowledge about the land and all that lived on it, and in return these small presents were as nothing. In the Ambulist's world the exchange of gifts was the warp which held society in its unbreakable weave. Living in nature, with nature, as he now was, Queedy began to appreciate the importance of maintaining the formal gestures of the bush; for here, where any man might take another's possessions, trust and solidarity were absolute values.

Queedy posted his sketch, as he had before, in the incongruous little red mail box at the remote crossroads. Even the sight of a metalled road now seemed like a modern, quite unnecessary intrusion into the privacy of the hills, even though he half-wished that M. had been there to meet him, as before. He craved chocolate and a hot shower, a light to read by at night; a table; how he missed something as simple and essential as a table. He longed for conversation in which he did not feel so inferior, so unable to contribute except as antagonist or pupil. It was true that in the matter of cosmology he could hold his own with the Ambulist; but even then, his dry mathematical explanations shrivelled before the Ambulist's primordial creation myths, the richness of the stories he knew from his years on the edge of the desert where the night sky was a circus, a cathedral, an amphitheatre of human dreams, fears and aspirations.

Queedy did not, curiously, miss his tent. Its loss had almost crushed him in those dark hours of terrible unprotected frailty when he had felt bereaved, slighted. His base desire to fly, to escape, to enjoy again the comfort, not of his own characterless apartment but the intimacy of the Tower-house kitchen, was overcome only by a presentiment of fate or destiny, which began to pervade his thoughts without him being truly aware of it. Fatalism, as the Ambulist knew, was the shield in the armoury of the wanderer, as it was to the sailor and the warrior: knowledge of the bullet with one's name on it; of the great wave or the rudderless ship, of the effortless power of nature to pluck any of earth's creatures from this world into the next. This was the reduction of the ego to an infinitesimal speck, the irreversible knowledge of one's irrelevance in the great scheme of the universe. It was a catharsis that might crush a man, or liberate him.

In making the long return journey to the camp from his postal mission Queedy experienced what others of a more metaphysical bent might have called an epiphany. His senses were completely alive to the moment: to the crunching of his brogues, now battered almost beyond recognition, on the dry stony dust of the path; to the call of the skylark above and the mewling of the curlew out of sight somewhere on the moor; to the sweet smell of fresh moorland grass and the dry, peaty musk of heather. The sun's living heat soaked his skin. His body, so often strained and aching, lost all awareness of what it was to walk and hurt and it was as if his mind became entirely detached from the mechanical action of placing one foot before the other. It floated above him. He might, indeed, have been watching himself from a distance, playing no part in the physical process of the journey except as onlooker. He tried to force himself to re-join the working parts – his heart and lungs, arms, legs, hands and feet – and found that he could not. He was unable consciously to operate the mechanisms, could barely oversee them. They knew how to walk, at what pace and in which direction, and he became as it were a passenger. He was outside of them, floating, present but not active. Was this what the Ambulist felt, this beatific detachment? Was this how all wanderers came to be? Was this what it was like to walk forever?

As far as Gaunt was concerned it had been a good day's business. Jumped before they could push him, he had. He'd not allowed M. the satisfaction of giving him the bollocking, of kicking him out of his office. He hadn't used the room anyway since the boss had seen fit to fumigate it. How could you work in a room that looked and smelled like a urinal? After all the years he had given to the *Courier*: what a kick in the teeth to be treated like that. Anyway, it was about time he moved on, pastures new and all that. He might give Harry Tanning a bell, see what the craic was, put a few feelers out. A good old-fashioned reporter was always in demand, knew the pack drill, all the wrinkles, no fuss. Albie Rooi would see him right anyway. Not that he expected Albie to come up with a fistful of readies, not as such. It was just that opportunities might arise in that direction and if he kept him on a shortish rope, well, Albie needed him more than the other way round. The direct route to cash and a small payback for M. and the snotty kid was to blow their cosy little Friday sketch out of the water. A quick call to another mate of his who had connections on the news desk at a redtop and Bob was your uncle. Yes, they had it coming, the whole bloody lot of them.

Gaunt went directly back to the *Courier* following his enlightening and potentially profitable meeting with Albie Rooi, missing the hurried departures of both M. and the distraught Miss Nixon. Miss Nixon, having abandoned her small office in a hurry, had left its door open and Gaunt, sensing that he might strike while the iron was hot, had availed himself of the key to M.'s room and acquired the editor's copy of the Ambulist's map, in possession of which he triumphantly left the building, never to return.

Gaunt had not left the *Courier* more than five minutes before he saw the copy almost type itself before his eyes. Gentle giant revealed as terrorist. No, not quite: Gentle giant was a bomber. Better. A quick résumé of Jäger's fabricated autobiography – the homely African friend-of-the-natives, quite Davy Crockett that had been, hadn't it, and they had all fallen for it. And the miracles, blimey, who would swallow that load of bull? Well Gaunt, for one, hadn't been fooled for a minute. Who did they think he was? Right from that first moment in the bar where they served that bloody awful beer and the Ambulist had been sitting in the corner reading Shelley. Oh yes, he had sussed him out there and then. What a give-away: Shelley was the original bloody anarchist masquerading as a romantic poet and wanderer; here was another.

So, yes, quick résumé, then the reveal: sources close to the South African Government have passed this reporter information, no, secret files, that would be more satisfactory, secret files which show that the so called Ambulist was wanted for mass murder and had been on the run for more than twenty years, disguised as... in fact passing himself off as... Jesus. Or a tramp. And here he was now, roaming the English countryside, begging food off innocent people, faking miracles and scaring children from a village school. A con man, in fact. Not only that, this reporter had just come into possession of a map, formerly belonging to Jäger, which showed he was planning a campaign of... yes, well that was a good question that was, planning a campaign of what? Difficult to say. There would be money at the bottom of it, there always was. Some giant con. Someone would leave him a fortune in a will after he pretended to cure their cat or some such. Sort of thing Yank preachers were always up to, only give him credit, Jäger looked the part. And even Albie confessed that he hadn't found the bank account. Yet.

The map Gaunt had liberated from M.'s desk was a bit of a poser. Did M. understand the code – the markings, circles, arrows? Perhaps leave it at that and promise more to come on the map, which experts would be deciphering for clues to the present whereabouts of this dangerous murderer. Meantime he would let Albie know he had it, maybe let him have a very quick shufti, just to get the juices flowing, then Albie would be in no doubt that he needed Gaunt's help. No doubt at all. Gaunt would take the map home, see what could be made of it and while he was doing that his old reliables, his network of narks, postmen, delivery drivers, publicans and newsagents who had stood him in good stead these many years would be out looking for Jäger and he would be buggered if they didn't come up with something in a couple of days. Meantime, he typed out the deadly copy which was to plunge M. and the *Courier* into crisis and despatched it by facsimile the three hundred miles to London.

Instead of catching the bus Gaunt walked home, stopping only for a quick one at the Blacksmith's, another old haunt of his. On this balmy April evening it was still light so he strolled back, enjoying a fag and the thought that he wouldn't have to go to work tomorrow though to be sure there was plenty to do. The sound of the starlings twittering on their telegraph wires and the spill of students on the pavements outside bars reminded him of his days as an NCO bashing youngsters into shape. They weren't a bad lot, most of them. Such was Gaunt's mood that he bought his wife a bottle of wine from the offie on the way. She liked a nice Cabernet Sauvignon, did the wife. He would tell her about the *Courier* nonsense another time, once a few offers had come in. No need to get the old girl excited. Pity he wouldn't see Mrs Fenwick again. Very ladylike, very elegant was Mrs Fenwick. A smile replaced the jutting lip for a second or two, unobserved by the distracted students chatting away loudly around him but noticed with interest by the red-haired man strolling casually along the pavement on the opposite side of the road, looking up from the street map that he was evidently consulting.

Queedy, in his apprentice bivouac, slept deeply in a state almost of grace with no thought either for the past or for the future. A breeze caressed the heather fronds of his roof; the dawn glanced in at his bower. A blue tit, curious, hopped inside and pecked at his feet for crumbs. Physical exhaustion overwhelmed him but his mind was free from burden, uncaring of danger and insensitive to pain or irritation. His dreams were of flying, of soaring effortlessly over the waveform hills of the Border with buzzards for company and with an extraordinary clarity of vision which scrutinised all of creation but did not judge it.

The Ambulist woke a little before dawn with a grey-blue misty light suffusing his vision. It was superbly cold after a brilliantly clear new-moon starlit night. With the passing minutes the sun's first yellow-white light ought to have penetrated the mist but the greyness persisted. The Ambulist raised himself and leant, confused, with his back against the wall of the old cottage. He rubbed his eyes. The mist was so dense that he could barely make out the far wall; the gables were lost in a dull continuum of the sky. The incidental thought came to him that he might be unable to see the immediate world around him not because of the mist but because he was himself blind. He reached out in front of him, held his hand up before his face. The fog was so utterly impenetrable that he could barely trace its outline, could by no means count his fingers. Was it perhaps still dark? Was the pale light itself an illusion?

The actual truth of his blindness did not come to him as a shattering revelation in a moment of poignant clarity so much as in a slow, insidious creeping sensation that began at the back of his neck and spread viscerally downwards to his bowels. The innate human instinct to cry out for help in such a moment of pure horror had, in the Ambulist, been suppressed through long experience to prevent him from exposing any sign of weakness. Even so, the primal urge to fly, to cry, to roar in defiance was strong in him and he had to feel for the wall behind him, and grip the stones with all his strength, to convince himself that the outside world, at least, still existed in solid form.

He had known. First in the woods on his way back to Halstane, the day when the fish appeared in the holy well on Good Friday. His eyes had blurred for a while then and although they had cleared soon afterwards a part of his consciousness had stored the uncomfortable fact; stored it somewhere safe, out of the way. By the fire, one night, he had struggled to see his hand before his face and it had scared him. He had stumbled, too, crossing the river, with Queedy on the bridge watching him, and he knew Queedy had been bemused. Yes, he had known something was wrong. His mother had known too, in the weeks and months before her sight failed. She had tormented herself in self-denial, said nothing until it was too late to help her. It was a family trait.

The man who walks forever does not have the luxury of retiring to his rocking chair and listening to the world pass by from his veranda while his progeny care for his needs. Like all wanderers and gatherers, he must die if he cannot forage. No institution stands ready to ease his passage through infirmity towards death. The Ambulist knew this and accepted it as the eland accepts its fate when the hunter runs it down. It turns to face its nemesis and stands there with neither hope nor fear but the purest knowledge of its future. It accepts. The Ambulist had no kin to look after him. Nor did he, in that moment, believe he could decide his own fate by walking into the bush and waiting to be taken mercifully by some other predator: it was not his privilege to know that he was being stalked by a deadly enemy. But the life of the wanderer does not allow room for cowardice or abject surrender. If he could not decide his fate, he could at least hold the reigns in his own hands. He must walk forever, and when he could walk no more through fatigue or ailment he would lie down and then, let others decide. The equation of time was, perhaps, returning to its starting point.

The Ambulist gathered his few possessions in his old grip. Although he could not see them, he had long experience of feeling for objects in the dark of night – not just the dark of the new moon or starless nights under heavy cloud but also the dark of the prison cell, where he had been kept without light as punishment, as policy. You like it black, they had shouted at him: you like it black, you can have it black. Blind he may now be; incapable he was not. He took strength from his sureness of touch, from the acuteness of his hearing which had also been honed in the bush and behind bars where any slight noise might herald relief, pain, threat or promise.

The Ambulist, falling back on these skills, probed his way from the cottage to the foot of the Rigg. He knew now that the sun had risen: he felt it hot and comforting on his right cheek and hand: just north of east. A breeze humming in the copse of Scots pines told him in which direction Queedy's camp lay and he skirted it, fearful of waking the boy who would be concerned, solicitous, would want to help, would be a nuisance and a distraction. The breeze, he knew, came from the north-west and so he kept it on his port quarter until he walked full square into the low drystone wall which bounded the improved pasture from the moor. He followed the wall, feeling for it with his hand until he reached the gate and was safely within the parallel lines of the old drove way. This would take him high up onto the Border ridge, for mile upon mile. In his mind's eye he was able to read the familiar nuances of the trail ahead, its subtle windings, its dips and crests, the smells of hedgerows and running water. He knew he would be able to reach down to the ground and rub his fingers in the soil, taste it, and know the land by its flavour. He would be able to sense the loom of each new horizon, the compass of the hills. He knew where edible roots, shoots and greenery were to be had at this season. He knew where a certain hazel bush grew, from which he would be able to cut himself a good stick. A stick would help. Even thus disabled, walking not with his usual imposing, rhythmic stride but like Queedy, like a dweller, self-conscious and cautious, he could make progress. By early evening he would be close to the highest point of the volcanic massif and Queedy would be sure not to find him there even if he should come looking. Where his feet would take him after that he did not at present consider. It was enough to be away and on the move, free from encumbrance and from the responsibility of leading the boy any further through his faltering steps towards self-knowledge. For neither man, that glorious spring morning, did the future exist.

Queedy rose in a state of euphoria which did not outlast his early attendance at the Ambulist's cottage bivouac. He anticipated with genuine pleasure the first cup of tea, brewed on the small camp fire; the spoonful of honey, the accompanying cigarette, the profound sensibility which the dawn brought to those who had chosen not to dwell. The intensity of the external world was now alive to him, pressed him, touched him on all sides, urged him to exist wholly within his own immediate experience of it. He wanted to tell the Ambulist that he had at least transcended the narrow fictions of journalism, had won the knowledge of his own uncertainty. The Ambulist might have listened, might have offered a non-committal grunt in return; might even have put Queedy down, dismissed his revelation as immaturity. But the Ambulist was not at his bivouac; the fire's embers were cold.

The realisation that the Ambulist had left him alone and then, gradually, that he might have wholly abandoned the camp and moved on without telling Queedy, came suddenly on him. The nomad had moved on from the Tower-house without a backward glance, walked away from his fire and shabby camp by the lake careless of social form: no goodbye, no thanks or acknowledgement. The immediate past was discarded along with its material evidence as if memory was leaf litter to be consumed by the worms. In this respect he was, like a wild animal, free from all obligations. In a sense this was what made him free. But for Queedy this new abandonment, this casting aside of the shackles of obligation, could be nothing other than a personal rejection.

In spite of a sort of factual appreciation of the Ambulist's beliefs, of his modus operandi, Queedy felt in that moment a stunning intestinal pain that forced him to his knees on the floor of the old shieling, where the sole evidence of the Ambulist's passing residence was the little heap of ashes where last night's fire had burned. It might have been Queedy's funeral pyre. The evidence of the Ambulist's premeditated flitting, an actual bodily insult, struck him like a blow, felled him, laid him out there and then. Shepherds had built, lived and died in this place, dwelt in it summer after summer over the generations, and finally retreated from it. Nature had come to reside here, stripping the stones of their status as building blocks in a human dwelling and reclaiming them as if the ruins were no more than a recent geological eruption, fit for colonisation like a quiescent volcano. Each tenant had left his mark save for the last. The Ambulist might never have been there.

Queedy's own journey now appeared tragically incomplete. He had, in his epiphany the previous day, deluded himself that he was being initiated into a sort of wanderer's club, that he had been incorporated into the company of those who did not belong. The Ambulist had taken to walking forever because he had once been loved. Queedy might join the same club because he had not. There were no rules, only the rite of walking and not dwelling. Now, with immense force, came the disillusioning thought that the cottage, the Rigg, the camp which he had shared with the Ambulist, had become for him a place of dwelling. The Ambulist was its patriarch; the patch of ashes was its hearth, the illimitable canopy of the heavens its roof and protection. Queedy was its son, the son who would stay at home.

The Ambulist must have known this too and so, Queedy now reasoned, that was why he had left, throwing his protégé on the mercy of the unsigned trail. Queedy had been cast off. Again. M., in his clumsy, kind, avuncular way had warned him and, in his way, Pieter had warned him too. His companionship had been incidental. He had not cared if Queedy were there or not. The Arnesens must have sensed it too, just as the headmaster who expelled him from school had. They, after all, had encouraged him to take this blind leap from comfort into danger and fear. And yes, even old Gaunt's tough love had in its way had the same purpose at heart. They had all seen that Queedy, the wounded orphan, must be weaned off his fatal dependence on the spectre of his father's non-existent love. But if he now saw these things for himself, who was there to tell, to seek approbation from? What was he to do?

In the dark of the night the Ambulist came upon the highest point of the Border ridge and reached the outer limits of familiarity. He could not read his map, try as he might. His wanderings had not before taken him further. A tramp wind came barging out of the northwest across the blunt dome of the Cheviot and chasing at its heels a pernicious chill tore at his greatcoat and his wild grey hair. Fear and fatigue came calling like ill-intentioned guests and the Ambulist, rigid with cold, knew he must find shelter. No tree grew at this height; no shepherd's hut or sheep stell had ever been built in such a wild place, the haunt only of the buzzard and the wild goat, where every step from the trail beckoned the unwary into sucking bog or endless seas of life-sapping bent-grass. Once, from near this place, the Ambulist had spied a refuge hut, a tiny wooden cabin built for those unwary souls caught out by sudden blizzard or storm. His remaining senses sought it desperately in the darkness of his plight, but in vain.

A dazzling ceiling of stars might have offered him succour or guidance, but he was blind to it. If he lay down at this place the night would take him and he must die. He did not wish it. He must come down off the high ground where the wind could not track and hunt him down. Now he squatted, face close to the ground, and reached out to the wind, probing it, interrogating it, examining its every twist and swerve, the subtle chaos of its changing contours, the rushing cataract of its onward flight. Here, his outstretched palm, scanning the air before him, came upon a turbulent clue, a forensic echo of some

obstacle, some fault or rift to windward. He let it draw him on, alert
to every small nuance in this tidal race of Arctic air. Before him, close
now, was a break in the leviathan mass of the Cheviot. With his stick
he tried the uneven ground before him: an outcrop of rock, too small
for shelter; a pool of water which might be a spring; a spring which
might lead him downwards. The land sloped away before him, tugging
at him to follow. A change, a faltering in the pitch of the wind's cry,
led the Ambulist on more urgently. His foot missed its step. Then,
nothing. Into the jaws of Hell the Ambulist plummeted, swallowed by
its yawning gape: the black mouth of Blizzen Gorge. The night and the
land closed above him and took him in their careless arms.

With the day came pain and light. The sun's heat and the trickle
of a tiny waterfall nearby roused the Ambulist to consciousness. Sleep
had not overcome him. He had lain senseless through the night, his
giant form racked and torn, legs bent beneath him, arms at his sides
but limp, almost as if detached. His great craggy, lifeless face was
shrouded by filthy grey-brown hair, lank and fronded with moss. The
greatcoat, drenched and smeared with black peaty mud, was like a
coffin. The Ambulist might have been some ancient stag-headed oak
whose heart had succumbed finally to disease, whose roots had in the
moment of defeat let go their fingertip grasp on the earth: crashing to
the ground, shattered, to become at last a part of the land from which
it had sprung.

He was not dead, though, and in the creeping acknowledgement
that he yet lived but was broken, there was also a sort of stupid
awareness of the fuzzy line of the ridge far above him, black against a
pristine blue sky. He could see, or at least tell the difference between
the earth and the heavens. He did not yet try to move: the pain was
overwhelming and could not be located with precision. His mind sent
emissaries to each part of his body, requesting information, assessing
damage. He wanted very much to raise a hand to his face, to wipe a
strand of hair from his mouth, but did not yet dare. He waited, and as

he waited the notes of a beautiful song came to mind. It was a song he had first heard many years before, as a child. There was nothing especially poignant about it; the tune was one of those which bushmen girls sang to while away the time spent digging in the dirt at the foot of a tree for an edible root. But the memory of the girl, the scent of the dark orange earth in that intense heat and the lilting, hip-swaying melody accompanied by the rhythmic thud of the digging stick in its hole, was as clear to the Ambulist as if the girl were there now before him. Its implication, its message, was equally unmistakable: he must be up and looking for food while the sun shone and the rain stayed its hand; while he could see.

The Ambulist had fallen far from the ridge but his headlong descent into the chasm had been broken by a boulder, an erratic glacial giant tossed capriciously down by the Gods to lie there in apparent anticipation of this meeting. The Ambulist, to be sure, had come off worse from the encounter. He had broken one of his ribs. There was a livid gash down his right shin such that the bone was exposed and would not support his weight. His right shoulder had been torn from its socket and although he had contrived to return it to its proper place the pain brought wave after wave of nausea with it. No pain could have masked his exultation at the partial restoration of his vision. He was able only to see with his left eye, and that imperfectly – the other brought nothing except a haze of light and shade – but for the moment he regained command of his destiny. His grip, which blinded he would have had little hope of retrieving, lay perched absurdly on top of the boulder more or less as if he had rested it there while taking lunch. Now that he was able to survey his condition and his surroundings, he understood both the folly which had led him here and the geography of the place. The wind must have backed while he was on the Border ridge and its false trail had led him toward the most dangerous defile in the entire massif.

Blizzen Gorge had taken many a rider, many a beast, swallowed whole and never to be seen again. No shepherd, no walker ventured there unless he was a fool or desperate for oblivion. It had been cut from the loaf-like dome of the plateau into a sharp V by a brute blade: ten thousand years of rain, snow and ice. Inverted, it would have resembled the ocean-slicing keel of a racing yacht. It was almost inaccessible from its base by virtue of a voracious bog of watery peat and from the ridge by the precipice from which the Ambulist had fallen. For much of the year parts of the gorge did not see the sun from dawn till dusk. Patches of snow remained clinging to the slopes. Below him the trickling streamlet tumbled away through moss and boulders. A hundred, perhaps two hundred feet further down a line of scrub birch trees clung to the slope and far, far below that the stream lost itself in the mire.

For the moment the remoteness of Blizzen Gorge was a virtue. The Ambulist could not in any case escape it while his wounds were so severe. He must have time to heal. Time and shelter. Fortune brought him the latter. A dark shadow beneath the ridge on the west side of the gorge suggested an overhang of rock which might provide some relief from rain and wind for a day or so. Water there was in plenty. In his grip the Ambulist had the scrapings of a jar of Queedy's honey and part of a loaf. It was paltry fare, but even in this bleak, beautiful place the wanderer had nature's means at his disposal. Moss he would collect to cleanse his wounds. He could set a snare for a rabbit, and at this time of year swelling bulbs of ramsons and the tender leaves of wood sorrel might be found if he could climb down far enough. For now he must investigate his shelter. He must dry his clothes or freeze, and there was no prospect of gathering wood here. Looking up at the sun he gauged its passage and saw that it must be the hour before midday. The stick which he had cut from the hazel bush the previous day in his blindness he was able to retrieve by crawling sideways on his bruised but uninjured left side. Now he must stand.

The shadow which promised the Ambulist shelter lay two

hundred yards and more away, high up across the stream and beyond
a lethal scree of volcanic rocks. He used his stick to brace himself
upright against the slope, the handle of the grip crooked in his left
armpit. More often than not he was forced to scramble on his knees,
breathing hard against his straining rib, wincing, his fractured body
fighting against each fresh insult, his leg bleeding and raw beneath his
improvised bandage. Twice he stopped to make himself a cigarette, to
recover his breathing and his wits, to press a finger against the broken
rib and check that it was not cutting at his insides. His progress was
tracked with interest by a pair of buzzards wheeling contemptuously
above the ridge in relay, alert for any prey to feed to their voracious
young. The Ambulist was not, as yet, willing carrion. Two more hours
it took him to reach the base of the scree slope that he must traverse.
Two more hours of cuts and scrapes, of panting, silently screaming
pain: five yards gained and ten lost; ten gained and two lost, five more
gained and lost. His reward was to find not an overhang, but a cave.

Selena was determined to bring M.'s message of warning to the
Ambulist and bring Queedy away, back to the safety of the Tower-
house. Her parents accepted that they could not dissuade her. The
protective instinct in her was strong and her will was not easily diverted. She had an aptitude for deflecting attention from herself; she
moved lightly and quietly on the land. She was a satellite, unjudging
of the world, barely interacting with it, unfailing in her steadiness and
always watching. She might, as M. had romantically supposed, have
been plucked from the Atlantic breakers, a tail-less mermaid who
cast her limpid eye with faint interest over the complexities of human
society but who cared little for its troubles. The animals in her charge
could rely absolutely on her because their needs were simple, direct

and unfailingly honest. They demanded her care and only that. They did not require to be analysed or for her to manage and judge their relations. Queedy had supposed that she saw him as one more of her charges, to be fed and watered and patted on the head like the goat, and he might have supposed that by extension she saw the Ambulist as a feral animal, yet to be domesticated but to be nurtured none the less.

To the extent that Selena did not care to judge human folly or to involve herself in engineering the society around her, M. and Queedy – and others before them – were right. For the most part this modest child did not tug on or try to break free from the thread which, binding her to the earth, yet kept her orbiting, detached from it. And yet, like an Artemis, she might on a whim reach down and play a pawn either with caprice or wielding the moral baton of constant watchfulness. Her parents knew her, knew that she was of them but did not belong to them, that she belonged only to herself and must answer only to herself.

Was it because of this watchfulness, this disinterested vision, that she alone noticed the photograph, that it caught her eye and drew her to it? The heap of images had lain there overnight on the kitchen table amongst a huddle of wine glasses, pots, pans and plates. M. had spread them out so that the Arnesens might judge for themselves the pictorial history that had accumulated to damn the Ambulist as a hunted terrorist: a photograph of Jäger as a young man graduating from the University of the Cape of Good Hope with his law degree: already the intense gaze, the smile lines, the strong mouth; touched even then by sadness and loss but not yet wise; a picture of the exterior of the prison in which he had been kept; a grainy press shot of the Ongandjera car bombing and an accompanying article naming Jäger as one of twenty suspects; a family photograph of him as an adult with his arm around his mother's waist – the years after his return to the farm; another of him with a group of bushmen grinning. Was one of these the wife of whom Queedy, but not M. or the Arnesens, knew?

The photograph that M. had not noticed, leafing through them on the train, which none of them had seen in the candlelight of evening and which the girl's eye now caught in the morning as she began to clear the kitchen table, was of Pieter aged, she supposed, about forty, dressed in a smart safari suit wearing one of those queer hats with the folded-up brim, quite the Boer. He was standing on the steps of what must have been a court of law – in Windhoek, perhaps: a classical portico, Palladian pediment and fluted columns, very legal, very colonial, an unreadable Latin motto carved in relief in the white limestone. Next to the Ambulist were two bushman women, mother and daughter possibly. The dress of the younger one just touched Jäger's jacket sleeve. On the other side stood a man about ten years younger than Pieter. He wore a white or maybe a cream linen suit, slightly crumpled, and co-respondent shoes. His hair was short at the back, the front brushed back and greased, and he wore no hat. The tie was tied with a thin knot, very sixties. Had not the ages, dates, times and place been so absolutely wrong, there was something about this man which suggested an older John Queedy. It could not be, of course. She slid the photograph out from the pile which half-hid it. The group, she now saw, was surrounded by reporters and photographers. It was an occasion. The two men were smiling, shaking hands in mutual congratulation. The women at their sides were smiling too, but looked uncomfortable with the cameras, with the attention, with the western clothes they wore.

Selena took the photograph over to the light of the kitchen window. She examined the face of the man who looked like Queedy. A little like Queedy, yes, but not him. Older, with intense eyes, with more lines and hair evidently already receding; a supercilious smile on the same thin, expressive lips. The same bones and posture, certainly, and those delicate, artistic hands. On the reverse of the photograph was written in fading pencil: Jäger, Smith, N!ai and Dil'ai, Windhoek, and the date. It was the year when the Western Kalahari Game Reserve was legally enshrined by the white government in Pretoria. It was the year in which the Ambulist was sent to prison for the second time. It was the year of the massacre in Ongandjera. It was the last time the Ambulist saw his wife. It was the year when Carew Smith unexpectedly turned up in Dublin after all those years with nothing, hoping his old friend would forgive and forget, would give him a job, help him get back on his feet. It was the year of betrayal.

Chapter Eleven

Blizzen

Selena Arnesen might have made a successful career as a confidential agent. Watchful and discreet, slight of frame and deft in movement, she neither courted the external world's interest nor made demands of it outside her family. The Ambulist read, in her unjudging gaze, her passivity and stoicism, a fellow wandering spirit. Neither was feckless; neither lacked a concept of home. Their shared secret was that they dwelt entirely within themselves so that, like the hermit crab and the tortoise, they carried their home with them. In one another they recognised those attributes which conventional society found so disconcerting. They needed no one. The Ambulist had reached this state through pain, endurance and enlightenment. In Selena it was innate. She was, in truth, complete. Like that other pale nomad, the moon, she seemed to exist only in reflected light, to be noticed only when pointed at; she and the earth tugged at one another faintly, and at a distance.

Often during her childhood she had vanished from the Arnesens' city apartment. She had never intended to run away, nor did she feel any sense of liberation or purpose in the act. She could not explain herself, nor did she desire to. The girl would take a notion to explore, or to meditate by walking, or merely to initiate a physical activity. She rarely had a destination in mind. On untold occasions her parents had fretted and feared for her safety. In her youth they remonstrated with her, after days when they thought she must have come to terrible harm on the city's streets. Always she would return, oblivious to their concern, bewildered by it, without any sense of shame or guilt but aware in their pain that she must have committed some fault which she could not identify. She learned that coming to the place where her parents dwelt gave them comfort, and so pleased them. She had no need of 'home' for herself because home was wherever she was. Freya and Jareld, for their part, learned through the passing years not to ask, not to argue but to let her loose, because if they did not she would gnaw and chew at herself like a caged creature and her spirit would die. She would grow to hate them. She had no fear of the city's dark corners, nor did she apprehend that behind every tree in the forest lay a monster or some other manifestation of evil. It was as if the atavistic human distrust of dark, empty or silent places, the panic fear of nature, did not touch her. No harm had ever come to her and it now seemed evident to her parents, or at least they were able to convince themselves, that she enjoyed some special celestial protection. No wonder that M. thought she must have come from beneath the sea.

Her father insisted on driving her in his battered old Land Rover to the crossroads where the little red post box stood sentinel. They went by the county's back roads, wary of pursuit, and arrived as the warm late April sun was at its full height. They did not know, could not know, that Queedy's last sketch and his list of requests – perhaps the only letter that had been posted at this place since his last – even now lay waiting in the box to be collected. They had, however, in some measure anticipated Queedy's needs in bringing a hamper of chocolate bars, honey and tobacco.

From the passenger seat Selena leant across, kissed her father on the forehead, and was gone. Jareld, biting his lip to stifle a sentimental declaration of paternal adoration, returned to the Tower-house with unprecedented thoughts of foreboding. He absolutely trusted his daughter; his love overflowed and his eyes filled with unchecked tears as he drove. He had always managed to convince himself, if not his wife, that Selena was safe. He had always been right. But never before had such evil been on her trail and he had a strong urge now to turn around and be with her in whatever adventure destiny might bring them all. He knew he must not. He began to sing himself a cheerful song but found he could not. He gripped the wheel tight with both hands and drove on along the county's sinuous ancient byways, regretting every yard that slipped irrevocably beneath the wheels of his vehicle.

For an hour or more, as her light step consumed the track unwinding before her, Selena could see ahead greyish clumps of smoke scurrying away to leeward. That it came from the shell of the old cottage high on the hill she did not doubt. Its extravagance did not seem congruent with Pieter's abstemiousness and as she drew nearer she began to wonder why the two men had lit a fire at all during the day. She did not share her father's sense of unease, however, and did not change her pace. This was the trail upon which Queedy had experienced his epiphany. The land's oceanic rise and fall, each crest opening a new view, each trough closing behind her, was in perfect sympathy with her own lilting rhythm. Selena was not, like Queedy, susceptible to the cathartic possibilities of such an intense experience. Nevertheless, she swam in the current of immediacy, exulting in the day, all her senses alive to the trail and the moment.

Queedy stood unmoving inside the shell of the old cottage, staring at an enormous bonfire, a snarling, spitting, hissing air-quake of a blaze. This was no back-garden dweller's pyromania; it was the unleashing of an animal spirit, cornered, scared and dangerous, whose cage door the young man had recklessly, carelessly thrust open. Queedy seemed transfixed by the roaring flames, rendered into a state almost of trance by the catastrophic promethean forces he had liberated.

He did not immediately notice the girl's arrival. He had just lit a cigarette, an inferno in miniature which he periodically drew on, exhaling the sweet grey smoke in its own tiny plume above him. Selena, pausing to watch him for a moment, saw with half-smiling approval that Queedy's hands were grimy with soot, that his fingernails were long and dirty, that his hair was lank and that he had not shaved in several days. She noticed also, with the concern of the experienced stock woman, that his cheeks were drawn, his eyes bloodshot and his posture tense. His arms were stiff at his sides, his shoulders hunched forward.

The absence of the Ambulist, who would surely have deprecated such conspicuous consumption, she immediately read as either a source or an effect of conflict. Had the two men fought? Had Queedy proved too demanding in his need for attention, for instruction? Her sharp eye noticed another absence. No camp functioned without a kettle or pan; moreover a pan with water permanently boiling or simmering in it ready for tea, for washing, for filling bottles. There was no pan, and therefore Pieter, wherever he was, had taken it with him.

How long had he been gone? That he should leave the vulnerable young man without means of boiling water was disturbing evidence of an irrevocable split. It was hard to imagine that this hopelessly impractical youth could already have learned to look after himself, to improvise, to survive out here alone. That he was burning so much precious wood in a single fire seemed in itself to prove his unfitness.

    - Hello John. (She says it softly so as not to startle him; he turns slowly and appears not to comprehend her presence immediately)

    - He has gone (he says, after a pause, not looking at Selena but past her, into the beyond).

- Yes. (Selena lays her pack down and takes out the gifts she has brought. She also removes from the pack a small camping gas stove and kettle, which she fills with water from a bottle. Queedy watches her light the stove and even he cannot help smiling at the sight of such a pathetic flame)

- For God's sake. I am bloody well dying for a cup of tea. (He scrapes out some hot embers from his bonfire, turns off her stove and places the kettle on them. He has not spent time at the Ambulist's knee for nothing) Your visit could not have been better timed. I was beginning to think I had been abandoned by the world.

- When did Pieter go?

- This morning, possibly last night.

- Did you fight?

- No.

- Did he say he was going?

- No. It must have been time to move on, don't you think? (At least, that is what he wishes to think; the alternative, that the Ambulist has walked away from Queedy because of Queedy, makes him feel sick)

- Do you know where he has gone?

- No.

- I think I have come too late.

- Why? Haven't you come to find out how your beasts are thriving in their summer pastures? As you see, one of them at least is still here and alive, if not exactly living off the land. You must come and inspect my camp. I am quite proud of it in a sort of city-boy goes scouting kind of a way.

- No, John. I am very happy that you are living well here. But I have come to warn Pieter that he is in great danger, and to take you home.

Queedy did show Selena his birch bivouac, in the manner of a child who believes he has tidied his room just sufficiently to bear parental scrutiny. He told her of his plans for improvements, of his desire to acquire more practical tools now that the Ambulist had left, now that he must become more self-reliant and independent. He would construct a better shelter next time, somewhere to hang a lantern and some sort of table to write on. He would make of his bivouac a dwelling. He led Selena on to the Rigg and, springing up from one black slab to the next as if he were showing her a newly-discovered badger's den or a stream that he had just dammed with boulders, he gave her a guided tour of the landscape inhabited by the ancestors. He told her of the hunters who had roamed these hills in millennia past when they had been shrouded in oak and pine, of the necessity for maintaining diplomatic relations with the motive forces of earth and sky.

The girl quietened him not by gesture or command, but by her passivity. She allowed him his febrile exposition, not nodding or looking him in the eye but, as once before in her yard, watching the ground as if the echo of his words off the path at their feet might offer a clearer comprehension of his cluttered, overflowing speech. And when he at last fell silent she walked away from the camp out into the heather, knowing he would follow her.

As he walked with her, Queedy heard, but did not listen. Selena told him the history of the Ambulist through the cuttings and notes which M. had brought to the Tower-house. She told him of M.'s disturbing Easter phone call and of the red-haired stranger who had appeared at the offices of the *Courier*: of Gaunt's apparent betrayal. She recounted M.'s distracted arrival at the Tower-house and the conversation in the sitting room. She explained the necessity of warning the Ambulist so that he might take flight.

The Ambulist's career as a terrorist and fugitive seemed not to register with Queedy; it bore, could bear, no tangible meaning or relation to reality or truth. He rejected it out of hand, would give it no room to settle, to fester. He refused to accept, too, that the Ambulist could be hunted down, that he might not be able to miraculously avert his fate by sheer force of moral authority. He had constructed an Ambulist who was a romantic hero, whose abandonment of him (Queedy must have offended him in some way, must have been inadequate as a pupil: too stupid, probably, too slow and weak to belong in his company) did not alter that truth. Selena did not require such a truth, or at least did not have to put a name to it. She believed that the Ambulist was incapable of an act of ideological violence, but not because she was romantically inclined. Was it, in her case, timid avoidance of the unpalatable realities of the world, or did she simply accept without judging? Had she constructed the foundation of her self on less shifting truths, or was she content to ride the flotsam and jetsam of existence and let the currents of fate take her where they would drift? She could not explain the Ambulist's disappearance; it added to the urgency of her mission, to her impatience, but she did not consciously interrogate the fact of his absence for its significance.

Queedy, finding that they had returned to the ruins of the cottage, insisted that they eat, that he make Selena a meal, a proper bush meal. There was a rabbit, caught and killed two days ago, which he would skin and roast; there was bread, honey of course. Selena refused, accepting that Queedy would take offence, even though he worried her. She would have liked very much to speak gently with him and at length, to calm him, to soothe or resolve the warring thoughts that raced through his mind that morning. But Pieter's ignorance of the immediate dangers he faced tugged at her, insisted that she move: to act, to follow and warn.

There was no time. Now, when she refused food and insisted that she must set out to find Pieter, Queedy began to prepare himself to accompany her. She could not allow it. He would be an encumbrance. It was true that he had begun to learn some of the ways of the hills, that he was physically more robust than he had been, that he might have some idea of the path the Ambulist had taken. But his discomposure made him lame like the straggler falling behind the herd, the weak animal who would eventually need to be carried or fatally compromise the herd. He would distract Selena from complete concentration on her task, which in any case seemed almost impossible. Her small hope was that Pieter's animal discretion would make him as difficult to track for his enemies as for his friends. Queedy, she knew, must return to the Tower-house whether or not he wanted to. Her mother and father would take care of him, distract him. She did not allow herself to worry that Queedy would feel himself abandoned again.

That Queedy did not immediately defer to Selena's calm insistence was, perhaps, an indication that he was not so weak as he seemed, but his manic scurrying around the camp, collecting more sticks for the fire, skinning the rabbit, preparing a spit for it, only reinforced her unease. Selena now saw that he would not listen to her. He could not listen. She could inflict a crippling wound on the young man with the weapon she carried in her pack; the photograph was like a knife in her hand: Queedy's father and the Ambulist, side by side, saluting each other before a courthouse. One of them about to betray the other. Selena had not told her parents about the picture. She did not yet know the whole meaning of it. It was possible that she did not want to know. But Queedy would. It might kill him or it might make him. But she could not allow the young man and the Ambulist to come face to face. Not now. Maybe not ever.

Queedy had run to fetch something from his bivouac. Selena took the photograph from her pack and looked at it once more. She felt a desire to toss it into the heart of his bonfire, to burn it so that its meaning should remain secret. But she did not. She thought of placing it on the ground against the wall of the cottage, where Queedy would shortly find it. She found that she could not. Instead she folded it and put it in her pocket. The tolling bell of its message must wait for another day. Even so, Selena must leave the boy with no option but to return to the Tower-house. She stowed her little gas burner and kettle so that Queedy should have no means of brewing tea or boiling water, picked up her pack, and was gone.

Gaunt pulled his car off the road that ran through the village, turned the engine off and lit a cigarette. M.'s copy of the Ambulist's map lay on the passenger seat. The day was warm. He wound down his window and let in the sound of a buzzing lawnmower and the perfume of freshly-cut grass. The only other sign of human activity was a man carrying the last of a stack of scaffolding poles from the back of a flat-bed truck into the grounds of the village school. The day-trippers and photographers, souvenir hunters and hippies, pilgrims and weirdos had gone. So had the fish, bought one and all by an American millionaire and flown at gigantic expense to his Baptist theme park in Arkansas. The story of the miraculous Easter fishes would become stratified in local folklore; the school would have its new roof and extension for a kitchen.

Picking up the map Gaunt located Halstane, which he had marked in red felt pen, with his finger. The symbol which the Ambulist had originally pencilled next to it, a bucket, took no great wit to decipher. Another bucket sign had been drawn next to Twyford, the village where the Tower-house stood. Gaunt, and M. before him, could not fail to notice that in centuries past the two settlements had been connected by a Roman road, now largely buried under fields and modern roads. Like M., Gaunt saw in the map a rich seam of possibilities for anticipating the movements of the Ambulist. Like M. he had so far been unable to parse more than a scattering of obvious symbols, which might have revealed the Ambulist's interest in certain places but which offered few clues to his itinerary, supposing he had one. In Gaunt's mind everyone had an itinerary. No one wandered just for the sake of it. Gaunt knew what the boss had not: that the Ambulist was wanted for terrorist crimes in South Africa. He was a man of violence; a man on the run. A whole swathe of wild moorland to the west of Halstane belonged to the army's artillery corps. On the map it was ringed with little red flags and if one drove along those roads one would find real flags fluttering at the roadside to warn unsuspecting walkers off the ranges during live-firing days. Now, why would the Ambulist be interested in the ranges?

Gaunt had set off early, just as he had each day since his departure from the *Courier*. That way he didn't have to explain anything to the wife. That way he could spend all the long spring days on the trail, feeding Albie little snippets as he came across them, sometimes offering him clues that were not strictly relevant – just to keep the pot simmering, so to speak. None of his reliable correspondents or informers had so far yielded a trace of the Ambulist. He had, in effect, vanished from the face of the earth. But he was out there somewhere, and now that Albie was getting impatient Gaunt must come up with something a bit more meaty: a sighting; a sniff of a sighting, even. He folded the map and put it in his jacket pocket, got out of the car and threw his cigarette stub onto the verge.

The path leading up the steep hill to the holy well, which had been bare at Easter save for scattering ewes, now dazzled with the pristine snowy blossom of the may tree and the less pure but more lively off-white scampering of spring lambs, darting at their mothers' udders and frantically wagging their tails. The spring grass was lush and moist, jewelled with daises and buttercups. The interior of the enclosure was even dimmer than it had been, for the exuberant green canopy of beech trees hanging high overhead shut out almost all sunlight. Gaunt did not expect to find anything here, did not expect to turn up clues. His only hope was that he might run across a native of the village prepared to yield intelligence. It was possible that the Ambulist, or Queedy, might have come this way again. Gaunt noticed the shabby wilted remains of the Easter bower and saw also that a determined pilgrim had waded to the centre of the pool and placed a small painted china figurine of the Virgin Mary at the base of the cross.

Gaunt ran Miss Davidson to ground in the school yard, where she was admonishing the scaffolding man – not for the first time – for the dreadful noise he made every time he dropped a scaffolding pole to the ground. Gaunt could see a row of eyes peering curious through the windows of the classroom. He would like to have a word with them too, but Miss Davidson would do. She would know if anyone did.

The red-haired assassin was not an impatient man, whatever Gaunt might think; he knew how to wait. But he did not like to wait for others. He had known Gaunts before, jumped up little non-comms, barrack-room big mouths who promised and did not deliver, small men who would always find a way of not being in the thick of the action. The sort that tapped the side of their nose, wanted everyone to think they had the gen, the inside knowledge, say no more squire. Ja, he might come up with something. Albie was not going to die not knowing. He had his own way of tracking a man down. Fifteen men and women had been named as suspects for the Ongandjera massacre. Fourteen of them were dead or in prison for the rest of their lives. One left, twenty-five years on. One left to pay for those innocent lives, to pay for the loss of his arm. For sure waiting was something he knew all about. But not waiting around.

Albie Rooi did not have the benefit of a car and neither did he possess Gaunt's enviable network of backwoods contacts. But he had hunted men across thousands of miles of veldt and coast, mountain and desert. The desert was where he had first come across Jäger, living out there almost naked like a beast with his filthy concubine. He knew how to persuade people to give him information. Of course in this country he must be discreet. He did not come with a legal mandate and he did not have the power of arrest. The police here could do nothing without being scrutinised. Man, you couldn't lay a finger on the worst criminal elements. But people everywhere liked to talk, especially of unusual events and odd people. No one who had seen the Ambulist would likely forget him.

In travelling the county by bus, in cadging lifts from farmers, postmen and delivery drivers, Rooi was tapping a source that spanned the whole region from the seashore to the Border ridge and beyond. It was only a matter of time. He had sat on the hill at the edge of the trees looking down on the Tower-house for the whole of a day, watching. He had been to Halstane before Gaunt, had spoken not to the schoolteacher but to the man delivering the scaffolding, who had given him a lift there. He read all the local papers assiduously, he looked at every advertisement card in every shop window – a missing dog, a watch found, any hint of the passing of his quarry. Sometime, someday Jäger would have to come down out of the hills to buy food. Where would he come? A tiny village, or a town? Did he know he was being tracked?

Days passed. A week. Two weeks. Rooi booked himself a room at an unobtrusive guest house in a small place on the north-east edge of the hills. Once it had been a thriving market town, growing wealthy on the profits from wool. There had been a railway station here and a hotel. It had boasted a dozen coaching inns to cater for all the horse-drawn traffic crossing the border or heading for the coastal ports. Now a few dowdy shops, a single bank and a marginal seasonal tourist business kept it from dereliction, but not by much. He called Gaunt's home, talked to his wife and left the telephone number of the guest house, in case. The wife seemed surprised that he was calling Gaunt at home; gave Rooi the office number. Interesting: the wife did not know Gaunt had been sacked. Most interesting.

Rooi spent a day chatting with the locals: shopkeepers, publicans. He allowed the landlady to bore him with a list of the best walks in the area taking in all the most scenic places. He made a temporary registration at the local doctor's, took time talking with the receptionist. He called in at a small estate agency that kept up a desultory list of local properties for rent: ten acres of rough grazing here, a worker's cottage to let there. What sort of cottages might be for rent in these parts? Did they get many requests for such things? He placed a card in the window of the last remaining newsagent. An old leather grip of his had been stolen, sentimental value more than anything; he offered a reward to anyone with information regarding its whereabouts. He gave an account of the grip by telephone to the local police office, of its contents and the time and place from where it had been stolen. As a tourist he was, he told them, particularly upset. The region had a reputation for friendliness and hospitality. The sergeant assured him that such thefts were very rare. He would keep an ear to the ground and contact him personally if he had any news. He hadn't heard of any outsiders in the town; he would be the first to know because his sister worked at the Co-op and, well, because he was the Police.

A dozen or so miles to the west, where no casual walker or policeman was ever likely to come across him, the Ambulist lay in his cave nursing his wounds, like a bear. There were days when he woke and could see nothing; some when he had some vestigial sight in his left eye, others when he thought he might recover more or less functional use of his eyes. Mostly they were worst in the morning, when they burned as if they had been sprayed with acid. With the passing of days the pain from them became more acute as his other injuries began to heal.

The first evening he ate scraps from his grip, bread and honey. Water there was in abundance in Blizzen Gorge. But the cave itself was dry. It reached back into the hillside three or four yards, its ceiling never high enough for him, or indeed for any man, to stand up; but he could sit or lie down. The floor of the cave was dusty, with the stench of a fox's spray and the droppings of rabbits hanging in the air. At first he had lain there on his left side, unable to act or think for some hours, just grateful for the blessed gift of shelter. His whole body had stiffened with bruising: his rib made every breath torture, the stabbing sensation in his shoulder was almost unendurable, his gashed leg immovably tender. He could not sleep, but must just survive. He forced his mind to take him back to the edge of the desert where he had first been taught how to overcome pain, not by fighting but by absorbing it, dissolving it into a subconscious solution of dream and trance. Beyond physical pain was the anguish of knowing that all was over except existence; that life, the life of the wanderer, the thinker, was over. It was ending not in enlightenment or acceptance but in darkness, in weakness, in fear.

Over many years the Ambulist had been permitted to learn something of the healing trances of the bushman: the giraffe dance, the liberation of the !kia energy, its dangers and applications. He had acquired a reputation as a man skilled in the use of poultices and medicines and the bushmen who knew him came to respect the potency of his n/um. Some took to calling him by a nickname which meant 'strong like the eland'. But no bushman ever practiced healing upon him or her self. The act of healing was a gift to the sick and the injured from the healer; one could not readily confer it on oneself: it exhausted the healer's own resources to the point of collapse. The energy must come from a body and mind with strength and potency. For now, the Ambulist must master his pain, and when deep sleep had overcome him and he woke again he would address the mechanics of his injuries.

The cave which the Ambulist had found was hidden from view partly by lush fronds of grass which hung down from above like extravagant eyelashes and partly by a large rock which had tumbled down from the cliff time out of mind and come to rest on the ledge that ran before it. From the opposite lip of Blizzen Gorge the cave would have looked like little more than a shadowy cleft, unworthy of investigation. Coupling foxes might use it in the spring, for they would never be disturbed here. In millennia past other, larger fauna might have come across it and used it as a lair. No human had been here in a thousand years and more. Now its inhabitant slept on and on, through a night of matt black darkness.

The sun, intensely white, rose above the far edge of the gorge and penetrated the slit of the cave's mouth two hours after a dawn of peerless clarity. The black air inside heated quickly and, had any soul been there to observe it, they would have seen a curious veil of steam rising through the eyelashes as the Ambulist's soaking greatcoat began to dry. Slowly, slowly the Ambulist drifted from sleep to consciousness. He was aware of pain long before he could calculate where he was and how he had come here. His eyes were red with fire and he could not bring himself to open them for some minutes. His limbs would not move and cramp strangled them in its sadistic ligature. But the heat soaking into him from his stewing coat finally brought him sweating into the world and memory's cruel hand smote him. In that brief but seemingly endless moment he wished to die here, to throw in his hand and surrender to the inevitability of the end game, the long trick played out.

Only humans enjoy the luxury of being able to choose if they die or not; all other animals must fight, or give in, or wait for death to come. The Ambulist, in common with the other great beasts of the bush, the lion and leopard, the buffalo and hartebeest, was stamped with a fierce inner mandate, an undeniable urge to play his hand out. In time he moved, manoeuvred himself into a sitting position, felt for his grip and from his tin flask splashed water in his face, and drank. He felt the cloth of his greatcoat, brought his fingers to his nose and smelt the warm damp mould. He wanted to take the coat off, to drape it on a warm rock in the sun and dry it thoroughly, but the thing was impossible unless he cut it off with a knife. He must dry it on, must get out of the cave and lie fully in the sun. If his sight returned sufficiently during the day he must collect dry heather for a fire, refill his water flask. If he was able to boil water on a small fire in the mouth of the cave he could brew himself a healing tea with herbs which he habitually carried in a leather pouch. He could make a poultice for the terrible wound on his shin and do something for his pain with the small mushrooms and cannabis leaves that he also carried. These were the objects that he must attain, or die. He now braced himself to accomplish them.

This first day, when instinct relieved him of the duty to contemplate his predicament, the Ambulist did no more than survive. He crawled on his left side using his stick as a lever until he could lean back against the boulder which lay before the cave. For an hour he bathed in the sun, now high and hot, letting it dry him and penetrate to his marrow. He could see little, but the purpling flowers of the new season's heather drew him towards them, and he managed to gather enough with his knife to crawl back to the cave and set a small fire to boil his water. The healing tea brought comfort and the hope that his wrecked body would respond. The mushrooms and cannabis leaves smoothed the crests of the pulsing waves of suffering on whose crashing slopes he tumbled helplessly adrift, and he lapsed into a deep senseless world of livid colours, swung back and forth on a monstrous fairground ride whose trilling music dulled even his sense of self. He did not wake again until it was dark, with a half moon rising in the east whose elevation told him it must be close to midnight. A breeze blew in at the cave's mouth and he could hear a faint burble of water plunging into the depths of the gorge. The moon's silver gilding light brought some small comfort but the familiar shapes of its craters and its starry background were lost to him and he felt bereft.

On the second day his mind cleared; his eyes were little better and stiffness made every movement a bodily insult, but he felt some strength returning in his muscles and was able to gather enough heather to store some as bedding, to ease his soreness and as spare fuel for his fire. Now he was hungry; ravenously so. He was able to set one snare near the cave but could not crawl far enough to set the several more which would have ensured a catch. He must survive still on his reserves. He had been close to starvation before, out in the bush. He was not yet starving. The weather remained kind to him. He was dry, and with a struggle he could wrestle the greatcoat from his shoulders, allow the sun to reach his skin. He ate nothing though, and a new pain pulled and twisted in his belly; small solace came from the herbs in his tea and from tobacco.

On the third day fortune favoured him. With the dawn came light, and although his eyes burned terribly, for the first time he had some vision in both. He was able to make out the lie of the ground in the gorge, marking on a mental map the small shrubs far below him, the places where he might in the next days set snares. He was not yet able to make out any useful ground plants; but then, he would not for some time be able to descend more than a few feet from the cave. He was a prisoner. Some time in the middle of that shimmering afternoon a white smudge came into his vision. A sheep had, like him, strayed too close to the lip of the gorge and fallen. It did not seem to be injured, but had rolled onto its back and now lay stranded, beached, legs pawing feebly in the air as it tried and failed to right itself against the inertia of its heavy late spring fleece. The Ambulist snatched his hunting knife from its sheath in the grip and crawled as fast as he was able towards the sheep, a hundred yards to the right and above him. The pain from his shoulder, rib and leg now was nothing: speed was all. He crossed the scree slope in a sort of one-armed swimming stroke, pulling handfuls of rocks towards him, careless of the noise he made and of the pain, sliding, rolling and bracing himself with his left leg until he reached the boulder-strewn grass. The sheep, sensing rather than seeing him, began desperately to try and fling itself over, twisting its spine in spasms, but it was so encumbered that sheer bulk prevented it from gaining any purchase on the ground with its feet. Now the Ambulist was upon it. With a swift movement he fell across the animal, weighing it down while with his left hand he swept the knife across its throat so that its struggling subsided with the pulsing of its blood down his wrist. He was utterly exhausted and lay there in fatal embrace with his victim while he recovered.

The Ambulist did not have the strength to drag the sheep back to his cave. He must butcher it where it lay, take as much meat as he could along with the fleece, bury the rest and return another time to salvage the carcass. That night he ate in style, oblivious to pain, roasting mutton steaks on his heather fire, gorging on slabs of fat and liver. The stinking fleece would make his bed and pillow. He sat late before his fire, watching sparks fizzing into the night sky. As the moon rose beyond the far wall of the gorge he lit himself a cigarette and with his uninjured arm saluted the return of a friend.

The Ambulist walked again for the first time seven days later. He had fashioned a strap which he attached to the end of his stick, binding it with a thong of the sheep's skin; now he could pull on the stick as well as prop himself with it. The rest of the carcass he had butchered; some of it he wrapped in grass and placed at the back of the cave under heather so it would last as long as possible. Strips of meat hung drying from a cord stretched across the roof of the cave. He had hammered the bones until they yielded their marrow, washed the tendons and stored them for later use, and made a broth from the skull. He needed green-stuffs now, and for that he would have to descend the gorge and seek roots, wild garlic and sorrel on the lower, more sheltered slopes. With the stick and a net bag he now made an expedition to reach those lower slopes, setting out early to give himself the full day. His rib hurt still, but he could feel it knitting. The gash in his leg he had been able to sew closed with no sign of infection; the bruising and stiffness still made movement difficult but he felt he could wait no longer for fresh food. His breath was rancid and his gums had begun to bleed. His shoulder was still so sore that his right arm was useless and would be for another two weeks, but now it was time to move.

On the fourteenth day, more than two weeks since he left the camp at the Rigg and at about the same time that Albie Rooi was arranging to take a room at the guest house, the Ambulist climbed from the pit of Blizzen Gorge back on to the Border ridge. It was a day of onrushing low white clouds scudding in almost at head height from the west, skimming the dome of the Cheviot before dashing onward to the sea. The light was milky blue, the air warm and moist. The Ambulist, with his stick in his left hand and his grip over his uninjured shoulder, levered himself up over the rim of the gorge and stood looking back down. From here he could not see his cave through the cotton wool mist which covered his eyes; he could make out a vague shadow and knew he would find it again that night. He had taken time to learn the shape of the gorge so intimately that he could navigate it without vision, should his eyes fail completely. He knew he must stay here until he was completely healed but he aimed within a few days to walk as far as the nearest village and supply himself with tobacco and whisky, bread, honey and fruit. Nourishment of his belly and soul was his urgent need. He had survived: his imagination now afforded him the luxury of thinking about life.

A spine of the Border ridge, he knew, would bring him gradually down into the valley of the Cuddy Burn. At the lower end of this remote and beautiful vale was a small hamlet which, though it had no shops, lay at the head of a tiny road which would lead out of the hills and into the country north of the border where a more substantial village lay. Along this spine stood the refuge hut he had sought in vain on the night of his fall. He could not yet make it out from the ridge, but he could see his path well enough and when the hut did come into view it would be his marker for the trail into the valley. To reach the hut and then return to the cave would be enough for this day. To reach the hut, to spread one's arms wide to the horizon across the distant hills and to breathe the hilltop wind: yes, it would be enough.

The hut had not been built with shelter from the elements in mind, but rather to make it visible to walkers. It stood on a saddle in the ridge exposed, to the southwest, to great swooping gusts of wind. To the north, spread out wide like a rippling blanket, was the Border: farm and vale, wooded dene, the formidable V of the Cuddy Burn whose little hamlet nestled in the bottom between two wooded, conical hills. A thin trail of smoke rising from the chimney of a cottage showed that down there the air was almost still. Up here, the un-braked wind tore at the bent grass, folded and pressed it against the earth. The Ambulist, hobbling towards the wooden hut, was buffeted this way and that and leant heavily on his stick. He would stop here, drink from his flask, chew on a piece of his mutton billtong and roll himself a cigarette. He would feed on the air, on the sky, on the distant horizon lost in its summer haze. The walk had drained his strength. He slumped to the ground in the lee of the hut and let his stick fall against the weatherboard.

A noise from inside: something like a tin mug falling against a concrete floor. The Ambulist, sitting absolutely still, listened intently for a moment, took a drag from his cigarette, levered himself to his feet and drew back the heavy wooden latch on the door. Inside, a human shape lay on the low wooden bench that ran along the back wall of the hut, with the wind whistling beneath the ill-fitting boards and rolling the enamel mug from side to side. Hearing the noise of the Ambulist's stick, the man had managed to nudge the mug onto the floor. The face, as the Ambulist probed it with his fingers, was sweating, the eyes half-closed, the hair matted, a few days of stubble on the chin. One trouser leg had been torn upward at the ankle to expose it. There was a stench of rot and even in that light the look of the leg told the Ambulist that the man had badly broken his tibia, had lain here for several days, probably in shock, now certainly in a fever. An infection had taken hold which would cost him the leg, if not his life.

The Ambulist did not say anything but fetched his grip from outside and, with the practiced swiftness of a surgeon, set to work upon the man. This was not a time for the craft or ritual of a healing ceremony; expediency was all. He removed his greatcoat, unconsciously wincing, and hung it from a nail. Noticing that there was a small gas burner on the hut's trestle table he lit it and boiled water in his pan. He rolled up his sleeves, felt the feeble pulse in the man's wrist and with his knife began to cut the boot off the foot. The man turned his head weakly towards him, registered his presence, gasped as if about to scream, and fainted.

Chapter Twelve

Third miracle

Queedy sat absolutely still, as he had for two hours. In that time his gaze remained perfectly steady on a small polished ivory figurine a few feet away. It might have been a voluptuously sexy pregnant woman had not the belly, the breasts and the genitals been so grossly distended as to make her monstrous; had the head and feet not been missing. Queedy had an idea to pick the figurine up, to hold it in his hand and trace its grotesque, sensuous form with his fingers. Self-control had so far won the day and his hands lay palm-down on his knees, symmetrical and unmoving. His breathing was slow and even. His eyes were bright, his skin a deep healthy brown. He had recently shaved but his now luxuriant hair had been left untrimmed so that he was almost unrecognisable from the gauche young man who had gone away some weeks before.

Queedy's other head was struggling to come to terms with this transformation. That is to say, Freya Arnesen was struggling to reconcile the clay head beneath her fingers with the Queedy who had returned from his apprenticeship with the Ambulist. For two hours now she had subjected it to what seemed like a severe form of massage in an attempt to change fundamentally the shape of the skull, to broaden it and give it more substance. It had taken a fistful of fresh clay to get the bulk just right; even so, the result was not satisfactory. A strand of the sculptor's dark blonde hair was plastered to her forehead by perspiration. The lines in her brow recorded like plough furrows the travails of her day. Freya was by no means sure the thing was yet right, that she had recaptured the essence of the boy/man whose frailty had so intrigued her, had so emphatically drawn her to him like a siren to a drowning sailor. Could Queedy's actual skull really have changed shape? Was it possible that the narrow, sleek and insubstantial face of the impossibly immature and damaged cub reporter could have evolved into that of a composed and mature adult after so short a time spent in the hills? The nose, for example, seemed less pinched, the eyes were now set deeper than they had been but without the ghostly hollowness she had first seen. The curve of the mouth kept its slight sneer and yet, was that not a mark of self-examination rather than superiority? Was there now just a trace of humility in the way he held his head? Did he not now look out on the world, rather than along his nose at it?

A barking of dogs from two floors below: Jareld returning from his walk. Dappled white light flooding through the windows of the studio and draping Queedy, the real Queedy, in alternate veils of light and shadow, reminded both sitter and artist that the morning was wearing towards midday, that there were chores to be done. Freya stepped back from her piece, draped a damp cloth over it – not in disgust at her efforts but to keep the clay moist – and dismissed her subject. She was disconcerted but, now that she held Queedy captive, there was time enough to explore this newfound beauty of his. Queedy rose meekly from his seat with no sign that he had suffered prolonged discomfort, and led the way below to the kitchen. Here a familiar uproar of dogs wagging tails, pans being clattered on the range, water running in the sink and Jareld singing a painfully cheerful song met the young man, banishing whatever thoughts had occupied him for the previous almost perfectly silent hours. He stayed in the kitchen long enough to ask Jareld where he had been on his walk, to put on his wellington boots and to ask how soon lunch would be ready before disappearing down the steps with the two dogs at his heels.

Since Selena's departure in search of the Ambulist and his arrival at the farm Queedy had, after a little encouragement, taken on her duties as husbandrywoman to the menagerie of animals. In a former life, it seemed, Queedy had been well-acquainted with the beasts – had been unable to avoid their acquaintance. Now the uneasy relationship changed. Their mistress unaccountably having disappeared, they must accept Queedy as their temporary keeper, like it or not. Unattractive as this new regime must have appeared, it nevertheless presented the animals with opportunities to exploit the young man's inexperience. The now robustly healthy donkey foal Tigger considered it her duty to bray at an immoderate volume if Queedy did not spend at least twenty minutes every morning and evening stroking her ears and scratching the patch of rough mane between her shoulder blades. The mother was not above aiming a swift kick at him with a rear hoof if he failed to provide ample straw for their bedding or bring her an extra carrot above and beyond her statutory ration of feed. Neither mother nor daughter could easily be persuaded either to leave their stall for the green pastures of the paddock first thing in the morning, or return at night, without deploying a full range of delaying tactics reserved for neophytes like Queedy. If, however, he was late for such rituals, both mother and daughter set up a most alarming racket, kicking, braying and biting anything that came within reach.

The chickens, ducks, cats and other small fauna who inhabited the yard were more or less unconcerned by the change of personnel. Their expectations, greed and indifference to any interests but their own allowed Queedy to deal with them in more or less mechanical fashion.

He had found that an escort of dogs was effective against most forms of avian ankle-biting. This was not true of the semi-domesticated geese, who nominally inhabited the lake but who were wont to graze the paddock and liked especially to graze on anything that wore shoes with laces. Against these frightful pests the dogs were no defence; Queedy rapidly became accustomed to wearing wellington boots outside unless he was accompanying Jareld on a walk in the woods to hunt pigeon or rabbit: Jareld with his shotgun, Queedy with snares and catapult.

The goat, his erstwhile antagonist, more imaginative and less stubborn than the donkeys, embarked upon an immediate campaign of sedition on realising that Queedy was to be, if not its new master, then its attendant for the foreseeable future. M. had reduced it to almost immediate submission because he had known goats as a child. He had learned long ago, in the rain-soaked pastures of Donegal, that with such malevolent spirits a pre-emptive offensive was the surest policy. But Queedy could not bring himself to punch the goat in the head and the goat, having achieved moral superiority over him at their first meeting, knew this. It thrived on conflict and on the principle of eating anything not cast in metal. It possessed genetic expertise at launching surprise attacks on its victim: from beyond hedges and fences, from behind walls, from within trailers and donkey stalls. The goat targeted Queedy with assiduous malice, front and rear, limb and body. It ate the coat off his back and the trousers from his legs. It could not be bribed with carrots, apples or any other juicy titbit from the kitchen table. It was resolute in its hostility, unfazed by Queedy's admonitions, threats or pleadings for peace.

In the end it gave in to nothing more sophisticated than Christian meekness. Queedy decided one day simply to ignore the creature, to pretend it did not exist, to turn the other cheek when attacked, to wordlessly forgive his trespasser. After a week of batterings and bruisings and the loss of an almost complete set of clothes, followed by three days of Queedy's stoical passivity, the incredulous goat began to yearn for attention. It took to licking and nibbling his hand and following at his heels, roughly shooing away any other creature, dogs included, that might compete for his affections. Queedy ignored it. The goat undertook to glare plaintively up at him in the vain hope of acknowledgement. Queedy affected not to notice. Finally it sulked, sitting with its legs folded demurely beneath it, in the far corner of the paddock, forehead butted up against a fencepost. The victor, after a suitable interval, noticed its existence and might thereafter be seen allowing it to search gently for a stump of carrot in his pocket. Queedy had acquired a devoted pet.

Jareld fretted for his daughter and worried for the safety of Pieter Jäger. It was almost a fortnight since he had left her at the crossroads by the post-box. She had sent a postcard, saying that she had not yet found Pieter, that she had spent some days walking in the hills, that she had dropped in to stay for a couple of days with some people she knew at a farm just the other side of the Border. Jareld telephoned and spoke with her for a few minutes, trying hard not to sound like a worried parent. The Arnesens knew the friend and her parents. They were fine decent people and he was glad Selena was safe in their company. Out there somewhere danger was following the man whom he had, so long ago it seemed, christened the Ambulist. He trusted them both. But impotence, the awful feeling that he should be doing something practical in the search for the wandering giant, that for want of action the giant might yet be hunted down and destroyed by his enemy, haunted him. He could not write music, had not even descended to his studio these past days. His mind was filled not with songs but with pictures from a film he wanted never to see. He distracted himself by cooking, walking the dogs, by talking to Queedy about the Ambulist, about his daughter, and by the resolute cheeriness which he knew irritated even his adoring wife at times. How Queedy had grown up since his last collapse! How much stronger he was, a fine new man indeed! Was this the miraculous work of the Ambulist; had he actually fixed the boy's heart, or was this simply the experience of self-reliance? It was true that scouting had given him great self-confidence as a boy; but this, surely, was different. Perhaps, Jareld suspected, this was the inner quality in the man coming out, released from the black weight of his father's guilt and the pain of being unloved. He also liked to think that something of the Arnesens' love for one another had softened Queedy's heart. Was it too much to hope?

M. lay in his bath with an empty gin glass on the side. He had lain there nearly three-quarters of an hour and the water was getting cold but he could still hardly be bothered to move. Inertia lay heavy on him. The casserole in the oven would be ready, he just had to put the potatoes on. His bath was still his greatest pleasure, especially now that his back was bad again from sleeping on the floor of the office and because he had not been for a good long walk in weeks. Since the arrival of a commissar, imposed from on high as a sort of punishment for his failings, there had been few good days at the *Courier*. He almost missed Gaunt; almost.

He supposed he ought to get out and get on with it, although the temptation to turn the hot tap on again with his foot was strong. Instead he looped the chain of the bath plug round his big toe and pulled, and the throaty sucking sound of the water whirling down the drain finally roused him.

As M. plopped the last peeled potato into the pan of water on the stove and turned the gas ring down he once again picked up Queedy's last dispatch from the Rigg, what would have been the fifth of John Smith's Friday sketches. It had arrived two days after Queedy's reappearance at the Tower-house all bronzed and athletic and, from what he had heard, quite a new man. The front page of Queedy's handwritten scrawl had suffered at the hands of a previous dinner and was stained with passata and the brown ring of a coffee cup. He ought, he knew, to treat it more carefully. It was almost a historical document, recalling the last days of the enigmatic wanderer's free roaming in the English countryside before... well, who knew what? M. liked to believe, still, that the Ambulist was a more or less innocent victim of apartheid bigotry and a personal witch hunt. He liked to think that when the truth emerged the Ambulist's own account, admittedly incomplete, would be accepted as a record of fidelity and integrity, the life history of an extraordinary man living in extraordinary times. The hack in him knew that the truth, whatever it was, might never emerge and if it did it might be too late to save either the Ambulist or the *Courier*.

Nevertheless... he read Queedy's piece again while he waited for his spuds. He liked it. The boy was showing signs, definitely showing signs. But sooner rather than later M. must go out to the Tower-house and see him. He envisaged an awkward interview. He must tell the boy that by order of the new assistant chief-editor to whom M. must now pay obeisance, Queedy was sacked and would never work for any of the group's papers or agencies again. The expensive flat overlooking the river would have to go and so would the sharp suits. M. was putting it off. Queedy had been back at the Tower-house for a week; more than a week. He couldn't put it off much longer. He wondered how he was going to break it to the boy and nothing came, no good way of saying it. Another part of him asked why should he worry? He was, as he had told himself many times over the years, emphatically not the boy's bloody father, Christ Jesus so he wasn't. It was time the boy made it alone in the world. Maybe he should cash that cheque from Queedy's father, give it to the boy as a sort of redundancy payment. It was all he would get. M. had covered the boy's tracks by making him turn freelance: he had no rights at all with the *Courier*. M. folded the sketch and put it in the pocket of his dressing gown. The spuds were ready.

M. slept well for a change. There was nothing like one's own bed and, now firm in his mind that he would go to see Queedy at the weekend, his conscience was clear. He would talk the whole thing through with the boy, not his fault and all that, make sympathetic noises about having a word with one or two people in the business, seeing what he could do for him. That would be for the best. When M. woke at seven the following morning he felt refreshed. His sacroiliac had eased somewhat – the gin had helped – and even the prospect of going to work and having to deal with an apparatchik from HQ looking over his shoulder all the time was not, in the cold light of day, all that depressing. It meant, for one thing, that he could blame her for next month's sales figures. They would be bloody awful.

The post came just as he was leaving: a large mud-spattered brown envelope, crumpled at the corners and with an illegible rural post mark; one of the towns on the other side of the Border, he fancied, one of those genteel Scots communities whose ruddy-faced rugger-playing youths were a match for any club side in the game. A tough lot. M. had no correspondents in those parts. The handwriting he did not recognise. It looked rather childish, the letters formed individually, rounded and too large for an adult, surely. He put the envelope in his briefcase, holding it with one arm against his raised knee while he crunched his marmalade toast between his teeth and pulled the front door behind him with his free hand. Marmalade dripped onto the briefcase, and as he walked into town he wiped it off with a finger and sucked it, rolling the sweet bitter orange flavour round his mouth. Good marmalade, that. Mary had sent it over with her usual generous Christmas hamper and he had only just got around to opening it.

The woman who bore the honour of being M.'s new assistant had taken up official residence in Gaunt's freshly-decorated office, but being a woman eager for promotion she had so far been found every day waiting outside the editor's office, keen to discuss the day's news events and potential stories with the man who, for a while, would pretend to be her boss. The more persistent she was in coming early to his office, the more tempting it was for M. to be late. He had almost forgotten the envelope by the time his new assistant departed having suggested some terribly useful ways in which M. might tighten his ship, make cash flow savings and reduce overheads while increasing the efficiency of the news gathering operation. M. considered offering her procreative advice, and walking out. Maybe it would come to that, although if he was smart he would wait another eighteen months, until he was entitled to early retirement. Then the whole bloody lot of them could go to blazes. That was a day worth waiting for.

Now, with a fresh cup of very hot, very strong coffee in his hand, M. walked over to the window where it had all started, envelope in hand. The exuberant foliage on the plane trees in the market place softened the grey backdrop of the cobbles. Office workers and lunchtime school children livened the place up with their bright warm-weather clothes. He opened the window and let the sounds of early summer flood into the office. Across the market place at the entrance to the alley where It, whatever It was, had begun, a busker was murdering Bob Dylan knocking at the gates of Heaven. M., unconsciously singing along, put the cup on top of the filing cabinet and slit the envelope with his thumbnail. Inside were a photograph and a note, hastily written. It was from the girl, Selena. She had written: I found this when you left us. I wanted to give it to John but couldn't, nor could I burn it. You must decide what to do with it.

M. looked at the photograph for a few moments and then glanced up at the world outside where he and Queedy, standing next to him right here on that freezing bloody night in December, had first seen the Ambulist stride into their lives. He looked down at the picture again, then turned it over and read what was written on the back: the names, the date. Christ Jesus, he thought. Christ effing Jesus.

M.'s arrival at the Tower-house that weekend coincided with Queedy's morning visit to the paddock. For once he was late rising – they had all been late rising after a night of flowing wine – and a

cacophony of indignant cries from his foster-creatures met the sound
of his exit from the kitchen door, boots scraping on the steps as he
nudged his stockinged feet into them. The sun had been up these
few hours and the day promised warmth, if not heat; but still the yard
was partially shaded and Queedy wore an old sweater of Jareld's,
his expensive woollen polo-neck having been consumed by the goat.
Now, as Queedy opened the gate to the paddock, M. trundling reluctant
along the lane in his car was met by the sight of his former employee
and ward leading a sort of biblical procession composed of dogs, two
in number, donkeys ditto, the goat on its own, various ducks, chickens
and geese and at a safe distance the curious but aloof black cat, who
could not resist the pleasure of shadowing the action from a position of
matchless superiority on top of the farmyard wall.

    - I'll give it to you straight, Son. (Queedy has fulfilled his
duties and they have retired to the kitchen) They won't let me
take your pieces any more and they won't let me have you on
the staff. Gaunt sticking his filthy bloody great boot in has done
for us both, I'm thinking.

    - I had rather thought of him as a harmless old curmudgeon.
(Queedy faces M. across the kitchen table, a mug of tea in one
hand and the other stroking a dog's ear; he has not yet taken his
wellington boots off. Jareld stands at the sink, listening. Freya
sits at the table between the two men. Queedy looks towards
the afternoon sun coming through the kitchen window as if he
has better things to do outside than waste the day away in idle
chat)

    - I suffered from the same delusion, sure (says M.). Thing
is, Son, you're on your own now.

    - It seems people are queuing up not to be the father figure
in my life. (Queedy turns and smiles at Freya and leans back
in his chair) Perhaps I shall come to like it. Perhaps I should
become my own father figure, what do you say? (M. shrugs,

and, in an unconscious imitation of Gaunt, sticks his bottom lip out)

- What will you do, John? (This is Freya, who touches him lightly on the arm with her hand, unconsciously comparing reality to the feel of her clay)

- I wonder if I should take up Ambulism.

- You what, Son?

- He means, he might walk forever, like our friend Pieter. You like walking fine, now, Queedy, don't you (says Jareld from the sink)?

- I'm not sure 'like' is the right word.

- There's no career in it, Son.

- Don't people still write novels, or travel diaries? I am certain I have heard of such things. Perhaps someone might give me a shilling or two now and then for a nicely-turned phrase.

- Have you thought about keeping goats and chickens, Queedy? (Jareld lets out a hoot of laughter from the sink; it is the funniest thing he has thought of to say in many weeks and he is rather proud of it)

- But seriously, John, you must stay here until you have thought what you will do; you are very welcome.

- Of course he is welcome, my dear. Queedy, you are more than welcome. (Jareld is still laughing to himself at the sink)

- The only thing I can offer you is a bit of money I have lying around. I don't need it. There's sixteen hundred quid to get you going. Do you want me to get rid of the flat for you?

- Thanks. I can sort the flat out myself. There is nothing much there that I want to keep. I hated the place anyway.

- The kitchen melted into a sort of after-lunch stupor. Queedy looked up at the clock as if he was late for something

and scraped his chair back against the floor. Before he could
rise, M. put out a hand to stop him.

    - There's one other thing, Son.

    - Only one other thing?

    - What I mean to say is, there's this. (M. pulls from the
pocket of his overcoat the envelope with the photograph in it
and places it in front of Queedy. The young man opens it and
pulls the picture out and Freya and Jareld lean over to see what
it might be; they recognise their daughter's writing and catch
each other's eye. The kitchen falls silent apart from the sound
of one of the dogs gnawing at a bone and the clock ticking away
on the wall above the range, so loud that each tick might have
been a punch aimed at Queedy's ribs)

Selena came upon the Ambulist at last in the tiny hamlet at the
foot of the Cuddy Burn. A grandiose house, built in the middle of the
last century by a baronet Member of Parliament as a summer retreat and
winter hunting lodge, sat complacent on a terrace above the burn. All
turrets and crenellations in soft red sandstone, it commanded a view of
the whole valley almost to the broad sweep of the Border ridge, which
masked it from Blizzen Gorge. On three sides its turrets were now
dwarfed by mature conifers, specimens from the Himalayas collected
on botanising trips during the baronet's years in India. A huddle of
estate cottages nestled below it on the single-track road that led north
from the valley out into the broader glen beyond. Behind it, the hillside
shone green with bustling oak trees in their best early summer foliage.
The smoke of coal fires hung in the still air of mid-afternoon.

    The hamlet marked the limit of the Ambulist's present ambitions
in venturing from his cave, testing the soreness in his limbs and chest;
yesterday's exertions on the injured walker in the hut had drained him
of energy, but today he had set himself the goal of reaching the hamlet
and beyond. He had not left the gorge by way of the ridge and the
refuge hut; he had descended its steepest slopes direct from his cave

and emerged from the bog at its entrance. His leg and rib were stronger but he was desperate for fresh fruit and vegetables notwithstanding the few early blueberries and odd patch of ramsons he had come upon these last few days. His eyes were poor. He could make out the loom of the big house from some way off and the little track that penetrated upstream alongside the burn was easy enough to follow, but the world had no detail for him today; he could not forage in the hedges or along the wayside. He would stop at one of the cottages and ask if he might buy some fruit, or bread.

Selena had spent two days with her friends, fretting all the while that she had not yet brought her warning of danger to Pieter. She could delay her search no longer. He must now be somewhere in the most inaccessible fastnesses of the Border. It was here that she would spend the next days looking for any signs of his camp or of his passing. His almost magical appearance on the track, walking towards her from some half a mile above the hamlet, made her heart glad. As he closed the yards between them she saw that something was wrong. He was too slow. His characteristic stride and rhythm were gone, he rocked from side to side, limping. He followed the track tentatively, feeling for it beneath his feet, when she could only imagine him bestriding it, parting the landscape before him as though he were sweeping aside a curtain on the future. The immediate thought came to her that Rooi had already found him, that the two men had engaged in some terrible fight, that he had been wounded. She waited until she was close, within a hundred yards, hoping for signs that she had misread his walk, before calling out. By then she realised that he must be blind; he had not seen her, this giant with eagle's eyes. This seer, this watcher, could neither see nor watch. Emasculated, his world had shrivelled and it came to her in an instant that his seeming abandonment of Queedy had not been dereliction or contempt, but flight.

>   - Pieter (she calls, with the same gentleness with which she had greeted Queedy at his bonfire. The Ambulist turns his

head to one side as if he is not sure what he has heard, as if her call might be an artefact of the wind).

- Ah, Meisje? Is it you? The air brings me a beautiful sound on its wings this fine afternoon. To meet another wandering soul and a friend on the trail is good cheer for my heart. I am happy.

- Pieter, you are broken. (He stops and holds his hands out. She runs up to him and takes them in hers) Whatever has happened?

- You are right. Not so good at wandering now. I am indeed broken in my body, but my soul is here still (he points a finger at his temple) and I have not died yet.

Selena took the Ambulist by the hand and they sat down on the side of the track. He pulled out his tobacco pouch, sighing, and rolled himself a cigarette. Tears came to her eyes. She could not look at him in case her heart broke.

- Mutton and tobacco. Not such a bad diet but it becomes boring after a while and I believe that like your old tars I may have the scurvy. Have you any idea how I wish for an apple, a tomato? (Selena, wiping her tears, smiles faintly and takes an apple and a brown paper bag full of carrots from her pack; the carrots are for any animals she might meet. She places the apple in the Ambulist's hand and he grasps hers and holds it tight)

- Meisje, thank you. (He finishes his cigarette first, then polishes the apple on his sleeve like a schoolboy and takes a huge bite from it. The tart juice stings his sore gums and his dry, cracked lips but as he crunches the apple's sweet flesh he lets out a sigh of simple delight)

- You are lucky I was passing this way with an apple, Pieter.

- Ja, klopt. And you also are lucky I was passing this way.

Not every man would have appreciated this apple as well as I. (Selena smiles again, and takes from her paper bag a carrot to munch on, for company)

The two wanderers sat in the mouth of the Ambulist's cave watching the last of the sun's molten light spark the rim of the gorge like the hammer strike of a smith beating down on his anvil. With the end of the light the day's warmth fled the land and cold's fingers crept inexorably up the sides of the valley. The flames from the small camp fire now began to illuminate the entrance to the cave, a fiery yellow-pink suffused with creamy grey smoke from the heather. The dark recesses of the shelter were banked high with sticks and branches which the girl had spent the afternoon collecting, and the wanderers' shadows danced across them. The two now shared their food. The Ambulist fried dried strips of mutton in Selena's butter with mushrooms which she had collected under his guidance from the wayside. The caramel fumes were intoxicating. Selena unloaded the pack of treasures that had been meant for him and Queedy, that she had been religiously carrying these last two weeks: honey – precious honey – whisky, more apples, bread and oatcakes, packets of nuts, currants and dried dates.

Had the Ambulist not already seen a vision of hell that day, he might have thought himself in heaven. Selena's description of the man called Albie Rooi had struck at his heart.

- You know of this man?

- Ja, I have come across him, many years ago. I have never seen his face, but I know the voice, it is the voice of a sadist. He likes to hear men scream. I think I will know his face when I see it. If I can see it.

- How can it be that you have heard him but not seen his face?

- He came to the prison in the night. He would stand outside our cells when we wanted to sleep and talk to us about what he was going to do. Always his voice was like a whisper.

And then the next day the man with the kind voice and the packet of cigarettes in the interrogation room would offer to make your life easy, you just had to tell him what he wanted to hear and he would protect you from this man Rooi. He has one arm, ja?

- Yes.

- Ja, that is him. He seems to think it was me who blew his arm off. So, he has come for me. Maybe I am the last one left.

- You do not have to talk unless you wish it.

- Night is the time for talking. But we eat first, eh Meisje? You have bread there, break some off and we share the meat from the pan. I will cheer myself with the idea of poor Mister Queedy thinking I have abandoned him. Dat is heel fijn, verdomme.

- My father tells me that John has taken my place, that he is now looking after all the animals. He tells me Billy has become quite tame in John's hands. But then, my father is a great storyteller.

- Ha, it would be a fine good thing to see, as your father would say. I would like to see that boy tame the goat. (The Ambulist almost chokes on a hunk of bread as he laughs a deep guttural laugh) Ja, that is a good one.

They ate the rest of their meal in silence with only the slow ascent of the constellations beyond the ridge marking the time. Presently the full moon rose, a stupendous yellow bull moon, so immensely heavy-looking that it seemed it could scarcely launch itself beyond the horizon; it must surely fall back to earth to try again on another night when it was not so fat. But climb it did, the livid grey scars on its flanks a reminder of its stormy migration through the aeons. Selena now laid out a banquet of her dried dates, the apples and the whisky and offered them to her host. He took them all and while she tended to the fire he smoked, took great gulps from the bottle and chewed dates. Slowly, the light came back into his eyes. Selena, searching his face, leant back on her hands, her feet pointing towards the moon. She watched his features with the wonder of seeing them as if for the first time: tired he was, close to exhaustion, the years of toil and hardship, fear and loss written deep in the lines of his skin picked out by the twin lights of the livid fire and the honey moon. But life was strong in him. Beneath her hand she felt the outline of a hard shiny angular stone and taking it in her hand she held it up to the glow of the fire. It was an arrowhead, made of pearl-white flint knapped with great precision and as fresh as if it had been made that day.

  - Did you pick this up on your travels, Pieter? (She presses it into his hand and he turns it over, picking out its shape with his finger and thumb)

  - No, Meisje. Have you found this just now, here in the cave?

  - Yes, I thought you must have dropped it.

  - No. Then the hunters have been here before me. They sat here long ago watching the full moon rise just as we have. They have sung their songs and told their stories, followed the elk up to the high ridges. Ja, they have followed him and camped here like us; they have repaired their arrows for tomorrow's pursuit. I am glad you found it, Meisje, this gives me strength. This is a place for hunters, not for their prey.

  - I hope so, Pieter.

Morning: first light; the cave deep in shadow, the air chilled and heavy with dew. Selena woke to the sound of the Ambulist tending his fire, the quiet clanking of his pan against the rim of mugs, pouring water into them with the concentrated care of a man who cannot see. From inside the cave the intensity of the light beyond on the slate grey of the crags, on the purple heather flower-heads and virgin machair grass, on the tumbling brown-black water of the burn, was breathtaking, enough to make one's head reel. A raven's caw echoed from above;

a pipit chirped from a few yards away hoping for a little bounty from its human neighbours. Diminished as he was by infirmity and age, the magnificent bulk of the Ambulist, his self-possession and his dauntless courage were a reassurance against an uncertain future. Selena lay for a few minutes, watching her thoughts play out on the microscopic universe of the cave's ceiling, before rising. Today she must walk right across the rump of the Cheviot plateau to the town where she could buy fresh provisions. She must call her father and tell him she had found Pieter, that he was not now capable of protecting himself, that he must be taken to a place where he could be safe. She must also unburden herself of a pain which gnawed at her insides.

 - Pieter...?

 - Ah, so you are awake. Yes, Meisje, what is it?

 - There is something I must ask you.

 - I will try to answer you, Meisje.

 - I have seen a photograph, taken many years ago. You are standing on the steps of a court house, I think. There are many reporters with notebooks and cameras and you are smiling. There are two women with you and a man. Will you tell me who they are?

The Ambulist did not answer her immediately. He had the flint arrowhead in his fingers and was rubbing its point against the palm of his hand, testing its strength and sharpness. Now he put the flint into his pocket and, reaching up, pulled from around his neck a string of small shells and semi-precious stones. Pulling the string round, he unpicked the tiny knot in the thong and, gathering the necklace in his massive fist, held it out for Selena to take. The beads were delicate, minute, polished by time.

 - The young woman you have seen in that photograph, she gave me this necklace when we were thirteen years of age. It had twenty-six beads on it then, one for every year that each of us had been on the earth. She gave me one more bead for every year that we were married. Sometimes we did not see each other for a long time, and then she would give me several at once.

    - What was your gift to her?

    - I gave her a bracelet for every year. Some of these she gave to her mother, who is also in that picture, and some to the other members of her kin. She always wore the ones I gave her when we married.

    - Did you have any children?

    - Meisje, it is hard to speak of these things.

    - I am sorry. Can you tell me about the man?

    - He also is hard to speak of. He was my friend.

    - I am glad of it.

    - The man with one arm, Rooi, he gave my friend a lot of money.

Selena, putting a hand to her eyes, found that she was weeping fresh tears and that she could not stop. She felt an overwhelming pain which no tending of wounds, no words of compassion could ever have prepared her for. She wanted to run from the cave, to escape, to flee from what she must now do.

    - Meisje, you are crying. I am sorry for it. What do you have to say to me?

    - You must tell me what happened to your wife, Pieter. I do not want to know, but I must.

    - My friend promised me he would take her to a safe place when they came for me. I did not know he had sent them. I did not know he would give her to them. Child, you must not cry, these are old wounds, only the scars are left.

    - Pieter, I do not cry for you but for what I have to say. Have you not looked at John Queedy and seen in him something of this man?

    - What you say disturbs me, child, but his name was Smith.

- Queedy is John's mother's name. He is the son of Carew Smith.

- How long have you known this, child?

- A few days.

- Does he know? Has he known all the time?

- No, no, he cannot. I believe he must know now, though.

No more words passed between them. The girl, distraught at being the instrument of such a mortal wound and unable to prevent the flow of her tears, ran from the cave, the fire and the Ambulist, stumbling across the scree and down into the gaping abyss of the gorge. The Ambulist now opened his own heart to the torture of his memory and, spreading his arms wide above him, roared his anger to the sky. Its echoes rang around the walls of the gorge, throwing his pain back at him again and again and crashing down upon the fleeing girl like the blows of her guilt.

Gaunt poked at the smear of ashes with his shoe. Nothing else in the tumbledown cottage offered a clue to its recent occupants. No litter, no debris from cooking or eating lay scattered about, so it was hard to say how cold the trail was. Gaunt sauntered over to the base of the Rigg, would have climbed it had he not been so unfit. Eventually he came upon Queedy's bivouac, evidenced by a single remaining artefact: the stub of a reporter's pencil lying on the flattened earth, half-buried. The shelter was much as the boy had left it except that by the smell a fox had been pissing in there. Gaunt knew how the fox felt and, looking around to be sure he was alone, he pissed into the shelter himself.

Gaunt knew he was no closer to the Ambulist than he had been before the tip-off from the postman, an old mucker of his who'd become curious about the enigmatic envelopes being sent periodically from this remote place to the editor of the *Courier*. Gaunt was sure to know, so the postman gave him a call. The twenty quid was an almost unforeseen bonus. Always appreciative, Mr Gaunt was, knew the value of local knowledge. Still, it didn't get him very far; not much use wandering up and down hill and dale looking for the next camp, it might be miles away the way that man walked. The map was no bloody help at all, neither use nor ornament. Gaunt challenged any man to make sense of it. Might as well be hieroglyphics.

On the other hand, Albie couldn't accuse him of sitting on his arse, could he? He had caught up with their man, even if he was a bit late. Time to pay a call on his mate Albie in his cosy little B&B. That is to say, on his friend Mr Walker, Rooi's current nom de guerre. Gaunt, driving up there the following morning with nothing better to do, ran him to ground after being re-directed by Rooi's landlady, who had seen him going into Mrs Graham's tea room not half an hour since. Through the window of the tea room Gaunt saw Rooi right enough, engaged in earnest conversation with a rural-looking character in a flat cap. Rooi made no sign of recognition and, discretion being Gaunt's watchword, he continued along the high street, looking in shop windows, every now and then casting a glance back at the tea room. A quarter of an hour later Rooi's correspondent left the café and Gaunt took his place.

     - Any news, Albie? I see you're in with the local intelligence agency, eh? (Gaunt permits himself a small laugh at the locals' expense and Rooi almost smiles back but not quite. Without waiting for an invitation Gaunt waves the waitress over, orders himself tea and scones and tells her to put it on Mr Walker's bill. Rooi stares at him but makes no comment)

     - What brings you here, Gaunt? You've been quiet these last few days. Your newspaper story has made quite a splash back home, I hear.

     - Good, glad to hear it. I've been busy sleuthing, old boy.

Hot on the trail, you might say. I know where they were this
time last week.

    - And where are they now?

    - Can't say just yet, but the hounds are baying, you know.

    - You mean you don't know.

    - Who was that chap then?

    - What chap?

    - Say no more, Albie, say no more. Mum's the word.

Rooi did not respond. He was more interested in looking over
Gaunt's shoulder at the police car which had just pulled up outside
the tea shop. He recognised the driver as his friend Sergeant Graham,
who was none other than the nephew of the Mrs Graham whose tea
cakes Gaunt was about to consume at his expense. The sergeant might
have been paying his aunt a social visit, or have been on important
community business. In fact he, like Gaunt, had run Albie to ground
thanks to the guidance of the landlady. And, like Gaunt before him, he
sat down at Rooi's table. His aunt, waving, called out that she would
bring an extra cup and some more hot water.

    - Sergeant.

    - Mr Walker, I thought I might find you here. Are we okay
to talk? (He nods in Gaunt's direction. Rooi introduces them,
somewhat reluctantly)

    - Please, Sergeant, do go ahead. I hope you have brought
me news of my stolen bag. (Gaunt is about to say something
but changes his mind)

    - As a matter of fact, I have. It's an odd sort of story.
Aunty! I might just have one of them teacakes meself, I've
been on shift since six and I'm gagging for me bait. Your lot
have been on the blower all morning (he adds, nodding first at
Rooi and then at Gaunt).

    - Our lot?

    - Press. Papers, TV, radio, all that lot. I was surprised not to hear from you, thought you'd want it from the horse's mouth. I suppose your wires have been buzzing anyhow and you've got all the gen already...?

- Do go ahead, Sergeant, Mr Gaunt and I are all ears.

- Oh, well, right then. I had a call yesterday evening from old Mrs Belson. Now she lives up at the big house along by Hetha, it's a hamlet, half a dozen cottages, that's all. It's a bleak kind of place, mind, down the bottom of the Cuddy Burn. You know it?

- Yes, I know it (says Gaunt).

- They don't get many visitors up there, mind, it's kind of off the beaten track.

- There's nothing there.

- Not a lot, no. Well, Mrs Belson tells me a man she's never seen before bangs on her door mid-way through the after-noon yesterday. She says he looks dead rough, like, she isn't sure if she ought to answer it, but she does. He's dressed like a proper walker, rucksack, waterproofs, the lot, except he only has one boot, he's just wearing a sock on the other foot and that's worn through with walking on it and stained with dried blood. Nasty blisters, too, she says. He tells her he has been out on the fells for five days, he's had a bad fall and broke his leg. You'd better come in and have a cup of tea, she says. Anyhow, he comes in and she sits him down, and he tells her he thought he was going to die, he'd broke his leg so bad it got infected, he was in a fever and hallucinating and all sorts. He managed to crawl to the refuge hut right up at the top of the ridge – you know it? – and lay down thinking that was it. He had a kind of a dream while he was in this fever, that a man came from out of nowhere and sort of laid hands on him, and then he doesn't know what happened but he woke up and his leg was, well, not perfect, but the infection had gone and he could walk okay with a bit of a limp, apart from the fact that the man had shredded his boot with a knife. This is his story, you understand, I'm not saying I believe it. So anyway Mrs Belson, she thinks he's not right in the head, so she phones Dr Marshall here in town, and he says to call an ambulance, and they take the bloke away. And then when he's been picked up and taken off to hospital she phones me and tells me the whole story. Guess what?

- What? (Gaunt and Rooi in unison)

- The quacks reckon he had a very recent compound fracture of his leg, but it's almost healed on its own accord in three days.

- Don't tell me (says Gaunt): they think it's a miracle.

- Aye, they do. Guess what else?

- You're going to tell us (says Rooi) that the man in the dream had a grip, just like mine.

- How did you know that (says the incredulous sergeant)?

- Just a hunch, Sergeant. I thank you for telling us such an interesting story.

- No bother, Mr Walker. Now, it's a bit delicate, see, because your lot are going to want to interview this bloke if they can find him and you know what they are like... I mean, you journalists want a good story, don't you? They are bound to go calling him the new messiah or something. Which leaves me in a bit of a sticky situation, and that's why I wanted to talk to you in person...

- Sergeant, I see your problem. You cannot arrest the new messiah for stealing an old bag, can you? You don't crucify thieves in this country even if they are the son of God, do you? Let's keep this to ourselves. There was nothing valuable in it, a few worthless items. He is welcome to them. Like you say, we journalists wouldn't want anything to get in the way of a good story.

The Sergeant, with a broad smile on his face, shook Mr Walker's hand warmly, nodded to Mr Gaunt and, waving to his aunt, left with his half-eaten teacake wrapped in a napkin. Gaunt, watching him go, raised an eyebrow to his friend Albie.

- Bit of a cheek, that, getting you to buy his tea, eh?

- Worth the money, I would say, Gaunt. And talking of which, I won't be needing you any more. Here is a fiver for the bill (Rooi walks out without another word, leaving Gaunt, mouth open, to contemplate his future at leisure).

Chapter Thirteen

Fog of war

The woman sitting three seats in front of Queedy reached up with her arm, struggled for a moment with the catch and then slid back the window. A swirl of cool air washed over Queedy's face and he opened his eyes. The stupefying heat, which had sent him almost to sleep, which had seduced him into a lair of unwelcome dreams, left him sweating and dazed on the back seat, before he remembered where he was and pulled off Jareld's old sweater. Now grumbling, now roaring as the driver changed down through the gears, the bus emerged from its last village stop into something like a new world where stone wall graced by lichen, humpback bridge, rushing burn and scrubby pasture gave way to tailored hedge and fox covert, bijou gate-house and beech-lined drive. Through the window at his side Queedy watched fields of spring wheat and hay sweltering in the unseasonable breathlessness of the day. Daisies, dandelions and buttercups littered acrylic lime verges which so recently, it seemed to him, had lain under a mantle of mud or snow, drained of all life and colour. Now the bus pulled out on to the main road and impatient cars dashed past them on the way to somewhere or nowhere. Queedy noticed a young man sitting across the aisle in a suit that was too smart for such transport, who was looking back at him in an old-fashioned sort of way. He realised that perhaps after his early morning chores he probably stank of straw and manure; it was difficult to tell. He rubbed his bristly jaw. He felt in his pocket for a handkerchief to wipe the sweat from his face and found only the stump of a carrot.

The city's pavements and office blocks, its parked cars and shop windows assaulted him with a confusion of images after the comforting shades of the country. The air was choking under a giant blanket which could not be shed. The sun's light was blinding. Noise boxed Queedy's ears on all sides: blaring, ringing, shouting, slamming. The unforgiving echo of granite, brick and stone made him wish for the silence of the breeze on the Rigg, the sympathetic crackle of the camp fire, even the flap of canvas when the wind blew hard. The unfamiliar-looking key of his apartment felt strange in his hand. Inside, the geometric order, the enervating immobility of the rooms and furniture were shocking in their modernity, in their impersonal brutality. The walls stared back at him. His bedroom might have been a suite in a hotel. This was no dwelling. Was it possible that the place could ever have felt like home, could ever have been his? In the kitchen he could not even console himself with a brew. Tea there was, but no milk; a kettle, but no honey. He wished for a pouch of tobacco so he could roll himself a cigarette. Should he shower? He seemed almost to infect the sterile air with his vernacular dress and odour.

Queedy sat on the bed in silence for some minutes and then, opening all the cupboards, set to conducting an inventory of his life. He laid his suits out on the bed. They might as well go to the nearest charity shop. The contents of the bookshelves would pack into a box; it was possible that Jareld might like to leaf through his books and keep a few. M. might pick them up for him – a last favour. The furniture came with the flat: it was nondescript, uncaring of style or substance. What else did he possess that he might take with him on his way towards tomorrow? A box file of letters and postcards, the sort of accumulation of family memories that in other lives would end up collecting dust in an attic. It had better go out with the rubbish; he had no need of family memories now. He went over to the window, to the proscenium vista of an urban theatre: today looked like another dress rehearsal. The same cars crawled in endless queues across bridges. Redundant cranes hung listless on half-built tower-blocks. Nothing had changed. Everything had changed.

Away into the distance stretched the line of the river, hemmed in by wharves, warehouses and apartments just like his. How the Ambulist would have deplored those six bridges which spanned it in defiance of its geological birthright. It struck Queedy that he had not crossed the river on foot a single time since he had come to the city. The thought came to him that it might be cooler out there above the brackish water than here in this empty pristine oven. He thought also that Pieter, wherever he was, would deprecate such patronage of the river's bane. A thin smile came to Queedy's lips, unnoticed by the players far below treading their unacknowledged boards.

Queedy dropped the key to his flat with the rental agency, his suits with a grateful charity shop. He threw the box file into the communal bins, leaving himself with a suitcase that contained his few, his very few essentials. Pulling this behind him on its vestigial wheels he walked back down towards the bridge. Past the cathedral, stranded almost on an island by the secular imperatives of a one-way traffic system; past the medieval barbican and the incongruous Norman keep that might have been a prototype for the Tower-house; past the old law courts and onward, with the sound of gulls, and rolling stock on the railway line above, clamouring for attention in his ears.

The High Bridge was a monument to another age. Its narrow roadway was caged by wrought iron rods and girders held together with fist-sized bolts. Trucks, cars, buses squeezed gingerly past one another a hundred feet above the river. On either side pedestrians might leisurely stroll across, wondering at each new perspective opening before them: arch beyond arch, the balustrade playing like a zoetrope, each elegant lamp post looming before and diminishing behind. The bridge had been built in long gone days when ten thousand men a day crossed the river in the early morning for work in the city and again in the evening, a monstrous herd of labour bent on launching ships, blowing light bulbs, building locomotives for the world. Now its patrons were tourists and late-night drunks.

Above the roadway and superior in every dimension was a second storey to this engineering marvel. Here ran the iron tracks whose master engineer had conceived the bridge not as a mausoleum of past glories but to serve notice on the future. Over these rails came and went the trains which had for the first time connected the distant ends of the country, conquering time and distance, emasculating land and water. Beneath them walked Queedy, suitcase ridiculously in tow. A cool breeze funnelled down the river and worked its way between pillar and arch as if they were no more than clothes on a line; but no wind would move them in a thousand years. Overhead a train lumbered, clattering rhythmically out of the station on its way south. Queedy stopped halfway across, leaned out over the balustrade and looked down. Behind him a taxi blurted its horn at a cyclist. Below, a turmoil of erupting brown water and white foam played out an interminable game: the battle between the moon's graceful, distant shove and the downward urge of all the Border's rivers emptying of their rain – a conflict as old as the hills.

Queedy took it in with an almost overwhelming sense of human frailty. In a sudden violent wave of vertigo an image of the improbable intimacy of his bivouac, the homeliness of moor and fell, burn and wood came on him. The epiphany he had experienced during his exile now, shockingly, revealed itself as delusion. This real world, the external world punished by irresistible elements and kept so ephemerally at bay by the pretence of dwelling, was inexorable and uncaring. It did not need him. It did not need any of them.

Queedy leant heavily on the parapet, feeling almost faint. As he did so his leg brushed against something. Looking down he saw it was a bunch of flowers: chrysanthemums of garish hothouse colours wrapped in cellophane and tied with pink string to the parapet. A small note was attached: the word Why? and an X in blue ballpoint pen, the ink smudged with tears or rain. It was a good question, thought Queedy. But then, Why not? He leant out over the river again and for another minute or two watched the water's swirling currents boiling to their diurnal resolution.

Inside the great glass and iron vault of the Victorian market the clamour of voices, the heat and the crowd were oppressive to Queedy. Smells of fresh fish, of fruit, meat, cheese and vegetables likewise crowded in on his senses. What had once seemed like homely bustle was now cheaply intrusive, claustrophobic. Queedy, trundling his case behind him, forced his way through the crowd of shoppers and dawdlers to a stall that sold clothes and equipment for the outdoors. Here he spent a concentrated hour trying on and purchasing a waterproof coat and a set of rugged boots, two pairs of trousers, two lined work shirts and two vests, several pairs of thick socks; a small torch and a steel for striking sparks; a lethal-looking knife; a set of cooking implements which included a pan and kettle. He also bought a sturdy rucksack, adjusting its straps and cords to his satisfaction and weighting it with his other purchases. Finally he disgorged the paltry contents of his suitcase onto the floor of the market and stowed them in the new pack, to the amusement of a huddle of onlookers thinking that perhaps this was some novel kind of street theatre. He offered the suitcase to anyone who would take it and an embarrassed woman, whingeing child in hand, took it from him and led it briskly away in the direction of the bus station. Queedy, almost satisfied with his morning's work, had one last stop to make. From the cobbler he bought two spare pairs of laces, extra long and extra strong. Thus equipped, he set off once more for the Tower-house. This time he travelled on foot.

M. might, if he had looked down on the market place that morning, have seen Queedy marching past on his way to the bridge and wondered what the suitcase meant. He might have opened the window and shouted down for the boy to wait. He suspected that his former ward was capable of some drastic initiative, some fatal step which would end in disaster. Life had thrown these many arrows at his meagre frame. Could this fragile boy take them? As it was M. did not see him pass beneath his window. For the short time he was in his office that morning he was engaged with his shadow, the assistant to whom he must defer now that the executive eye was focused on him from its all-seeing tower in the other City.

Had M. been younger, less intolerant, less preoccupied, more reasonable or patient, he might have come to like the woman. Who could blame her for the sin of ambition? She might even be said to possess virtues. She avoided the pretence of being more male than her male colleagues. She disdained the power suit and the big hair; her appearance was, if anything, mousey with the slightest trace of an incipient moustache which M. could not quite bring himself to admit was oddly attractive. Miss Nixon, poor Miss Nixon, had scrutinised very carefully both her coiffure and the way M. looked at her, and had mentally prepared herself for war. She need not have worried. Life was complicated enough for the editor: he did not wish to complicate it further.

Mrs Crowther – in her late thirties but dressed frumpy, so she might even be in her early thirties: divorced, widowed, married? Should he ask, would it be polite, was it the done thing these days? – stuck to her routine with admirable persistence. Here she was, waiting for M. with a sheaf of conspicuously well-organised files under her arm and her reading glasses hanging ready from a chain around her neck. M. wondered whether she would take offence if he had a chair placed outside his door so that she would not have to wait standing all that time. It gave him the creeps knowing she would be there every morning, ever so patient. The alternative, that he should tie himself to her inflexible morning schedule, was too awful to contemplate even for a few weeks. The seditious thought came to him to enter his office by climbing a ladder and coming through the window. He made a mental note to have a word with the caretaker. She couldn't possibly take it wrong if they got her a really comfortable chair, could she? Mary would know about that sort of thing. He hadn't spoken to Mary for weeks. He didn't like to bother her. Perhaps a small coffee table and a vase of flowers on it in the corridor: give the place a bit more of a homely feel. But then, he wasn't sure he wanted her to feel at home. He would be happier if she went away again. As his wise uncle Diarmid had said, he would as soon have her space as her. Time for another miracle, maybe.

A smile and a Good morning, which he unfailingly returned. An apology for the fact that the building had no air conditioning, hopeless in this hot weather; one would rather be in the country, or by the sea. A Won't you come in Mrs Crowther, I'll put the kettle on and we'll begin with a coffee. The ritual response, A little too early for me, Sir, thank you. Perhaps later. The Sir was genuine deference, even if his superiors had made it plain why she was there. A gesture to her to sit down while M. attended to the kettle, arranged himself in the chair behind his desk and aligned his unused pencil and pad in front of him. He was ready for her.

- What can we do for you this morning, Mrs Crowther? (The We sounds patronising; where had he got that from? From Queedy, probably, sort of thing he would say. Christ, what a thought.)

- Jeanette, please. I hope you don't mind, Sir, but I have been spending some time down in the print room. (M. doesn't

mind at all but he's damn sure the old boys down there do,
having an outsider watch over their shoulders all the time when
they would rather be at the racing form; he suppresses a smile)

- Ah.   What interesting things have you found down in
the dungeon? No monsters, I hope. They are a law unto themselves, but we indulge them. (There is a hint of a smile from
Mrs Crowther, just a slight wrinkle at the corners of the mouth).

- Well… (At this point M.'s phone rings and with a small
private glance upward in gratitude to whatever spirits reside in
the sky, he halts Mrs Crowther's flow with a hand and, pressing
the flashing yellow button that tells him it's the direct line from
the newsroom, picks it up)

- Jimmy, what's happening in the world? No, no, not at all,
go on. Yes… (M. gestures to Mrs Crowther to pour his coffee
now that the kettle has boiled. It is a gesture of superiority;
he can't help it) Who's this from? Oh, sure, yes I know him.
When (he looks at his watch even though he knows exactly
what the time is)… Where is this chap now…? Not a bit…
Christ Jesus I bet they are. I don't see how we can cover it, do
you, under the circumstances? No. No. They would only give
me the boot, eh Jimmy? (He aims a wink at the nonplussed
and now unsmiling Mrs Crowther even as she places his mug
of coffee on the corner of his desk) File it away, Jimmy, give it
a quarter column under Local, but send Stokes to get a picture
anyway. I don't bloody well care where he is supposed to be
today, send him up there. Right. (He slams the phone down,
grabs his jacket from the back of his chair and heads for the
door)

- Anything I should know about, Sir (says Mrs Crowther,
a slight flush appearing on her cheeks)?

- No, Mrs Crowther (says M. from the doorway). No.
It seems there has been an unusual incident in the Borders

which requires my personal attention. We often get reports
of improbable happenings but, as you know, this newspaper
doesn't report miracles.

   - May I come with you, Sir?

   - No, Mrs Crowther, you may not. (M. turns, runs down
the corridor towards the stairs, clatters down them like a fifteen
year-old and out into the glaring heat of the day, leaving both
the door and Mrs Crowther's mouth ajar)

The crags and pastures, ruined shielings and wooded gorges of the hills
basked in the premature summer heat. The throbbing air was thick
with a blue-green shimmering haze, the earth beneath it perspiring. All
sound was deadened; no breeze stirred the tops of the trees, nor the
ragged seed-heads of the bent grass. A soporific mood settled on the
land; only the buzzards, riding their invisible spiral elevators upwards,
ever upwards, kept watch. Even the peaty brown water in its river bed
seemed somehow lethargic, running in slow motion. In the hamlet of
Hetha at the foot of the Cuddy Burn no fires had been lit that morning;
it might, indeed, have been deserted. Lines of coloured washing left out
overnight hung motionless. Curtains were closed against the day and
blinds drawn to keep the sun out, unless perhaps the residents feared
another sort of intrusion. It was Mrs Belson at Hetha House whose day
had been invaded. Her gravel drive was overrun with cars which had
been coming and going all morning. She had, in fact, felt constrained
to telephone Sergeant Graham and ask him to send someone down to
deal with the chaos – or at least give her a hand in the kitchen. She
could not very well make tea and sandwiches for a dozen reporters
and photographers and be interviewed by them at the same time. It
was really too much: and one of the photographers – not Stokes, who

had only just been diverted from the opening of a refurbished school playground – had taken the liberty of climbing from an upstairs landing window onto her roof to take a picture. Did they think she had people come in and clean for her, just like that?

High on the ridge above the burn, unnoticed, the man with the red face walked at speed through the crackling heather. He carried nothing; his hand was free and it swung mechanically at his side. The wiry shoots caught at his ankles; flower heads crept into his shoes and began to itch. Underfoot the peat hags, pitted and riven by rain, snow and ice, lay in wait to trip him. A buzz of insects pirouetted before his sweating brow and every now and then he vainly beat them away. At the edge of the hag he stopped, removed his shoes and shook them out. In front of him, like the aftermath of some reckless battle between invisible armies, lay a blackened wasteland plateau of burnt stalks where the heather had been fired by the tweed-clad gillies of some estate. Beneath the soot and ash fresh green shoots were even now beginning to push through the charcoal crust. Now he could move at even greater pace. He looked at his watch, then up at the sun. He still had not got used to the length of the days here; dusk seemed to last forever.

Often in his native land Rooi had seen the bushmen burn off the dead grass of the veldt on the edges of the desert, and when the rains came tender new leaves would grow, irresistibly attractive to the eland and the gemsbok; in their shadow waited the hunter. The secret of fire was not offered to humans so that they might frighten animals away in the dark of night or learn to cook, but as a gift to the hunter. The man whom Rooi now hunted, the last of them to evade him, knew all the bushman arts, living out there with them in the desert like a dog. Like the bushman he had lured his prey, innocents drawn to a market place with the promise of bounty just like the eland to his fresh green grass. Ja, the man he had sought these many years knew the bushman's arts; just as he had known their women.

They both preyed on the weak, he and Jäger. You had to have a taste for it. Now, closing in on his man at last after the long chase, Rooi was barely aware of a tensing of his muscles, a super-heightening of senses as his mind became completely focused on the immediate future. He had heard those Bushmen describe this feeling as though the blood of the carcass they would carry home upon their shoulder was already dripping down the backs of their calves, muscles twitching in anticipation of success.

The afternoon heat pressed down upon him. Every tiny sound was now amplified by his state of alertness; all movement was exaggerated. His footfall slowed, became measured, effortlessly silent from long practice in the pursuit of men. Way in the distance ahead, through the haze rising off the ridge, he could make out the squat shape of the refuge hut. Any human figure that far away would be too tiny to identify; nevertheless, he kept his eyes fixed on it.

At about the time when Stokes was arriving at Mrs Belson's house in time for fresh tea and scones, Rooi came to a stile where the heather was fenced off from a young plantation of pine trees. In their trifling shade he stopped for a few minutes to drink water and look at his map. Another hour's walk along the spine of the ridge and he would come to a rocky pinnacle called the Shiel; from there he would be able to see any movement close to the hut, and from that time on he would have to move with greater discretion. The dull fatigues he wore would allow him to approach it almost invisible to any watcher. Rooi knew his man would have a bivouac somewhere, a discreet place in a fold of the land, behind a koppie maybe or in a patch of young wood like this where he could watch without being watched. But it was not so easy to be discreet out in the open on the ridge. Ja, his man knew all the tricks just as he did. It would be a contest worthy of its antagonists. It was a contest due him after all this time. He felt his heart rate rising and in response he slowed his breathing, closed his eyes for a minute or two as he squatted close to the earth, so that to a casual observer he might be meditating. In his pocket he felt for his hunting knife, ran his thumb across its bright blade, drew a few drops of blood which he sucked at, tasting the salt.

The morning had not gone well for him. Leaving Gaunt in the café he had walked straight to the post office, where he knew a package would be waiting for him. It had been wrapped to look like a drab parcel, though a heavy one. Taken from its wrapping it would fit neatly in the moulded compartments of the wooden case which lay on his bed back at the guest house. Wishing his landlady a good morning, Rooi climbed the stairs to the landing, opened the door of his room and put the package down on the bed next to the case. He took a small hunting knife from his pocket and slit the cardboard open, removed the packaging and laid the parts out. Everything was clean and beautifully polished, just as he expected from a professional gunsmith. He would give the weapon a thorough inspection anyway before he assembled it. Only... where was the trigger-pin? How could the man have failed to pack it? It was not possible.

For an hour and more as he neared the refuge hut Rooi's gaze hardly left it except to scan the flanks of the hills beyond for any sign of human movement. So far only the odd white speck of a sheep had distracted him. Into this remote valley walkers rarely ventured. Even the press's greedy photographers, Stokes among them, were preparing excuses for their editors; who could expect them to walk the several miles from the end of the road up onto the ridge? It was too much to ask. High above, in the deep unsullied sapphire blue of the heavens, only the silent outline of a glider soaring enviably towards the summit of the Cheviot compromised the buzzard's monopoly of surveillance over the land below.

Rooi did not approach the hut until the light began to fade behind him in the west. The wait had seemed endless. Now the sapping heat drained from the land and something of a breeze began to seep up from the valley. From a quarter of a mile away he sat in the shade of the

Shiel's granite outcrop, unmoving. His view took in the hut and the ridge beyond, the deep scar known as Penharl that bit into the western edge of the plateau, and the trail that led to it from the hamlet. The gully was narrow, its chiselled walls crowding in on it, leaning inward from either side as if at any moment the scar might heal, might close in upon itself. The late sun shot a bolt of orange light into it, splintering on the gushing waterfall at its mouth. On Rooi's map a small track led up through this canyon and on to the plateau beyond, though he could not make it out at this distance. It was the sort of place a man could hide if he wished, and not be found.

Now Rooi came on the hut, as good a place as any to spend a night on the hill. He moved silently even though he was certain it must be empty. Inside, the shredded boot on the floor and the abandoned gas ring on the trestle showed that no one had been here since the injured walker. Rooi had slept in worse places: ja, it would do. As twilight's shadow draped itself across the moors and the last drops of orange light were squeezed from the jaws of Penharl, Rooi watched from the door. For the merest moment, silhouetted on the brow of the ridge above him, Rooi caught half a glimpse of a figure before it disappeared. His reaction was instant. Leaving the door swinging on its hinge he ran: along the path that wove lazily up the ridge onto the plateau with Penharl grimacing on his left; just light enough to see his footfall. He no longer cared for discretion. He did not sprint but his pace was relentless: up and up with the soft pounding of the peat beneath his feet, unceasing, until he worked around the top of Penharl and crouched briefly at the point where he had seen his quarry.

Rooi knew, Jäger knew, that the most celebrated hunters of the veldt and the bush were not those skilful with the bow or the spear, nor those who could run fastest but those who could run the farthest, for days if necessary. A wounded beast might fly for many miles until it sank with exhaustion to the ground, and only the finest runners would be able to pursue it. When they caught up with the eland it would stand

and turn on them, acknowledging their superiority in the chase. Then the runner must take his spear and end it quickly out of respect. He would light a small fire for smoke and the other hunters then knew where to find him so they could butcher the carcass and carry it back to camp, sometimes many days walking away. Ja, the runners, the ones whose bodies never gave out, they were the equal of any animal in the bush, even the leopard. Rooi was a runner.

In the blurred purple-orange flames of his fire the Ambulist saw an image of the photograph which Selena had described to him. He had never seen this picture but it filled his vision now: not as the photographer but as himself, with the courthouse steps behind them; N!ai next to him in those strange-looking western clothes, that crisp linen dress whose sleeve brushed against his; next to her Dil'ai, her mother; all those bracelets around her wrist, her wiry hair scraped into a bun; the shoes which tortured their feet: the smiles, the relief, the dancing and singing at their waterhole for a full week afterwards. On his right his friend Smith, the young journalist who had fought their cause in the white press, in Windhoek and in Pretoria.

How had the Ambulist not seen this man in Queedy? But then, how had he not seen the betrayal in Smith's eyes? When had Smith turned? Was it Rooi, with his government money and his clever words? Had his friend been that weak? It seemed that everyone Smith touched and more besides bore some of his guilt: Selena, for knowing; Queedy, for being unloved. Ja, and himself. The guilt for what had happened to N!ai whose toothy grin he now saw before him, whose hand now stretched out as if to take his, to ask him to come and bring her home. The guilt for being too late. The guilt for the curse he had laid upon his betrayer. How was he to live with that?

The Ambulist rolled himself a cigarette and took the top off the bottle of whisky at his side. Ja, too much guilt all round, and now Rooi was coming to tell him the end of the story. What a lucky man, to live without guilt; to believe yourself an instrument of a god. The Ambulist raised the bottle to the fire and the invisible night sky and toasted his enemy: To live without guilt! And as if in direct response a disembodied voice from above spoke softly to him, almost whispering. It might have been the *Kaggen* lying in his waterhole or the spirit of the hunter in the branches of the acacia tree. He might even have been talking to himself.

- A fine sentiment for a guilty man.

The Ambulist, without conscious thought, reached out with his hand and felt for the pan of water that laying cooling by the fire. He doused the flames with it, sending up a hiss of steam: reply enough to his visitor. With his other hand he felt for his stick and ran his hand along it. The arrowhead, which Selena had found by chance in the cave and which he had hafted to the stick by its tang with a tendon from the sheep, felt sharp against his finger. He rested the shaft of the stick, his improvised spear, across his knees, and waited.

- You knew I was coming?
- Seker.
- I wonder how.
- I have friends.
- So. Good friends, I hope.
- Maybe.
- Have we come to it now?
- Ja, we have come to it now.
- You have found a good place to hide.
- I do not hide from any man.
- 'turlijk, if you say so. (The Ambulist, his ears keen to all sound, fancies that Rooi is lying face down upon the grass bank above the entrance to his cave, perhaps leaning a little over the

edge. He wonders if now is the moment to strike in the dark of night and, in wondering, knows the moment is lost) It is a fitting sort of reunion, this.

- Varrom?

- You in your dark cell, me outside. Neither of us can see. Only one of us can walk away.

- Ja, we are both blind, you and me Mister Rooi.

- This time you cannot run.

- Do you have the keys to my cell, Mister Rooi? I have whisky and cigarettes. Maybe you want to come and join me. There is plenty of room for two.

- Maybe and maybe not. Do you still sleep badly?

- I sleep fine when there is fresh air.

The Ambulist received no response. Only the hissing embers of the fire disturbed the noiseless air. The Ambulist lit another cigarette and allowed the sweet smoke of the grass he had put in it to envelop him. In the dark before his eyes he now saw another picture. The same darkness. A prison cell. A smell of smoke, not sweet but rancid, the foetid ammonia stink of piss-soaked mattresses being set alight all along the corridor. A choking, blinding curtain of poisonous blackness and men coughing, the sound of a set of keys fumbling in the cell door and an urgent shout to run. Movement without thought or hesitation. Bodies in the corridor; a forearm in the face; a body check and the winding thump of his body against the corridor wall. Angry, fearful shouts from guards blinded too, and the wail of a siren. Shots fired. Batons clanging against bars. Choking again, the desperate clawing of the lungs for breath; unravelling a mental map of the building, the panic of disorientation and visceral fear of recapture, then the clean air of the night, the sound of the chase diminishing in his ears, the raw tearing pain in his chest. Ja, they had all been blind that night, too.

Dawn's first inhalation of breath, the moon long set and the grass fronds hanging down over the cave's mouth, barely moving in the slightest breeze; a violet halo crowning the eastern horizon; the Ambulist, half-sitting, half-lying, hand resting on the shaft of his new-wrought weapon; eyes closed and at rest but the trigger of his conscious self set on a hair's breadth; the minutest noise filtered by the practice of year upon year in the bush: the scratching of a small rodent and the lilting whine of a hover fly; faintly, very faintly, the lethargic stumbling of burn over moss and boulder. All else seemed still.

The Ambulist's first movement, reaching out for a handful of kindling and setting a spark to it as the silent light of day ascended the rim, was watched from the distance of a bow shot across Blizzen Gorge. The red-faced man lay motionless, concealed in the dark shadow between two boulders.

Far away at the foot of the valley the sleepy inertia of the hamlet allowed the noise of the Land Rover's idling engine to be heard by those cottage-dwellers who, from long habit, rose early. One elderly man, bent and bow-legged, capped like a trucker, hobbled along the passage from his kitchen and drew back the chintz curtain at his sitting room window while his kettle boiled, to see who these early walkers might be; more reporters, he shouldn't wonder. The discussion taking place inside the Land Rover could not be heard or seen: its windows were misted by breath. Now one of the back seat windows was slid back and a cloud of vapour rose from it. Voices could be heard, but indistinctly. The back door opened and a man got out: a large-framed man in his middle years, hair receding and showing signs of grey, dressed as a walker and carrying a stick more suited to fighting than to hiking; grim-faced and determined. As he shut the door behind him the window of the passenger seat slid back and if the cottager had bothered to look he would have seen a pale-faced girl with plaits saying something, too softly to be heard; and in the driver's seat another man of middle years with a beard. The first man leaned in at the window and said something, then straightened and set off up the track towards the head of the valley. And now the Land Rover's engine was switched off, the window slid shut again. Silence returned to the hamlet.

If M. had been decisive in his conversation with Selena and her father, it was not because he had any very clear idea of what he was going to do. He did not, to begin with, know what or whom he might face. He did not know if the Ambulist was still alive or if Rooi had already got to him. He did not even know if Rooi was up there too, was perhaps watching him now from some vantage point. He could not have articulated his fears, nor could he explain to any but himself why he must go alone into danger. He half-regretted his adamant refusal to let Jareld to accompany him. Jareld, he knew, was desperate to be part of the action, to help their friend Pieter in any way he could. But Jareld had a wife and daughter who loved and needed him. Jareld had not brawled in the back street bars of Dublin, had not broken his knuckles on a man's face; had not been glassed; nor did he know how to anticipate the coming blow, to read it and get his own head out of the way. If nothing else, M. knew how to fight a man and he feared no-one's fists. His fear was that Rooi had a gun. He had always hated guns, the weapons of the bully and the inarticulate.

As he walked, M. half-formed an idea that he might pose as an innocent walker, might stroll right up to Rooi, supposing he found him and found him in time, and wish him a wonderful Donegal top of the morning before laying him out cold on the ground. Sure, it might just work. The hunter's skill was in his silence, his invisibility. M. would enter the stage loud in garb and voice. He might even sing.

This was bravado and he knew it. He also knew that no plan of his would outlast first contact with the enemy. He would have backed the Ambulist, uninjured and with sight, to overcome the assassin. But by Christ he needed help now. For Queedy's sake and for the girl's, and maybe for his own sake too. M. had suffered for Smith's sins for most of his life. He had married and raised children with a woman who did not love him because of Smith. He had rescued him from poverty and set him on the road to tyranny. He had taken on the boy when he was outcast and disinherited. And now, now he knew Smith had betrayed the Ambulist too in some as yet imperfectly understood way; that he, M., had been the means by which the Ambulist had been identified and tracked down. If the Ambulist now died broken and blind somewhere on the hills M. must accept that guilt too. There was a time for watching and a time for writing, and there was a time for getting oneself a set of bloody knuckles and maybe a broken head. But then, if there was redemption in the thing, whose was it?

M. had never climbed Blizzen Gorge, though he had walked past its open crocodile jaws many a time and shuddered at the sight of its glowering cliffs, the atmosphere of brooding hostility it gave off. He had never spotted the cave where the Ambulist made his camp after falling from the ridge, but with Selena's description he would find it all right. The mouth of the gorge, often so boggy that only the most determined fool or sheep would attempt its passage, came slowly into view as M. rounded the foot of the ridge. Although the day was still cloudless above, a thick blue-grey haze lay in the bottom, creeping down towards the burn. The bog which M. had anticipated was almost dry underfoot and he found he could pick his way through it, aiming to get high enough above the burn to walk on solid ground. Now, as he climbed through the thin layer of haze into clearer air he saw the cause of it. High up where the concave sides of the gorge must rise almost vertically, where the map showed only scree and cliffs, there was nothing to be seen but a dense pall of smoke. The origin of the smoke was immediately obvious: fire raged through the heather in the bowl of the gorge and on the slight breeze. Fed by its own sucking, roaring draught, the ground had become a furnace feasting on dry roots and on the peat beneath. The cave, or where M. supposed the cave to be, was wreathed invisibly in billowing angry clouds of choking grey. If the fire had been deliberately set its purpose was either to blind or to suffocate, or both. It was impossible to believe that any man could breathe or see inside it. Into the maelstrom M. now ran with his stick held out before him in both hands.

Towards the middle of the morning the attention of the cottagers of Hetha was drawn by old Mr Ridley to the umbrella of smoke which he had seen rising above the ridge, funnelling out of Blizzen Gorge. On another day it might have been mistaken for a storm front, so angry and dense was the atmosphere over the plateau. But old Ridley had seen many a peat fire in his time. It would be a bad one, that, he said to himself. The last of the press photographers – it was Stokes – could be seen breaking off a chat he was having with the occupants of the Land Rover, still standing there with its engine off but now with the windows slid fully back and the doors half open. Stokes, wondering what all the fuss was about as four women almost simultaneously emerged from their back doors to take their washing in, looked up at them and then at the skyline. The driver, following Stokes' pointing arm with his eyes, could be seen waving him into the back of the Land Rover, whose engine he now started. It roared off up the valley with its own little cloud of blue smoke following behind.

Some minutes later Sergeant Graham, beginning to wonder how much more excitement he could take, drew up in his police car having been summoned – again – by Mrs Belson. He had no intention of investigating the site of the fire; his intention was to prevent the public from venturing up the valley until the arrival of the fire brigade, who would probably let the blaze burn out by itself. Not much you could do once the peat under the heather was lit; it could burn underground for weeks and then surface again somewhere else. It would have to wait for rain. No one would have any sheep up in the gorge anyway. He hoped it would not be like this all summer. They had plenty of fires up here caused by careless walkers but he could not remember a fire in the gorge, nor any fire so early in the summer. In any case he'd like to catch the bugger who had lit it, whether by design or by mistake.

Mid-day: Jareld leaning helpless against the bonnet of the Land Rover, his clothes stained with soot and grass, his tear-streaked face and beard black; Selena dabbing away at the few slight burns on his hands and knees with water and antiseptic; the senior fire officer walking across from his idling tender. No, Jareld did not need a doctor, he would be fine well in the morning. An Air Ambulance, mobilised when it became clear that there would probably be casualties, whirred overhead, churning up the smoke into angry grey vortices. Since Jareld's return from his hopeless attempt to penetrate the gorge the officer had forbidden any further entry: it was too dangerous for his men, and if there were casualties up there they would probably already be dead. He would keep the tender here until it was too dark to see and they would return tomorrow to assess the state of the ground.

The hours of the afternoon wore slowly on as if the day must be dragged from its purchase on the watching, dreading audience. The tide of smoke which for three hours had poured up over the lip of the gorge to be wafted northeast on what little breeze there was, began to settle back into its abysmal hole, no longer driven by flames and now pressed down by the cooling air above. The extent of the devastation caused by the fire was not yet apparent. Nothing within its grey blanket stirred; no bird called out, no insect buzzed.

As dusk insinuated itself across the land, the fire officer called time on his vigil and withdrew his engine, gingerly reversing it down the track. Stokes, tired, hungry, dissatisfied and late for his dinner, begged a lift and said his farewells. The helicopter had long since returned to its pad.

- How long shall we stay, Papa?

- How can we leave, my darling?

- It is hard. Would you like to stay?

- Yes, I would. We can sleep in the car if you do not mind.

- No, Papa, I don't mind. Mama will worry.

- Yes, she will. But our friend Stokes will call and tell her we are waiting and she will understand.

- Yes, Papa.

With the very last light two dark figures might just be seen emerging from the haze, picking their way with great care down the steep bank beside the burn. They were supporting each other, the two men, unnoticed by Selena and her father behind the Land Rover's misted windows. One would lose his footing momentarily and be caught by the other. In different circumstances they might have been mistaken for a pair of drunks, father and son perhaps, except that one was only ten years younger than the other. Both of them looked too old or infirm to be out after dark. A keen ear might have picked out the odd word which passed between them in low voices but they did not converse; they did not discuss. What might have been said was private to each man; what could not be said would remain between them and neither would ever speak of it.

M. rapped on the window of the Land Rover, shouting as loud as his feeble voice was able.

- I hope to Christ Jesus there's still a bottle of whisky somewhere in this vehicle.

The door opened; an interior light shone feebly on to the black faces of the two men, almost unrecognisable except as refugees from some terrible disaster; an earthquake it might be, or at the very least a volcanic eruption. Into the Land Rover they were bundled by Jareld and Selena, father and daughter laughing with grief and crying in happiness. Selena passed them back a bottle of whisky, and chocolate, and tobacco; and after that water and cotton wool and antiseptic and bandages for them to minister to themselves while Jareld, beaming through his own grizzled face, drove the car down out of the valley and home, singing a song of his own composition. M. ate and drank like he had not seen food or whisky for a month, all the while passing his companion the bottle or some chocolate. The Ambulist, his raw red eyes burning from within and without, was silent either from exhaustion or pain or because he was overwhelmed by the gifts of love and emancipation. Seeing his anguish even in the dim-lit vehicle, M.

now leaned across and bathed the Ambulist's eyes gently with cotton wool moistened by water. Who could tell if the streaks running down the old man's face and onto his cracked swollen lips tasted of salt? And who could tell how M. had broken the hands with which he clumsily went about his job?

> – Meisje?

> – Yes, Pieter.

> – I would like you to have this. (He puts his closed fist out towards the sound of the girl's voice and she feels for it, taking the tiny flint arrowhead from his hand and feeling its sharp smoothness)

> – Thank you, Pieter.

Later, when the hum of the engine easing through the country night towards the Tower-house along roads empty of traffic had become a sort of lullaby, Jareld spoke to M. over his shoulder.

> – You know, they will ask you, was there anyone else up there in that fire?

> – Sure they will. They'll not find anyone.

> – That is not what they will ask you.

> – They'll still not find anyone.

Chapter Fourteen

Dwellings

M. felt the weight of the gun in his hands. It came back to him easily enough. It must have been forty years and more since he had braced a stock against his shoulder and squeezed the trigger, enjoyed the thump of the recoil, the split-second wait and the double crack of the shot and its echo, watched the flight of a bird collapsing in its fatal arc. It was a nice gun, an expensive gun, on the light side but well-balanced. Without loading it, M. traced the imaginary path of a target across his eye line through the trees, and in his mind's eye brought it down. As the sight between the barrels came to rest on the trunk of a slender beech sapling a hundred yards ahead of him, a slight movement caught his eye and, panning back, he brought the gun to bear on the head of a young doe who, picking up his scent on the slight breeze, paused in her browsing to gaze steadily at him before continuing demurely on her way, unperturbed. Another movement: this time the quick-fire applause of a pigeon flapping in sudden alarm somewhere high up in the forest overhead. M. instinctively followed the noise with the gun but could not see the bird through the green vault of branches overhead. Now he broke the barrels open, handing the gun back to its owner, and the two men, dogs at their heels, moved off deeper into the wood.

- I think maybe I'd better leave the hunting to you. We'll end up with a precious small haul if it's left to me.

- Nonsense, some moments practising and you will do fine well, you handle the gun like a veteran, so to say. Perhaps that is a little like an insult, but I cannot offend you, I am certain.

- Sure, I've been offended worse and by uglier men. And then again you have the gun, not me. My uncle Diarmid was fond of telling us in the early days of the Provisionals coming over the border that a man with a gun may say pretty well what he likes, unless you have a bigger one. And always to call him Sir.

- You are playing fun with me.

- I am, sure and sorry for it. Will we find some game to shoot at now? Otherwise the women will be serving us a plate of spurs for our supper?

- Yes, let us play at being hunters. Some pigeon and a few brace of rabbits before we deserve our breakfast! Come dogs!

A companionable silence. Before them lay an iridescent ocean of bluebells, perhaps just passing the high tide of their glory but nonetheless heavenly; white firework flower-heads of ramsons and yellow celandine star-bursts. From the melodious racket above and around them Jareld picked out the territories of blackbird and chaffinch, great tit and warbler and, off in the distance, the suicidal jack-hammer drumming of a randy male woodpecker at his favourite hollow birch tree. The urgency of the soundtrack harmonised oddly with the lazy dance of shifting light and shade that played across the floor of the wood, projected by sunlight through the kaleidoscope shutters of the canopy; centenarian oak trees in their noble prime gorging on its rays.

- You know, I don't believe Smith knew absolutely what would happen to the wife when he handed her over.

- That would be his way, sure, not to know the consequences. He was a great one for Nothing to do with me.

- I forget, of course, you knew him better than anyone.

- At one time, perhaps; I knew nothing of his time in South Africa. I thought I knew him before then and was wrong. I was wrong about that man a few times and it looks as if our friend was too. When he turned up on my doorstep in Dublin I thought it would be a girl he was running from.

- You think he suspected what Rooi would do with the woman.

- I'm bloody well sure he knew what Rooi was like, what he was capable of. I dare say money changed hands. I dare say Smith persuaded himself there was some higher motive. Maybe he even believed Jäger had something to do with the massacre. But to hand the wife over to that bastard... Did you ever see so much evil on a man's face? Christ Jesus it gives me the shudders just thinking of it. (M. crosses himself, a gesture from his Donegal past which surprises even him)

- My dear fellow, I am sorry to talk of it. I never saw him myself. I have wondered if our friend was capable of planting a bomb and persuaded myself that he was not.

- Sometimes even a cynical old hack like me does not want to know.

- I suppose you will not tell what happened up there in the valley?

- Not to any man.

- I do not think you are quite so cynical as you would like us to believe.

- They all say that, sure.

The boundary of Twyford Wood, its long sine chased into the

earth by a ditch and bank crowned with ancient pollarded oaks, had marked the limit of the township time out of mind. At its farthest point, where the wood seemed to be folded back on itself, was a fork in the stream after which the village had been named as far back as history would tell. In days gone by, and into the lifetime of the oldest inhabitants, small boys had been led to this place every year at the spring equinox. In long-polished and reverend lines the local squire had intoned the names of the boundary markers of the parish, and at each named point a boy, or boys, were dealt a sound beating so that they might not forget. The last of the hereditary squires having failed to set good seed some thirty years since, the privilege technically fell on whoever dwelt at the Tower-house. It was Jareld Arnesen's right and duty to convene and legitimise this barbaric rite of territorial passage. The two men paused for a nip of whisky and to take breath. Jareld, cradling his shotgun, drew the outline of the parish in the air with it.

- So you see I am not a very good English squire. I have not yet done my duty by giving the local boys a good thrashing. You think I should be more conscientious in my role as the head man of the village?

- There is something to be said for it, sure. You might persuade them to bring you rabbits and pheasant in lieu of punishment...?

- Ha! I like your thinking, that is a fine good idea. In the meantime we shall go a little way along the old track, there will be plenty rabbits there. (The two hunters and their tail-wagging escorts leave the cover of the wood, tread gingerly across the little plank bridge which spans the stream and climb a stile onto a wide grassy lane sunk between high hedges on either side; a dozen or more young rabbits scatter before them into the undergrowth)

- Just here, you can see? (Jareld thrusts his head through the hedge and points with the barrel of the shotgun towards a small foetid-looking pool encased in a square stone cistern. M. is unimpressed; one of the dogs barks) This is a very ancient holy well, as old as the village and older. And the lane, you notice the straightness of the lane? This was a Roman road.

    - Sure it is the straight true track. I always worried about the Romans, this obsession with right angles and straight lines, it would never do in Ireland. How is a man to discover the world if he knows where he is going all the time?

    - Well, you may have a point. You wouldn't be thinking of starting off on a long walk yourself, would you?

    - No I would not. I will bide my time and let them put me out to pasture on a decent pension in another year or so. I like the hills and the valleys and I like them even more when I have a warm bath and a bed to contemplate.

    - Where do you think this lane comes out?

    - I have no idea.

    - It comes out right next to the holy well at Halstane: what do you think of that, my friend?

    - I think the rabbits will be there before us.

Mother and daughter for once had exclusive possession of the kitchen at the Tower-house. A dusting of flour, which coated the table thickly and the floor less so, together with collateral hand prints on the backs of the chairs and on the stone lintel above the range, was firm evidence of a determined campaign of baking that had been planned these few days and now saw its decisive phase. A deeply seductive odour of rising bread, crisping tart and browning pie-crust emanated from the ovens and wafted with provocative sloth through the upper storeys of the tower. Queedy, uncharacteristically liberated from outside chores and busy with a piece of writing, detected it and thought very seriously about engineering an excuse to visit the kitchen. Higher still Pieter, recuperating alone in Selena's apartment at the top of the house, was awakened from his slumber by its beckoning whiff. In spite of such temptation, neither man dared disturb the well-advertised exertions of the mistresses of the household.

- Pieter seems to be eating a little better these last few days, don't you think?

- Yes, Mama, I have seen it too. I think the pain from his eyes is not so bad. I brought his tray down last night and he had eaten most of his dinner.

- Have Pieter and John spoken yet, Mette? I mean, spoken of John's father?

- I cannot tell. I have heard them saying the things men say to one another when there are things they ought to talk about but can't.

- I wonder, has John forgiven Pieter his abandonment? Has he understood?

- I do not know, Mama. John is quiet. They have been discussing an eclipse of the moon which they are expecting this weekend. (Selena, who has been standing next to her mother, both of them leaning back against the great white sink, puts down her cup of tea. Picking up a tea towel, she goes to the smaller oven and opens the door. Steam erupts from it in a ballooning cloud, followed by a divine emission of doughy perfume) They seem quite excited by it.

- Oh, that is very good; they will be so happy. Is it to occur on Saturday night?

- Yes, I believe so.

- How perfect. I hope the weather will keep fine.

- I am sure it will, Mama.

- What time is it? The hunters have been out for hours. Did they take food with them?

- Yes, Papa made sandwiches and a flask of tea. I wonder if they will have killed any poor animals yet?

- Oh I do hope so. (Freya unconsciously times her response so that the word Do is emphasised by the slamming of a fat ball of dough onto the marble slab on the counter. She pummels it so vigorously that a strand of her yellow hair falls over her eyes. She restores it to its proper place with a floury hand, and her daughter giggles as she wipes the white dust off her mother's face with the teacloth)

Neither Queedy's writing nor the baking, nor yet the difficulty of the task, prevented a resumption of Freya's endeavour to render the young man's soul in clay. Every day, towards the end of the afternoon when the sunlight was at its most lustrous and perceptive, Queedy would take up his inscrutable pose. Every day Freya repeated the ritual removal of the cloth which covered the head; every day she would walk around it to begin afresh, hoping that in some way it had been tamed overnight, had come to an acceptance of what it ought to be. Every day she added more clay: daubing, smearing lumps onto the head so that she might then reveal the truth by a process of excavation. Sometimes she went to her subject to peer at him, holding his head between her hands and closing her eyes. At such moments he would close his eyes too and try to empty his mind, to allow the sculptor in, but he could not dispel the warring images which played to him insistently and in some way, unspoken, Freya must have sensed this.

The clutter of the studio crowded in on Queedy's thoughts like the jostling shoppers and traders of the market place. The staccato pounding of clay in the sculptor's hands seemed almost to physically assault him. If Freya sensed his discomfort, his wish to be anywhere else, it was as an undercurrent to her frustration. To cede possession of his soul was not easy. She could not yet admit to herself that her subject was impossible, that he could not be rendered in clay; that is to say, his soul, which she believed was confined inside that proud, hurt, angry head, could not be rendered. By anyone... or just not by her?

    - And how is your construction coming along, John? (He does not turn towards her but continues to stare at the ivory palaeolithic Venus on which his eye seems always to rest)

- I am not sure I am qualified to judge. I do not think it will blow down. I intend to make it proof against the elements.

- How will you do that?

- Jareld has found a recipe for daub, a mixture of clay, animal dung and straw. When it is thrown against the woven laths and smoothed over it can be proofed with lime and then I think it will last.

- Ah. So you are to become a sculptor too.

- So it seems. We have been pounding the mixture in a tub with our feet. Jareld believes it to be therapeutic. (Freya lets out an indulgent laugh in syncopation with the thumbs which knead Queedy's temples)

- Perhaps I should try it too. Will it be ready by Saturday?

- Yes, I think so.

- You are a faster worker than I am, John. I must say it sounds almost as if it will be a real home.

- It will occupy the higher end of the market for such residences; but I promise it will not have a door. A door makes the difference.

- If you can shut out the night it is a dwelling, is that how you nomads think?

- Yes.

Queedy's thoughts floated gently downward like motes of dust in the patient air of the studio. A part of his mind insisted on listing the chores his needy animals would shortly require; another part reminded him that they were no longer his, that their mistress would probably already be attending to them. Into these thoughts a razor-sharp monochrome image of his smiling father standing next to the Ambulist was a constant intrusion. Queedy's imagination insisted on playing and replaying the image unbidden, like a fragment of a movie in which the camera lens zoomed in on his father's hand grasping a fistful of dollar bills, then panned up to frame his irresistible smile, on an endless loop. Time passed too slowly to come to his rescue.

For Freya the passage of time meant nothing: all was in the moment, in the manipulation of the sitter whose head seemed to become less and not more plastic as she kneaded and shaped it. At length the intrusive ring of a small alarm clock, which sculptor and subject had agreed must mark the end of their sessions, intervened, tugging them both back into the present. Freya stood back with an exhalation which was intended to convey satisfaction but which sounded to Queedy like an admission of defeat, and threw her damp cloth over his uncontrollable head.

Selena, the goat trotting contentedly at her side, found Queedy down by the lake at the site of the new shelter, stripped to his white-skinned waist and with arms brown not from the sun but smeared up to his elbows with richly stinking brown mud. The remnants of the Ambulist's bivouac, now little more a than a few sticks propped against each other, lay nearby. A small fire crackled, its flames almost invisible in the piercing light of late afternoon. The goat, instantly curious and keen to assert its proprietorial rights, nudged Queedy aside and scampered into the half-moon shelter, its frame hooped with hazel rods interwoven with thin oak laths which Queedy had soaked to make them pliable. A particularly astute or learned historian of architecture might speculate that the shelter's heritage was part Anglo-Saxon and part bushman; and not entirely suited either to local culture or climate. Queedy apologised to the goat for not having yet provided it with straw bedding, and promised to atone for his sin. The goat took a stray end of one of the laths in its mouth and started chewing to show its disapproval. Selena called it out and gave it a carrot stub.

- John, we have come to inspect. I hope you will make us some tea?

- Selena, you are welcome. And so is Billy, if he behaves. It is a beautiful afternoon, don't you think? I will make tea for us shortly. Will you just fill the pan while I plaster the last of this daub before it goes hard? You know, I have to find something to do now you have taken my foster children from me.

- Oh you mustn't say that, John, they would be very sad if you went away. And so should I. (She sets the pan on the fire and as she kneels on the ground she watches Queedy, his back to her. How can one know what he is thinking or feeling?)

- Thank you, Selena.

- I have not seen you take your medicine, John, in these last few days: have you run out? Would you like me to drive you to town to get some more?

- I have thrown it all away. (He slaps a last fistful of daub onto the laths and presses it in with his thumbs and then, wetting his hand in a bucket of water, smooths the surface of the daub. The runny brown slip spills down his arms and he wipes them on his shirt)

Selena's gaze followed him as he stooped over the fire to brew their tea. Her moral presence demanded that he look her directly in the eye. Months ago, even such understated interrogation would have precipitated a physical and emotional crisis in the young man. Now he returned her gaze, and smiled. The goat, sensing that relations in the human world had returned to harmonious rectitude after recent disruptions, took the opportunity to aim its lowered head at the small of his back off a short run. But Queedy was too quick and sidestepped with an ease and suppleness which reduced the girl to almost helpless delight as the goat crashed headlong into fire, pan and tea mugs, scattering them with a hiss and a clatter, leaving the creature unharmed but utterly humiliated.

Darkness did not fall on the lake until a late hour. The latent heat of the day sweated from the earth and the air, though still and clear, was not cold. A fire had long been lit, though, and in deference to the dwellers among the party, and the occasion, it had been constructed on a suitably impressive scale. A large heap of seasoned wood had been collected over the last days and lay piled nearby so that the blaze might be kept going for many hours. On a night of conspicuous consumption the efforts of many had gone into the preparation of a feast. The hunters provided wild game in abundance: some to be spit-roasted, some crammed into sumptuous gravy-filled pies. There were pasties with shiny polished crusts, savoury flans and tarts filled with curds, with sorrel, wild garlic, woodland mushrooms; cheese from a local dairy; loaves, rolls and plaits of fresh bread. The lake had donated trout and bream in bounteous quantities. Beer, wine and whisky flowed without calculation. This celebration of the Ambulist's deliverance, of life, of summer and abundance, of the generosity of nature, seemed to the Arnesens an affirmation and expression of their own overflowing love; an affirmation also of the solidity and permanence of dwelling, of home, of returning and rest. Only by dwelling could humans, it seemed to say, create a culture which was generous.

It was Queedy who, complicit in the planning of the feast, was to fetch Pieter from his eyrie high, high up in the tower where with the windows always open and the skies wide he might feel himself almost free from confinement. During his recuperation Selena had made herself a bed down in her father's studio. Now, Queedy was to bring Pieter to his new shelter by the lake, not so that he would remain there, but that he might know his welcome was permanent. Down through the house Queedy led the old man by the hand, each step warily taken. The abnormal silence of the kitchen, the absence of the happy chaos which made even the stoutest nomad yearn for its pleasures, confused the Ambulist, but he said nothing. Down the kitchen steps and through the yard he was led, to the more reassuring sounds of hay being munched in manger, chicks clucking amiably. Here too he was greeted by the bleating of the goat, thrusting its muzzle into his hand as he passed through the gate into the lane beside the paddock.

The Ambulist sensed the presence of the gathering as he neared. He felt the heat of the fire, and its roaring light penetrated the dark clouds before his eyes. He smelled the roasting meat and the rich melange of foodstuffs. Here too were sounds he knew: the opening of bottles, the sawing of bread and pastry with knives and, behind it all, the familiar backdrop of the lake with its shuffling nest-builders, squawking landings and take-offs, its mating calls and angry squabbles. There was a more muted reception from the humans, uncertain how the once-titanic wanderer, now hobbled by injury and infirmity, would respond to the gift of their friendship.

Queedy brought Pieter to his new shelter, guiding his hand towards it so that the old man might trace its shape in his mind. There was a hush in the conversation splintered by cracking sparks and by noises off. A quiet word of explanation from Queedy. The Ambulist examined Queedy's efforts with a sort of professional detachment which gave no clue to his emotions. Freya and Jareld watched him with indulgence and hope; M. with the thought of their shared knowledge in his mind; Selena with the keen eye of the shepherdess watching for signs; Queedy, as tense as he had felt in many months watching and listening for disapprobation, for criticism. The Ambulist, aware that he must play his part, shook the frame of his new bivouac; appeared to shake it very firmly. He felt the texture and material of Queedy's daub, probed the lath-work on the inside, kicked with apparent ferocity the hazel stakes that held it to the ground.

> - Mister Queedy, I thank you for this gift. I hope you will now roll me as fine a cigarette. That young girl will not let me smoke in her rooms.

Indeed, the Ambulist played his part that night. He praised the feast and the company, raised many a bottle to these his friends, sat in the entrance to his abode as if it were his throne, magnificent once again in the light of the camp fire, wearing his ancient greatcoat and with his grip at his side. His particular friend the goat curled up behind him in the shelter on a fresh bed of straw, its malevolent eye falling possessively on Queedy's movements.

At midnight the full moon made its appearance above the trees to the east, casting an eerie light on the lake. It did not possess its customary brilliance but looked sickly, anaemic, without lustre. Queedy watched it keenly and knelt for some time next to the Ambulist, describing what he saw so that the Ambulist might picture the moon exactly in his mind. An hour passed; the fire burned lower and more wood was put on. Its embers spread, like the seething rump of a volcano, over the ground between the camp and the lake shore.

The life of the lake now quietened with apprehension. The breathless air seemed to tremble, the leaves of the trees to twitch as though they had suddenly become prone to some tic. The humans circling the fire fell quiet too. Queedy, who had been watching the moon with great attention for some minutes, checking his watch, moved back from the fire to sit on the ground next to Pieter. Now, a blood-red glow began to suffuse its surface, seeping into its craters and flooding its vast barren plains one by one until the whole of the perfect disc looked as though it were bleeding from some awful internal wound. The earth seemed to hold its breath, to brace itself for some cataclysmic event, fearing perhaps a cosmic act of portentous theft. Around the dimming moon stars began to shine with more than usual brilliance. No one was able to move. For more than half an hour, while the earthly fire subsided, the moon sacrificed its blood to the heavens. Slowly, slowly the red faded to terracotta, then to a dull yellow ochre; then it lightened to a creamy pastel as the moon struggled free of its parent's umbra. Sounds of life, of relief, began to come once more from the lake and its shore. M., breaking the spell under which the revellers had been held, raised a glass to the moon and welcomed its return as that of a friend.

- Sure in Donegal they used to tell us it was a sign that a changeling had been placed in a family by the fairies.

- It is a beautiful thing, a sensuous message from the gods, if you are not scared of it. This night reminds me of our time in the far north, Jara.

- Yes, my darling. It makes my own blood run a little cold but I like it fine.

- The Ambulist, whisky bottle at his side, rolled himself a cigarette and lit it while his companions mused on the significance of the blood-moon. Now, almost for the first time that night, he spoke.

- The moon is crying tears of blood for her lost companion.

- Who is her lost companion?

- The comet. (The Ambulist lights his cigarette and draws on it, breathes deeply and sighs) Many generations ago, the moon had a half-sister, a fiery spirit who followed her always through the sky. When the moon was resting and could not be seen from earth the fiery spirit still shined so the hunter could find his way by night. To make sure the spirit stayed constant the hunter used to sing her a song, a love song.

- Have you heard this song? What does it sound like?

- I cannot say. It was a very beautiful song, but a great secret and only the hunter and the fiery spirit knew its meaning. Now, the hunter had a friend, a lizard, who used to share his camp fire to keep warm and who in turn protected him from spiders and scorpions. One day, the lizard overheard the hunter sing his secret love song to the fiery spirit. (Selena has laid more wood on the fire; the Ambulist's eyes shine in its light and it is almost impossible to believe that his sight has been taken from him. He seems to look beyond mere material vision to other realities)

- Now, the lizard was also friendly with the hyaena, who was the enemy of the hunter. One night the lizard crept away from the hunter's camp while he was sleeping and sang to the hyaena the love song which the hunter sang to the fiery spirit, the comet. The very next time that the moon was not looking and the hunter was asleep, the hyaena sang this love song to the fiery spirit and seduced her. When the hunter found out that the spirit had another lover he shot an arrow into the sky with his bow and she fled. Now the fiery spirit only comes back when a great hunter is about to die, to cry over his body. (The Ambulist feels with his hand for the bottle of whisky and drinks from it; his eyes are wet with tears and his voice is laden with sadness for the story he tells. All eyes watch him and no one moves) You can see her hair streaming away from her as she approaches.

- Tell us, Pieter, why does the moon turn red?

- These are tears of guilt, Meisje, for the moon knows what the lizard has done and tells the hunter, whose heart is broken. She cries tears of blood for the knowledge which she has, which she gives away and cannot take back.

- And what, my friend, happens to the lizard when the hunter learns of his betrayal?

- Ja, the lizard. (The Ambulist reaches his hand out and feels for Queedy who, he knows, is next to him, now sitting very tensely upright. He grips Queedy's arm tightly so that he cannot move away and holds him there. Queedy looks down at his arm, and then at the old man's face; the coldness clutching at his heart, squeezing it, almost robs him of breath) The hunter is angry, you understand Mister Queedy, seker, he is very angry. He lays a terrible curse on his friend, so that the lizard's children will be forever cast out of man's society. He is angry, you see, the hunter. Maybe he would take back his curse if he could, but he cannot. He must live with it always. And so must the children of the lizard.

Morning came lazily to the Tower-house. Even the creatures who inhabited the lake seemed to have been stricken with lassitude. The animals, impatient to be fed and liberated and angry at their neglect, set up a racket which did not penetrate the great stone fastness of the Tower-house for many minutes. Freya and Jareld Arnesen heard nothing, deeply asleep in each other's arms in their bed. The Ambulist, stirring first at his bivouac, wondered that no-one had attended the beasts. From close by he heard the noise of a man snoring by the burnt-out fire. M. had fallen asleep late into that fateful night with a bottle of whisky in his hand, and someone had covered him with a blanket. The Ambulist was making his way stiffly along the track towards the yard when the kitchen door opened and Selena, no more than half-awake, emerged with the two dogs barking at her heels.

The young man calling himself Queedy did not appear as the morning wore on and the other inhabitants of the Tower-house convened for breakfast. He departed before first light, and was not seen again. No one knew what he made of the gift which he found in his pack: a beautiful shiny flint arrowhead hanging from a necklace of beads.